D0962591

brary
Street
Fallon, Nevada 89406
(775) 423-7581

TERRAN TOMORROW

TOR BOOKS BY NANCY KRESS

TERRAN TOMORROW

BOOK 3

OF THE

YESTERDAY'S KIN

TRILOGY

NANCY KRESS

TOR

A TOM DOHERTY ASSOCIATES BOOK

NEW YORK

This is a work of fiction. All of the characters, organizations, and events portrayed in this novel are either products of the author's imagination or are used fictitiously.

TERRAN TOMORROW

Copyright © 2018 Nancy Kress

All rights reserved.

Map by Rhys Davies

A Tor Book
Published by Tom Doherty Associates
175 Fifth Avenue
New York, NY 10010

www.tor-forge.com

Tor® is a registered trademark of Macmillan Publishing Group, LLC.

The Library of Congress Cataloging-in-Publication Data is available upon request.

ISBN 978-0-7653-9035-6 (hardcover)
ISBN 978-0-7653-9037-0 (ebook)

Our books may be purchased in bulk for promotional, educational, or business use. Please contact your local bookseller or the Macmillan Corporate and Premium Sales Department at 1-800-221-7945, extension 5442, or by email at MacmillanSpecialMarkets@macmillan.com.

First Edition: November 2018

Printed in the United States of America

0 9 8 7 6 5 4 3 2 1

For Jack, always

MONTEREY BASE

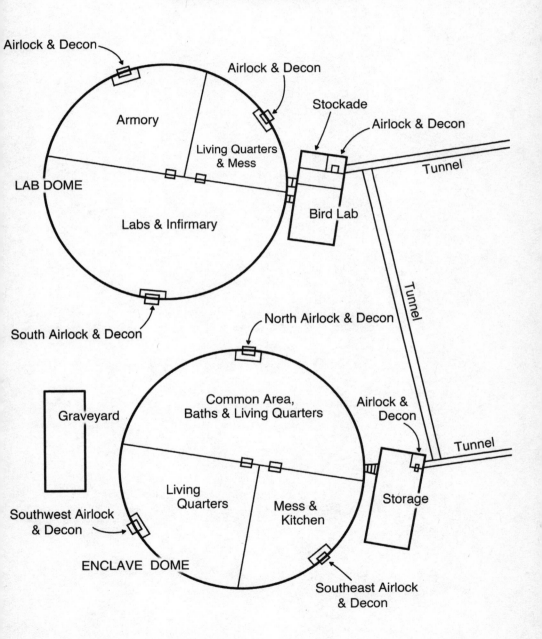

The major advances in civilization are processes that all but wreck the societies in which they occur. . . . It is the business of the future to be dangerous; and it is among the merits of science that it equips the future for its duties.

—Alfred North Whitehead

The brain is wider than the sky
For, put them side by side
The one the other will contain
With ease, and you beside.

—Emily Dickinson

TERRAN TOMORROW

PROLOGUE

Jason stood in a small enclosure between two doors, leaned forward, and touched the tip of his finger to the pad mounted on the door in front of him. The door said, "Retinal scan and digital chip match. Colonel Jason Jenner," opened to a long flight of metal steps, and locked behind him. His boots rang on each step.

At the bottom was a small windowless space with three doors. Two were unmarked, one of heavy wood and one of alien metal. The third, fitted with a decontamination chamber and the soft whoosh of negative pressure, bore a sign:

BIOHAZARDOUS MATERIAL
DANGER!
AUTHORIZED PERSONNEL ONLY

Jason keyed his way into the unmarked wooden door and closed it. In a tiny, sound-baffled space, a soldier jumped up from a stool and saluted.

Jason said, "Any trouble, Corporal?"

"No, sir. Sleeping, breathing, saying nothing."

The guard room led to two cells, both with a single barred plastic window. Jason opened one of the cell doors and entered. The cell stank. The prisoner, naked, lay on his side on the bare floor in a stain of his own dried piss. His wrists were manacled with a short chain; another secured one ankle to the wall. Both had bloodied strips of skin. He opened his eyes to stare at Jason, who had to restrain himself from kicking him.

This was one of the men who had broken the world.

"Dr. Anderson, are you ready to talk to me?"

The prisoner said nothing. He had water within reach but had not eaten for three days. Only a few of the people in the base above, none of them civilians, even knew he was here. It had taken Army Intelligence—such as it was, since the Collapse—eight years to find this man. He was the last Gaiist they would ever find.

"If you don't talk to me . . ."

Jason didn't have to finish the sentence, which was good. He was weak enough—that's how he thought of it—to shrink from torture, even though this man deserved anything that Jason's men could do to him. But the sentence was such a cliché, even if the situation was not. Never before in the world had there been a situation like this. But always somewhere in Jason's mind, inescapable as the dull throb of headache, was what Colin would think.

The prisoner finally spoke. "We saved the Earth."

Anger surged so strong that for a moment Jason's vision filled with red haze. He regained control.

"Are you going to tell us their plans? New America is your enemy as much as ours."

Anderson went on gazing at him from pale blue eyes. For a moment Jason thought that Anderson was actually going to give up. But all he did was repeat, "We saved the Earth."

Disgusted, Jason turned to leave. To Anderson he said, "You have until tomorrow morning to talk voluntarily." To the sergeant, "No change in treatment."

"Yes, sir."

We saved the Earth.

Nothing could be less true.

Or more so.

CHAPTER 1

Her name was Jane.

She told this to all nine people aboard the spaceship *Return*, her own people first. Her father, reading in a corner of a big room that ten people could not fill, looked at her calmly. "Yes, Jeg^faan, if you prefer. 'Jane.'" He did not ask why the change. He knew. When you go to live on another planet, you must adapt. Worlders had always, of necessity, been good at adaptation. It was in their genes. And now adaptation was Jane's mission: she would be the translator, the bridge between worlds.

Glamet^vorɟ, with whom Jane once thought she might sign a mating contract, frowned. "I will keep my identity on Terra, and that includes my name. I am Glamet^vorɟ," he said, emphasizing the rising inflection in the middle and the click at the end, the way children did. In many ways, Jane thought, he was a child, although the most brilliant biologist on World, after her father.

"As you wish," she said mildly. It was good that she had changed her mind about the mating contract. "Changed her mind"—that was a Terran expression, as if a mind was something that could be removed and replaced like a body wrap. English words came more easily to her now, after constant study for so long, but the meanings revealed by the words still astonished her.

She found Glamet^vorɟ's sister with their brother in a sleeping cabin. La^vor, the same age as Jane, was devoted to the boy, who could not speak more than a few words. Something had gone wrong at

Belok^'s birth; his mother had died and Belok^'s brain had been damaged. Not, of course, that that made any difference to his siblings' decision to bring him to Terra. They were lahk.

"La^vor," Jane said, "I will be called 'Jane' now."

"Why?"

"It's a Terran name."

La^vor, nowhere near as intelligent as her older brother, frowned. "You are not Terran."

"No. But here, I will be called Jane."

"All right," La^vor said. She was never argumentative.

Belok^ laughed, but not because he understood. He often laughed or cried inappropriately, following vague ideas in his vague brain. Jane smiled and touched his arm. Like all Worlders, Belok^ had coppery skin, plus the huge dark eyes that had evolved on World to better gather Skihlla's orangey light. As tall as most Worlders even though he hadn't finished growing, Belok^ was much wider. If he had been as prickly as Glamet^vorɪ, his baby mind in an almost-man's body might have been difficult to lead, but Belok^ had the same sweet, accommodating disposition as his sister.

None of the Terrans, Jane suspected, fully understood why Belok^ had been brought with them. Terrans did not understand the unbreakable bonds of a lahk. Not even Marianne Jenner, whom Jane sought out next. Marianne sat on the bridge with Dr. Patel and Branch Carter.

Jane said in English, "My name here will be Jane, please. And I will call you Dr. Jenner now, not Marianne-kal, if that is all right."

"Just call me Marianne," the older woman said. Jane looked at her more closely. Marianne-kal . . . no, Dr. Jenner . . . no, *Marianne* looked sad. That was to be expected, perhaps. She had left behind her son Noah, married to a Worlder, and her granddaughter. She had two more children on Terra, but when she arrived there, twenty-eight years would have passed since her departure. Marianne's daughter would be a Terran-year older than Marianne. Jane could not imagine how that would be.

"I feel your sadness," she said, and Marianne looked at her sharply, started to say something, and then did not.

Dr. Patel said quickly, "'Jane'—pretty name. Call me Claire."

"I will," Jane said, hoping she would remember. Branch Carter ignored her, but since he hadn't ever called her by her Worlder name in the first place, it hardly mattered what he called her now. He was thin, intense, a young Terran who preferred machinery to people. He said to a wall screen, "Come in, Terra, come in. This is the spaceship *Return*, coming from World . . . I mean, Kindred. Come in, Terra."

No one answered. The *Return* had jumped—another strange expression, as if bypassing a hundred light-years of space was no more than a dance step—shortly after liftoff, three days ago. Since then the ship had been flying toward Terra and Branch had been trying to make contact.

"I don't understand why no one is answering," he said for perhaps the hundredth time. But, then, there was so much they didn't understand about the ship, which operated on forces none of them, neither Worlders nor Terrans, understood. Jane less than the others. The *Return* was not Terran technology, nor World's. Jane regarded this gift, made eons ago by an unknown race, as a sort of illathil, but there was no explaining that to any of the Terrans aboard. Jane didn't try. It was going to be her job to learn their ways, not theirs to learn hers.

She left the bridge. Just outside the door, Private Kandiss was "on duty." The soldier scared Jane a little—there had been no army on World until the Terrans came with their four soldiers. She had grown used to them, but they had always made her uneasy. Only Lieutenant Brodie had tried to learn World language or customs, and he had stayed behind. Kandiss-kal didn't smile. His weapons were terrifying and distasteful, in equal measure. But there would be soldiers on Terra, many more soldiers than just this one returning home, and Jane must accept them. Acceptance of the new was the price of what World could learn from Terra.

And the Terrans knew so much more than World! Without their

intervention, Jane's society would have perished. A debt was owed, to the soldiers no less than to the scientists.

She said, "I will be called Jane now, please." Kandiss nodded and turned away. Like Branch Carter, although for different reasons, Kandiss seldom looked directly at her, or at any of her people.

She found the fifth Terran, Kayla Rhinehart, on the observation deck, watching unmoving stars in the black sky. Jane didn't like Kayla, who was one day too weepy and the next too excited, both without reason. However, Jane tried to be compassionate because Dr. Patel-kal—Claire!—said that Kayla had a "mental condition." So did Belok^, but Belok^ was never mean.

"You're going to love Earth," Kayla said.

"Tell me about Earth," Jane said, careful of her tenses. Although that was far easier than in World, since there were fewer tenses: just past, present, and future. Nothing to distinguish tentative, absolute, rotational, or in flux states of being. A simple language, English. Jane had learned it quickly.

Kayla said, "Earth is *beautiful*. Not dark and drab like World. Blue sky, green grass, cities with buildings that touch the sky!"

World was also beautiful. Jane did not say this. She was here to learn, not argue. "Did you have lived in a city?"

"Yes." For a moment, Kayla's face darkened; she was remembering something unpleasant, although Jane knew that Kayla would never say anything unpleasant about Earth. Her face brightened. "New York is the most exciting city in the world! It has Central Park, full of trees—green trees, Jane, not those ugly purple things on World—and flower beds and paths full of humans going exciting places: movies and VR palaces and boxing matches at the Garden. I know you don't have those on World, being so backward and all."

"Where did you go in New York City?"

"Oh, everywhere! But you're missing the point. Earth is *beautiful*." She stuck out her lip and glared.

"It sounds wonderful," Jane said.

"It is! And people there don't all look alike, because they come from all different countries. Not just one dinky continent, like on World, with everybody the same coppery color you are and with the same black hair. On Earth you can tell people apart."

Jane said calmly, "Please tell me about the different countries."

"No point. Everything you could want is in America."

"Okay." Jane had discovered that "okay" was a very useful word. It could mean almost anything, even polite disagreement. "Tell me about your favorite of things to do in New York City. You have said there was a place called McDooned?"

"McDonald's," Kayla laughed. "But you don't eat meat, do you?"

"No."

"Another reason to leave World! You don't know what you're missing!"

"We believe—"

"All those primitive beliefs will change once you've been here a while. You'll be astonished at how much you'll learn."

"Okay," Jane said.

Marianne needed a real lab.

The *Return* was huge. It had been a colony ship, had killed everyone on it, and had returned empty to World, contaminated and overgrown with flora. But, scoured and disinfected, it was the only ship available for the journey back to Earth, incomprehensible ships from long-departed aliens being in short supply. The star-farers had room for ten labs, and adequate equipment for none. Marianne's "lab" consisted of a microscope, fifty years behind Earth tech, that Ka^graa had brought with him; fifteen smelly leelees in their cages; and a collection of cultures growing the virophage that had neutralized *R. sporii* on World. Which, on Terra, was now called Kindred. Or had been twenty-eight years ago.

"Hold that animal tighter," Marianne said irritably to Branch, whom she'd all but dragged from the bridge to assist. "I can't get the knife in the right spot when it wiggles so much."

"I'm no longer a lab tech," Branch said. "I'm the captain of the *Return*."

"Only because you're the only one who can make sense of the ship's hardware."

"I can't make sense of it. I can only use it—a little bit, anyway. God, this thing reeks." But he held the chittering creature closer while Marianne slid in the knife to sacrifice it.

"Marianne," Branch said quietly as she laid the leelee out for dissection, "you should wait to do that. We don't have an unlimited supply of leelees. And you'll have better equipment on Terra."

"I need to be doing something. And who knows what we'll find on Terra?"

Branch said nothing. They had gone over and over this already, with Claire. The other two Terrans aboard, Mason Kandiss and Kayla Rhinehart, had refused to participate in the discussions. Marianne knew that Private Kandiss was too fearful of what might have changed, and Kayla refused to admit the possibility that anything had.

Twenty-eight years. No one had known that taking the alien ship to Kindred would involve time dilation. If she had known, Marianne would not have gone, not even to see Noah one last time.

For Claire, Branch, and Marianne, the discussions had evolved into a morbid game about how much things would have changed while they had been gone. "In the twenty-eight years from 1950 to 1978," said Marianne, the geneticist, "we decoded the shape of DNA and sequenced an entire microorganism."

"In the twenty-eight years between 1940 and 1968," said Claire, the physician, "we got antibiotics, organ transplants, and vaccines for polio, influenza, mumps, and measles."

"In the twenty-eight years between 1990 and 2018," said Branch, the hardware wonk, "we got the Web, cell phones, and drones."

"From 1770 to 1798, the United States was formed and royalist France fell, completely changing the political realities."

"From 1955 to 2025, the CO_2 in the atmosphere went from three hundred and ten parts per million to six hundred."

"No fair, Branch," Marianne said, "that's seventy years, not twenty-eight."

Branch looked mulish. "The rate of CO_2 increase was accelerating. We could be going back to massive climate change."

"Or," Claire said, "to innovative tech that solved that problem."

"To a wrecked ecology."

"To a high-tech utopia, with free energy and cheap food."

"You wish. To an empty Earth because everybody built more alien ships and left."

"Seven billion people? Come on, these are supposed to be realistic possibilities."

"Such as free energy? Uh-huh. To a world at atomic war."

"I think," Marianne had said quietly, "that I don't want to play anymore. I have a headache."

Now she carefully removed the dead leelee's brain and began to prepare slides for the microscope. Leelees, purple malodorous fauna native to World, had been just as susceptible to the spore cloud as mice had been when *Respirovirus sporii* hit Earth thirty-eight years ago. But these particular leelees had not come from World. They had been on the infected colony ship when it returned from the aborted colony run. The ship had been lousy with spores, yet these animals had survived because they had been lousy with a virophage evolved to counteract *R. sporii*. The leelees had poured from the ship, chittering and scampering and stinking, and dissection had showed that something weird had been happening in their brains.

But Marianne had no idea what, because she had no proper lab equipment.

But soon they would reach Terra. And then—what?

Twenty-eight years was a long time.

———

Another bright day in late summer, the sky a blinding blue, maple trees just starting to tinge with red. Zachary McKay left Enclave Dome, thinking about zebras.

Both processes were complicated. Monterey Base consisted of two separate domes, and simply going from Enclave Dome to Lab Dome fifty yards away required going through the north airlock, being escorted by two of Colonel Jenner's heavily armed soldiers, and then reversing the entire process at Lab Dome's south airlock, plus passing through decontamination. Or, he could have taken the underground tunnels, which also required airlocks and decon. At least Zack, a plague survivor, didn't need to don an esuit.

Both domes were made of shimmering alien energy shields, looking like upturned blue bowls about to shed glitter on the weeds at their bases. Young forest pressed toward both bowls despite the Army's constant efforts to keep a cleared perimeter; everything grew so fast now. From above, Zack thought, the whole setup probably looked like two fluorescent breasts surrounded by beard stubble, a genuinely unsettling image.

As Zack finally reached decon in Lab Dome, Toni Steffens's voice sounded in his earplant. "Did you succeed?"

"No. Didn't try."

"Then you owe me another five dollars. Why didn't you try? It's a serious bet."

"Zebras," Zack said. Let *that* shut her up for a while.

Zack and his colleague had a long-standing bet: Who could get one of Colonel Jenner's elite squad of soldiers, whom Toni referred to as the "Praetorian Guard," to say something, anything, as they escorted scientists to and from Lab Dome. So far, Zack owed Toni $345, which was a problem in an "economy" that didn't use money. Toni was good at getting the soldiers to break silence, usually by provoking them to outrage. Zack did not do outrage, but he enjoyed hers. Usually.

She appeared in the doorway of the esuit room just beyond decon, a plain woman in her forties, dressed in ancient jeans grown a little tight and a top of flexible brown plastic fabric, the only cloth that the 3-D printer, running out of polymers, was still able to produce. "Zebras?"

"Caitlin was drawing them at breakfast."

"And how does a four-year-old even know about ungulates not found within a thousand miles of what used to be California?"

"From a picture book on her tablet. Toni, what was that Latin you quoted yesterday for Occam's razor?"

"'Numquam ponenda est pluralitas sine necessitate. Frusta fit per plura, quod potest fieri per pauciora.' It means—"

"I know what it means. The simplest explanation that fits the facts is usually correct."

"Not exactly. A literal translation—"

"Show-off."

"Ill-educated barbarian. So you think we're looking for a zebra when the hoofbeats we're hearing are from a simple horse?"

"No. I think we're looking at horses when we might need a zebra."

Toni considered this. "We would stand a better chance of finding one if Jasonus Caesar would let us experiment outside, where the meta-phorical ungulates actually are."

Zack said, "Colonel Jenner is just being cautious."

"Or just exercising his accidental power. Ave, ave, Caesar imperator. I don't understand how Lindy could have been married to him for so long."

Zack started for the corridor. Toni, who had the tenacity of a suck-ing tick, did not give up. "You think we need a whole different approach to the gene drive?"

"I don't know. But we—everybody—have been working on this problem for ten solid years and we're not making much progress."

Toni said quietly, "There used to be a lot more 'everybodies.' And it's really three problems."

"Yes. Let's get to work."

"Staff meeting this morning. Everyone's already in the conference room."

"Oh, God, I forgot."

"That's what comes of indulging zebras at breakfast."

Zack didn't pick up this gauntlet. Toni was not fond of children; she and her wife, Nicole, did not want any. More than that, Toni believed it was wrong to raise children who could never go outside the domes, not unless the microbiologists succeeded in their mission. One of their missions. Whereas for Zack and Susan, little Caitlin was the whole point of this struggle.

On the way to the conference room, Zack said, "Is anyone in there going to report any actual progress?"

"We're not going to."

"No kidding. Come on, Toni, you always hear everything. Any significant developments on the immunity questions or the vaccine?"

"No. I tell you, Zack, our team's project is going to be it. The last resort, and Jenner will have to use it."

Zack glanced over at her. Toni's usual sarcastic sneer had given way to a thoughtful sadness. He said quietly, "Maybe not. Sometimes a wild card turns up."

"Uh-huh. Or a zebra."

"Or a zebra."

They went to the conference room. This section of Lab Dome had been divided into corridors and working spaces by the usual makeshift combination of sleek painted walls from before the Collapse and rough wooden partitions erected since, mostly by the Army. Monterey Base had just begun to operate as a national laboratory, like Fort Detrick or Cold Harbor although much smaller, when the Collapse came. The equipment was—or had been, ten years ago—state of the art, but space was limited due to the constraints of domes. But if the domes hadn't existed, there would now be no Monterey Base at all. Nor would the base still be functioning if Colonel Jenner hadn't been so quick-witted and resourceful. Zack kept that constantly in mind, even if Toni didn't.

In the conference room, three dozen scientists jammed themselves around the long table, with lab techs standing along the walls. It was as bad, Zack thought, as a high-school cafeteria: like sat with like, with no mingling. The immune-boosting team sat with immune boosters, the vaccine team with other vaccinators, the gene-drive team made room for him and Toni. At the front of the room, Chief Scientist Jessica Yu, who dated all the way back to the *Embassy* team thirty-eight years ago and was now in her eighties, frowned at Zack and Toni's lateness.

"Now that we're all here," she said pointedly, "maybe we can—"

An air-shattering alarm started—*blatt blatt blatt*—and went on and on. Three blasts, repeated every five seconds.

New America was attacking.

CHAPTER 2

Zack tore out of the conference room, running at top speed to the south airlock. He was keying in the code when Toni puffed into the tiny space.

"Zack! Where the fuck do you think you're going?"

"Back to Enclave. To be with Susan and Caitlin."

"You know that's against orders and anyway they're safe!"

"Not if the attack is nuclear." Nuclear bombs were the only thing that could destroy an energy dome. That had first been demonstrated in DC eight years ago. And New York. And so many other places.

Zack said, "Then I want to die with my family."

"That's stupid! Dead is dead!"

Zack punched in the last of the manual code and touched the pad for his finger chip to register. Nothing happened.

"Damn! Jenner has us in lockdown!"

"Of course he does. Zack—"

He pounded his fist against the wall, which of course did nothing except make him feel stupid. Toni said, "Come with me to Observation."

"I'm staying right here until the all clear."

"All right. We know what an attack looks like anyway." Toni dusted off a bench in the esuit room, plopped herself down on half of it, and said, "You're behaving like an idiot."

"I know." He sat beside her. But Caitlin was scared of the sirens;

she screamed whenever they started. Zack couldn't communicate with Susan because each dome incorporated something like a Faraday cage. No electromagnetic radiation in, and none out. It was one of the things that made life here so complicated.

At the observation deck on the top of Lab Dome, the opaque bluish shimmer of the dome became a clear shimmer. Colonel Jenner had his command post at the top of Enclave Dome. But Toni was right—Zack knew what an attack by New America looked like. Warheads carried by drones would be exploding near and even against the domes, on which they would have no effect whatsoever. Birds would fly up from trees; animals would flee in terror. Fires might start in the forest, but probably not, because it had rained hard just last night. Heat-seeking drones would look for any targets outside the domes: soldiers, scientists, advance-warning equipment. Esuits used the same basic principle as the energy domes, but the suits were far more vulnerable. The basic principle had taken Terran scientists over twenty-five years to understand and duplicate. Before the Collapse, the military had had only two years to construct the first domes, including Monterey Base, as well as a large supply of esuits. It was well that they had the suits, which somehow let in pure, breathable air but filtered out everything else, because there might never be any more.

"I just wish," Zack said to Toni, "that the bastards would run out of either missiles or drones."

"They might. Someday. They can't have an infinite supply. It's not like anybody can make more."

"How long has this been?"

"Five minutes. Down, boy. We're here at least another hour."

A little less than an hour later, the airlock door began opening from the outside.

Zack and Toni sprang from the bench. The alarm was still blatting. Had the enemy somehow obtained the airlock code? Was Enclave Dome invaded?

A soldier entered, an esuit over his uniform. Not one of the survivors, then. Private Somebody—Zack paid as little attention to the military as possible. The soldier said, "Dr. McKay?"

"Yes. What is—"

"Come with me, please. Colonel Jenner has requested your presence."

"Me? What happened? Is Enclave safe? *Is it?*"

"Yes, sir."

A closer look, and Zack realized how young the soldier was. Eyes open wide, color high, a seedpod ready to burst with information.

"What is it, Private?"

The soldier said, "A ship is coming in. A spaceship. From that other planet. It's here."

Stunned silence. Then Toni said, "Well. A zebra, after all."

Jason, in his command post at the top of Enclave Dome, had received news of the attack from his master sergeant, who received it from the perimeter patrol, who received it from Lieutenant Li at the signal station.

Signaler was the most dangerous position in this transformed warfare. Domes that could not be penetrated by electromagnetic radiation meant that advance-warning equipment must be hidden somewhere outside, and so must the two soldiers who manned the station at all times. The station was equipped with radar and the ability to transmit to orbit. If the station detected incoming, the signalers contacted by earplant the soldiers on constant patrol outside the domes, who then had to go inside to sound the alert. All this limited the intel coming from the outside as well as making communication with HQ in Texas clumsy, but there was no way around it.

Since the war began eight years ago, Jason had lost three signalers. Information Tech Specialist Amanda Stevens and Private Luis Almadero had died when a New America missile hit the previous signal station, before the new one was built beneath a hill. Private John Unger, unwisely giving in to boredom, had gone exploring in his esuit and been killed by a cougar. Now Jason staffed the signaling station with a trusted J Squad officer in addition to the IT specialist.

Even at the new station, the early-warning equipment remained outside. No way around that. This was not NORAD, or what NORAD had once been.

Everything about running Monterey Base was complicated. The domes could be constructed only to a given size, with three airlocks above ground and one in the underground annex, which also had a predetermined size. Any deviation from this blueprint and the entire energy-based structure simply disintegrated. No physicists knew why. They might have learned if the Collapse hadn't come, but it did, and Jason spent hours each day maneuvering around the limitations of the structures that had saved all their lives. First from the bird plague, and then from New America.

It used to be that the signal station received news from orbiting satellites, both military and civilian. But over time, the satellites had failed. No maintenance, no orbital adjustments, no personnel. The US Army was down to one functional comsat. New America also controlled a comsat, and so far neither side had figured out how either to destroy the other's or to hack its encryption.

"Sir," Master Sergeant Hillson said over the blatting alarm, "message from Lieutenant Li at the signal station."

"Go on," Jason said. Hillson, a thirty-year lifer whom Jason would have trusted with his command if necessary, always spoke slowly, sometimes with pauses between his words. This was not, Jason had learned long ago, because Hillson didn't know what he thought. The sergeant paused because he was reluctant to let words go. Dragged up dirt poor in some God-forsaken corner of the Ozarks, his instinct was to hold on to everything as long as he could, even words. But his statements, when they finally emerged, were always true. Always.

"Sir, the station has received direct contact from a *spaceship*."

Jason said sharply, "The *Stremlenie*?" No one knew what had happened to the Russian ship.

"No, sir. Lieutenant says the ship claims to be American, coming from World. Calling itself the *Return*."

Jason stared. For a long moment, Hillson's words refused to form themselves into coherent thought. They jumped around randomly, pixels on a deranged screen.

The American ship *Friendship* had departed Earth twenty-eight years ago. Its mission had been to establish trade relations with the human-aliens who had arrived on Earth ten years earlier, warned Earth about the spore cloud, deceived everyone, and abruptly departed. The *Friendship* and its twenty-one passengers, including the grandmother that Jason had finished mourning decades ago, had never been heard from again. Perhaps the Russian ship, which had launched shortly afterward, had destroyed the *Friendship*. Perhaps the alien star drive on both ships had failed. Perhaps World, that unknown planet, had decided to keep the ships and kill the Terrans. After the Collapse, no one on Earth had cared. Only survival mattered.

Pixelated thoughts cohered into solidity and hardness. "The *Return*? Not the *Friendship*? What were Lieutenant Li's exact words?"

"'For immediate emergency relay to Colonel Jenner, priority one: Contact by an alien ship calling itself the *Return* and claiming to be carrying Americans and coming from World. I have not responded. Do not know if the message is connected with the drone attack. Please advise.'"

It could be a trick by New America. Get a detachment of soldiers outside the dome, mount a second drone attack. Although New America had tried something similar before, and had not succeeded. Jason rose from his desk and scanned the sky through the clear top of the dome.

The missiles had spent themselves uselessly against the domes and then ceased, leaving debris lying around the cleared zone but no fires, not this time. As soon as the drones stopped coming, perimeter patrol had returned outside, although staying close to the airlock and ready for snipers. Jason squinted into the distance.

Overhead a hawk soared, dark against the clouds.

A breeze stirred the treetops, a hundred yards away and level with the top of the dome.

At the edge of the trees, a deer appeared, startled, and vanished.

Sergeant Hillson waited.

The alarm still sounded: *blatt blatt blatt*.

"Tell them to turn off the alarm, but don't sound the all clear. Get Major Duncan up here."

"Yes, sir. Sir . . . Corporal Olivera."

Jason turned. Rosa Olivera, assigned to patrol, held out a tiny data cube. "Sir, Lieutenant Li sent this. A longer message from the spaceship. The lieutenant relayed it to record for you."

Jason popped the cube into his wrister. A male voice said, "Come in, Earth. This is the World ship *Return*, Captain Branch Carter. We are coming from World—Kindred, I mean—the planet that the *Friendship* left Earth for twenty-eight years ago. Some of that original mission are aboard here, including me. We're coming home."

Jason's forehead wrinkled. The message sounded in no way military. He touched his finger chip to his wrister and said, "Identity, Branch Carter, *Friendship* mission, text only."

Carter continued, "A lot has happened to tell you about, but right now we just want permission to land. Last night we didn't see any city lights from space, which sort of concerns us. Also, no one has responded to our hailings. I don't really know how to direct this communication very well, it's not our ship and I'm not really an engineer, but—"

BRANCH CARTER scrolled across the small screen on Jason's wrister. Member of *Friendship* diplomatic mission, lab technician. MS from Yale, employed at CDC from—

A lab tech? As captain? Jason turned off the wrister.

"—but we're relaying this message through what looks like an American comsat. I think. If you give us coordinates to land, latitude and longitude, I think I can get this system to recognize those enough so we can set down. I hope."

He hoped? What kind of Mickey Mouse operation—

Then, with surprising dignity, "I know this message must sound strange. There was time dilation that we didn't know about—and I guess you probably don't, either—both going to and coming from World. Twenty-eight years, total. There are only ten of us aboard here, and to us, it's like we've only been gone a few months. We're five Terran and five Kindred, and none of us understand the ship. We are doing the best we can."

Corporal Olivera blurted out, *"Five aliens?"* She turned a mottled red. "Sorry, sir."

Jason was thinking faster than he had since the Collapse. It could still be a trick and "Branch Carter's" voice a pretense. The *Friendship*, he remembered, had been equipped with classified alpha-beam weapons capable of firing ship-to-ground; this ship, if indeed there was an actual ship, could also carry that ordnance. If he denied permission to land, what would the ship do? If it *was* permitted to land, it could carry various forms of contamination. Or, given that Kindred was so much more advanced than Terra, the ship could contain incredibly valuable tech. Or it might hold both: contaminants and advanced tech. But then why didn't this Branch Carter seem to know anything about the ship, and why weren't the alleged aliens aboard the ones captaining her? They had invented the technology! That argued for a trick. But—

Then another voice sounded on the recording, and the probability waves in Jason's mind collapsed into certainty.

"This is Dr. Marianne Jenner, from the *Friendship*. I'm a scientist; I worked in the *Embassy* with the original team for the spore cloud. My son Noah and nine others left on the *Embassy* for Kindred, and he is still there. May I speak to the president, or to his or her representative, or maybe to the UN? I also want to say that we have with us a virophage that counteracts *Respirovirus sporii*."

No one spoke.

Then Jason said to Hillson, "Equip two FiVees. One goes to the ship with J Squad, to rendezvous at Point Tango Delta. Bring ten extra es-uits. Pick up all star-farers for transport to the signal station, it's closer. The other FiVee to transport me to the original station with doctors Ross and Yu. No, not Yu"—the chief scientist was too old—"Dr. McKay. Orders are that if anything impedes transport progress, shoot it."

Major Elizabeth Duncan, Jason's second in command, strode into the command post. Jason said to her, "Major, we have a situation. Brief you in a minute." And to Hillson, "Go!"

"Yes, sir."

It was the first time Jason had ever heard the veteran sergeant's voice tremble. Jason hoped that his own had not. But—

A spaceship. And what did you say to a grandmother who left for the stars when you were eleven, twenty-eight years ago?

"Why aren't they answering?" Branch said. "Why isn't *anybody* answer-ing?"

Marianne said wearily, "Are you sure you're doing it right?"

"Of course I'm not sure I'm doing it right! None of us knows what we're doing!"

Jane looked from one Terran to the other. They were tired—every-body was tired—and they did not have bu^ka^tel to guide their behav-ior, as any Worlder would. She said softly in her still-slow English, "You did this thing wonderful well by now. We are here, and they maybe will answer soon."

Marianne smiled at her, a smile so full of anxiety and exhaustion that Jane longed to take some of the burden off the older woman's shoulders.

They stood on the bridge of the vast *Return*, all ten of them. Mason Kandiss wore his armor and carried all his weapons, although Jane did not understand why. Kayla lay asleep on a mat in the corner. The five Worlders stood behind Marianne, Branch, and Claire, who clustered around a screen filled with a huge planet.

Terra. Blue and white, incredibly beautiful. And so much land! Thirty percent of the surface was land, Branch had said. Unimaginable room—except that it held an equally unimaginable and terrifying population of over seven billion people. Or by now, Marianne had said, even more.

Ka^graa said to his daughter, "What do they say?"

Jane translated. "They still try to greet Terra and do not understand why no one replies. Branch-kal wishes he understood more about how the ship works."

Ka^graa, who did not understand it either, said, "Have they discovered why they see no city lights on the planet?"

"No."

"Come in, come in, Terra. This is the World ship *Return*, Captain Branch Carter. We are the—"

"Captain Carter, this is Colonel Jason Jenner of the United States Army."

Marianne made a small sound.

The voice continued, "Can you provide positive identification that you are who you claim to be?"

Branch said, "What kind of proof?"

Marianne stepped forward. "Colonel Jenner, this is Marianne Jenner. Are you Ryan Anthony Jenner's son? I know Jenner is a common name, but—"

"Yes. Ryan Jenner is my father. Can you provide positive identification that you are actually who you claim to be?"

Marianne, her voice thick, said, "When you were a small boy, you had an ant farm that fascinated you. It broke and there were ants all over the house. Colin ate one."

Silence. Jane had a sudden qualm. If this man was a soldier like the ones that had come to World, there were very strict rules about what you could and could not say. Jane didn't understand those rules, but no one had ever spoken so informally, so naturally, to Lieutenant Lamont. Although they did, eventually, to Lieutenant Brodie. It was all very confusing.

"Jason?" Marianne said.

The unseen soldier spoke again. His voice was still formal, but Jane could hear emotion underneath. "World ship *Return*—welcome home."

Claire Patel laughed, as much from relief as mirth. Then they were all smiling. But it was Ranger Kandiss who astonished Jane. His body held as rigid as ever, his lips moving silently—in prayer?—he let tears course silently over his face.

Both smiles and tears both stopped at Jason Jenner's next words. "*Return*, we have a situation on Earth, developed since the *Friendship* launched twenty-eight years ago. You said that you are equipped with a drug that can counteract *R. sporii*?"

"Not a drug," Marianne said, while Jane struggled to keep up translation for the other four Worlders. "A microbe, a virophage. It . . . why do you need a counteraction for *R. sporii*? When we left, Terrans were either immune or had already died from the original spore cloud, and a vaccine had been developed and—"

The voice cut her off. "*Return*, you must land now. You've been detected by the enemy. Latitude and longitude to follow immediately. When your ship touches down, do not—repeat, do not—attempt to emerge unless you have sufficient esuits for everyone aboard. Do you?"

Carter said, "Yes, but—what enemy?"

"Are your esuits the same as the ones we've made from plans left by World scientists on your previous expedition?"

"Yes, they are, but *what enemy?*"

"We are at war. Put on your esuits immediately, land, and cycle through your airlock to exit the ship. Do not let Terran air invade the ship or it will be contaminated. Stay under cover of trees, if you can. Troops will meet you and conduct you to safety. Go with them immediately. *Now*, Captain Carter!"

"But I'm not even sure if I—"

Some numbers, a burst of static, and then nothing.

"Do as he says," Branch said. His young face had paled. "Go to the airlock and suit up. I'm going to land where he said."

Jane ran with the others to the closest airlock. Did Branch know how to land the ship at a specific place? Would the ship help him? A war— why was there a war? With who?

Esuits lay on shelves in the vast room. Glamet^vor¡ and La^vor struggled to get Belok^ into his. He started to cry and La^vor comforted him.

The screen on the wall brightened, and the planet on it grew larger and larger until blue and white filled the whole screen. Suddenly a burst of red, eerie in its silence.

Kandiss said, "Enemy fire. We are under attack."

Ka^graa grabbed Jane's arm. "What did he say?"

"It is a weapon. It tried to hit us."

The ship lurched. Somehow, Jane was more shocked by that than by anything else—the *Return* always flew sedately, even when it had launched, without perceptible motion. Belok^ cried out.

The screen now showed nothing but white—they were inside clouds. A moment later, the ground flew up at terrifying speed. Then they broke through trees—green trees, not purple!—and came to rest quietly on the ground.

Mason Kandiss activated the airlock.

"No, wait!" Marianne cried. "Branch!"

"Orders are to get you out. He can recycle later. Go now."

It was, Jane realized numbly, the longest speech she had ever heard Mason Kandiss make.

He pushed them all into the airlock. Air, the good air of World, which Jane had probably breathed for the last time, was sucked out. The outer door opened and six soldiers rushed in. The leader's eyes widened when he saw Mason Kandiss, but he didn't slow. "Come with us! Now!"

They ran from the ship. There was no need to get under trees; a big cart waited, made of heavy metal. One man sat in a small housing in the front; the back was open. A *truck*, Jane remembered—it was fueled in ways forbidden on World. A soldier picked up Jane and threw her into the back.

"Wait!" Marianne cried. "There is one more person coming! The captain, Branch Carter—"

"We'll come back for him if we can. Orders are to get you out." He threw Marianne into the truck. She landed on top of Jane.

Something exploded with tremendous sound and fire in the trees beyond. Wood, leaves, dirt, even rocks flew into the air. The soldiers leaped into the truck, the back closed, and it sped away—so fast! Unlike the ship, it lurched and bounced on the uneven ground, crashing through bushes. Jane hung on to metal protrusions in the wall. Belok^ never stopped screaming.

Over the din, Kandiss yelled, "Destination, sir?"

"Signal station. Close now."

The truck drove past more trees toward a hill. A section of the hill opened and the truck drove downward into a cave and stopped. The hill swung shut behind them. Lights came on.

Abrupt silence. Even Belok^ stopped yelling.

"Decon is this way, and it's also the airlock," a soldier said, leaping down from the truck. She was talking to Kandiss. "Bring your people through in groups of five, that's probably all that will fit. Esuits stay on at all times."

"Yes, ma'am."

The soldier thought Kandiss was in charge. But since Marianne said nothing, Jane merely translated for the others, who nodded. Belok^ clutched La^vor with one hand and touched the truck with the other, his eyes wide and mouth open in a wide O.

Decon—Jane would have to ask what the word meant—was a small airlock abruptly bathed in violet light. When the far door opened, they walked into an underground room, windowless, with walls of wood and metal. One wall held a bank of strange equipment. Four men and two women, all in uniform, waited until everyone had come from the airlock. The room was not meant for so many.

One of the men, the only soldier in an esuit, stepped forward. Jane, shaken by the rough ride, the violence, the strangeness of everything, nonetheless felt another tiny shock. His eyes, clear gray flecked with gold, were Marianne's.

"I am Colonel Jenner, commander of Monterey Base. Do not remove your esuits, not yet, for your protection and ours. You must have questions, and I think we have much information to exchange. Almost nothing on Earth is as you remember it. But first . . . again, welcome home."

Jane had never heard a greeting so weary and regretful. Jason Jenner's face looked like petrified karthwood at home, set in hard ridges instead of supple in the wind. And so formal—this was Marianne, his grandmother and surely the mother of his lahk! Although there were no lahks here—but there *were* "families." He did not even look at Marianne.

She had expected things on Terra to be different from World, but not like this.

Quietly, keeping fear and sorrow to herself so as not to increase theirs, she began to translate for her father and the other three.

Zack had been designated the explainer, a role he did not want. Jenner was busy barking orders to the two signal officers in person and the Praetorian Guard remotely, presumably trying to save the ship and the station from drone attacks, if that was possible. Probably it wasn't; Jenner was breaking radio silence, which of course had already been broken by contact with the ship, and New America would be tracking him through their comsat. Zack hoped that nothing stronger than a drone-carried missile would be fired at this underground bunker. During the Collapse, when Army bases were all charnel houses of the dead and dying, all sorts of organizations had taken over the bases. What eventually became New America had gained nuclear capability—and used it two years later, during the war. But if they had any nukes left, wouldn't they have already used them? And wouldn't they want to capture this ship from the stars, not destroy it?

It wasn't as if the New America survivalists were as psychotic as the Gaiists had been. Just as evil, but not as deranged.

Zack sat on a hard, straight-backed chair—trust the military to think comfort unimportant—and waited while Dr. Lindy Ross examined the nine star-farers. No, not examined—she could hardly palpate anything through an esuit, let alone take blood samples. These people would have to be introduced, or reintroduced, to Terran microbes. Did Lindy have the means to do that at the base? Meanwhile, she passed her portalab over their hearts and heads, studied the results, talked to humans and aliens.

No. They were all human, including the Worlders. Zack, who had been five years old when the Worlders left Earth thirty-eight years ago, had of course seen pictures. At university he had studied the reports of blood and tissue samples. The Worlders—Denebs, Kindred, the names kept changing until the Collapse, when nobody was interested any longer—were human, brought from Earth to their planet 140,000 years ago.

By whom? Unknown.

Why? Unknown.

They looked human, with minor evolutionary adaptations. Copper-colored skin, like aged pennies. Coarse black hair, all of them. Tall and slender—was gravity less on World? Zack couldn't remember what he'd read about that. The only strange thing was the eyes, much larger than Terrans, genetically selected to gather as much light as possible under a dimmer sun. He did remember that much.

One of the two young girls was translating. A fine-boned, very pretty face. The other Worlders were a scowling young man, an older man, and a large boy. The boy turned, clutching at the other girl. Zack startled—the boy's features were unmistakable, even across cultures and light-years. Why bring a mentally challenged kid to another planet?

Marianne Jenner broke away from the group and walked over to the colonel. Zack was glad to not overhear that conversation. Her face went through changes: questioning, shock, anger. She stalked away.

What was that all about? It almost seemed as if they already knew each other. "Jenner"—were they related? It wasn't that uncommon a name. During the hectic ride in the FiVee from the base to the station, the soldier in charge had refused to answer any questions at all: "You will be debriefed at the appropriate time." Lindy had made a moue of disgust.

Now Lindy walked over to Zack and smiled wryly. "You're on. Jason wants you to give them the abbreviated version of the past twenty-eight years. They're all healthy as far as I can tell through esuits, but bewildered and upset, especially Kayla Rhinehart. She's the one sobbing. One of the Terrans got left behind at the ship, Branch Carter. Claire Patel—she's the Indian-American woman—is a physician and says they're all asymptomatic from the virophage they're infected with. She says that on Kindred, it counterattacked *R. sporii*."

"Really? And they're all infected?"

"So she says. We have to get them to quarantine stat, but Jason is still trying to save the ship from drone attacks. Apparently it's not e-shielded. Everything's all fucked up out there still. He—Shit!"

A direct hit on the hill. The bunker shuddered, but nothing fell from the ceiling and the station held. They were probably all right down here. Probably.

Lindy, who had nerves of titanium—and most likely needed them to have been married to Jenner—said, "You want me to stand by while you do the dismal?"

"Yeah. Thanks. About this virophage—"

"I don't know any more than that," Lindy said.

"Are the ali—the Worlders fluent enough in English to understand me?"

"Jane is, if you talk slowly. She's the translator."

"'Jane'?"

"Apparently self-chosen. She seems very bright. Come on, they're waiting."

"Just one more thing—did you happen to see Susan and Caitlin before they brought you here?"

"No. But Caity will be fine, Zack. She's learned to cope with her condition remarkably well for a four-year-old, and she's getting better all the time."

Zack walked across the underground bunker to the waiting starfarers. How did you explain in a few paragraphs what Earth had become? Especially to people who must have expected something far different.

"Hello," he said. "I'm Dr. Zachary McKay, a virologist. I'm sorry for this upsetting arrival. Colonel Jenner asked me to tell you about Earth and to answer the questions you must have."

"Yes," Marianne said. "This is Dr. Claire Patel, Kayla Rhinehart, and Private . . . no, I guess he's over there with . . . with the colonel."

A catch in her voice. So she and Jenner *were* related. How? Zack said, "I've read your paper on mitochondrial haplogroups, Dr. Jenner. Seminal."

She grimaced. Okay, a sensitive subject. It had, after all, started so much. She continued. "This is Jane, our translator. Ka^graa and Glamet^vor͓, both biologists. La^vor and her brother Belok^."

He would never remember the names, which involved rising-and-falling inflections and, for one, a click at the end. Zack settled for a friendly nod. Jane murmured in low, musical translation.

"All right," Marianne said, "tell us what happened that we need to wear esuits, that there are no city lights visible from space, that missiles are falling on California. Start at when the *Friendship* left Earth."

Zack looked at her. Late sixties, maybe, although she looked older. Clearly braced for the worst, yet she asked, clear-eyed and ready to bear whatever she must. Admiration flooded him.

He plunged in. "After your ship left, climate change on Earth accelerated, even worse than had been predicted. Feedback loops became engaged. CO_2 levels rose, ice at the poles melted, there was severe coastal flooding and increasing superstorms and radically decreased ocean phytoplankton—that was why the *Friendship* was originally built, wasn't it? By that entrepreneur who thought we only had a few generations left and the best hope for humanity was to start spreading to the stars?"

"Yes." Short and clipped—she didn't want to talk about Jonah Stubbins. Zack could only remember part of that story; he would look it up when they got back to the base. If they got back to the base.

"Stubbins was actually right. The entire global ecology was on the way to destruction, or at least to being drastically altered. Then a group of environmental fanatics—"

"Please, slower," Jane said. "And what is 'fanatic'?"

Claire Patel said, "Hubon^tel," and Marianne glanced at her in surprise.

"This environmental group," Zack continued, "called themselves Gaiists. They—"

"Please," Jane said, "I am sorry—but how can people be too much dedicated to environment? It is Mother Earth and without care, it will not support life."

My first insight into World culture, Zack thought. Too bad they hadn't been in charge of Terra when carbon-emission caps and all the other pathetic stopgaps had failed.

He said, "The Gaiists were 'too much dedicated to the environment' when they decided that humans were a deadly parasite on the planet, and only if we were gone could Earth recover. So they tried to kill off humanity, or at least most of it. And they succeeded."

No one spoke, and Zack had a hard time looking at their faces. "The Gaiists had started as a group of scientists dedicated to stopping global warming, and to reversing it if they could, no matter what the cost. But a group of fanatics seized control. Their numbers grew, people were desperate. Gaiists cells formed in a lot of countries, not just scientists anymore although a few gifted, deranged scientists remained. They were convinced that the only way to save humanity was to destroy it. They weaponized *R. sporii.*"

"*How?*" Marianne said.

"Are you familiar with the experiments—they go back over fifty years—to dramatically increase the virility of pox viruses by insert-ing human immune-boosting genes into the virus, so that the body gets overwhelmed by its own antibodies?"

"Yes, of course. But *R. sporii* wasn't—isn't—a pox virus. It's related to the paramyxoviruses."

Marianne, this indomitable old woman, seemed to Zack the only one capable of speech. Jane had stopped translating, overwhelmed either by the technical language or by horror. He said, "Yes. But the Gaiist scientists—they were brilliant, you have to give them that—did something similar to *R. sporii*. They then combined it with another paramyxovirus, avulavirus, whose natural host is sparrows. Avulavirus shares spore disease's structure and entry protein, glycoprotein. Avula-virus is usually transmissible by direct contact, but now it's airborne from bird droppings, with a dual reservoir—humans and several species of sparrows. The birds are asymptomatic carriers."

"And the humans?"

This was the hard part. "The weaponized microbe was released ten years ago. It was deadly. The incubation period is incredibly short. Ninety-six percent of humans died within a few weeks."

Kayla Rhinehart screamed and fell to the floor. Jane translated that, her voice quavering. Claire Patel made a small sound and turned away.

Marianne, her face pale and waxy, said, "So there were left alive—"

"Something like two hundred and eighty million worldwide, four-teen million in the United States. Not so many now." Starvation, disease, suicide, gangs, war.

Marianne, very pale, said, "Go on. Why the war?"

"After the Collapse, that's what we call it"—because no one could bear the more accurate names—"the survivors were, and are, two groups. The four percent who survived *R. sporii avivirus*—we call it RSA—and the people who were inside energy domes and have not gone outside since without esuits. The weaponized virus is still out there. It didn't die out because sparrows serve as the alternate host. That's why you were told to put on esuits. Things in America would be much worse if it weren't for domes and esuits, both technology we gained from the Worlders and finally figured out." Zack nodded at Ka^graa.

Claire said, "It wasn't theirs."

"What?"

Marianne said, "Never mind that now. Go on."

Zack said, "The survivors, some of them anyway, formed various paramilitary groups. There were intragroup warfare and South American–style coups, including among some ex-Army. You have to understand that entire military bases were empty and vulnerable. One group emerged from the fighting, New America. They seized control of critical Army bases, all equipped with various weapons. They want the rest of the bases and weapons, including ours at Monterey Base. They think we might have control of some really big stuff."

She didn't, thank heavens, ask what big stuff. Zack had heard the rumors, and feared they were true.

Marianne said, "The federal government?"

"DC was nuked even before New America killed off its rivals. No one knows if it was a homegrown group, Russia, China, North Korea— anyone who had the bomb. Although when Congress still existed, it was New America they declared war on."

"US retaliation?"

"Yes. And counterretaliation. Much of the East Coast, plus Seattle, LA, and Chicago are radiation holes. And most key military bases as well."

"How many of these energy-shielded domes are left?"

"Not sure. There may be small ones with no ability to communicate. There is no Internet anymore—it was designed to survive attack, but nothing was designed for RSA."

"So who does my grandson report to?"

Grandson. Well, at least that meant she had one family member left. No, two—the colonel's brother would also be her grandson. Zack hadn't been that lucky. He'd lost everyone, until he met Susan and they had Caitlin. He would die before he lost this second, precious family.

He said, "The American military government, which is what we have now, holds a few domed bases across the country. Headquarters is at Fort Hood, Texas. Colonel Jenner can tell you more about that."

"These protective domes—can't you make more?"

"Energy dome manufacture was just starting when the Collapse came and the factory went up with LA. We can't even alter their size or shape—essentially, they're prefabs. But now that World scientists are here, with their more advanced—"

Jane spoke, in English, with the look of a person focusing on what was most important. "The Earth, now . . . is the globe warming stopped? Is the environment saved?"

For a moment, red rage flooded Zack. Then he got control of himself. She couldn't know, this human girl cousin from the stars, that she had just named the Gaiist and New America justification for mass murder of nearly an entire species, and that species their own. Even now there were people who said, *But what would have become of all of us on an unsustainable Earth if 96 percent hadn't died? Wasn't 96 percent better than everyone? Even now.*

"Yes," he said to Jane. "Global warming has stopped increasing. Earth is slowly returning to healthy forests and savannahs and wetlands and jungles. To lovely pristine wilderness."

"Zack," Lindy said warningly. Jane looked as if he'd slapped her— had his tone been that savage? Maybe. He was an RSA survivor. When he'd emerged from the fever high enough to cause delirium, his first wife and two sons lay dead on the bedroom floor, their lungs drowned in their own bodily fluids.

Lindy took Jane's hand. "You'll be okay, Jane. All of you. As soon as Jas—Colonel Jenner says it's safe, we'll take you all to quarantine and adjust your gut microbes to Terran air. The process is much easier than it once was. We've learned a lot about the human body since you left. And inside the e-shields your people gave ours, you'll be safe."

Marianne said, "I had two other children and another grandson . . ."

Zack watched realization dawn on Lindy. He saved her from having to make explanations. "Marianne, Colin Jenner is an RSA survivor. He lives at the coast."

Tears clouded her eyes. Zack knew, already, she was a person who would hate that public display of weakness. He took a stab at redirection. "You said you're infected with a virophage against the original *R. sporii?*"

"Yes." He watched her face steady. "But I doubt it will have any effect on this variation. If the virus has been merged with a bird virus, the two versions will be too different."

"Yes, but we can try. Have you cultured the virophage?"

"Yes. But those cultures are aboard ship. There are anomalies in infected native animals—I want to talk to you about that. Later."

Yes, later. Zack turned to the physician, Claire Patel. "We're doing work here that will interest you I think. And now that these scientists are here from World"—he nodded at the two men—"with their much more advanced knowledge, the work will probably go much better!"

Silence. Then Claire said in a flat voice, "There is no 'much more advanced knowledge.' World science and technology are about fifty years behind ours. Ours when we left Terra, I mean."

"But . . . but . . . the energy shields! The spaceships!"

"Not theirs. And they don't know whose, any more than we do."

Zack considered this, while the world turned itself inside out, like a sock. World was not ahead of Terra, but behind. There would be no help from the stars.

But there would be no advanced weapons, either, which was undoubtedly what Jason Jenner had been talking to the star-faring soldier about. Jenner would gain only the ship itself, if he had managed to save it.

That, and five transplanted refugees who probably wished right now that they had never left home.

CHAPTER 3

"Sir," Lieutenant Seth Allen said in Jason's earplant, "we picked up the starship captain, Branch Carter. He'd left the ship in an esuit and was following the FiVee's tracks here. He says he thinks he can move the ship. It hasn't been hit yet, although one missile came close. But sir, it's a whole lot bigger than we expected. Maybe twenty times the size of the one that launched twenty-eight years ago."

Jason said, "Okay, stand by." He tongue-flicked off his mic and turned to Mason Kandiss, the soldier from the *Return*. Jason wanted a debrief about the whole situation, but there was no time for that now. Zack McKay and Lindy had the other nine refugees in a far corner of the signaling station, checking them out and answering questions. Outside the signaling station, the drones still attacked—how many more missiles were the fuckers prepared to expend? Jason would have to have the signaling station moved again, assuming the external equipment survived. If it didn't, they'd lose contact with the comsat as well as the ship, and communication with Headquarters would be reduced to the uncertainties of long-distance radio.

Private Kandiss stood at attention, a faded Ranger tab on his shoulder. Jason said, "At ease, Private. I need information. Does that ship have its own e-shield?"

"No, sir."

"What can destroy it?"

"On World, a shoulder-launched missile blew a big hole in it. It was repaired."

World had shoulder-launched missiles? Jason thought it was supposed to be peaceful, without war. But no time to go into that now.

"To the best of your knowledge, can Captain Carter lift the ship again?"

"He says so, sir."

"Can he park it in a stable orbit high enough to preclude a drone attack? Earth no longer has space-missile capacity." Long gone. But at least Earth no longer had fighter jets, or they would have hit the spaceship already. The world's remaining jets sat rusting on cracked tarmacs, all fuel long since expended and no people to make more.

"I don't know, sir. Carter isn't really a pilot. He's a lab assistant with a knack for hardware."

Christ. The only starship on Earth and it depended on a lab assistant with a knack for hardware. But it wasn't like Jason had much choice; they had no additional dome to put the ship under, even if it would've fit, and a direct missile hit could take out the signaling shield at any moment. Jason flicked on his mic.

"Lieutenant Allen, take Carter back to the ship and stay in it while he takes it up to low orbit. Take IT Specialist Martin with you. Up there, both of you learn everything he knows about the ship—maneuverability, communication capacity, fuel stores, weapons—particularly weapons. Await contact with us—we might wait to contact you, to avoid giving away the position of the next station. If you hear nothing in a week, it means the contact equipment has been destroyed. Land somewhere and hope. Go now."

"Yes, sir. Out."

Jason scanned the station. Sergeant Hillson stood with more of J Squad, awaiting orders. The star-farers huddled with Zack McKay and Lindy in a corner. As soon as he deemed it safe, Jason would send them all to the base.

"Sir," Kandiss said, "permission to speak."

"Go ahead."

"What happened to the Seventy-Fifth?"

The Ranger Regiment of the United States Army. Of course Kandiss would want to know; he must have assumed he would return to it, albeit twenty-eight years later than he'd expected.

"I don't know. They were headquartered at Fort Benning, weren't they?"

If Kandiss felt surprise that Jason didn't know this, it didn't show. "Yes. And the Second Battalion at Joint Base Lewis–McChord."

"Benning is gone. Pretty much the entire East Coast was heavily nuked during the war. It's not livable. Seattle and Portland were taken out, too, as was Creech Air Force Base. There are a few other Army bases left and staffed, or at least the parts of them that were under domes, notably Fort Hood and Fort Campbell. We are in communication with them. Headquarters is Fort Hood, ranking officer is General Ethan Lassiter, who is the military head of the United States under martial law." Jason didn't add that Lassiter was eighty-three and sickly. Let that information wait.

Kandiss said, "Commander in chief?"

"There is no president anymore. Chain of command starts with Lassiter." Whom Jason would have to apprise about the *Return* as soon as possible.

"Yes, sir," Kandiss said. His face was stone.

"You are hereby officially attached to J Squad of this company," Jason said, knowing that what men like Kandiss needed was structure. "When we return to base, see Sergeant Tasselman about billeting. After that, report to me for full debriefing."

"Yes, sir."

"Dismissed."

Kandiss joined the other refugees. A Ranger in such superb physical condition would be an asset to the elite J Squad. And Kandiss was probably the most reliable source for learning in military terms what had happened on World, including to the rest of Kandiss's unit. And hadn't there been an ambassador along?

His grandmother would know.

Jason turned his back to the group of refugees. He had never before considered himself a coward. He had seen military service in Congo, he had come through the horror of the Collapse, he had fought New America. He had taken control of Monterey Base when there was nobody else left to do so. He was a colonel in the United States Army. He could steel himself to do what was necessary to the man in the underground prison in order to further protect the safety of those in his charge.

But faced with his grandmother, the woman from the stars whom he had long thought dead, a thousand memories flooded his already stressed brain: Grandma making him and Colin peanut butter and jelly sandwiches. Grandma teaching him to read. Grandma believing Colin could superhear what Colin said he could, when no one else believed. Grandma was the same as Marianne Jenner, world-famous geneticist—Jason's childish pride when he had first realized that! Grandma—

But he had lacked the courage to tell her outright that her daughter, his aunt Liz, had vanished during the Collapse. *R. sporii*, the scourge that his grandmother had once successfully defeated, had been weaponized by madmen to roar back and defeat the victors.

Only—Jason did not feel defeated, and that was going to be the hardest thing of all to explain to her. Ninety-six percent of humanity had perished, but humanity was recovering. The remaining three large Army bases were winning the war against New America, even though the enemy had guerilla mobility on their side and a continent-wide returning wilderness to hide in. The scientists in Lab Dome, which Jason would do anything at all to protect, were going to figure out a way to neutralize RSA. He believed that. Villages and farms, at least those he'd had contact with on the West Coast, had not descended into preindustrial barbarism. The United States had working technology, and enough brilliant minds to restart heavy industry as soon as the war was over and factories could be restarted or built. Children were being born. The oceans and atmosphere were recovering.

Would his grandmother see all that? Could he make her see it?

He knew what she would see at the base, what it would look like to her eyes. Two domes packed with too many people, divided into mazelike warrens by walls of wood harvested from the burgeoning forest or metal from before the Collapse. The result was a functional, unlovely, ramshackle hodgepodge surrounded by blue shimmering walls.

Once Lindy had said, "It's a mess. But what can you expect in a postapocalyptic world?"

"This is not a postapocalyptic world!" Jason had flared, before he even knew he was going to say anything.

She'd stared at him in astonishment. "Of course it is. The Collapse was an *apocalypse*, Jason. The Four Horsemen, every last rider."

"No. We are not scavenging for canned goods. We are not eating dogs. This is an Army base, orderly and growing. We are not some cheap horror film cliché. This is a thriving base of the United States Army."

"You always have to think you're in control, don't you? Have to prove to yourself again and again that you can handle anything because nothing is stronger than you are, not even reality."

"That is not true."

"It is, and don't take that measured and superior tone with me. I'm sick of it."

The fight had escalated from there. One of their many, many fights. Until the last one.

He could not expect Lindy to tell Grandma about Aunt Liz. Jason would have to do that himself. And this old woman who had come home from so far, who had endured so much over the years, who looked so worn—was she strong enough to bear this double blow?

"Sir," Li said, "the shelling has stopped and the outside equipment wasn't hit."

"Good. We'll wait for confirmation of liftoff from the *Return*, then convey the refugees to base. I'll leave three of the squad here to help you move the station tonight." Li would already have the next location picked out, and it would be the best fit possible, the borer bot already on site.

Jason needed to call General Lassiter at HQ and brief him, now, before the station's equipment was either hit or moved. Radio contact among the domes that did not go through the one remaining com-sat, and so did not call further attention to the signaling equipment, was fitful. It depended on the use of codes and coding machines, and no one knew when or if New America had broken the latest code. It had all been so much easier when the Internet had existed, along with quantum encryption, cell towers, and eyes-in-the-sky. But if they existed, then New America would have access to them, too. Maybe this way was actually better.

You always have to think you're in control, don't you?

And she had always said that he wasn't. Jason was better off without her.

He straightened his back to go talk to his grandmother.

In the outer cave, Jane climbed into the back of the big self-moving cart—a "fighting vehicle." Huge guns, much bigger than anything Lieutenant Lamont had had on World, were mounted on the front. The FiVee had no windows along the sides but there was a big window along the front. The shield between front and back was now gone. Five soldiers, one of them driving, and nine people from the *Return* crowded the space. Kayla still sobbed. Zack McKay perched at the edge of a bench that ran along the inside, talking intently with Claire. Marianne had jammed herself into a corner, her face turned away from the rest of them.

Jane maneuvered to squeeze in beside Lindy Ross, who seemed the most willing to answer questions. "Lindy, are you of Army, too?"

"No, I'm a civilian. That means 'not in the Army.'"

Jane noted the word. "The soldiers here don't wear esuits, but Lieutenant Jenner does wear one. Why—"

"*Colonel* Jenner," Lindy corrected. Her face took on a fleeting expression that Jane could not interpret.

"Yes, I am sorry. Colonel Jenner." She had not heard that title from the Terran soldiers on World; the soldier leader there was "lieutenant." It was confusing.

"Oh, I don't mind, but he will." Again that face. "About the esuits— some people at the base are survivors of RSA and so are immune. Like me, and all of the soldiers here although not all of those at the base. Some never had the disease and aren't immune, and since the virus is airborne, those can't go outside without the esuits. Is your English good enough for scientific translation?"

"I hope so. My father and Glamet^vorᵢ are biologists."

"I see how eagerly they're listening. Any English?"

"Not many words."

"They'll want to talk with Zack, not me. He's the virologist. I'm a physician."

Abruptly the FiVee roared to life, startling Jane. Belok^ clutched his sister.

Jane said, "Will you tell me about the place we go? Are many of people there?"

"About seven hundred, which is more than the domes should hold. They were erected and equipped as an Army base before RSA, a sort of West Coast Fort Detrick—never mind, you can't know what that was—doing biological research along with basic military functions. Inland, because coastal flooding and superstorms were ravaging the coast. When RSA hit, families and some other scientists not yet infected were flown here on an emergency basis—that was the colonel's foresight, I have to admit that much—and quarantined until . . . I'm going too fast, aren't I? You're not getting all this."

"No," Jane said. "I am sorry."

"My fault, not yours. Let me drop back several notches. Monterey Base, where we're going, has two domes, one of living quarters called Enclave Dome and one for scientific research, called Lab Dome, although some scientists live there, too, and the Army has a whole quadrant for the armory. We're all pretty jammed in, but we manage."

The FiVee rumbled but did not move out of the cave. Colonel Jenner seemed to be talking to the driver, or maybe to the air, since he wasn't looking at the other soldier. Jane said, "If the domes are . . . are closed up against air like esuits are . . ."

"Sealed," Lindy said. "And like the esuits, they're equipped with some mechanism that purifies the air of everything, even nanoparticles, instead of keeping air out completely. Nobody understands exactly how they work, even though we can—*could*—make them. From the plans that we thought were your people's. Jane, I have a lot of questions, too. Can I ask some?"

"Of course. I did not intention to be rude."

Lindy smiled. "I don't think it's in you to be rude. Is it true that World has no war, no violence?"

"No wars, no, although there were some small ones back in history. Violence, yes, sometimes. Quarrels, personal fights. We are human, you know."

"Of course. But . . . no, that's too complicated to ask in a moving FiVee. If we ever actually move, of course." She made a funny face.

"Where do—Oh, we move now!"

The back of the FiVee slammed closed, the hillside opened, and the truck tore out at tremendous speed. Jane rose to her knees to look through the forward window, which seemed to be made of something thicker and cloudier than glass.

"Lindy, what is the window stuff?"

"Plastic. Bulletproof. This whole vehicle is heavily armored."

Through the plastic, Jane watched trees slide past as the FiVee lurched and rolled. She grabbed a metal protrusion and hung on. So many trees! The road wasn't really a road at all, just a rough track through the trees, mostly hidden by leaves overhead and plant life underneath. There was no place on World, not even in the central mountains kept for hiking, this wild.

"It looks like . . . like Ranger Kandiss's weapons."

Lindy smiled. "Dangerous?"

"Yes." Another new word.

"It is dangerous. The wilderness has rushed back. So has its wildlife, bears and cougars and all kinds of rodents that—"

Something hard smashed into the FiVee's front plastic window. Belok^ cried out. Jane clutched her bench and said, "Was that a weapon?"

"No. A bird."

A long dark smear ran diagonally down the window. The FiVee did not slow. Jane translated for the others. To Lindy she said, "Belok^ thought it is something dangerous."

"It is," Lindy said. "That sparrow is the most dangerous thing on Earth."

Zack said quietly to Claire over the roar of the FiVee's engine, "Will Marianne be all right?" He remembered, all too painfully, losing his wife and two sons to RSA. Marianne's daughter was only presumed dead, but still . . . if he ever lost Caitlin . . .

Claire said, "Marianne is the toughest person I've ever known. You wouldn't believe what she's survived. The best thing is to get her back to work." She grimaced. Small and delicately made, with skin the color of wet sand, she looked spun of silk, but Zack suspected that Claire Patel had survived just as many horrors as Marianne. Spider silk, strand for strand, was stronger than steel.

She said, "The virophage destroys *R. sporii*, and it does it fast. The two seemed to have coevolved. All of us from World are carrying it, asymptomatically. It's unusually easy to culture from blood samples. On the ship, we used a culture of leelee tissue—"

"Of what?"

"A native mammal. But, Dr. McKay—"

"Zack, please."

"Zack, I doubt the phage will be effective against this weaponized version of *R. sporii*, not with all the genemods you told me about."

"No, probably not. But there might be something in the virophage genome we can use."

"Use to do what? What are you trying to do?"

"Later. It's complicated, and we're here." Zack wasn't sure how much he was supposed to reveal. This was classified work, after all. Toni wouldn't have hesitated, but Zack had more respect for Jenner's orders. Slightly more, anyway.

The FiVee drove into Lab Dome's vehicle airlock, a tight fit, and everybody climbed out to go through decon. Zack had only been here a few times before; this quadrant was Army, tightly restricted. Soldiers called it the armory. It held FiVees, three low-flying quadcopters, tank-like things that Zack didn't know the name of, and huge, e-locked, reinforced metal containers. Some probably held ammunition. Zack didn't know what was in the rest and wasn't sure he wanted to know. The Army drones were elsewhere, off base, although they were launched and controlled from Enclave Dome's command post. Everything stood around the walls, leaving an open space for drills or calisthenics or whatever else the soldiers did here.

One of the things that made life so difficult at Monterey Base was the prefab, unchangeable design of the domes, inherited from—whom? Apparently not, as everyone had believed until today, from technologically advanced humans on World. If Claire and Marianne could be believed (and Zack did), World had received these plans from some other, long-gone "super race"—even thinking the words made Zack feel unreal. But the domes were real enough, with their prefab forms that Jenner, and everyone else, had to work around.

Each dome was divided by internal, unchangeable, alien-energy walls into three sections, one taking up half of the dome and the other two one-quarter each. Internal airlocks connected them. This was undoubtedly a safety measure. On the *Embassy*, for instance, thirty-eight years ago, Worlders had lived in their own section, with their own air, emerging only in esuits. Now, however, the internal airlocks were a nuisance, standing open most of the time except to the restricted-area armory that Zack walked through, escorted by armed soldiers as if they were royalty, or prisoners. The five star-farers still wore their esuits, shimmering faintly and looking exhausted except for Jane, who looked around so eagerly that her head might have been mounted on a swivel gun.

The other smaller quadrant—the name had stuck even though there were three sections, not four, go figure—housed living quarters, the Army mess, and a kitchen. Some scientists were quartered here and some soldiers; Jenner wanted a military presence in both domes. The large quadrant held the labs that were Monterey Base's initial reason for existence.

Enclave Dome was similarly divided into more living quarters, the main kitchen and mess, communal showers, and nonmilitary store-rooms. The large "quadrant" included a common area that was supposed to be an open, airy relief from the crowding everywhere else, a sort of park with no plants. But partitions were always being put up for one reason or another. Big pieces of equipment that there was no room for anyplace else littered the area; some of the equipment no longer even worked but was kept for the scrap metal.

To complicate matters even more, Jenner's command post was located at the top of Enclave Dome, not Lab Dome, although the armory was in Lab Dome. This arrangement was the result of pre-Collapse plans, presumably to allow two effective areas of command in case of attack. Or something; military matters didn't interest Zack much. He had his own worries. He could, however, imagine the difficulties that Jenner encountered in getting orders from the command post to Lab Dome when no electromagnetic radiation could penetrate either, although sound could. There was an underground tunnel running from one subterranean cave to another, but it was not part of the dome design. Dug by an Army borer, it wouldn't be usable by anyone who hadn't either survived RSA or donned an esuit. RSA spores were everywhere, long lived, and deadly, except where kept out by alien energy shields.

As Zack emerged from the armory airlock, Toni pounced on him. "Well? What are our star-farers like?"

"Christ, Toni, you're a vulture."

"Are they . . . okay, here they come. Exotic. What advanced tech are they bringing us?"

"None."

For once, he had surprised her. It was a mean-spirited surprise, but Zack was already tired. He didn't feel up to explaining that the Worlders were behind Terrans in science, not ahead, and that they didn't know who had given their planet the ships and e-shields that Earth had inherited from them secondhand. Third hand. Whatever. Let someone else give the details to Toni.

He said, "We need blood samples from each of them before they're given any treatments. Lindy will do that. She's going to take all nine to quarantine and give them the pills to adjust their microbial signatures to ours. She says they can sleep through it. Apparently when their microbiomes were adjusted on World, it was a horrendous process."

"Because they're so far behind us scientifically. You want to explain that to me?"

No escape. "Can I go home and see Susan and Caitlin first?"

"No. They're fine; I saw them in the mess at lunch. We didn't lose anybody in the drone attack. Come on, Zack, spill. I can't wait for the all-hands-on-deck meeting. Are any of these aliens scientifically literate?"

"Two geneticists. There's also a young translator who seems very bright, and one of the scientist's younger sister and brother. The brother seems to have some variation of Down's syndrome."

"And they brought him here why?"

"Not sure. Jane—that's the translator—says that the Mother of Mothers decreed that the lahk should stay together."

"Oh, well, *that* makes everything crystal clear."

"Toni," Zack said, "if I have to satisfy your unprofessional impatience, can I at least have a cup of coffee first? And something to eat? I haven't had anything since breakfast and, as you just pointed out, you got to eat lunch."

"I'll walk you to the mess," Toni said. "Just keep talking on the way."

Late in the evening, Jason received a panicky, private-frequency call from the stockade. He jammed on an esuit, crossed to Lab Dome, and ran down the long flight of metal steps. In the fetid prisoner cell, Corporal Yunez bent over Dr. James Anderson. The prisoner's naked form lay distorted in a position Jason wouldn't have thought even possible for a human body. Somehow Anderson had looped the chain of his wrist manacles behind his neck and then hooked each knee beyond the opposite wrist, straining the tether that held one ankle to the wall, turning himself into a pretzel whose slightest movement to free himself would result in strangulation. And then he had wriggled.

"Sir," Yunez said, shaken, "I was watching, sir, I only went to use the head, not gone more than three minutes . . ."

Jason knelt and entered the code to release the manacles. They fell away and the prisoner unfolded limply. Under the grime, his face was deep purple, even the swollen tongue that protruded through parted lips the color of blueberries. Jason groped for a pulse and didn't find it. But Anderson gave a long, shuddering breath and so maybe . . . Jason started CPR.

He tongued his mic. Dr. Holbrook would already be asleep in Enclave Dome and would need an esuit and escort to come through the tunnels . . . no time. But Jason had passed Lindy on her way to the infirmary. "Dr. Ross, to the bird lab immediately, code one!" To Yunez he said, "Bring her into the stockade the second she comes down the steps. Go!"

Yunez sprinted from the cell. Jason kept on with CPR.

This was his own fault. He had waited too long to extract information. If he hadn't wanted to give the prisoner every chance to cooperate . . .

Breathe, damn you!

If he hadn't tried hunger first but had gone right to torture . . .

Breathe, you fucker!

If he hadn't tried so hard to play by rules of engagement set by a world that didn't even exist anymore . . .

Lindy burst into the room. "Jason! What the fuck is this undergroun—oh my God."

She dropped to her knees. "Stop CPR for a minute." Pulling a stethoscope from her pocket, she listened to his heart and lungs and pushed a knuckle hard onto Anderson's sternum. "I'm not getting anything. Jason, try again!"

He resumed CPR while he pried up Anderson's eyelids. The pupils were fixed. Jason said, "A defibrillator?"

"No time. Let me check him again." She did, while Jason waited.

Lindy said, "It's too late. He's gone."

"No, I heard him give a breath just before I started CPR!"

"Agonal respiration—the lungs trying one last desperate thing. But he's gone." She sat back on her heels and wrinkled her nose. "What is this—a dungeon? What have you done? Who is he? Jason!"

"Anderson. Of the Gaiists."

"*James Colson Anderson?* Of the original eight?"

"Yes."

"And you captured him and were torturing him for information about New America? Their movements? He was with them now?"

"I'm not discussing this with you." He stood. His legs felt wobbly; he clenched his ass cheeks to steady them.

She leaped to her feet. "You sure the fuck are discussing it! Torture? You were torturing—"

"No. I wasn't." But he would have, tomorrow morning. "Anderson did that to himself."

"And I suppose he starved himself, too, and was willing to piss and shit himself and—What the fuck did you think you were doing down here?"

Something rose up in Jason, knotted and complicated as gnarled tree roots, sharp as thorns. He said with deadly quiet, "What do you know about it, Lindy? It's my job to defeat New America so you and people like you can stay all holy and above the dirty work necessary to accomplish that. Who the hell do you think you are? You want the war to end but condemn the tactics necessary to get there. You—"

"This isn't a 'tactic,' it's a war crime! Couldn't you have just used truth drugs?"

"Do you think we didn't try? God, this is you jumping to condemnation and conclusions before you even—"

"No, this is *you*, Jason, trying to prove to himself once again how he can handle anything thrown at him!"

"I couldn't handle you, could I? Couldn't handle your smug self-righteousness, your holier-than-thou—"

"No," she said, her voice dropping into glacial cold, "you couldn't handle me. Or anyone else who has the guts to speak truth to you. You want a doctor to certify that the prisoner is dead so you can stay within all your stupid rules? Okay, I so certify. He's dead. Congratulations."

She turned and stalked up. Her shoes rang on the metal stairs, leaving behind an embarrassed Yunez, who tried to look as if he had not heard all that. Jason knelt beside the dead man, this Gaiist scientist, one of the eight who had helped create the most horrendous weapon of mass destruction ever let loose on the world.

Carefully, Jason closed Dr. Anderson's eyes.

CHAPTER 4

Jane stood in the . . . courtyard? lobby?—no English word she had learned
for the Terran structures on World fit this cluttered area of Enclave
Dome—and let six children look at her. She knew that she was like
nothing they had ever seen before.

Earth was like nothing *she* had seen before, or had imagined. Lindy
Ross said there was hardly anyone left after the plague, but then she
said there were perhaps two hundred million people still alive on the
planet. Two hundred million! All of World contained, on its one small
continent, only fifteen million people. Lindy said that many might be
left in the "United States," a subdivision of this continent that Jane had
trouble grasping. It didn't seem to be based on lahks or families. And
the head of government, who had not been a Mother but a man, was
dead without anybody else taking that role except the Army.

These children had lahks, of course. Four little boys and two girls.
The smaller girl came shyly forward, held out two chubby fingers, and
touched Jane's hand below the "sleeve" of the "shirt" that had been
given to Jane to wear over her wrap. "Are you real?"

Jane laughed. "Yes. What is your name?"

"Caitlin."

"I greet you, Caitlin. I am Jane."

Emboldened, two of the boys inched forward. One said, "Do you
come from a star?"

"Yes."

Murmurs, wide eyes, wiggling. The boy said, "Does it have a really big dome?"

"No dome."

"You went outside with no dome? You'll die!"

"Here, yes. But not on my planet."

They digested this. Jane had no idea how much they understood. Two adults, a barefoot man and a woman with startlingly red hair, stood nearby, talking to each other and ignoring everything else. Jane said, "Do you children go now to the school?"

"Yes." Caitlin, her brown hair in two bunches on either side of her head. "Where are you going?"

"I come now from Lab Dome. I wait for someone to take me to see Colonel Jenner."

The boy said importantly, "You need soldiers to go to Lab Dome. And an esuit."

"I know."

Caitlin said, "Can you hear the ground?"

It must be an idiom. "Hear what?"

"The ground," Caitlin said. "The air. The machines. The sky."

"I hear it, too," one of the older boys said.

"You're a liar!" another said.

The first boy punched him. Jane, shocked, waited for the adults to rush over and be severe with the child. No adult did, so she said, "Stop! You cannot hit people!"

"You're not the boss of me!" The boy ran off.

"Scott!" the man called after him. Scott did not answer. Reluctantly, the man jogged after the boy.

Caitlin said, "I do hear the ground and everything! I put it in rows!"

"Okay," Jane said, that useful word. Caitlin stopped scowling.

The other girl, who had not so far spoken, demanded, "When are you going back to your star?"

"I don't know."

"We don't have enough room for more refugees. Daddy said. You can't stay here." She turned her back.

Caitlin cried, "You shut up! I like her!"

The woman walked over. "Kids, time for school. Come on." She smiled briefly at Jane. The children followed her, threading their way among crates, machines, benches, all of which seemed as permanent as the mysterious lines on the floor beneath a broken string basket on a tall pole.

Why had the children been permitted to be so rude? On World, children were always accompanied by adults until it was certain they understood bu^ka^tel and could be trusted with consideration for others and proper reverence for Mother World. Jane had burst with pride the first day she had been allowed to walk to a shop alone, relied on to behave properly. Even without bu^ka^tel, manners and restraint were important when a lot of people had to live together with no room to expand. And what had the children meant: Caitlin saying she could hear the ground, the other girl saying there was no room for refugees and Jane would have to leave? Where had she gotten that idea?

Jane rubbed her forehead. The headache, a vague presence since she'd woken up from having her microbes changed, had increased to a dull ache just above her eyes. It had not, however, kept her from asking Zack and Lindy and anyone else she encountered questions about Terra. She wanted to know everything about how life worked in this bewildering, alien place.

Food was brought in from outside. Soldiers went into the wilderness and killed large animals for their flesh. However, most food, Jane was glad to hear, was made of plants grown on farms and collected in Fi-Vees. It was irradiated to kill *R. sporii avivirus*. Outside, the virus multiplied in bird droppings, dried to dust, and was blown up into the air, turning every breath deadly. Water was taken somehow from the air by machines. Most of the Terran clothing had been made by "3-D printers," whatever those were, although not so much now because "raw material" was in short supply. Sometimes "foraging parties" of soldiers brought new garments in through decon.

All the dome areas that Jane had seen were crowded with inanimate things. Nowhere were there any plants or flowers or parks or anything alive except humans. Little Caitlin had never sat on grass, never picked a flower, never stroked or fed a pet animal. She had never seen graceful and spacious houses, like the lahks built of karthwood on World. Those had soaring curves following the natural curves of the wood, sides that could be opened to the sweet air, views of purple valleys thick with crops and orchards and people bicycling on white roads under the calm orange sun. The light here, inside and out, was so bright. It hurt her eyes.

"Ugly, isn't it?" Glamet^vor¡ had come up behind her. "I greet you, Jeg^faan."

"Jane," she said.

"Not to me. I am so sorry that we came to Terra. I think your father regrets this as well."

"He does not," Jane said, although she didn't really know. Her father, La^vor, and Belok^ all had a harder time with the microbe adjustment and the vaccines against Terran diseases. They were still recovering in Lab Dome.

Glamet^vor¡ said, "Where are you going? I can't work with any of the Terrans in Lab Dome unless you're there to translate."

Jane wasn't sure he would be of any use in the labs even if she did translate. She said, "I am waiting for someone to take me to Colonel Jenner. He wishes to see me."

"Why?"

"I don't know."

"Find out if Branch Carter has landed the ship and when it will return to World. I will be on it."

Startled, Jane said, "The ship is returning to World?"

"I hope so. Where else is there for it to go?"

A reasonable question. But reason was absent from the sneer on

Glamet^vorȷ's handsome face. How could he be so different from his sister? La^vor had the sweetest nature Jane had ever met. Once again, Jane was glad that she had refused the mating contract with Glamet^vorȷ, even though he was so brilliant. That she had "changed her mind."

A soldier approached them. "Ms. Jane Ka^graa?"

"Yes," Jane said, even though her father's name had nothing to do with hers; they did not even belong to the same lahk. Glamet^vorȷ snorted.

"Come with me, please. Colonel Jenner will see you now."

He led her through a bewildering maze of corridors to a closed door guarded by a soldier in armor, with a gun strapped to her side. Why? The first soldier saluted and said something Jane didn't catch. They were allowed to pass, climbing a flight of stairs to the top of Enclave Dome, and another closed door. Her escort said something to the air. Then he opened the door, led her in, and saluted.

Colonel Jenner rose from behind a big desk in the middle of the room. "Dismissed, Private."

"Yes, sir."

Another salute and he left, closing the door. Tentatively, Jane imitated the salute. Colonel Jenner's eyes narrowed, but then he smiled. "No, Ms. Ka^graa, only soldiers may do that."

"I'm sorry, I didn't know."

"That's all right. Weren't you around the soldiers we sent to World?"

He was watching her very carefully. Tall, straight-backed, brown hair and his grandmother's eyes. Sometimes Marianne's eyes looked like that: weary but determined.

Jane said, "Yes, a little. At the end of their time on World. My father worked with the Terran scientists on World. My lahk mother permitted this. She is the lahk's 'colonel.'"

"The leader. Your society is matrilineal."

"Yes."

The room was an upended bowl. In the center sat a big wooden desk, facing a few chairs. The only items on the desk were a plain white coffee cup and a carved wooden box emblazoned with a red-striped white square, with an inset square of pointy, white-on-blue symbols. Equipment and screens, none of which Jane could identify, lined the curving walls waist-high. Above them, the curved dome was clear to the sky, a blinding blue fringed with green trees. Jane blinked and looked down.

Colonel Jenner said, "The brightness hurts your eyes."

"Yes," she said, surprised that he'd noticed.

"Try these." From his desk he pulled out a pair of dark spectacles. Jane put them on. "Better?"

"Yes! Thank you. What is their word?"

"Sunglasses. Sit down, Ms. Ka^graa."

"Only 'Jane.' We don't use names of our fathers."

"Of your mothers?"

"On papers and for ceremonies, yes. But not for everyday." She didn't explain to him the courtesy titles of "mak" or "kal," because it would involve explaining so much else.

"Why did you pick 'Jane' for a name? You don't have to tell me, I'm just curious."

"I like the sound." Jane sat on the chair he'd indicated. Like the desk, it was too tall. Worlders, a tall people, liked cushions on the floor and low tables.

Colonel Jenner was not what she'd expected. Lindy Ross and Zack McKay didn't seem to like him. Jane's father regarded the colonel with suspicion—but then, on World her father had always been happier with the Terran scientists than with the soldiers, although he'd come to respect Leo Brodie. Colonel Jenner seemed milder than Jane had envisioned, more curious and open, although not relaxed. A tiny patch of skin at his temple twitched constantly.

"If you were only around the Terran diplomatic mission for a short time, how did you learn English?"

"I learned for years from my cousin Graa^lok, who was friends of Austin Rhinehart, a Terran. I practiced very much."

"Why?"

She said simply, "I hoped to come to Earth. To where my people became taken, a hundred and forty thousand years ago. I didn't know if that will happen, but I wished to prepare."

"I see. And now you are here. I know it must not be what you expected."

"No. It is a . . . ," she searched for the word. ". . . a tragedy. But I can see that it will became better. After war ends. The wilderness is beautiful."

Colonel Jenner stared at her. Oddly, this didn't make Jane uncomfortable.

The door opened and a woman in uniform entered. Colonel Jenner said, "Ah, Major. This is Jane. My second in command, Major Duncan."

Jane said, "I greet you, Major Duncan." Another title? There had been no "majors" among the Terrans on World, and Jane thought the word meant "large" or "important." But Major Duncan wasn't in command here, so she couldn't be more important than Colonel Jenner. Also, she was tall but not particularly large. It was very confusing.

Major Duncan looked strong and severe. Her hair had been scraped back under a soldier hat; her boots shone blindingly; her face bore no expression as she nodded at Jane. She said nothing, and evidently Colonel Jenner didn't expect her to. He said to Jane, his tone less warm and more detached, "Even though you only met the Terran soldiers at the end of their deployment to World, I'd like you to tell me what happened with them."

"It will be better to talk to my father. He was there, in the compound, much longer. Or to . . . to Dr. Jenner."

He didn't react to the mention of his grandmother. "I will talk to all of them, but they are all recovering still from microbial adjustment. Only you and Glamet^vor¡ are out of the infirmary . . . that's not how you say his name, is it? I'm sorry, I'm not good at languages."

"That is okay. He should to choose a Terran name."

"But I see from your face that he will not."

The colonel was quick-witted. Jane said, "No, he will not. He doesn't like it here."

"But you do."

"I don't know yet. But it is interesting."

Colonel Jenner laughed, a short bark that seemed to explode from him without his choice; he looked astonished that it had. Major Duncan didn't change expression. The colonel said, "I'm sorry—I wasn't laughing at you. There's a silly Terran curse: 'May you live in interesting times.'"

"And you do," Jane said. He looked much different when he laughed.

Again he studied her intently, and again he turned formal.

"Yes. Now please tell us everything you know of the Terran expedition to World, starting at the beginning. Even if you only heard it from others."

She did, careful to include everything and in the right order: the attack by another Terran spaceship ("They said it was Russian") that destroyed the *Friendship* and killed most of the Terran expedition. How the survivors, four soldiers and five others, had not known about the time jump. How they tried and failed to find a vaccine against the same spore cloud that had hit Earth earlier. How Branch Carter had made contact with the colony ship launched decades before; the ship had been contaminated with spores that had killed the colonists but not the leelees aboard—

Major Duncan spoke for the first time. "What is a leelee?"

"A animal that Marianne used by experiments. Like your mice."

"I see. Go on."

Marianne and Claire had realized there must be something aboard the colony ship that killed the spores. Branch discovered how to call the ship back and it contained the virophage, airborne, that had saved most of World's people by counteracting *R. sporii*. That ship was the *Return*.

"Thank you," Colonel Jenner said, "but what did the soldiers do?"

"Did not Ranger Kandiss tell you?"

"He did. I want to hear your version."

There were no different "versions" of truth, only truth and lies. Jane's headache was worse. She said, "Lieutenant Lamont was the leader soldier. They built the compound to protect the lab from people who tried to steal the little amount of vaccine Claire brought from Terra. But it was stealed anyway, by Lieutenant Lamont. He also tried to destroy the device necessary to call back the colony ship. He wanted the spore cloud to destroy World. He hated us. I didn't know why. I also now don't know why, but I heard that he believed Worlders did not tell Terra the truth about the spore cloud. That Worlders caused it, to hurt Terra. Or maybe not that we caused it, but that we knew it would kill so many on Terra and did not say. Or something bad. I don't know what he believed, or what the Russians believed when they destroyed our cities. I know that Lieutenant Lamont tried to destroy the call-back device so we cannot call back the colony ship and save World."

She could not tell from Colonel Jenner's face whether or not he already had this information. Wouldn't Ranger Kandiss have told him all this? Why was he making Jane relive it all? She had lost members of her lahk in the destruction of the beautiful capital city, Kam^tel^ha. They had all lost so much to the Russian attacks, including their only other starship.

Colonel Jenner said, "And what happened to Lieutenant Lamont?"

"Lieutenant Brodie—"

"Lieutenant? Did he give himself that rank?"

Jane tried to remember. "No, I think no. He said he was 'corporal.' But his soldiers—his World soldiers and also Ranger Zoe—called him that. Later, I mean."

"I see. Then what happened?"

"Lieutenant Brodie killed Lieutenant Lamont. To stop him of shooting another Terran so Lieutenant Lamont can obtain the device and destroy it. Then Lieutenant Brodie and Ranger Zoe stayed on World. They are there now."

"Thank you, Jane, for all that information. I can see you're angry. Why?"

"You already knew this."

"Yes. But confirmation of intelligence is important. And I learned a new fact: You don't like talking about violence."

"No."

"Let me ask you this—do you think Lieutenant Brodie was right to kill his commanding officer?"

For the first time, Major Duncan's face changed; she showed surprise, almost immediately gone. Jane wasn't surprised; this was a question of ethics, and so had been endlessly discussed on World. Jane had discussed it with La^vor, who said no, violence was never justified. But . . .

Jane said slowly, "Yes, I think Lieutenant Brodie was right. Lieutenant Lamont was ready to shoot another Terran, a *child*. And Brodie-mak saved so many more of lives on World by to obtain the call-back device before it was destroyed."

"Did he stay on World to avoid court-martial?"

"What is that?"

"A judgment about the killing, with possible punishment."

"No, he did not stay on World because of that. He stayed to help rebuild, and to make an army on World for if the Russian ship comes back. Also, he signed a mating contract with Isabel Rhinehart from the *Friendship*. You asked me many questions, Colonel. May I ask now?"

He looked surprised. "Yes, I suppose so. But first—Major, do you have any additional questions?"

"No, sir."

"Dismissed."

When Major Duncan had gone, Colonel Jenner turned back to Jane. "Ask your questions."

"When I waited for a soldier to bring me to you, I talked to some of children. They were very unpolite. One said there is not room enough in the dome for us and we will became told to leave. Is this true?"

"No. Absolutely not."

"Two adults stood near. They permitted the children to be unpolite and they did not tell the children we can stay. Why?"

"Jane, politics—do you know that word? Good—are complicated here. Not everyone agrees on everything. Surely that was true on World as well?"

"Yes. But no one goes against bu^ka^tel." Not quite true, but she was angry now.

"What is bu^ka^tel?"

He was the first Terran at Monterey Base to ask. She said, "It is what makes us human. To serve and protect Mother World, to obey the Mothers who gave us life, to put the good of others equal with the good of us-selfs, to honor the ancestors, to understand that to give is the only way to receive, in the Great Web by which we all need. That is best I can say it in English. There is more, but it does not translate. Every child learns this down to the bones before they may walk alone outside their lahk."

"And everyone keeps to this bu^ka^tel? What about the Worlders you just spoke about who tried to steal vaccine?"

"No. They did not keep to bu^ka^tel. I am sorry—I did not say true. But bu^ka^tel is the right path, even when a Worlder breaks it. To violate bu^ka^tel is to . . . to violate others and Mother World. It is to become outside the lahk. Nothing is worth that. Even those people who try to steal vaccine had their lahks with them in the camp. Even the Worlders in Lieutenant Brodie's new army have permission of the lahk Mothers."

Colonel Jenner rose and gazed out the window. Jane didn't see anything happening out there, but she rose to take in more of the view. The sunglasses deepened the wilderness to an even lovelier green. Branches waved gently and puffy white clouds drifted through a blue sky—so blue! A flock of birds flew overhead.

He finally spoke. "So you think that Leo Brodie was justified in breaking bu^ka^tel when he shot Lieutenant Lamont."

"Yes. But it hurt him, I think."

"And you don't think he stayed on World to avoid court-martial."

"No. He wishes to rebuild, and he signed the mating contract with Isabel for five years."

"Five years? Marriage expires after five years?"

"Expires?"

"Is ended."

"Yes, of course. Some contracts are for two years or three."

"On Terra, marriage is supposed to be for life."

She heard but did not understand the bitterness in his voice. She said gently, "That must be difficult, I think. Sometimes people change, or what they want changes. To force people to stay married . . . that would not show them respect. It would not be bu^ka^tel."

Abruptly Colonel Jenner turned away from the window, back to her. "You are going to be our translator and you should understand our life here. When my grandmother recovers, I'm going to take her outside the base to a coastal settlement. We'll go by quadcopter, which is not completely without danger but not too bad—we fly lower than New America's radar can detect. I would like you to come along. There is someone I would like you to meet."

"Yes," she said instantly. A chance to see Terra outside the domes! More than she had hoped for. "Who will we be to meet?"

Now his voice held even more complicated layers. "My brother Colin."

Marianne stuck one bare foot out of bed and put it on the floor, then the other foot. The floor, made of alien-dome material she had not touched in thirty-eight years, tingled faintly, just as she remembered. She stood, relieved to feel neither weakness nor vomiting. Expanding her lungs as far as they would go, she took in a huge breath of Terran air.

No weakness or gastric distress. When her gut microbes had been changed on World, the more primitive process had nearly killed her. Score one for Terran science, marching forward even as everything crumpled around it.

Her cell in quarantine—you couldn't really call it a room, too monastic—held only a bed, sink and toilet, and an array of monitors. Sometime in the night, someone must have unhooked her from them. Marianne wore a thin hospital gown open in the back—okay, not everything on Terra had progressed—and didn't see her clothes. Before she could figure out how to ring for a nurse, Lindy Ross came in.

"Dr. Jenner! You look much better."

"Yes. No. But I can't . . . I need to talk to Jason. Colonel Jenner."

"He probably isn't available. Let me examine—"

"I need to talk to him!" To her own horror, Marianne heard her voice rise to a shriek. "I need to! Now!"

Dr. Ross gazed at her a long moment. "Okay, I'll send for him, if you let me examine you now."

"Yes! Just . . . I need to talk to him."

Dr. Ross left, speaking in a low voice to someone in the corridor. After a moment she returned. "I've sent someone to Enclave Dome to tell him. Dr. Jenner—"

"'Marianne.' I'm sorry. I just need to—"

"I know. I'm Lindy. Would you like something to calm you a bit?"

"No." Marianne tried to steady herself; she must have appeared hysterical. Maybe she was hysterical. "How . . . how are the others from the ship doing? Where *is* the ship?"

"Back in orbit. You're the last to wake up from the microbe adjustment. Everyone is doing fine except for Kayla Rhinehart. Physically she's well but she seems deeply depressed, maybe dangerously so. She cries constantly. Was she like that on World?"

Lindy's tone, soothing but not condescending, was helping Marianne. "Kayla varies. Claire says she's bipolar. Do you have lamotrigine?"

"We use something newer now. There's no psychiatrist on base, unfortunately, and the meds can have rare but powerful psychotic side effects. I've prescribed them here only once. Let me consult with the Army doctor, Captain Holbrook."

"You're not in the Army?"

"No." Lindy put a stethoscope to Marianne's chest. "Cough, please."

Marianne coughed. "Will Jason come here?"

"I've sent for him."

Not an answer. Marianne had to keep talking or she would disintegrate. "I want to know more about what Jason did at the . . . the Collapse. Do you know him well?"

Lindy took a step backward. "I think you must not have been told, Marianne, that Jason is my ex-husband. We're divorced, or at least as divorced as you can be when there is no government except the military."

No, Marianne had not known that. "Do you . . . did you have any children?"

"No. If you'd rather have Dr. Holbrook attend you . . ."

"No. I . . . no. I just need to see Jason."

"I'm here," he said.

Lindy said something to him, too low for Marianne to catch, and then left, closing the door behind her. Marianne clutched Jason's arm. "It's all gone, all of it?"

Pity flooded him. He didn't have to ask what she meant. He had been there, in the place she occupied now, ten years ago, and then again eight years ago. They had all been there, all the survivors of both the Collapse and then, for those who lived through the first horror, of the war. Her hand, veined and liver-spotted, tightened even more on the sleeve of his uniform.

"Yes," he said gently. "Most of it is gone. Not all, but most."

"Yesterday I was too stunned to really understand all the . . . New York? DC."

"Yes."

"NIH? Fermilab? The CDC? CERN?"

Leave it to his grandmother to think first of the scientific facilities.

"All the biotech firms in Boston and Maryland and Seattle—"

"Yes." And US Strategic Command, NASA, Andersen Air Force Base in Guam, Fort Bragg, Creech, Vandenberg, Fort Benning, the labs at Livermore . . . The list went on and on.

She let go of Jason's arm. Her face looked not only old, but ancient. "I can't believe it. But . . . what about fallout? From the nuclear bombs— didn't we have thousands? And other countries, too?"

"Most of them weren't even used. Remember, the Collapse from plague came first, and fast. Nearly everyone died then, including the people with access to weapons, expertise, launch codes. US Strategic Command could only launch on direct order of the president. He died early on, and then his successors, along with the military who were supposed to receive or execute retaliation orders. When the war started two years later, most weapons weren't usable by either side."

"There were enough to take out all the places you just mentioned!"

"Yes. But it was such a confused time. I'm not even sure who bombed which specific targets: Russia, China, Korea, New America. Even the details of our retaliation are murky."

"But when there were so few people left anyway . . . to senselessly kill more . . ."

She stopped. Jason understood that she, more than most people, knew how senseless some people could be. He said, "It isn't—"

"Fallout? Even from a few nuclear strikes there would be—"

"Yes. But most of it blew west to east. And the new bombs aren't as dirty as the ones you remember. The mechanism is different. Even the Seattle bombs didn't harm us much here."

"I can't get my mind around it. All gone. And Elizabeth . . ."

"We never found out what happened to Aunt Liz," he said gently. "I'm sorry. Grandma, the only thing you can do is not think about it. Think about now. Try to not remember."

Jason exerted a lot of energy to not think about the Collapse. To not remember his frantic efforts to save what and who he could, bringing in biologists from the closest biotech firms and universities. To not remember the dying he left behind, and—much worse—the still healthy he denied a place on the copters because they could be of no use in battling this strange new plague. To not distinguish his own failures from those of the civilization disintegrating all around him. To not remember when the last of his copters was shot down, taking three good soldiers and six evacuees with it.

Lindy, he knew, remembered everything. She had remembered it over and over, until the memories somehow became bearable to her, like bloody cloths bleached lighter and lighter by sunlight. Jason couldn't do that. He'd shut the bloody shrouds away in darkness, and only for his grandmother would he have brought them even briefly into light.

She let go of his arm and pulled at the skin of her face, and he knew that she was herself again. Battered, scarred—they were all scarred, forever—but she was not the quavery, crushed old woman he'd seen when he entered the infirmary.

"I'm sorry, Jason. I know I can't just summon you like this—you're in command of this base. But thank you for coming."

He nodded, and offered her the only thing he could. "Tomorrow, I have to see Dad and Colin at the Settlement on the Coast. If you're feeling strong enough, would you like to come?"

She raised her face to his, and her eyes glinted with tears. "Yes. I would. Please."

CHAPTER 5

In the armory Jason waited with several soldiers and, to Marianne's surprise, Jane. Jason, Jane, and one of the soldiers wore armor under e-suits. Jane looked like a tall coppery flower encased in a clear vase and incongruously wearing sunglasses. They stood beside a contraption like nothing Marianne had seen before. It had four rotors resting on the vehicle bay floor and, in the center and a few feet above, a dome of clear, heavy plastic housing four low seats. The whole thing looked assembled from Tinkertoys. Somewhere in Marianne's forehead a headache simmered, kept at bay by the same meds that made her willing to even consider riding in such a flimsy-looking vehicle.

She said, "What is it?"

"Quadcopter. Fast and efficient."

"What powers it?"

"Electric batteries."

"Where do you get your electricity?" And why hadn't she thought to ask this before? She'd had a day of resting and asking questions.

"Generators. This is an Army base, Marianne. We have supplies of very advanced fuel cells, although not an indefinite supply."

Marianne. Well, all right, he didn't want to call her "Grandma" in front of his troops, and "Marianne" was probably better than "Dr. Jenner." She said, "How high can it go, and how far, on battery power?"

"Maximum height is half a mile, although we won't be going that

high. With full passenger load, battery lasts six hours before re-
charging."

"Jas . . . Colonel, it doesn't look safe. What about a drone attack?"

He looked at her steadily, from eyes so much like her own. "It has
happened. But we fly under New America's radar, and over open country so that we won't be ambushed from the ground. Scouts have
cleared us for today's flight. But the choice is yours. However, this is
the safest way to see Ryan and Colin."

"Can't they come here?"

"They won't," he said in what she'd come to think of as his Army
voice. It allowed no dissent. She'd used the same tone in another lifetime, when she'd taught undergraduates. "Do you still want to go?"

"Yes. But should *you* go? If the . . . the enemy knows that the commander is outside the domes . . ."

"They don't know," Jason said. "And my second in command is
very competent. Put on this body armor and then this esuit. Sergeant,
have the quadcopter readied in the airlock."

Two soldiers pushed the Tinkertoy contraption toward the oversized
armory airlock that the FiVee had driven through yesterday. Jane helped
Marianne put on the light armor and esuit. Marianne desperately
wanted to see her son and her other grandson. Her daughter was
gone; she needed to hold fast to what she still had. If everyone else at
Monterey Base could rebuild their lives after unthinkable loss, that
was what she would have to do, too.

It was more thrilling than the spaceship, where everything had
to be viewed on screens. In the quadcopter—strange word, even for
English—Jane could look down and see Terra, separated from it only
by her esuit and a piece of glass. No . . . *plastic.* She craned her neck forward and to the side.

The quadcopter skimmed over forest, over field after field filled with weeds and bushes. No crops in the field; this was wild land. Jane shouted over the noise of the quadcopter, "Look! What are those? Look!"

Colonel Jenner, piloting with Jane beside him and the other soldier with Marianne in the back seats, smiled. "Deer."

"They're beautiful!"

He said nothing, and Jane remembered that he ate deer. Oh, how could they? These beautiful animals, running so fast and free! They . . . "Oh, look! What's that?"

"Monterey Bay, part of the Pacific Ocean."

It was a thin curve on the horizon, growing larger as they flew toward it. Jane had seen the ocean at home, but under a dimmer orange sun, with purple seaweed floating near the shore, World's ocean had looked nothing like this dazzling, clear blue. "Blue" wasn't even the right word for it, not if "blue" meant the dye used on World. There must be a better, more wondrous English word.

Marianne said to the colonel, "Oceanic dead spots?"

"Dissipating more each year, from what we can tell. Colin will know more."

"Jason . . . can he still superhear?"

"Yes."

What did that mean? From the look on the colonel's face, nothing good. The closer they flew to Monterey Bay, the more rigid his jaw grew, the stronger the little quiver of flesh at his temple. Did that mean the danger to the quadcopter was increasing?

Jane clasped her hands in her lap and recited one of the first bu^ka^tel chants taught to children: *Death enriches Mother World, who takes us to her breast for peaceful sleep. Be not afraid, dear heart, for you are eternally loved.*

Mother Terra? Well, in a phrase she had learned from Claire Patel: why not? This was the original Mother of all Worlders, after all.

Monterey Bay grew larger and more dazzling. A single dome like those at the base came into view, less blue and shimmering than the ocean. Beside it stretched cultivated fields and orchards like those at home. A river splashed through a small waterfall surrounded by wooden structures. More structures extended from the mouth of the river out into the ocean; those were filled with intensely green slime.

Small figures ran from fields and bay into the dome. Colonel Jenner set down the quadcopter beside it, and the figures, people-sized now, ran out again. Jane was shocked to see that the airlock to the dome stood wide open. Didn't RSA spores contaminate everything inside?

The quadcopter noise stopped. The armed soldier jumped out, followed by Colonel Jenner. In the sudden silence, someone spoke: an older woman, gray-haired and scowling. She wore what Jane still thought of as normal clothes: a simple wrap of undyed cloth that looked homespun, with sandals of cloth and thin wood. No esuit. She said flatly, "Colonel Jenner. Such an honor. Something wrong with the last shipment?"

"No. Hello, Sarah. Nice to see you, too."

She snorted. Then Marianne and Jane climbed out of the quadcopter and Sarah's sunken eyes went round as buttons. "Oh my God, you're *Kindred*."

"I greet you," Jane said in English. Sarah stared and shook her head. What did that mean?

Marianne said, "I'm Marianne Jenner. Hello, Sarah."

Sarah found her voice. "The *Friendship* returned to Earth?"

Colonel Jenner said, "Not exactly. Is Colin around?"

Sarah said, "He'll be on his way here. Dr. Jenner . . ."

"Yes?"

Sarah seemed to have found not only her voice but also a commanding stance. Was she then the mother of this lahk? She put her hands on her hips and demanded, "Are you staying here? Are you with us or them?"

Colonel Jenner said, "With us. She's a scientist, Sarah. And Jane is our translator."

Sarah said to Marianne, "You choose death over life?"

Marianne, bewildered, turned to Colonel Jenner. He said tightly, "Here comes Colin."

A man ran toward them from the beach. Jane watched the pounding figure grow larger and stockier; a thickset, short, heavily muscled Terran deeply sunburned. He wore the same type of wrap as Sarah but was barefoot, his long graying hair tied back with a strip of cloth. When he spied Jane, he stopped dead.

His gaze moved to Colonel Jenner, and he smiled, a grin of such unself-conscious sweetness that Jane felt her own lips curve in response.

He saw Marianne, gasped, and burst into tears.

Marianne took an uncertain step forward. Colin Jenner closed the gap between them in five huge bounds and threw his arms around her, lifting her off the ground in a hug so tight that Jane was afraid it might break her old bones. But Marianne was hugging him back and laughing like a girl.

"Grandma! You're home! But how—"

"There was a time dilation, it—"

Sarah shouted, "Incoming!"

Everyone moved toward the dome, but not very quickly. Colin took Marianne's hand and led her. Jane hurried behind. Again she was shocked to see that the airlock stood open on both sides, and even more shocked that Colonel Jenner's guard took time to climb into the quadcopter, start it, and fly it around to the other side of the dome and, presumably, inside an airlock as big as the one in the armory of Enclave Dome.

Still no explosions.

She said timidly to Sarah, "I don't hear anything."

"Oh, it'll be another ten minutes at least."

There hadn't been ten minutes warning at the base. "How do you know?"

"Grasses," Sarah said, which explained nothing. "Would you like some tea?"

"I . . . no, I can't drink in this esuit."

"Oh, of course. I forgot. Poor you."

Jane didn't think that Sarah had forgotten, or that her remark had really been aimed at Jane. Colonel Jenner frowned at the old woman.

Marianne was answering Colin Jenner's questions about his uncle, Noah, left behind on World. Jane turned in a slow circle, inspecting this quadrant of the dome. Although identical in size and alien material to the two domes of Monterey Base, this one looked entirely different inside. Plants grew against the curved walls. There was no flat ceiling of wood or metal making a second story, and through the clear upper dome sunlight poured in. Between irregularly shaped beds of grass or seaweed, woven mats lay rolled up or not; they looked like the sleeping mats on World. Children came shyly from behind trees; men and women in little knots stared openly; two people stirred a pot of something on the metal stove where Sarah brewed tea. The stove had a glass or plastic window with actual fire burning behind it.

Colonel Jenner came up beside her. "Not like the base, is it?"

"No. It's like . . . an unplanned garden."

"Oh, it's planned, all right. My brother might be a lunatic tree-worshipper, but he's capable."

"Really? They worship the trees here?"

"Not literally. I meant that they're vegetarian, refuse to slaughter animals for leather, eat a lot of seaweed—that's a kelp farm down at the beach—and offer thanks to any tree they cut down for fuel or any vegetable they put into a stew. I think they atone for all the food they send to us killers at the base, too. Trying to make up for our sins."

Jane tried to follow all this. "Food to the base comes by here?"

"Plus hunting and foraging by the Army. Colin's people don't approve of hunting, of course. We send FiVees to collect their produce and grain, varying the collection days to avoid drone attacks. In return, we supply them with medicines and such metal as they'll accept, like the stove. We get fed and they get to keep morally clean from all the disgusting military practices that make their lives possible. Not that we get any credit for it. My brother— Hello, Dad."

A man, walking with a cane, emerged from an internal, standing-open airlock. An older, frailer version of Colin, he trembled as he lurched along, but he grinned widely and his eyes shone. Marianne's son, Jane remembered, the father of both Colin and Colonel Jenner. Wordlessly he patted Colonel Jenner's arm, then stumbled toward Marianne. To Jane he looked older than Marianne.

"Is your father sick?"

"Parkinson's. That's a neurological disease we never did figure out how to cure. Jane, I know how strange this must seem to you."

Actually, this place seemed less strange, more like World, than the base did. This wasn't bu^ka^tel, but the respect for Mother Terra, the abundant plants and simple furnishing, were all echoes of World.

She said, "I don't . . . aren't drones coming?"

"Yes. Any minute now."

"Do they have radar here? Like the base?"

"No. Colin and Sarah and some of the others are superhearers. You don't know about that, do you? About five percent of children born from mothers infected with the original R. sporii carry a gene that gets activated in the womb. The kids hear way above and below the usual range of human hearing . . . do I need to say that more simply?"

"No." Little Caitlin saying I hear the ground. "But will this also happen with children born on World? The spore cloud came only a little time before our ship left."

"I don't know. You need to ask a geneticist."

Colin Jenner broke free from the group around his father and grandmother. "Jason!" He hugged Colonel Jenner, who didn't immediately break free.

"Hello, Col."

"How are you? You okay?"

"Fine. Everything all right here?"

"Yes. Haven't lost anyone."

The brothers liked each other. They might agree on nothing, but their affection was just as clear to Jane as their wariness. Colonel Jenner's disdain for the way of life here did not include his brother, the architect of this place. The colonel said, "Colin, this is Jane, from World. A translator."

Colin turned. He took her hand and his gaze met hers. His eyes were mud-colored in a sunburned, strong-nosed face, and she was staggered by their intensity. Something flashed between Jane and Colin: more than interest, less than recognition.

She said, almost timidly, "I greet you, Colin Jenner."

Instantly he said, "I greet you, Jane," just as if the World greeting were natural to him. He still held her hand.

Outside, the first missile struck, with noise and fury. Everyone ignored it.

She said, "Will you tell me, please, about . . . about the life here?"

"Yes." A quick glance, humorous but not mocking, at his brother. The colonel shrugged and moved away to talk to a group of three people carrying a huge basket of red vegetables.

Colin said, "Jane, here we try to live free on the Earth, while it repairs itself from what humanity did to it. We respect every living thing, even the vegetables and nuts and seaweed we eat. We try to tread lightly, and always in harmony with nature."

He had gone beyond her knowledge of specific words, but she understood the ideas. "And you can hear the ground? That is how you knew that the drones . . . how *do* you know?"

"There are changes in the air. Birds react and so do other animals—they always know if an earthquake is coming. Also, trees and grasses register incoming. Plants aren't sentient but they can, over time, develop warning signals, pheromones or vibrations, to let others of their species know that danger approaches. Botanists have known that for nearly a hundred years. Everything is connected underground, through grass roots and fungi, and sound moves really well through soil."

Another missile strike outside. Colin finally let go of her hand. Jane said, to cover her regret at the absence of his warm fingers, "You can hear all that? From plants and air and animals?"

"If I'm paying attention. Six of us can."

His eyes held hers. Abruptly, Colonel Jenner crossed his arms over his chest. Jane barely noticed. "Nobody here wears an esuit."

"We don't need them. We're all survivors of *R. sporii avivirus*."

"But . . . you have children not ten years, born since the Collapse—they survived RSA, too?"

"Yes."

Colonel Jenner had returned to listen. He said harshly, "But not all of them. Colin would rather expose his newborns to RSA and let most of them die than live inside esuits and domes—right, Colin?"

Colin said quietly, "I have no children. Parents make that decision, not me."

"You're the leader."

"This is not a military base, Jason. I don't control anyone else's choices."

Colonel Jenner turned to Jane. "Children here die, over ninety percent of them, shortly after birth. Or else the pregnant parents defect and come to live rationally at the base."

Colin said, "Living sealed up, surviving only by killing—that's not living rationally."

"You wouldn't be living at all if it weren't for us. New America would already have wiped you out."

All at once Jane realized this was an old argument, as worn and saggy as some of the Army uniforms at the base. The brothers did not need to argue it again; neither would change the other's mind. They were arguing now only because of her. Even the way they stood—she had seen male skalethį on World stand like that, facing each other with their heads slightly lowered and their bodies tense, during mating season.

No, that couldn't be right. She must look so strange to them: coppery skin, too-big eyes, taller than Colin. But—

To cover her confusion, she said, "Why doesn't New America come at night and burn your crops? Or . . . or poison them? If they want to destroy you."

Colonel Jenner smiled, not pleasantly. "They want to destroy people, not farms or domes or weapons. Those that want to take over. Only they're not going to, here or at the base, because some of us are fighting back."

"And some of us believe that over time, nature always wins, and we are part of nature."

Colonel Jenner snorted. "Don't go into too many forests armed with just your ideals, Colin."

"Don't kill so much life that you become as bad as your enemy."

"I think," Jane said firmly, "that I would like to talk to those children over there."

The children were shy, but she got them talking to her, and then they were charming. The missile hits stopped. Colin's gaze kept meeting Jane's. She thought that he looked bewildered. Well, she was, too. She detached herself from the children—a small girl clutched her legs—to ask him more questions, to have more time with him.

Colonel Jenner, who'd gone outside, strode back into the dome. "We have to go back now."

Marianne said, "Oh, no, not yet!"

"I'm sorry, Grandma," he said, the first time Jane had heard him use that word, "but I just got an urgent message from my master sergeant."

In his wrist thing, of course. No one asked what the message was. The quadcopter was pushed out of the large airlock, they climbed in, and it lifted, the noise covering Jane's silence. She had a headache and she felt so confused about . . . everything.

Living in harmony with Terra, without killing.

Letting nearly all children die of RSA, so that the survivors could "live free."

Fighting and killing . . . but killing people who were trying to murder you.

Hearing the whole, huge plant world, the air, the ground itself as it shifted in its own mysterious life.

The dome, without which all of Colin Jenner's people would already be dead.

Colin Jenner . . .

Her headache worsened.

"I'm tired," Marianne said to Jane over the rotors. "Are you?"

"Yes," Jane said. She watched some large gray animals jumping out of the water of the bay, falling back in, jumping again. Somehow, they reminded her of Colin. She said, "I am tired. It is hard to experience so much at once."

Jason left his grandmother and Jane at the base. He and Specialist Kowalski flew the quadcopter to the new signal station. This was doubly risky. New America might have picked up Hillson's coded radio message. Even without decoding it, they would know where Jason was and might guess at his route back. Or they might be able to trace the quadcopter to the station, which would then have to be moved again. But Hillson's message had been urgent.

He would have left Jane and Marianne in the relative safety of Colin's dome, but neither woman would have agreed willingly. Jane was needed to translate, and Marianne to work at Lab Dome with the science teams. Besides, he didn't want to leave Jane at the Settlement with . . . No, there was no "besides." This was the best plan. And he'd gotten them both back safely.

The new signal station lay farther up the slope of the southern Diablo Range. Jason flew low over maples, oaks, gray pines, all taller and older than the sapling forests invading the valleys since the Collapse. In a field thick with wildflowers stood a herd of elk. The quadcopter startled them and they bolted. Farther on, a mountain lion sunned itself on a rock.

Robot-dug, the station was burrowed into a rocky hillside. Jason frowned. More difficult to reach by FiVee but easier to approach without detection. Still, the signal equipment was better camouflaged up here. On the rocky and uneven ground, the track of Li's FiVee was faint.

He landed the quadcopter at the coordinates Li had given him, and waited. Ten minutes later IT Specialist David DeFord appeared. He wore armor but not an esuit; like all members of J Squad, DeFord was an RSA survivor. He saluted smartly and led him to the station. Kowalski remained with the copter.

Inside, Jason braced himself. He'd never seen Li look this tense.

"Sir, three items of intel came in. First and worst, the enemy has taken Sierra Depot."

Fuck. Sierra Depot, northwest in high desert near the border of what had been Nevada, was essentially a 36,000-acre shopping mall for Army equipment. For decades it had been staffed lightly by Army officers overseeing civilian contractors. It stored uniforms, goggles, generators, radios, scopes, vehicles. Just before the Collapse, the depot had received an influx of Army, including a company of Marines, and a new, maximum-security building. Jason and Li both knew why. Their eyes met.

Jason said, "They don't have the launch codes. And the ordnance isn't housed there."

"Yes, sir. But now they have—"

"I know what they have. It will self-destruct if they try to access it."

"Yes, sir."

There hadn't been enough Marines left after the Collapse to adequately defend the depot. In the first few months, Jason had sent all the troops he could spare. New America did not take prisoners, unless it was to torture them for information. But at Sierra, none of them except the CO had any intel to give up. Everyone else who knew what lay underground had died of RSA.

Jason didn't need to ask about current casualties; he already knew. He asked anyway, listening to the names as Li read them off his wrister. Some of them he had served with, before the Collapse. Two had been drinking friends. Major John Burchfell had been best man at Jason and Lindy's wedding.

He said, throat tightening, "The other intel?"

"General Lassiter died this morning. Heart."

Not unexpected. The general, whom Jason had never met in person, was eighty-three and had been failing for at least six months. That left General Colleen Hahn as CO. Jason knew her slightly and respected her; he could work with Hahn.

It also made Jason the fourth highest ranking officer left in the United States Army.

"And finally," Li said, "a piece of good news. New America's comsat has failed."

Jason nodded. That *was* good news. Of the two functioning comsats in orbit, New America had used theirs to track signals between the remaining Army bases and, although no one had expected this, the *Return*. They could not piggyback on the US comsat, which used advanced-state, heavily encrypted software. New America still had short-range surveillance drones, ground movements, and radio interceptions, but no communication through space. Very good news.

He said, "Contact the *Return* in orbit. We're going to bring the ship down. Corporal Kandiss tells me it's vulnerable to ground attack, but it's no good to us upstairs and anyway, the scientists say they need research items from aboard. Make contact while I figure out where to land it."

"Yes, sir."

"Tell them they've done well."

But his mind was on Sierra Depot. The quantum computer was set to self-destruct if anyone without authorized entry tried to use it. Only the q-computer had the computing power to calculate and try the launch codes without taking a hundred thousand years to accomplish the task. The only other way to launch what were, as far as Jason knew, the only remaining viable nuclear weapons in North America, was from either Jason's command post or General Hahn's. But if New America *was* able to use the q-computer . . .

No. Unthinkable. He would do anything, anything at all, to keep that from happening.

CHAPTER 6

Zack hovered over Caitlin's bed, Susan on the other side. "Does she have a fever?"

"No," Susan said. "She just complains that her head hurts. Where on your head, Caity? Show Daddy."

Caitlin lay in a tangle of twisted sheets and a green Army blanket. She touched the center of her forehead and tried to smile. She clutched her stuffed toy, a foot-high rabbit named Bollers, so ancient and much laundered that its pink had faded to gray and one amputated paw had been replaced with a substitute sewn from a military-issue black sock. Her trundle bed, stored during the day under Zack and Susan's, now took up most of the cramped bedroom in their two-room quarters in Enclave Dome.

The other room held a table and chairs, battered sofa, and a wall screen hung on the rough wooden walls that partitioned this "apartment" off from others just like it. Storage closets were made from the same rough wood. Neither room had any windows. Zack had been meaning to borrow tools from the Army and spruce things up a bit, maybe sand the closet doors, even paint something, but there was always too much to do in the lab. Susan was equally busy, often bringing Caitlin to work with her. The only decorations in the tiny apartment were a few pictures drawn by Caity, plus a startlingly ugly collection of plastic zinnias in a willow basket, which had come from God-knew-where. "Leave it," Susan always said. "At least it provides a spot of color. And Caity likes it."

Zack put his hand on Caitlin's forehead. It didn't feel hot. "Should we send for Lindy?"

"No, I don't think so. Not unless she develops a fever. But can you sit with her for a while? I have a staff meeting." Susan, a former CPA, was now the civilian quartermaster for both domes. Her military counterpart had not lived through the Collapse. Susan had the thankless job of stretching dwindling supplies of nearly everything to meet too many requests from too many people.

Zack said, "I'm supposed to be at Lab Dome to brief Marianne Jenner and the other scientists off the *Return*."

"Okay," Susan said. "Star-farers outrank incoming vegetables, which is what this staff meeting is supposed to be about. I'll postpone it."

"Thank you, love." God, he was lucky. Susan was inevitably cheerful, always fair, and far more fearless than he was. When his first family died from RSA, Zack had cursed the immune system that hadn't let him die with Tara and their sons. He'd thought his life was over. Susan showed him that it was not. She, too, had lost much—there was no one who survived the Collapse who would not bear emotional scars forever—but her natural sturdiness let her carry on, and she carried him with her.

Caitlin said, "It hurts, Daddy."

"I know. But if you go to sleep, it will be better when you wake up." *Let that be true.*

"It will be better if you print my zebras."

Susan smiled. Zack heard her unspoken words: *She can't be that sick if she's haggling to use the printer.* Paper was a hoarded commodity; no more of it would be manufactured until the war ended.

Caitlin said craftily, "Bollers wants to look at my zebras while I'm sleeping."

"Well, just this once," Susan said. She carried Caitlin's tablet to the quartermaster's office, printed from it, and returned. Zack duct-taped the picture to the rough wooden wall. The base was well supplied with duct tape, even if everything else was running low. Three zebras, one with only two legs but all with magnificent purple stripes, cavorted across a yellow field.

Occam's razor did not apply to a child's imagination. Zebras abounded.

The conference room at Lab Dome was actually an all-purpose gathering room too small for most of the gatherings it hosted. Space was too valuable to ever sit unused. Zack ousted some soldiers lounging at one end of the long table, plus a small knot of immunologists arguing earnestly at the other end. Two of the scientists left for their lab, but the other two stayed from curiosity about the Worlders, even though they now knew that World was far behind Earth in science.

The room had two walls of metal and two of rough slats, with metal Army-issue chairs and a table of what had once been exquisitely polished wood. After ten years, it bore cup stains, gouges, and a long crack in the middle vaguely resembling the east coast of Africa.

More people filed in and seated themselves. Marianne sat beside Zack and set down a cup of what passed here for coffee, mostly made from chicory. She said to him in a low voice, "I'm astonished by how smoothly—how *normal*—work seems to proceed here."

"Well, no, not exactly. We lost so much data and equipment." The understatement of the year. Maybe of the century. They'd lost the CDC, the US Army Medical Research Institute for Infectious Diseases, the gene labs at UC Berkeley and Harvard—and that was only in biology. Fermi Lab, CERN, the Laser Interferometer Gravitational-Wave Observatory, Livermore, and Cold Harbor. . . . Some of these places still existed as rusting and abandoned facilities in which everyone had died; some had been nuked in the first chaos of the most ill-defined war in history. Participants hadn't even been sure who were the other combatants.

And what was "normal" about three Worlders and two Terrans, who had all jumped twenty-eight years and a hundred and three light-years, sitting on metal folding chairs around a table, waiting to hear about a weaponized microbe? Marianne, looking tired and rubbing her forehead. Claire Patel, who was not a geneticist but a physician. Ka^graa, demoted by circumstances from being the most celebrated scientist on his planet to a nobody on this one. Glamet^vorɪ, looking sulky. Jane, the translator, who might or might not have enough scientific terminology to actually translate.

Zack plunged in, stopping after each sentence for Jane to translate. "I'd like to first talk about how *R. sporii* was weaponized, and then what we're trying to do about it. As you know, *R. sporii* is related to the paramyxoviruses, a diverse group. Humans and birds were always the natural hosts for the paras, and the human and avian forms share structural features and replication mechanisms. In fact, the *Respirovirus* may be basal to the bird form, the avulavirus-rubulavirus clade."

Was he already beyond Jane's translation ability? He wanted to include enough technical terms to brief Marianne and Claire, but he had no idea what Ka^graa and Glamet^vorɪ could grasp. However, Jane didn't interrupt, and the two World men seemed to be following. She must have really prepared for this. Zack was impressed with her intelligence and determination.

He continued, "The whole family of paramyxoviridae is genetically stable, but it does have a P gene that can produce multiple proteins not needed for replication. The Gaiists used that, plus histone modification and a host of other tricks. It's a beautiful piece of work, really."

Jane looked up sharply at that, but Marianne nodded. She, at least, understood impersonal admiration for a complicated, if evil, piece of scientific work.

"*R. sporii* lent itself to modification because it was a pretty large virus to begin with, as viruses go, and now it's bigger still. The genemods to *R. sporii* did three things. First, they combined the spore virus with the bird virus. Second, they boosted the virus's virulence in humans, while leaving birds as infected carriers who don't get sick. Third, genemods aerosolized *R. sporii avivirus*, making it airborne. It thrives in bird droppings, and when they dry out in warm summer weather, the air is full of the most deadly disease ever known to human beings. Its exposure time plotted versus parts per million is very small, even for an airborne pathogen, which means you don't need much of it to infect a population. Its kill rate is higher than smallpox.

"The Gaiists were trying to wipe out most of the human race, not just now but in any foreseeable future. That's why they needed the birds as a second reservoir. *R. sporii avivirus* kills so many of its human hosts that the disease would die out if birds didn't keep it alive to infect the next generation."

Glamet^vor; spoke angrily to Jane, who said, "He asks what you will do about this terrible evil."

"I'm coming to that. We have three scientific teams here at Lab Dome. Let me describe them briefly, and then, if you like, you can question me or find the team members and question them. First, the vaccine team is trying to develop a vaccine against RSA. So far, no luck.

"The immunology team is trying to change or bolster the human immune response to better cope with *R. sporii avivirus*. They hope to develop a drug that mimics proteins that seem to protect the small number of people with natural immunity, as well as the survivors. Apparently, you can't get this disease twice. So far, no luck.

"The gene-drive team is working on two gene drives, on a last resort. The first—"

Jane said, "What is 'last resort,' please?"

"Something we will do only if all else fails. We're trying to create a gene drive—that's a bit of engineered DNA that will paste itself into the chromosomes of both male and female sparrows, so all the offspring inherit it. The first gene drive would make it impossible for sparrows to contract RSA. That's the harder drive to create, and so far we haven't succeeded. The second drive, which we haven't succeeded at either but we're closer, produces changes in the DNA of the next generation of birds that makes all males sterile. The computer model says that within fifty generations, all sparrows would be gone from North America. Longer for the rest of the world, but selective genetic sweep will eventually get there."

While Jane translated, Claire said, "*All* sparrows? You'll wreck the global ecology all over again!"

Zack said, "I said it was a last resort."

Marianne said, "This was tried in Africa with Anopheles mosquitoes before I left Terra. It was working. What happened?"

"The Collapse happened," Zack said, more harshly than he'd intended. "I said that the sterility drive was a last resort."

Claire echoed herself. "*All* sparrows? Didn't they . . . wasn't that tried once in China?"

Jane finished translating. Glamet^vor¡ said something to her, his face twisted. Jane frowned at him. Glamet^vor¡ turned to Zack and demanded in heavily accented English, "All things you do? Three things—no things work? Now?"

"No," Zack said. "None of them work now." And looked to be a long way from ever doing so.

Glamet^vor¡ said something in his own language. It needed no translation: his contemptuous face and hand gesture were graphic. He stood and stalked out.

Jane said, "Please to excuse Glamet^vor¡'s unpolite. He . . . has the headache."

No one spoke until Marianne said, "The virophage in our blood . . ."

"The immunology team is working with it now. It would help if we had the samples you already cultured on your ship."

"Yes. Meanwhile, I'd like to ask you more about both the potential vaccine and the gene drive. Have you found a homing endonuclease to reliably cut or insert—"

Zack listened patiently. He wanted to go back to Enclave Dome and check on Caitlin. He wanted to go back to work with Toni Steffens on the gene drive, even though it meant putting up with her calling it the "bird basher." He wanted these scientists, who could not contribute to any of the desperate and unsuccessful trials going forward under this inverted alien bowl, to leave him alone.

And if he had to sit here and patiently answer Marianne's questions, he hoped to hell that she didn't know too much more about the mosquito trials in Africa just before the Collapse. They had been on the point of cancellation because it was discovered that the gene drive had transferred itself to at least one other species of arthropod. A fairly *distant* species. Zack did not want to discuss the possible risk of his sterility drive transferring from birds to other warm-blooded species.

Like, for instance, mammals.

No, he did not at all want to discuss that possibility, not until he and Toni had found a way around it. Horizontal gene transfer of a drive that interfered with reproduction—that would be a zebra fatal enough to do what RSA had not, ending human life on Earth.

Unthinkable.

Kill all the birds? Was killing all that these Terrans ever thought about?

Disgust flared Jane's nostrils, knotted her stomach as she rushed along the corridor. World was not like this. Every small child knew that each species needed the rest, that all of Mother Nature was a harmonious whole and could no more function smoothly, optimally, than could a human body if you cut off its arm. And if what you sliced out was not a limb but a liver or heart . . .

And she had liked Zack McKay. How was he different, really, than the Gaiists who'd tried to kill humans? Were human lives so much more valuable than birds? The hawk she'd seen from the quadcopter, swooping over meadows and forest—wasn't it sentient to some degree?

Murder. The soldiers with their weapons, the scientists with their genes. All Terrans were so—

No. Not all. Colin Jenner and his group were different. When Jane had looked at Colin, she'd seen a Kindred, not a killer. Although he let the babies at his dome die—but he did not make that decision—

"Jeg^faan!"

Glamet^vorɿ stopped her headlong race to the privacy of her sleeping room. He was a convenient target for her anger and confusion. "Don't call me that name! I told you!"

"I greet you, Jeg^faan," he said, not courteously.

"Let me pass, please."

"You are becoming as demanding as the Terrans. I—"

"Jane!" A shrill, grating voice behind her. Jane went immobile, but this World signal for privacy did not stop Kayla Rhinehart. Nothing stopped Kayla.

"I want to talk to you, Jane!"

"I greet you, Kayla."

"Yeah. Whatever. I heard that you—"

"This is Glamet^vorɿ."

"Hi. I heard that you went to Colin Jenner's Settlement!"

"I did go there, yes." Kayla's eyes looked almost as big as a Worlder's, although of course they were not, and too shiny. She had been given some sort of Terran medicine for her crying sadness—had the medicine made her like this, talking too fast and unable to stay still? If so, maybe the sadness was better. More human.

Kayla breathed, "What is it like? Tell me everything!"

"It's a farm. Everyone is RSA survivor so no person wears esuits. They have a dome but the airlocks are open except of attacks. They live very simple. No weapons, no killing animals. They—"

"It sounds like Eden!"

Jane didn't know what that was. She said, "But children—"

"What is Colin Jenner like? Is he handsome?"

"I am sorry, I don't know that word but—"

"Is he good to look at?"

Jane saw again Colin's smiling, expressive face, his strong hug to his chilly brother, the affection in his eyes for Marianne. The way he'd gazed at Jane. "Yes. He is good to look at."

"Mated?"

"No, I don't think . . . no one said . . ."

"I hate living in this dome," Kayla said. "It's worse than World."

"It is different. But Colonel Jenner is trying to—"

"He's the worst thing about this fucking place!"

Jane was silent. Her head ached. She wanted to be alone to think.

Kayla said, "Colin Jenner's dome sounds wonderful. How far away is it?"

"I don't know. We went in a flying machine."

"A plane? A helicopter? A dirigible—what?"

"I don't know those words."

"I wish it wasn't so hard to talk to you!" Kayla flounced off.

Glamet^vorᵢ said in World, "What did you and Kayla say?"

Jane didn't want to repeat the entire pointless conversation, nor talk about Kayla's mental condition. "My head hurts, Glamet^vorᵢ. Excuse me, please."

"My head hurts, too."

That caught her attention. Were the Worlders becoming sick with some Terran microbe? She said swiftly, "Do you know if my father or La^vor or Belok^ have headaches, too?"

"I don't know. You were talking with Kayla about Colin Jenner."

"Yes. Glamet^vorᵢ, I must go. Where is my father?"

"In the other dome, you can't go there without an esuit and 'military escort.' Fah!"

La^vor and Belok^ weren't at the other dome. They were here. Jane pushed past Glamet^vorᵢ, but he caught at her arm. "When you said 'Colin Jenner,' you didn't look like your head ached."

What? How had she looked? Jane felt warmth rise from her neck through her face, and knew that her blush was only making things worse. She broke free of Glamet^vorᵢ's hand and went to the tiny sleeping room shared by the three World siblings, their own small lahk.

La^vor and Belok^ weren't there. But there were only a few other places where they could go. Jane began to search, hoping that both of them felt fine, that her own headache and Glamet^vorᵢ's were due merely to the newness and tension of everything in this terrifying, fascinating, always tense world.

All at once the dome exploded into activity. Soldiers ran toward airlocks. Lindy Ross tore out of the corridor leading to sleeping rooms, followed a moment later by more people and a robot carrying heavy medical equipment. From another direction, Claire Patel sprinted past.

"Claire!" Jane called. But no one answered.

The *Return* had landed.

Jason hadn't been sure that Branch Carter, who admitted that he didn't understand the alien ship, would be able to follow Li's directions to land on an upland meadow a mile from the signal station. Carter wasn't, after all, a trained pilot, not even for Terran craft. But Carter had succeeded, and Jason and Li slapped hands in a high-five gesture that Jason hadn't made since the Collapse. Jason was surprised that Li, younger, knew the high-five at all.

Jason spoke to the *Return* through the comsat; communication was so much easier with New America's comsat out of commission and unable to pinpoint their location.

"Lieutenant Allen, are you also able to lift and land the *Return*?"

"Yes, sir."

"Good. You, Carter, and Specialist Martin will remain aboard. Dr. Jenner says she needs some supplies and specimens from the ship. I'll send a FiVee to pick up whatever Carter thinks the scientists will need, everything suitably protected from contamination."

"Yes, sir."

"And then—"

Jason's earplant erupted into sound. "Colonel Jenner, Hillson here. Perimeter received a report of an attack on the Colin Jenner Settlement at the coast. New America ground troops. Play recording?"

"Yes. Allen, stand by." Jason's guts twisted. He'd insisted on providing Colin with radio equipment to contact the base if necessary. Reluctantly Colin had agreed to leave it hidden in woods beyond a bean field. The equipment had never been used before. Contact now meant that at least one person was outside the dome and that the attack was severe.

The recording came on. A woman's voice, shrill and terrified, gunfire in the distance. "They're here! They're shooting at us, at everybody who couldn't get to the dome in time . . . some people are dead—please come help! Please! Help us! They—"

A burst of automatic fire, deafeningly loud, and a dull thud. She was gone. Then Hillson's voice. "Sir?"

"Any more intel? Did anyone on site say how big the attack force is?"

"No. That recording is all there is."

Jason couldn't risk quadcopters; New America had shoulder-launched missiles. He said, "Load the FiVees with two lockers of C-11w's. Full complement of both infantry and medical. Have them drive to that flat place by the river three miles from the dome, unless New America is too close to there. If so, have them stop farther away at some largely open area and wait."

"Yes, sir." Hillson was too experienced to question orders, but Jason heard the puzzlement in his voice.

To Allen he said, "Belay previous orders. Do not leave the ship. I'll be there in a few minutes. Prepare for liftoff."

"Yes, sir. What—"

"Attack on the Settlement. FiVees are arriving with aerial bombs. The *Return* is now a warship."

CHAPTER 7

Jason had never thought he would leave Earth for space. The era of space travel, like so much else, had died with the Collapse. And yet—here he was, on the bridge of the *Return*, watching on a wall screen as the ground fell away below. A thousand pictures over a lifetime, a hundred rotating holograms—none of it did justice to the reality. His world, blue and white, looking as pure and unsullied as if humans had never built and destroyed and polluted and warred over its forests, oceans, soaring mountains. Jason blinked hard.

"Sir?" Branch Carter said. "I don't know how to do any evasive maneuvers."

Jason turned from the screen to the pilot's console, which didn't look like any cockpit Jason had ever seen. Carter sat on a wooden bench that had once been a wooden table, facing screens, mostly blank, above an array of oddly shaped protrusions and recesses, most of which he never touched. Jason said, "We're well above the altitude of any known enemy surface-to-air weapons. Lieutenant Li at the signal station will give you landing instructions. Be prepared to lift again immediately on my word, if we spot any ground activity. What is your fuel situation?"

"I don't know," Branch Carter said.

"And you are sure that this ship carries no air-to-ground weapons?" He had already asked this, along with everything else he needed to know, but the lab tech turned starship captain seemed to Jason so skittish that perhaps repeated questioning would elicit a different answer.

It didn't. Carter said, "Not that I've found. It was a *colony* ship. And Kindred don't believe in weapons."

The river came into view, a shining ribbon. Open meadows, woods, then individual trees. No people. The *Return* set down, gently as a soap bubble, beside the river. It took the FiVees longer to arrive, and every minute was agony—what was happening at the Settlement? Hillson, at the base, had no more information. When the FiVees roared into sight, Jason and the two members of J Squad he'd had with him at the signal station ran from the ship's airlock. Lindy leaped from the back of the truck crowded with her medical crew. Dr. Holbrook, so much older, climbed down more slowly.

Lindy said, "How bad is it?"

"Don't know. Radio contact broke off and someone was laying down fire. The Settlement dome may or may not have been breached. Stay here until I call you."

Goldman had taken charge of the FiVees filled with soldiers; Kowalski was overseeing the loading of ordnance into the *Return* airlock. Lindy stared at the carry-bot trundling crates marked DANGER—EXPLOSIVES. "Jesus. Aren't we going to use the spaceship to move casualties to the base?"

"Only if we have to. Depends on the numbers." Lindy nodded; she'd always been quick. Colin's people lived in, walked through, breathed RSA. Their presence in the ship would contaminate it. But you could not intubate, suture, or operate through an esuit.

When the bombs were aboard, Jason returned to the airlock but didn't open the inner door or close the outer one. He twisted the weird, curly protuberance that let him talk to the bridge. "Captain Carter, *go*." Then he held his breath.

Jason hadn't known if the ship would lift with the airlock open. It did. Everyone in the open airlock lashed restraining ropes around their waists and put on portable O_2 masks.

Carter lifted the *Return* to an altitude higher than shoulder-mounted missile launchers could target. On the wall screen—and thank God the unknown aliens who'd designed this thing had put wall screens everywhere—the main body of the enemy came into view. Maybe two hundred soldiers, lounging by the river, probably laughing at how easy it was for such a small number of their fighters to slaughter unarmed farmers. Hatred rose in Jason's throat, bitter as bile. He'd seen other raids. New America would kill the men, rape the women, take the youngest and prettiest with them. Portable R&R. Sometimes they murdered the children, sometimes left them to die.

"Carter, hover. Ordnance, first strike."

He hoped the fuckers below had looked up, astonished to see a starship gliding above their heads. The ordnance specialist armed and dropped the bomb.

It exploded in a fireball that consumed the troops below. Swiftly Jason directed the ship to drop lower and fire out the airlock door at those fleeing. Most of the enemy dropped.

A missile left the ground; Jason had wrongly assumed that those would be with the main body of the enemy. "Lift!" Jason cried, and faster than he would have thought possible, the *Return* lurched and soared. If Corporal Olivera had not been lashed to the bulkhead, she would have been shaken out the door. The missile missed the ship, but not by much. Carter had told him that the ship could be damaged by an explosion—*had* been damaged that way on World—but not what would happen if it took that explosion while in the air. Nobody knew.

Swiftly he directed the rest of the attack. They flew over the dome, taking out all the enemy they saw. But some fled into the dome, which meant the farmers had not secured their airlock before the first of the New America troops were inside. Jason cursed and contacted Goldman. "Bring in the FiVees and prepare to take the dome. Medical personnel to begin aiding casualties in the field." He could see bodies scattered among the field crops, along the river, at the kelp farm on the coast.

"Roger, sir." The FiVees, which Jason could just see on the horizon, moved forward.

"Take two or three prisoners if you can, preferably officers."

"Yes, sir."

Lindy, who was not supposed to be on this frequency, said sharply over the rumble of the FiVee, "And the rest of the enemy wounded?"

"Shoot them."

"Roger that, sir."

"Jason—"

"Shut up, Dr. Ross. This is a military frequency. If you don't leave it immediately, I'll have you arrested."

"Try," she said, just before he heard the click of her changing frequencies. For the hundredth time, he wished more Army medical doctors had survived RSA. But all he had were the elderly Holbrook, formerly a cardiologist and now without cardiology equipment, and two civilian physicians, Lindy and Claire Patel.

But Lindy was a damn good doctor. He watched her jump from the back of the truck and run toward a woman twitching on the ground. Then the *Return* was on the ground and Jason forgot those already wounded as he directed the attack that might save the rest.

He was counting on two things: that the enemy had not brought more missile launchers to the dome because they were useless against its shield, which would mean he had destroyed any real threat to the ship. Also, that while the remaining New America soldiers were inside the dome, they could not fire out.

It was not easy to take a dome. So far, only nuclear bombs had ever destroyed them, including the dome over the White House. The alien energy, whatever it was, formed itself into an upside-down bowl and then went rigid and unmovable. However, the visible bowl was not the only thing it formed. Long ago, when Jason was a child, his grandmother had told him about the underground submarine bay in the *Embassy* when it floated in New York harbor. Like Monterey Base, the Settlement dome had a subterranean extension. With any luck Colin had gotten his people underground when New America attacked. The door at the top of the stairwell inside the dome would not hold against military breaching—if this particular cell of New America knew which

door it was. They might or might not. Enemy cells were loosely orga-
nized and sometimes too rivalrous to share intel.

The underground annex came with an airlock, and Jason had insisted
that Colin allow a tunnel to be bored away from it, with a hatch hidden in a peach orchard a quarter mile from the dome. The Lab Dome
tunnel at the Monterey Base was how Jason had gotten James Anderson
into the base stockade without anyone except J Squad even aware that
the Gaiist had been captured. Colin used the tunnel only as an additional, cool storage area for fruit, vegetables, and grain. It was, he'd
said with the misplaced gratitude that drove Jason crazy, perfect because
the metal reinforcing helped keep out mice and vermin.

Jason left soldiers guarding Holbrook's medical corps, their weapons trained on each of the dome's above-ground airlocks in case of a
rush. Jason led the rest of J Squad to the tunnel exit. When the brush
had all been removed, two soldiers lifted the metal hatch, which wasn't
locked; for once Jason was grateful for the Settlers' casual carelessness
about security. Someone below screamed. J Squad raised their weapons. Jason looked down and said, "Christ!"

Three men crouched on the top step, holding shovels and hoes. Below them were jammed more men, women, and children. Did these
idiots think they could hold off New America with the weapons of
thirteenth-century serfs, and from a position *below* their attackers?

"US Army!" he shouted. "Come out of there!"

Some did, some ran back down the stairwell, some just cowered.
J Squad yanked them all above ground. Jason said to the first adult out,
a big man dressed in homespun shorts and nothing else, "How many
enemy inside?"

"I don't know. Maybe two dozen?"

Not good. "Colin Jenner?"

"Inside. Too hurt to move. He told us to come here and—"

"Take charge of these people. Keep them here, don't let them go back
inside the dome until you get an all clear. Understand?"

"Yes." And then, "If you give me a gun, I'll defend everybody."

So they're not all idiots, Colin. Jason handed over his SCAR. Jason would be in the rear, anyway, and he had his sidearm. The man, in homespun cloth and wooden sandals, held the rifle expertly and checked the magazine in the chamber.

Well.

J Squad poured down the stairwell, sending people back up behind them. Jason followed. The only light came from the tunnel opening, except . . . what the hell was that? A weird green glow . . .

People standing in the defense alcoves, or what were supposed to be defense alcoves, holding wooden trenches of biofluorescent bacteria or mold or some damn thing. But the glow helped as J Squad pounded up the stairway to the dome. Rice grains crunched under Jason's boots. A peach rolled past, leaving juicy smears on the steps. At the top, the metal doorway was barred with wooden slats. No e-locks here. The enemy could have breached this door at any time, which meant they hadn't known it was there.

He was wrong. But J Squad was ready.

As soon as the point man flung open the door, the enemy fired. J Squad returned fire. Two of Jason's soldiers went down, but there were only three New America fuckers there and the squad dispatched them and kept going. Experts at clearing rooms, they flowed in three-man stacks from area to area. Gunfire echoed off the metal partitions, thudded on the wooden ones. Jason bent over his fallen soldiers.

Private Sendis was dead. Specialist Lena Tarrant was hit in the chest. "I'll get medics to you as soon as I can."

She tried to nod.

Jason ran through the dome, following his troops, issuing orders into his mic. There weren't two dozen of New America inside, only half that. J Squad, sustaining one more nonserious casualty, killed them all. No chance to take any prisoner.

Settlers cowered where they could. Some lay dead or wounded on the dome floor, smearing it with blood. Jason found Colin unconscious beside an indoor planting bed, a wound in his side and his leg bent at an impossible angle. Bone showed through. A teenage boy crouched beside him, desperately pressing a cloth against Colin's side.

"Keep doing that," Jason said. "I'll send a medic as soon as I can." He ran toward an airlock.

Outside, all looked quiet. He said over his mic, "Kubetschek, report!"

"No one emerged, sir. All visible enemy here are dead. It's possible some escaped into the woods but none have fired. One prisoner."

"Lieutenant Allen?"

"No action at the ship, sir."

He switched frequencies. "Dr. Holbrook?"

"A lot of casualties. More dead. Inside?"

"Casualties. Send medics and Dr. Ross."

Lindy ran to the dome and Jason met her at the airlock. "This way. Colin. Multiple wounds."

He led her to Colin and went back outside, watching the medics work on the helpless farmers shot for the crops they had labored to raise, or shot to bring Jason's military running so they too could be slaughtered, or shot just for the thrill of killing.

He strode toward the captured New America prisoner.

It was a boy, no more than fifteen, the beard on his face wispy and childish. He wore old boots and a new uniform, its cloth still stiff with the original sizing, possibly captured from the Sierra Depot. His eyes glared at Jason in defiance, hatred, and fear, but mostly fear.

A boy, a private in this undisciplined army. From his age, a new recruit. He would not have any valuable intel.

But Jason would have to find that out for sure.

There were too many wounded to take back to the base in the FiVees. Lindy said, "Some of them couldn't stand the jolting anyway, over those nonroads." She waited, looking at him, arms crossed on her chest, blood smearing her jeans and cotton shirt.

Jason gazed at the wounded scattered over the fields, the orchard, by the mill and estuary. The Settlers from the dome and its underground annex had all been brought outside, bending over the injured and the dead or huddling together. Some wept. A heavy-duty medbot transported Colin, still unconscious, on its stretcher. Tubes and wires sprouted from him like the weeds he unaccountably loved.

Lindy said, "Jason—"

"I know." He would have to contaminate the *Return* with RSA.

He had Carter lift the ship and set it down in a field of broccoli. Jason and Lindy walked beside Colin's bot. "He's lucky," Lindy said. "The side bullet missed his vital organs. The leg injury is actually worse, a comminuted open fracture. When was his spleen removed?"

"He was just a kid," Jason said. "I don't really know much about it." Another life, like everything before the Collapse. He turned to face her. "Thank you for saving him."

"You don't think I did it for you, do you?"

"Not for half a second. But thank you anyway."

"Damn it, Jason, don't turn humble on me! That was always your most deceptive move!" And then, a moment later, "I'm sorry. That was uncalled for."

Before Jason had to answer, Luke trotted up to him. Luke, another superhearer like Colin, another reminder of Before. Colin, Jason, Luke—the three kids who'd been inseparable, who'd had adventures together, who'd pinkie-sworn brotherhood forever. Luke, mentally challenged, had followed Colin to the Settlement, although Jason didn't know how much Luke actually understood of Colin's ridiculous Luddite philosophy.

"Colin?" Luke said, his face twisted with anxiety. "Colin?"

Lindy said, "He'll be okay, Luke. But he has to go to the base. You all do. It's not safe here."

"I will go. But not Sarah. She won't. Not some other people."

"Christ," Jason said. Holdouts.

Lindy half turned to look at him; he could see the curve of her cheek filmed with sweat, a strand of hair sticking to it. The sight brought back a hundred inappropriate memories of how she looked after sex. He knew, too, in the way that married, or once-married, people understood their partners' thought processes, that she was waiting to hear how he would handle those who did not want to leave the dome. Let them stay here and die if more New America's troops returned here, or manhandle them into the ship?

Of course, the refuseniks could hole up in the dome, sealing themselves in, living off the stored crops, while New America plundered their fields and burned the kelp farm. Maybe they could outlast the enemy, who was not known for patience. But unlike Monterey Base, which used converters to create freshwater from air, the anti-tech Settlement obtained all its water from the river above the falls. If the enemy dammed or poisoned the river, the holdouts would soon run out of water. Also, Jason doubted that they would actually seal themselves into the dome and stay there. The moment they couldn't actually see an enemy soldier, they'd go outside because going outside was the entire point of their existence. "Live free on the Earth." And then New America would shoot more of them and maybe take the dome again.

Jason said into his mic, "Goldman, Kowalski, Hillson—everyone goes onto the *Return*, by force if necessary. Hillson, radio Major Duncan to prepare for about two hundred temporary refugees." He flicked off the mic and, prepared for battle, turned to Lindy.

She said, "You did the right thing," and turned toward the next wounded Settler, leaving Jason staring after her.

Damn it, Lindy, you can still surprise me.

Luke suddenly cried out. He heard it first—the Superhearers always heard everything first—and dropped to the ground. Jason seized Lindy, threw her down, and hurled himself on top of her. A second later the explosion shattered the air.

But no flying debris, no smoke, and the ship—the first thing Jason raised his head to see—was intact. The explosion had been inside the dome, contained by it, its rounded top no longer clear but darkened with ash. Smoke drifted out the open airlock.

J Squad had sprinted to defensive position, but there was no one to defend against, no one to attack. New America had set off a delayed-action bomb—probably more than one—inside the dome, timed to allow them to murder and loot. Jason knew without checking that nothing would be left except the indestructible alien-energy walls that divided the dome into quadrants. Plants, seeds, tools, living quarters, hand looms, candles and homemade soap and carved wooden bowls and every other seventeenth-century contrivance—all destroyed. Anyone returning here to live would have to start completely over, from nothing. Still—Colin was capable of that.

He stood. Lindy scrambled to her feet beside him, putting a hand on Luke's shoulder. Her green eyes were wide.

Jason said grimly, "At the base, the Settlers will all have to accept military rule."

"Yes," she said, and he was surprised to feel her fingers brush his hand before she ran toward the FiVee.

CHAPTER 8

Marianne sat with Ryan beside Colin's bedside. Colin, freshly out of OR and still sedated, slept deeply in one of the tiny, windowless rooms in Lab Dome that had actually been intended to be part of the infirmary. Less severely wounded people were jammed into a makeshift ward nearby. Because every single Settler was contaminated with RSA, they had had to be brought in batches through decon, even the dangerously wounded.

Marianne and Ryan shared a wooden bench, dragged into Colin's room from the Army mess. Luke lay curled asleep on the floor, his huge body taking up most of the floor space. He'd refused to leave Colin.

To Marianne, the entire scene felt unreal. Ryan was now only three years younger than she was, and looked ten years older. His right hand shook with Parkinson's. After he'd asked about Noah and his family on World, Ryan fell silent. He'd always been a quiet, even secretive, person, but as he gazed at his younger son without speaking, his left hand rested on Marianne's and she was comforted by its veiny, callused touch.

She said, "Lindy says that Colin will be all right."

Ryan nodded.

If Marianne wanted information from him, she was going to have to pry it out. "What went wrong between her and Jason?"

"I didn't ask, Mom."

"But you know."

Long silence. Then merely, "Jason and Colin are very different people."

She wanted to say *Duh*. She did not. Was "duh" even understood slang anymore? She said instead, "When did Jason grow such a turtle-plate?"

"A what?"

"A hard shell. Colin was always a gentle kid, but Jason wasn't always this hard."

Another long silence. When Ryan did speak, it clearly cost him pain. "You don't know what the Collapse was like, Mom. People dying, dead in just a few hours, nearly everyone. The cities were full of stinking corpses, industry gone overnight, some places with just a handful of survivors in an entire town. People reacted in different ways. They gave up, or started fighting each other, or went crazy, or started organizing what was left. Jason was already a major in the Army. He took control of Monterey Base, which had been under a dome less than one year. Everybody above him in the chain of command was dead. He sealed the base and used copters to bring in scientists from all over California, either before they were infected or after they survived, along with any surviving families. He sent soldiers in esuits to get whatever additional equipment the scientists asked for, plus more supplies and weapons and I don't know what all. He moved fast and efficiently, and he made enemies doing it because he could not take in everyone, and because some people wanted to mourn instead of moving on. He did what he had to, and none of us might be here at all if it weren't for him."

Ryan stopped. Marianne waited, sensing there was more to come.

Finally Ryan said, "Some of what he did might be called brutal. *Was* called brutal. His first goal was to not contaminate the base with RSA, because he needed the scientists who were not immune to stay alive and find a way to combat the weaponized disease. He kept out sick people begging to get in. They died, some of them, just outside the airlock, including children. Lindy wanted to go out in an esuit and do what she could to at least ease their dying, but he wouldn't let her, even though she's an RSA survivor. He couldn't risk some crazy survivor killing one of his two doctors. He instituted strict control of the birds brought into Lab Dome for research, and he enforced it with weapons when he had to."

She said, startled, "There are RSA-bearing birds inside Lab Dome?"

"There's a biohazard lab in the underground annex, with its own decon. Not a biohazard level 4, unfortunately, but an engineer rigged up negative pressure. Everybody allowed to work there is an RSA survivor, I'm told, which pissed off some scientists who aren't and feel their hands are tied, relatively."

Ryan had once been a scientist, too, long ago. A botanist concerned with invasive species, especially purple loosestrife. Not relevant now.

He went on, "When the war started with New America, I think Jason did . . . other things. I'm not sure what. But that's when Lindy left him. She doesn't understand that Jason is doing what he thinks is necessary. So is Colin. Mom—what about this virophage you brought back from World?"

She could have asked why Ryan chose to live with Colin instead of at the base, but she didn't. Ryan's tone said he was done discussing his sons. She said, "Zack McKay told me that the virophage from our tissues has proved useless against the weaponized version of *R. sporii*. The leelees—that's an animal native to World—aboard the *Return* were also infected with both virus and virophage, but they all died when Terran air filled the ship. The cultures that Claire and I made on ship died, too. None of us refugees is going to be much help to Zack and his people."

"You are a help. You brought the ship."

"Well, yes, there is that. We— Come in, Jane."

The Kindred woman stood uncertainly in the doorway. Marianne saw that to Ryan, Jane still looked alien. Marianne had been around Worlders so long that now they just looked like another group of Terrans, no stranger than people with red hair or brown skin.

She saw something else, too: the way Jane looked at Colin. Unlike

Ryan and Jason, Jane was not guarded. Her whole young heart shone in her big eyes.

She said in her musical English, "Will Colin become completely well?"

"We hope so. Dr. Ross says he's recovering as well as can be expected."

Jane glanced at Ryan and then at Luke, snoring loudly on the floor.

Marianne said, "This is my son, Ryan Jenner, Colin's father. And that's Luke, a friend of Colin's from the Settlement."

"I greet you, Ryan Jenner." Apparently Jane had decided to resume the World greeting; for a while she had dropped it. It must be difficult to decide how much of your culture to keep or shed in such different surroundings.

Ryan said, "Hello."

Lindy suddenly pushed past Jane. "What are all you doing in here without so much as a face mask? Where's Amy—why did she let you in? Out, all of you!"

Marianne said, "Don't blame Amy. She has too many to nurse in the ward. We snuck in, but we'll go now if you say so."

"You and Ryan can stay, with masks, but not until after I examine Colin. And get this big sleeping lump out of here, now. You, Jane: don't come back until I say so, and—Jason? No, you can't come in, stay out there in the corridor, and the rest of you—*out*. This is a vulnerable patient, people. I wish you would all remember that!"

Ryan woke Luke and got him out of the room, although only by constant soothing murmurs as he tugged Luke along. Jason and Jane left, followed by Marianne. Jason and Jane stood at the end of the corridor, talking in low voices. Sooner than Marianne expected, Lindy emerged from Colin's room.

"He's doing well—everything looks good. Find Amy and get a face mask before you go back in there. Jason, I need to talk to you."

He said stiffly, "Colonel Jenner, please."

Before Marianne heard Lindy's reply, she left to find a face mask.

Marianne had no intention of leaving Colin until she could see for herself that he was awake and rational.

Although the more she thought about it, the less rational everything seemed. Why should Colin be any different?

At least her headache had lessened. That was something.

"What did you do with him?" Lindy demanded.

Jason didn't have to ask whom she meant. Her green eyes, shadowed with fatigue, glared at him. Jane glided discreetly away. Jason didn't let his gaze follow her.

Just beyond the infirmary corridor, Zack McKay conferred with two other scientists. Boxes of God-knew-what lined the walls and narrowed the hallway; one of the scientists sat on a tall crate. By last count, 203 Settlers had survived the attack by New America, and all of them had been jammed into the base wherever they would fit. Families in two-room apartments were now down to a single room. Storerooms had been emptied to use as quarters, which was why the corridors were now crowded with crates and shelving. All but the main conference room in Lab Dome had been commandeered, and most other such amenities had been eliminated. Sergeant Tasselman, the billeting officer, had done the best he could. Susan McKay, quartermaster, had stretched blankets and cots and kitchenware as far as they could possibly go. Jason was sleeping on a cot in his command post. But, then, he'd often done that since he and Lindy divorced.

Lieutenant Allen had taken the contaminated *Return* back to orbit, along with Information Technology Specialist Ruby Martin and J Squad soldier Corporal Jeffrey Michaelson. Jason had hesitated over the decision to park the ship upstairs, even though that would keep it safe from attack. Branch Carter had no idea how much fuel was left, or even what fuel the ship used when it wasn't jumping through time and space. Carter was not aboard. With no immunity to RSA, Carter lay in the infirmary, having his gut microbes adjusted back to Terran.

Also aboard the *Return* was Monterey Base's only physicist, Major Thomas Farouk. Jason wasn't happy about that, either, but Farouk, an RSA survivor, was more eager to investigate the *Return* than to do research on the ground. During the frantic days after the Collapse, Jason had concentrated on gathering up biologists, virologists, doctors, anyone who could help with *R. sporii avivirus.* He had not anticipated needing more physicists to reverse-engineer an alien starship. But maybe Farouk would learn something useful about the alien technology.

In addition to the Army personnel, the *Return* now carried more weapons from the armory, transported to the ship in heavily guarded FiVees.

Lindy folded her arms across her chest. "That prisoner is underground, isn't he? In your dungeon?"

"This is none of your business, Dr. Ross."

"It sure the hell is! I'm chief medical officer here and—"

"You aren't an officer at all."

"—torture is against *your* rules of engagement that—"

"For Christ's sake!" he hissed. Two of the scientists glanced their way and Jason cursed himself. Nobody could make him lose his temper like Lindy. He lowered his voice.

"The rules of engagement no longer apply in a world without rules. But no, I am not going to torture that kid. He won't know anything valuable. A simple truth drug will be enough in this case, and since you're here and Captain Holbrook is in surgery performing a cesarean delivery, you're going to administer it. That's an order, Dr. Ross."

She wasn't an officer, but the base was under military law. Too bad so many civilians forgot that.

Momentarily distracted, she said, "A cesarean? Who's having a baby?"

"One of the Settlers." A baby that, because it was born at the base and not at the RSA-exposed Settlement, had a hugely increased chance of living more than a few hours. Would the new parents appreciate that? Would Colin?

Lindy was never distracted for long. "You promise? No torture?"

"Did you not hear me, Dr. Ross?"

"Yes." She calmed down. "Now?"

Why not? A hundred details clamored for Jason's attention, but everyone except the signal crew and patrol detail were safe inside the two domes. Private Sendis had been buried in the graveyard beside Enclave's seldom-used southwest airlock. Specialist Lena Tarrant was recovering from wounds sustained in the firefight at the Settlement. The base was not under attack, and Elizabeth Duncan sat in the command post at the top of Enclave Dome, ready to receive any messages from the outside patrol. His second in command was one of the best soldiers Jason had ever seen, although almost unknowable. Always she sat so straight that her back never touched any chair. Her expression seldom changed: alert and unemotional. Sometimes she seemed like a machine, except that nobody was a machine. Least of all, Jason thought, himself.

Jason said, "All right, now. Get whatever you need."

After Lindy fetched her supplies, he led the way to the secure door leading underground. Private Garson sprang up. "All quiet, sir."

"Good." He opened the door.

She said, "Don't you need a retinal and digital match?"

"Both off during daytime if a guard is on duty. Too many scientists and lab techs coming and going from the bird lab."

At the bottom of the stairs, Jason keyed them into the stockade. No one, fortunately, emerged from the bird lab opposite the stockade. Building the bird lab inside the dome, even underground, had troubled Jason, but the scientists had insisted. They needed easy access between the bird lab and the research facilities directly above. Jason also hadn't liked the scientists' bringing in live birds infected with RSA, even though the sparrows that had been captured outside were brought through the tunnel airlock sealed in esuits, and then taken directly into the negative-pressure lab. The birds weren't, of course, exposed to decon, which would have negated the whole point, and only RSA survivors were allowed to work in the bird lab. At first, Jason had argued for killing the birds outside and only transporting tissue to the lab. However, the scientists had all protested so stringently that he'd had to give way. Apparently, living and breeding sparrows were necessary to develop vaccines or gene drives. But if any of the scientists got careless for even a second . . .

So far, none of them had. "Colonel," Dr. Steffens had said, not bothering to hide her disdain, "I've worked with Congo hemorrhagic fever, Marburg, and Ebola. Dr. Yu headed the team for the *Embassy* work on *R. sporii*. Zack McKay is an expert on Lassa. We will not get careless."

"Everybody is careless sometime, Dr. Steffens," he'd said. She didn't like him, nor he her.

Nor did he like putting the stockade in Lab Dome underground annex. But there was no other place. The underground annex in Enclave was used to bring in Settlement crops and forest game, and kitchen staff were in and out constantly.

The private on stockade duty opened the cell door for Jason and Lindy. The New America soldier sat in the same cell where James Anderson had killed himself. Nothing indicated that fact; the alien material of the floor was as impervious to stains as to ordnance. A plate of untouched food sat beside the teenager. One wrist and both feet manacled, the kid glared at Jason and Lindy from defiant, scared eyes. His wispy beard had become neither fuller nor longer.

"I'm Colonel Jenner and I command here," Jason said. "Your name and rank?" Some New America cells kept to old rules for POWs; some did not.

The boy said nothing.

"Corporal, secure the prisoner."

Thompson expertly pinned the boy with a choke hold. Before he could even struggle, Lindy wrapped a tourniquet around his upper arm and slid a needle into a vein on the inner surface of his elbow.

Jason neither liked nor trusted truth drugs. They hadn't advanced much in fifty years; they usually produced an unsortable mishmash of fact, fantasy, and gibberish; a personality with strong defenses and even minimal conditioning could withstand them. They had not worked with Anderson. Jason wasn't a trained interrogator, and he doubted that this boy had any useful information. But he had to do this, just in case.

Or was this interrogation, done this gentler way, to demonstrate to Lindy that he was not a monster?

To demonstrate that to the image of Jane in his mind, more than she should be?

To demonstrate to Colin?

"He's under," Lindy said. "Just a minute . . ."

Jason said, "Corporal, dismissed."

"Yes, sir." He left, closing the door.

With narcosynthesis, timing mattered. The subject fell into sleep, and then partially aroused from it. Questioning needed to happen during the brief period of twilight consciousness, when inhibitions were lowered and the cortex no longer functioned as a control over what was said. Maintaining that state required frequent, carefully balanced doses of Lindy's witches' brew of depressant, barbiturate, and ataraxic. She had proved to be surprisingly good at this.

"Okay," she said.

Jason said, "What is your name?"

"Tommy. I am Tommy."

A lucid response, but thick and mumbling. "Tommy what?"

"Tommy knockers. Grandma said . . . tom toms . . . magic . . ." His body in the clean uniform twitched and then he was asleep. Lindy gave him more drug.

"Where did you get the uniform, Tommy?"

"Grandma. Sewed my . . . sewn shut . . ."

"Where did you get the uniform? Where?"

"Sierra Depot." Suddenly clear and crisp. But only for a moment. "Night . . . Blackie said . . . that girl . . ."

"Who was at Sierra Depot?"

"Danced with her but she wouldn't . . . they all . . . Grandma sewed it for me. Her big table, so big . . . why did Blackie do that? Why wouldn't she dance with me?" His face twisted, about to cry.

This was pointless. Bits and pieces of this pathetic kid's lost life, floating to the surface like jetsam after a shipwreck. He must have been only five or six when the Collapse happened.

Fragments of lost life mingled with bits of erotic fantasy. "I licked her and fucked her . . . tits and ass and cunt . . . Grandma said . . ."

Jason put his hand on Tommy's shoulder and squeezed hard. "Who was at Sierra Depot?"

"Sierra . . ." He lapsed into sleep.

"More, Lindy. . . . okay, Tommy, *who was at Sierra Depot?*"

"Unit Nineteen. We killed all the fuckers, we . . ."

"You what? What did Unit Nineteen do at Sierra Depot? Tell me!"

"There's a password. Blackie said . . ."

"A password to what?"

"A key."

"A key to what?"

"To the locked room."

"What's in the locked room?"

"Full of gold and jewels and silver and girls . . . Blackie said . . . gold and myrrh and Frank-in-his-senses . . . Frank is dead. . . ."

Christ. This was pointless.

Until all at once, it wasn't.

"Frank who?" Jason asked, because he had to ask something.

"Frank Shuh . . . Sug . . . yama. Frankie. The little one."

Shock jolted Jason, electricity that flashed from his head through his entire body, a lightning stroke that left him momentarily paralyzed. When he could speak again, he said, "Frank Sugiyama? Dr. Frank Philip Sugiyama?"

"They chopped him up. Little Frankie. The doctor screamed but . . . I couldn't look and Blackie said I'm a coward. . . ." The boy started to cry.

"*Tell me,*" Jason ordered, but Tommy kept on crying.

Lindy took his free hand and stroked it. She said gently, "Tell me, Tommy." He grabbed her arm as if he were drowning. "Blackie said . . . Blackie said . . . Grandma . . ."

"It's all right, Tommy. You can tell me. Grandma wants you to tell me . . . damn. Asleep again. Just a minute . . ."

She gave him another injection with her free hand. A soon as his eyes opened, she said, "Tell me about Frank Sugiyama. Was he at Sierra Depot?"

"Yeah. Only they chopped up little Frankie and the screaming . . . the screaming . . . why wouldn't she dance with me in the room with gold and jewels and Blackie said—"

"What is the password to the room with gold and jewels?"

"Through the back door, Blackie said. But Grandma . . . they chopped her up?"

Jason said, "Who was at Sierra Depot with Frank and little Frankie? Was his family there?"

"Three kids, only she wouldn't dance with me. They won't let her dance with me unless he tells. Tits and ass and cunt and . . . Grandma said!"

"What is her name, Tommy? Tell me!"

"Sewn shut, but Blackie said . . ."

"Her name! The girl who won't dance with you!"

"Flower. Don't hurt me, they always hurt me . . ."

"Which flower? *Which?*"

"Grandma said . . ."

"Iris? Pansy? Lily? Tell me!"

"Tell me her name," Lindy said softly into Tommy's ear. "The name of the girl who won't dance with you."

Tommy said, "Rose," and burst into loud sobbing, snot running onto his uniform, his body with its drugged loss of coordination twitching on the floor.

Lindy looked at Jason. "Do I . . ."

"Let him sleep."

A few moments later, he did. They were the longest moments of Jason's life. Whole continents of thought rose, lived, and fell in those moments.

Lindy waited. Finally she said, "What does it mean?" And when he didn't answer, "Come on, Jason. Does he mean Frank Sugiyama the famous physicist? What does he have to do with New America?"

"He's the genius behind a working quantum computer. He's supposed to be dead."

"I thought nobody succeeded in making a reliable quantum computer before the Collapse. You're saying the military did?"

"Yes."

Lindy was the most intelligent woman he'd ever known. She put it together. "There's a quantum computer at Sierra Depot. And New America took the depot. Sugiyama is there—"

"We thought he was dead. They must have found him and brought him there."

"And little Frankie . . . oh, God, they have his family. They chopped up his son to gain his cooperation, and Rose is—his daughter? 'Three kids,' Tommy said. What do they want from Sugiyama? Tommy mentioned a password . . . what's in that computer?"

"It will self-destruct," Jason said. His lips felt numb. On the floor, Tommy snored. "It will self-destruct if anyone but Army command accesses it. Sugiyama doesn't know the password."

"So they'll torture his family in front of him and kill him for nothing?"

"Yes."

"Tommy said 'back door'—is there a back door into the computer code?"

"No."

Unless Jason had not been told everything he needed to know by a US Army command that barely existed anymore. Or unless Sugiyama, under terror about his family, used the fine mind that made him the twenty-first century's equivalent of Albert Einstein to find a way around the self-destruct feature.

"Jason," Lindy said, "what information is in that computer? Why do you look like that? What can New America do if they get into the quantum computer?"

Jason didn't, couldn't, tell her. Classified. He looked at Tommy, snoring on the alien material of the floor. When he woke, he wouldn't remember what he'd said. That was how truth drugs worked. For a brief moment, Jason envied him.

Lindy said, more insistently, "What's in that computer?"

"Classified."

The launch codes for the only three viable nuclear missiles that the United States had left.

CHAPTER 9

Zack sat with Caitlin in the Enclave dining room, called a "mess hall" even though the Army had its own mess in Lab Dome, as the little girl fished the last of her vegetables out of the broth in her bowl. A bit of broccoli dropped onto her pants. She picked it up and ate it.

"Good girl. Now drink the broth."

"I don't like it."

"Drink it, pumpkin. You know we don't waste food." There was not as much of it to waste now.

Caitlin made a face and drank her broth. A pair of children from the Settlement entered the mess, surprising Zack; he thought that all the Settlers had been crammed into Lab Dome. Maybe Susan, as quartermaster, had moved some of them over here. Well, that would make sense—the school, such as it was, occupied a single room in Enclave Dome.

Caitlin's eyes went wide. "Daddy, who's *that!*"

The six children of Enclave Dome—that was all Caity had ever seen. Maybe that was all she thought existed in the world. He said, "The new people who came to live at the base. Do you want to say hello?"

She turned shy, pressing herself against his knee. "No. Where's Mommy?"

"She's at work. You know that."

"Okay. Can I eat my peach now?"

"Go ahead." A woman in a homespun tunic rounded up the two kids and led them away. Compared to the few people in the mess in midafternoon—two uniformed soldiers on duty in Enclave and four pale civilian staffers in old, 3-D–printed jeans—the three sandaled and suntanned Settlers looked as exotic as Fiji Islanders.

Caitlin put down her half-eaten peach. "I don't feel good."

"Is it the headache again?"

"No. My tummy." She turned and vomited onto the wooden bench, then started to cry.

"Oh, sweetie. It's all right. Here, let's get that icky shirt off you."

Zack took off the child's shirt and wrapped her in his own. Her head lolled against his bare chest. A janitor, sister to one of the lab techs, rushed over. "I'll take care of that, Dr. McKay. Do you need a doctor?"

"No, she saw Dr. Patel yesterday. It's just a stomach bug, but I thought she was over it."

"I'm over it," Caitlin mumbled against his chest.

"You take her home. I'll get this."

"Thank you so much."

He carried his daughter "home," which meant an eight-by-ten cubicle that Zack had been moved to after the influx of Settlers. Susan had been careful to not show any favoritism to her own family. Her and Zack's bed occupied four-by-six of the space; when Caitlin's trundle was pulled from underneath, there was barely room to stand beside it. He extricated the trundle and laid her on it, gazing down worriedly. "Does anything hurt now? Tummy? Head?"

"Nothing hurts. I'm sleepy."

"I see that." She was, it seemed to him, sleeping too much lately. But in the last few days, both Claire Patel and Lindy Ross had examined her. Neither had found anything unusual. Zack was supposed to turn Caity over to the two teachers who babysat children as well as taught them, but he wasn't going to leave his daughter until he was sure she was all right. Anyway, neither Karen nor Marissa would appreciate being saddled with a vomiting child. He intercommed Susan.

Caitlin yawned and said, "Tell me a story."

He began *The Three Bears*, a Caitlin favorite, but it was clear she wasn't listening. In the middle of Goldilocks's discontent with porridge, she said, "Daddy, who made the domes?"

"The Army made the domes. You know that."

"No, who *made* them. Devon says the Army doesn't know how the domes work."

True enough. How to explain to a four-year-old what physicists didn't understand? "The Army built the domes. But they didn't invent them. Somebody else told them how to make domes. Like when your teacher tells you how to add up numbers."

"Who told the Army how to make domes?"

"People from another planet. People like Jane—you met Jane."

"She's pretty."

Was she? Zack realized that he hadn't ever noticed. Susan was the only woman he'd noticed that way in years. Talk about your long-married clichés.

Caitlin said, "Jane must be really smart if she showed Colonel Jenner how to make domes."

"Well, it wasn't exactly like . . . you see, sweetie, some other people showed Jane's people how to make domes."

"Who?"

"Nobody knows. Nobody has ever seen them. They're . . . they're like super-aliens. Like in your book about Jerry and the Space Puppy."

That woke her a little. Caitlin sat up. "There are super-aliens? Where?"

"Nobody knows. They left a long time ago."

"Where did they go?"

"Nobody knows."

"What did they look like?"

"Nobody knows."

"Why did they go away?"

"Nobody knows that, either."

She stared at him doubtfully, this father who didn't seem able to provide answers to anything, and then lay back down on her trundle bed. *"I know."*

"You know what the super-aliens look like?"

"Yes."

"Then tell me! I really want to know!"

Caitlin frowned, and her eyes roamed the room, jammed with her family's few possessions, most heaped on shelves hastily affixed to the wooden walls. Her gaze fell on her own drawings. Triumphantly she said, "The aliens look like zebras, 'cause they are zebras!"

When you hear hoofbeats, think of horses not zebras.

"Maybe," he said, but Caitlin was already asleep.

Zack hurried through the tunnel connecting the domes. This was just as complicated as going through two ground-level airlocks, but right now Zack didn't want to deal with delay of the required military escort. It had taken too long to find someone to stay with Caity, and he was already late.

He ran down the long flight of stairs leading from the kitchens. The large, alien-metal room at the bottom was Enclave Dome's storeroom, jammed with produce, eggs, and grain from the Settlement and forest game shot by the Army. Semi-successful cheeses ripened on a shelf, the result of a semi-successful experiment with capturing and milking wild sheep. Two men were filling tote bags with apples from a crate; the smell made Zack's mouth water.

In the corner stood the door to decon and the airlock. "Retinal scan and digital chip match: Dr. Zachary McKay." The kitchen workers watched him with an expression Zack couldn't read: envy or pity or maybe just puzzlement that anyone would risk exposure to RSA. *I already had it, boys,* he thought, and pushed the memory away.

The airlock gave onto a tunnel with two branches. One, sealed a short distance along, was an escape hatch that Zack hoped fervently would never have to be used. He hurried, holding his flashlight, along the much shorter tunnel. It connected to a similar branching outside Lab Dome. Airlock, decon, and he stood in the small space outside the bird lab and the mysterious, heavy third door. Up the stairwell to the young soldier on guard (didn't they ever get bored, doing essentially nothing?), who unlocked the door to Lab Dome.

Zack raced into the conference room jammed with chairs, people, and the odors of too many bodies. Colonel Jenner sat at the head of the table. Was Jenner's command post at the top of Enclave Dome more spacious than this? Zack had never seen it. Almost no civilian had, and only the most trusted soldiers.

"Sorry I'm late," Zack said, squeezing into the only empty chair, beside Toni. Jenner frowned at him. Present were the heads of each research team, with some of their colleagues both military and civilian, plus some of the lab assistants. Four newcomers: two Army captains, Marianne Jenner, and Claire Patel. Neither of the Worlder scientists, which surprised Zack. Either Jane would not be able to keep up with the translation for this more technical meeting, or Jenner had decided on security grounds to exclude Ka^graa and Glamet^vorʲ from what was essentially a military briefing. Theoretically, these monthly briefings were classified, although in such close and crowded quarters almost nothing stayed secret very long. Major Duncan, whom Toni referred to as "Stonejaw," wasn't here; presumably Jenner had left her in temporary command at the top of Enclave Dome.

Surrounded by all those uniforms, Jenner looked tired but even more powerful than usual. "The emperor in state," Toni said to Jason under her breath. She had the disconcerting ability to speak sotto voce without moving her lips at all.

Jenner said, "This briefing is in session. I'd like to introduce captains Mott and Darnley from Headquarters. Their mission is to update General Hahn."

Zack blinked. Sending brass from Headquarters was a big deal, complicated and dangerous, unless these captains were already in the area.

Why would that be? Something in Jenner's posture suggested that this visit had been a surprise to him as well.

Jenner said only, "Captains Mott and Darnley will need to be brought up to speed on progress to date, so please start with the basics of your work. Dr. Yu?"

Dr. Jessica Yu, chief scientist for the base, also headed the vaccine unit. It seemed to Zack that she had always headed the vaccine unit, since the beginning of time. She'd been with the original *Embassy* team with Marianne. They had succeeded in creating a vaccine against *R. sporii*, and now Dr. Yu was trying to do the same for its weaponized cousin. At eighty-two, however, she turned more and more of the work over to others. She said, "Dr. Sullivan will present for the team."

Major Denise Sullivan, once of the United States Army Medical Research Institute for Infectious Diseases, stood diamond-fiber straight, facing her listeners as diagrams from her tablet appeared on the wall screen behind her. Despite the lack of advance warning, her presentation was meticulous and detailed. Zack couldn't tell how much of it the visiting captains understood, but by the end, one thing was clear: there was still no vaccine against RSA.

"Thank you, Major," Jenner said. "Major Vargas?"

Juan Vargas, a brilliant but disorganized researcher perpetually in trouble for disregarding military protocol, headed the human immunity unit. His uniform, which he hardly ever wore, was missing a button. Toni, who respected both Vargas's ability and his laissez-faire attitude toward spit-and-polish, changed her expression from fake to genuine interest, even though both she and Zack knew that Vargas's unit had nothing real to report. They had made no progress toward tweaking the human immune system to cope with RSA. The variant of the protein that conferred natural immunity on a very few people was their hope; they had not been able to mimic it.

Marianne and Claire both asked a lot of questions. Zack watched Mott and Darnley. He became certain that they understood little of what they were hearing; Vargas was being too technical for laymen. Well, Zack could remedy that, maybe earning some brownie points for his team.

When Vargas wrapped up his presentation, Jenner said, "Dr. McKay?" And to the newcomers, "Dr. McKay heads the experimental unit. Please keep in mind that his research is the fallback position and may never be deployed, even if successful."

Zack got to his feet. Before he could begin, Jenner added, "Since your area is the least familiar to all of us, Doctor, I hope your materials will begin with basics."

"Yes," McKay said. Definitely brownie points. He picked up a marking pen and pressed the button that retracted the screen into the ceiling. Behind it was an old-fashioned whiteboard on which someone had written "I WANT FUCKING REAL COFFEE!" There was no eraser. Zack swiped his sleeve across the board, leaving a smear. The marking pen had gone dry. Toni looked like she was suppressing giggles.

Two pens later, when he got one that actually wrote, he drew a diagram, talking as he sketched.

"Sparrows inherit two copies of every gene in their bodies, one from each parent. We are trying to alter one or more of those genes in order to develop two separate and distinct gene drives. Let's call a sparrow carrying one copy of any altered gene 'capital G.' The other copy of the gene, plus both genes in unaltered wild sparrows, 'small g.' If the altered gene is dominant, then usually inheritance will go like this through successive generations:

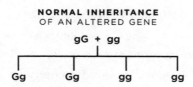

NORMAL INHERITANCE
OF AN ALTERED GENE

gG + gg

Gg   Gg   gg   gg

"As you can see, fifty percent of the offspring carry the altered gene. Now each of these birds mates with wild sparrows, who are all small g:

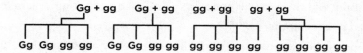

"Now only one-quarter of offspring carry the altered gene. In the next generation, it will be only one-eighth, until the genetically engineered change effectively dies out. But with a gene drive, the situation is different. A gene drive utilizes a so-called 'selfish gene,' which is a bit of parasitic DNA that circumvents the laws of normal inheritance. It gets itself propagated preferentially by pasting a copy of itself into the matching chromosome inherited from the other parent, so that *all* of the offspring carry two altered genes. By piggybacking on a selfish gene, a gene drive always gets inherited, like this."

He sketched another diagram, suppressing the insane idea to draw birds instead of letters. Too bad he hadn't had Caitlin "prepare his briefing materials."

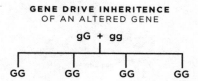

"Then those birds mate, and every one of their fledglings carries the alteration, on through the generations."

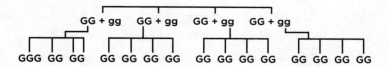

Zack turned back to the table. "A gene drive creates a 'selective sweep,' spreading like wildfire and so eventually wiping out all other versions of that gene. This is a known phenomenon, occurring both naturally and through lab creations pre-Collapse, although there it affected insects, not birds."

One of the new captains said, "But Dr. McKay, what are these two gene drives you're trying to create going to *do*?"

"I was coming to that. One of the gene drives we're working on would hinder birds' ability to carry RSA. The other—"

The captain interrupted him. "But you haven't achieved that gene drive, have you? In fact, Monterey Base research hasn't advanced on any of your three fronts."

"Well—we get closer every week."

Toni raised her eyebrow at this blatant exaggeration. The captain looked skeptical, or unimpressed, or something else that annoyed Zack. All at once a new thought hit him—was he in the middle of some sort of turf war between Jenner and HQ?

No way to know. He turned back to the board. "The other gene drive will render male sparrows sterile. The result will, eventually, be this."

There was silence. His attempt to lighten the atmosphere had fallen as flat as his dead bird.

The captain said, "And just why hasn't this gene drive succeeded so far?"

"The main difficulty of the complex gene drive is resistance to it that develops after a few generations of bird breeding. We're hoping to get around that by combining three different gene drives, so that resistance by mutation is minimized. But obviously that's a difficult task. Sometimes the alterations interfere with each other. The gene-editing tool doesn't cut or insert where it's supposed to. Or it cuts the target but doesn't complete the delivery."

Marianne Jenner said, "But . . . apart from the difficulties . . . May I ask questions, too?"

Zack braced himself. Marianne, undeterred by considerations of either rank or turf wars, was probably going to put her very capable finger on every reason that Zack's research shouldn't even exist.

She did. "I'm wondering how you can create a gene drive capable of being carried by more than one species of sparrow, since their genomes do differ."

Zack said, "We're piggybacking on RSA itself, which infects all species of sparrows, and only sparrows."

Her voice rose. "You're further altering the virus that killed so many people?"

"Yes."

"What if your alterations—"

"We're doing extensive testing." Both of them, and probably everyone else in the room, knew that "extensive testing" wasn't possible with their limitations of resources, personnel, time, birds. Zack was doing what he could with what he had.

Marianne said, "You mentioned pre-Collapse gene drives in insects. I'm sure you know that when the bacterium *Wolbachia* was used to create a gene drive to infect mosquitoes that carry malaria, the researchers also discovered that some strains of the bacteria were capable of transferring horizontally to other arthropods. What if your gene drive—either of your gene drives—jumps to other species and changes their reproductive biology?"

"I think," Zack said, "that you already know it can't jump to humans. And that the chances of it jumping to species more closely related to birds is small."

"But not zero. Altered genes have been transmitted through bacterial and parasitic plasmids."

"Yes. We are trying to build in safeguards."

"Doctor—you know that isn't possible."

Zack hadn't wanted to do this. But if he didn't, his entire team might be shut down by HQ. And nobody present except Toni would know he was about to utter a half-truth. "It wasn't possible in your time, Marianne. We know more now."

She was silenced.

The visiting captain was not. "But even if this gene drive can't jump species, wiping out all the birds on Earth will wreck the entire ecology, won't it?"

As if it weren't already wrecked. Zack put both palms flat on the table and leaned forward. "Look, I've tried to make clear that this is last-ditch, final-resort, hope-to-God-we-don't-need-it research in case the work by the other two scientific units fails. We cannot stay cooped up for generations in the few remaining domes. Ninety-six percent of children being born aren't immune to RSA, and we can't even discover which six percent *are* immune without exposing our children to overwhelming odds of a horrible death. If someday the choice comes down to the death of all birds or the death of humanity, which would you choose? I know my preference. And what I want is for us to have the means to *have* a choice, if it comes to that. That's what this research is about."

"Thank you, Doctor," Jenner said. "I think we're done here. Captains, this way, please."

The room emptied. Toni lingered, but Dr. Vargas called her aside to ask her something. When everyone had gone, Zack hunted for an eraser to wipe the board of his clumsy diagrams. There still wasn't one.

As he used his hand to erase, smearing his palm with black ink, he saw that in the second diagram, he had misspelled "inheritance."

The briefing left Marianne feeling shaky. Not that she hadn't known most of it before, since Zack's first explanations in the signal station, but somehow this meeting had made the full horror more real. At night she dreamed not of the Collapse she had never seen, but of the result that she also hadn't seen. Cities overgrown by wilderness, or else

H-bombed into rubble. Vast empty stretches of farmland reverting to prairie. Primitive settlements of survivors trying to hang on. And in Europe and Asia and Australia and Africa and South America, probably more of the same. A mixture of technology from Bronze Age to late twentieth century to alien artifacts like domes and esuits, used but not understood. The mind had trouble grasping it.

And yet people went on, replacing abysmal loss with everyday activities: prepare communal dinner, work in labs, educate children, prepare for dome defense. The new normal.

She made her way through the crowded, overpopulated Lab Dome to the infirmary. Children from the Settlement, who evidently had no trouble adapting to a change of "normal," pushed past her in some sort of excited game. Their parents looked bewildered and unhappy, although Marianne knew that the more enterprising of them had already begun to plant a vegetable garden right outside the dome walls, under the watchful eyes of Jason's guards, where they could be hustled back inside in case of attack.

Halfway to the infirmary, Kayla Rhinehart grabbed Marianne's arm. "Where are you going?"

"To see my son." Marianne peeled Kayla off her.

"I want you to get me in to see Colonel Jenner!"

"I can't do that, Kayla. I almost never see him myself and I have no authority."

"You're his grandmother!"

Marianne wanted to say *And this is not a matrilineal lahk*, but she didn't. Kayla looked dreadful. Claire must have adjusted her meds again, still without finding the optimum dose. Mania had been replaced not with depression but with desperate anxiety. Kayla had lost weight, and her thin face looked cadaverous. Marianne said, "Can I help?"

"No! Only Colonel Jenner! I want him to send us back to World on the *Return*!"

Marianne said as gently as she could, "That isn't going to happen, Kayla."

"It has to! I hate it here! And so does Glamet^vorɟ and La^vor and . . . and everybody!"

Marianne had not observed La^vor hating Earth. Jane's friend was mostly occupied with her younger, mentally challenged brother: playing with him, teaching him, looking after him. At fifteen Terran years, Belok^ had the lively curiosity of a three-year-old, although not as large a vocabulary. La^vor seemed the most loving of caretakers, the sort of woman born to be a wonderful mother.

Kayla said, "I want to go back to World! This isn't the Earth I came here for!"

As if it were for any of them. "Maybe someday we'll go back. But for right now—"

"You won't help me! You're no different from the rest of these fuckers, Marianne!"

"I—" But Kayla punched her on the shoulder, turned, and stalked away.

Marianne rubbed her shoulder. She would need to find Claire and tell her about this. But first she was going to see Colin, still in infirmary.

In the infirmary corridor, she met Lindy Ross. Lindy's face was creased with worry, and Marianne's heart clenched. "Colin? Is he—"

"No, no, he's fine. Healing well." Lindy hesitated. "Marianne, can I ask you something?"

"Sure. Go ahead."

"When Jason was a child, was he vindictive? No, that's the wrong word. I mean, did he feel that scores had to be settled even if there was no immediate threat?"

"No, never. He valued fairness and got indignant when people weren't fair, but he was never mean, if that's what you're asking."

Lindy nodded, her face still troubled. On impulse, Marianne said, "Forgive me if I'm overstepping boundaries here, but I think Jason still cares for you. I've seen the way he looks at you."

Immediately Lindy's face closed. "I've seen the way he looks at Jane."

Jane? Really? How had Marianne missed that? Or was Lindy mistaken? Marianne said, "Don't be too hard on Jason. He looks exhausted. He's holding this place together with spit and duct tape and sheer will."

"With all due respect, Marianne—do you think I don't know that? Plus a lot more that you don't know?"

"Yes, of course. I'm sorry."

"No, I'm sorry." Lindy's mouth twisted. "We're all just taut as catgut."

"I know. And you're all doing a wonderful job."

"Trying, anyway." Lindy forced a smile and walked away.

Marianne watched the back of Lindy's upright figure. Such a formidable young woman: intelligent, tireless, but unforgiving. Had Marianne herself ever been like that? She had. Maybe that was why she liked Lindy so much, despite Lindy's prickliness. Well, in this situation, prickliness was a reasonable response. Much better than hysteria or despair or fanaticism.

But . . . what did Lindy mean by *Plus a lot more that you don't know?*

CHAPTER 10

Jane sat alone with Colin Jenner when he woke from sedation.

His bed, her uncomfortable chair, and medical equipment crowded the tiny room in the infirmary, a place of hard edges and square angles and too bright lights. Each night Jane dreamed of the soaring curves of karthwood, of purplish orchards, of the broad soft sky of World. Each morning she had to find in herself the determination to face the next day without inflicting her fear and sadness on La^vor and Belok^. They did the same for her, of course, even Belok^. Bu^ka^tel.

But at least Lab Dome held Colin Jenner. He lay under an Army blanket drawn over most of his body, but she could see that one leg bulged with wrappings or machines of some kind. One hand lay under the blanket and one on top. If he had been a Worlder, she would have taken that free hand and held it in solidarity and comfort, even though he was a stranger. But Colin was not a Worlder, and Jane was bewildered by her attraction to this stocky, sun-burned Terran with the uncut hair and mud-colored eyes that no Worlder had ever had. She knew well what her feelings were; she was not a thirteen-year-old virgin. It was the strength of the attraction that surprised and upset her.

Sometimes, her lahk Mother had said back home, *delight comes unbidden and should be honored.* But this was not delight. It was all mixed up with her homesickness and Colin's beliefs and the maternal feelings that Jane had denied too long now—she was already twenty-seven, more in

Terran years, and had not provided her lahk with the first of the two children that were her duty to create for the good of all, while her eggs were still at their best.

Her lahk was 103 light-years away.

But—

Colin stirred and opened his eyes.

They focused slowly, and when they did, they gazed at Jane. A smile came and went on his lips. He tried to speak, croaked something unintelligible, tried again. "Settlement?"

Jane hadn't expected to be the one to tell him, but anything less than the truth was unthinkable. "Many of your people died, but the rest are here, in the domes. I am told that the inside of your dome is destroyed by . . . by a weapon. I don't know the word."

Colin squeezed closed his eyes, opened them again. Jane said, "I am sorry, Colin Jenner."

"We will start again. How . . ."

"Colonel Jenner destroyed the ones who attacked you and then bringed your people here in our spaceship."

"Is Jason hurt?"

"No."

"Mary?"

"I don't know who that is." A woman's name. His woman? Jane's throat tightened. "I will get Claire. She will want to examine you."

"In a minute. I'm fine."

His voice was stronger now, but he winced when he tried to turn his body. Jane said sharply, "Lie quiet!"

"Yes, ma'am." A tiny smile. "Jane, we'll build again. Will my brother let us return to the Settlement? The crops must still be in the fields, they couldn't have destroyed everything."

"I don't know."

"Will you find him and send him to me?"

As if Jane could send Colonel Jenner anywhere! How did it happen that she knew more about life with this Army than Colin did?

He said, "Okay, you can't do that. Sorry. But we need to leave here. Leave this sterile and ugly environment. Get the children out of here and living free on Terra again. Anyway, Jason will need the crops."

She said, before she knew she was going to say anything, "I wish I can come with you!"

His gaze sharpened, that upsetting gaze that seemed to see right into her brain. "You miss your planet."

"Yes."

His hand moved across the blanket and she took it, accepting the offered sympathy. Another electric jolt ran through her at the touch of his fingers. He said, "I understand about homesickness. You Worlders— you believe the same things we do. We Settlers, I mean."

"Some of the same things. Maybe not all."

"I want to know about World. I want to know about you. I wish you could come with us, too. But you're not immune to RSA, are you?"

"No."

Alarm crossed his face. Jane said, "You were decontaminated. All your people, when you were brought inside Lab Dome. Colonel Jenner was careful."

"He always is. Jason is a good man, just badly misguided."

"Yes." And then, "Colin, do you have a mate?"

He seemed startled; maybe that wasn't a proper thing to ask on Terra. He said, "No." And then, "Do you?"

"No, I was meant to sign a mating contract, but I didn't."

"A contract? Is that what you call it? Tell me about World. How do you keep an entire planetful of people from ruining the environment? I—"

"Colin!" Claire Patel pushed into the tiny space, her little medical box already in her hand. Jane turned to ease out and give Claire room to approach Colin's bed. Glamet^vorį stood in the doorway.

How long had he been there? What had he heard, and did he have enough English to understand any of it? Had he seen her holding Colin's hand?

Claire said, "Okay, everybody out, I need to examine my patient."

Jane and Glamet^vor¡ faced each other in the corridor. At the other end, a group of Settler children hunched over some game involving colored stones.

"I greet you, Jeg^faan." His voice was tight, his face stony. It occurred to Jane that in this mood, he looked more Terran than World. She must not say that.

"I greet you, Glamet^vor¡."

"Will Colin-mak recover from his injuries?"

"The doctors say yes."

"And will you copulate with him when he does?"

Definitely Terran. The demands, the anger, the lack of bu^ka^tel. Mating contracts were public, but copulations were private matters. Maybe people had to come to a new environment to reveal their true natures.

"I'm sorry, Glamet^vor¡, but that is not your concern."

"You have no lahk Mother here to approve a mating contract."

"There is no contract. Please let me pass."

He didn't move, blocking the corridor. Beyond, the children shrieked in delight over their game. "These Terrans are rotten." He used the word for decaying unburned flesh, a word that not only conveyed putrid odor and texture but was also a filthy oath.

"They are not."

"Why can't you see? You won't see! Terrans nearly destroyed their planet, the planet that was our original home as well, and were stopped from doing so only because instead they destroyed each other. They continue to fight. The Gaiists were right—Terra should be cleansed of the disease that is Terrans! Then she can recover, and someday World can come back to colonize her as it should be done, with respect and care for Mother Earth. You believe that, too, Jeg^faan. You must believe it!"

"I do not. Not all Terrans are a disease on the planet. The Settlers—"

"Cannot survive. New America is wiping them out. You saw that.

And then, if right prevails, New America and the United States Army"—
he all but spat the words—"will destroy each other."

Jane stared at him, appalled at his anger, his contempt, his lack of
manners toward their hosts. She said, "You are wrong. Even if New
America and the Army did destroy each other, four percent of Terrans
survived RSA. Do you think this little corner of the United States is all
that exists? I thought better of your mind, Glamet^vorɉ. There are almost three hundred million people left on Earth and—"

"There are not. Many of those will have died of war or hunger or
disease."

"—and they will start over—*are* starting over. This time, they will
do better."

"No. They will not. Do the math, Jeg^faan. If only four percent of
each new generation survives, how long will it take for Terrans to become powerless? They have already lost their industries, their planet-
wide communications, their technology. Probably all over Terra they
are merely surviving. They were ahead of us, once, in science and technology, but they abused both. Terrans are finished. And yet they treat
us with contempt!"

"They are not, and they do not."

"Yes? I was attacked yesterday by two soldiers." He pulled up his
sleeve—Jane had wondered why he wore a Terran shirt over his wrap—
and she saw ugly bruises and cuts on his arm. "They said that we are
taking their food, bringing to them our diseases, polluting their blood-
lines. They said we should go back where we came from. And they were
right."

Jane was shaken. "Did you . . . did you report this to Colonel Jenner?"

Glamet^vorɉ laughed. "Do you think he has control of his people?
Like a lahk Mother would? There is no bu^ka^tel here, no respect, no
solidarity. They are rotten animals."

Claire emerged from Colin's room. "He has remarkable recuperative
powers, I'll say that for him. You can go back in, Jane, if you like, but
don't stay too long. He needs to sleep."

Jane turned her back on Glamet^vorⱼ and squeezed herself into Colin's room. She didn't look back as she firmly closed the door behind her.

A half-moon shone as Jason climbed from a quadcopter in front of the signal station. Flying the copter at night was risky, but if Jason wanted to talk directly to HQ, it had to be from here. Specialist Kowalski was a good pilot even on visual only and by moonlight, and two heavily armed J Squad soldiers rode with them. Any snipers that New America had in the woods had either been asleep or inept. They'd flown under ground radar. Jason was here.

He glanced at the sky. Vega, Deneb, Altair: the Summer Triangle. He'd spent his thirteenth summer stargazing, making star charts, researching arcane celestial data on the Internet. He had hoped to be an astronomer, before he decided on West Point instead. Another, unlived life that probably would have ended abruptly at the Collapse.

The hillside tunnel opened and they entered the airlock. On the other side of decon, Jason shed his esuit. Neither Li nor DeFord saluted; things tended to be less formal at the station. Elizabeth Duncan would not have approved.

"Nothing to report, sir," Li said. "No new intel to us, and New America's comsat still offline."

"Good. Get me HQ. And a cup of coffee, please." The station had the last real coffee from base stores. They deserved it. "Do we have visual with HQ?" This report should already have been made, but before Jason had been able to get to the signal station, the visiting brass from HQ had shown up. Darnley and Mott had made the long, dangerous journey by quadcopter, and Jason still didn't know why. That disturbed him. It didn't seem like Colleen Hahn to not brief him that her representatives were in the Pacific Northwest.

Then something had gone wrong with the satellite software.

Li said, "No, sir, Fort Hood says that they've only been able to re-store audio."

"Good enough."

IT Specialist DeFord said, "Sir, I tried to repair the visual component from this end, but there's something wonky about the program . . . it's like the code has been altered to block visual."

Jason frowned and accepted a cup of coffee. "Altered? By the enemy?"

"No, sir, not hacked. Just rewritten at HQ, and in a way that won't let me override it."

That didn't make sense, but Jason was no computer expert. "Audio will do."

Li made the contact, requesting General Hahn. "One moment, Mon-terey Base," said a disembodied voice. Jason had finished his coffee be-fore another voice sounded. "Monterey Base, this is General William Strople, acting CO at Fort Hood and martial law commander in chief. Go ahead, Colonel Jenner."

Startled, Jason said, "Sir? I was reporting to General Hahn."

"General Hahn is gravely ill. Proceed, Colonel."

Was this a New America hack of the satellite? Catastrophic, if so. Jason had never heard of a General Strople, although that proved nothing. He glanced at DeFord, who mouthed *I don't know*. Jason said, "Request security protocol, sir."

"Certainly. You are commended for your caution."

They went through the classified oral exchanges until Jason was sat-isfied. He said, "Thank you, sir."

"Begin your report."

Colleen Hahn had had a definite format for briefings: one-sentence summaries followed by narration and Q&A. Jason stuck to it. "Three items to report. First, the Settlement of farmers on the Monterey coast was attacked by New America and survivors are now housed at Mon-terey Base. Second, one prisoner was captured and interrogated. Third, the spaceship *Return* remains safely in orbit."

"What was learned from prisoner interrogation?"

"New America has captured Dr. Frank Philip Sugiyama and is holding him at Sierra Depot. They also have Sugiyama's three children. One child has already been killed in an effort to force Sugiyama's cooperation with retrieving the Q14 launch codes from the quantum computer. Unknown whether Sugiyama is now cooperating, or whether he is even able to retrieve the codes. Access protocol says no, and the computer will self-destruct if tampered with. But—well, this is a physicist with a mind equal to Albert Einstein's."

Silence. The dilemma was clear: Take out Sierra Depot with one of their three active Q14s, and you removed the possibility of New America's gaining access to the codes for the other two. However, you also gave away the secret location of the Q14s, which would be clearly visible to New America's ground radar. The nukes could be destroyed in their silos. If you did not take out Sierra Depot, and Sugiyama was able to get into the quantum computer and willing to cooperate with the enemy in order to save his children from torture, then New America had all three codes. It came down to trust in the quantum computer and lack of trust in Sugiyama. An impossible choice, given the lack of hard intel.

"Colonel Jenner, you are closer to the situation. What is your advice?"

Jason's right hand, hidden on his lap, curled into a fist. Li shifted on his chair. Strople's tone did not sound like a genuine request for additional information. Strople was covering his ass in case the situation went wrong. *On the advice of Colonel Jenner, who had close knowledge of the factors involved* . . . Generals Lassiter and Hahn would never have done this. Jason's respect for Strople dropped a notch.

"Sir, it's a difficult decision. But pre-Collapse classified materials are insistent on the integrity of the quantum computer's protocols. The most likely scenario—not definite but most likely in my opinion—is that Sugiyama will be unable to crack the computer. He will try, from desperation, and it will self-destruct."

And hopefully take out not only the physicist but also both his kids before they could be tortured. And destroy a bunch of New America fuckers as well.

Strople said, "So you suggest waiting to see how the situation develops."

"Yes, sir. Maintaining both vigilance and readiness to shift strategy."

"So ordered. What have you done with the prisoner?"

"Put him to hard labor."

"At your discretion, Colonel."

The disapproving tone meant *Shoot the prisoner.* Jason was not going to do that. He said only, "Yes, sir."

The briefing continued. Jason explained that the *Return* was contaminated with RSA. He did his best to push from his mind the images of the two Sugiyama children still alive, a three-year-old boy and a four-year-old girl, Louis and Amanda. *Frankie was all chopped up . . .*

When Jason finished talking, Strople said, "Thank you, Colonel. Anything more?"

"No, sir. Sir, is General Hahn expected to recover? May I ask the nature of her illness?"

"The prognosis is uncertain. She contracted RSA."

Stunned, Jason said, "How—"

"That is all, Colonel."

"Yes, sir."

RSA victims, as Jason well knew, died within a few days. Colleen Hahn's infection must be recent, and inexplicable. In order to contract RSA, she would have had to leave the HQ dome without an esuit, or been in a firefight or accident that tore her suit, or come in contact with someone already infected inside the dome—but then all of HQ would be contaminated. Surely Strople would have briefed Jason on any of those events? And DeFord had said that visual communication with HQ had been deliberately blocked. Jason met Li's eyes and saw his own doubts mirrored.

On his wrister, he called up the file on General William Strople.

There wasn't one, but ten years ago there had been a Major William Strople on active duty. No other Stroples among the officer corps.

No one in the United States Army had been promoted since the Collapse.

What had gone on at Fort Hood during the three days of the "software glitch"?

Two days later, Zack watched a hunting party leave through Lab Dome's tunnel airlock. He only saw them go because he happened to be coming out of the bird lab, headed to Enclave Dome to see if Caitlin felt any better. The child was sleeping more and more. Claire Patel still could find nothing wrong. She told Zack and Susan that sleeping a lot was good for recovery from any illness, something that Zack already knew. "You might as well take the day off," Toni said to Zack. "It's not like we're making any progress here, and didn't you say Susan had to be somewhere for some meeting?"

"Yes," Zack said, wound down his work, and took the rare chance for a whole day away from the bird lab, where sparrows cheeped and shat and bred and were sacrificed to, so far, no avail whatsoever.

The soldiers of the hunting party carried rifles with scopes, belts of ammunition, larger weapons intended not for game but for encounters with the enemy. That was also why there were so many hunters: once, a lone man had been picked off by a New America sniper and his body not discovered for days, by which time there had been little left of him. As the wilderness had returned to California, so had its big predators. On the other hand, it was no longer difficult to find deer, rabbits, even bear. Zack loved venison stew, and so wasn't it hypocritical of him to shudder inwardly at the young men and women laughing and joking as they prepared for bloody killing? It was hypocritical, yes, as well as specieist, or whatever the word had been when Zack had been young. *Let me eat meat and wear leather but don't let me see how it's procured.* The eternal dilemma of the nonvegetarian liberal.

Leather—yesterday Zack had seen a civilian wearing a crude-but-new leather vest. Did the base now possess tanning facilities? Or did a tannery exist outside in the woods someplace, part of some Army-civilian black market? Zack worked so much that he didn't keep up with what passed here for trendiness. He'd heard a rumor that two soldiers had shot a mountain lion and kept the head mounted on a wall somewhere, but this seemed doubtful to him. Surely taxidermy was now a dead art?

The chief importance of the rumor was its widespread belief. It showed that Jenner, who surely would have forbidden a mounted and decaying wildcat head, didn't have complete control of the base he commanded, despite what Toni still called the "Praetorian Guard." She had a name for Master Sergeant Hillson, too—"Varys," who was apparently some sort of spymaster in an old epic.

The last of the hunting party entered the airlock. When it was empty again, Zack made his way through the tunnels to Enclave. Susan sat beside Caitlin, who clutched the tattered Bollers even while she slept.

"No change?"

"No. I think I'm worried."

"Claire says it's normal. So does Lindy." Neither had been pleased to discover that Zack had used up their precious time by having both of them examine Caitlin at different times on the same day. Sometimes the lack of central scheduling was a good thing.

Zack put his arms around Susan and kissed her hair. "I miss you."

"I'm right here."

"You know what I mean."

"I do. But I'm already late." She gave his cock a friendly little squeeze, at once too much and far too little, smiled wickedly, and left.

Zack settled onto the bed beside Caitlin's trundle, legs stretched out straight in front of him, and read an old scientific journal on his e-reader. There were no new scientific journals, and soon there might be no e-readers left. But while his existed, Zack tried to learn as much as he could of what had been cutting-edge science when the world Collapsed ten years ago.

The new normal, Marianne had said, with wonder and pain.

Hours later he was deep into an article on epistasis through epigenetic methylation, when someone pounded on the door. Zack leaped off the bed, tripped on Caity's trailing blankets, and grabbed the doorknob to pull himself upright. It came off in his hand. He flung the door open by the hole and said in a fierce whisper, "Shhhh! My daughter's sleeping!"

"Dr. McKay," a soldier said, her eyes wide in a very young face, "Colonel Jenner says to report to Lab Dome. Right away, sir."

"I can't leave my daughter. She's ill."

"The colonel said immediately, sir."

"Why? What's happened?"

"Some people were killed."

"An attack?" He hadn't heard drones.

"No, sir. A bear."

It didn't make sense. If anyone outside—the hunting party or the Settlement garden diggers or the patrol—had been attacked by a bear, Zack wasn't needed. He wasn't a physician. And both perimeter patrol and the hunting party were heavily enough armed to take out a rhinoceros.

The soldier—and now Zack recognized her, a kid who'd grown up inside the base and now apparently joined the Army or been conscripted into it—said, "The colonel said Dr. Jenner wants you, ASAP. I don't know why. I'm to escort you to Lab Dome."

"But I . . . all right."

He wrapped Caitlin in her blanket; she didn't stir. He carried her into the corridor and to the "school," a ramshackle area where two young women taught children of different ages whatever they could from tablets, a few handmade children's books, and chalk on rock slates in lieu of paper. Before the Settlers arrived, the school had six pupils. Now there were an indeterminate and shifting number, depending on the day. Or sometimes the hour; Settler parents didn't seem big on formal education. The cramped space looked like a mad version of America's little red one-room schoolhouse.

"Karen, can I leave Caitlin with you? I'm sorry but there's some sort of emergency at Lab Dome—no, not anything dangerous but Colonel Jenner has issued orders."

"Well . . . I guess so. Is she contagious?"

"No, not at all," Zack said, hoping this was true. But in such close quarters, whatever one child caught, they all got eventually, anyway. He laid Caitlin in a corner and arranged the blanket to partially hump up as a pillow for her head. "I'll be back as soon as I can."

"Okay. Devon, did you finish that math problem yet? No? Why not?"

Outside, escorted by the young soldier, Zack was startled to see an evening sky. He had been reading, and Caitlin sleeping, longer than he'd thought. Cool breezes ruffled dark trees beyond the perimeter, bringing the odors of mint and loam. One bright star shone directly overhead. He breathed deep, enjoying this too-brief taste of autumn twilight.

It was his last enjoyment for sixteen hours.

The corpses lay on open body bags on top of rough wooden tables. Zack recoiled; they were horribly maimed. His first thought was *Torture. . . . sadistic fuckers!* But then he saw that the young soldier had been correct. Even a layman could recognize the long claw marks of animal mauling. Kayla Rhinehart and Glamet^vorj had died horribly.

But why had they been outside? And why were the bodies here, in the virology lab?

Marianne Jenner, looking every year of her age, was at the one electron microscope. Lab assistants seemed to be preparing slides. Toni spotted Zack and walked over, the usual sardonic lip curl gone from her face.

"Toni, what the hell happened?"

"Those two idiots went outside. Rhinehart left a note—they planned to steal the spaceship and go back to World. Apparently neither of them realized that of course Emperor Jason First of His Name had already moved the ship to safety in orbit. Anyway, they didn't get very far. Wildlife got them first. Esuits might protect against microbes but not against a mother bear with cubs. A hunting party found them."

"But—"

"They were both crazy, Zack, in different ways. And that's not just a metaphor. Marianne suspected something about their brains. She says that everyone who came from World has been having headaches and, just lately, sleeping too much. She and Claire Patel convinced Lindy Ross that there was something weird going on. They did autopsies and prepared slides of brain tissue."

Sleeping too much? It must be just a coincidence; Caitlin had not come from World.

Toni continued, "You're going to ask how they got permission to autopsy. They didn't. Lindy says she'll take responsibility with His Majesty. Zack, you need to see these slides."

She led him to the electron microscope. Marianne, so deep in her work that she didn't hear them approach, jerked in surprise. Then she wordlessly rose and let Zack at the eyepiece.

Toni said, "Remember, everyone on that spaceship was infected with the virophage that destroyed the original *R. sporii* on World."

Zack peered into the eyepiece, adjusted it for better focus, looked again.

"Oh my God!"

"And that's not all," Toni said. "There's more."

CHAPTER 11

Jason said, "How did this happen? How did those two get out of the dome?"

In the command post, the entire outside patrol stood at rigid attention, six soldiers whose blank faces didn't quite hide their fear. Elizabeth Duncan stood beside Jason, hands clasped behind her back. Jason said, "Corporal Michaelson?"

Michaelson said, "Sir, I was on duty at Lab Dome vehicle bay airlock. Ms. Rhinehart and Dr. Glamever didn't leave that way."

Major Duncan said, "Sergeant Hillson led the hunting party, sir. He says that tracks indicate Rhinehart and Glamet^vor¡ left through the Enclave Dome southwest airlock."

Out of sight of the main route between the domes and the Settler gardens. Jason said, "Who was patrolling the Enclave southwest airlock?"

A soldier spoke. "I was, sir."

Private Perry. He'd screwed up before. Jason said, "Do the other three of you have any information to add about this?"

A chorus of "No, sirs."

"Dismissed."

They left. Jason said to Perry, "Well?"

"I'm sorry, sir, I don't know how it happened but it won't—"

"You don't know how it happened? Where were you that you didn't see them leave?"

"I . . . I did see them leave, sir. They said they were going to help the Settlers digging the vegetable garden around the other side of the dome and—"

"The vegetable garden? Was the prisoner-at-large there, as well?" Jason, who'd had to do something with the captured New America kid, Tommy Mills, had finally decided to label him a prisoner-at-large and set him to work with shovel and hoe under the watchful eyes of the perimeter patrol. But if Mills had somehow escaped and waited in ambush in the woods . . .

Perry said, "Yeah, Mills was there. Anyways, when those two said they were exiting the dome to go help dig some damn garden, I believed them. I mean, they believe in all that stuff, right? The Reddie's a fucking Worlder!"

Jason stared at Perry, whose brief puff of self-justifying and racist bombast dissipated like dandelion fluff in a gale. Jason said, "Private, you are confined to quarters until further notice. Dismissed."

"Yes, sir." Perry slunk out.

Duncan said, "Sir, if you'll permit me, they were only able to exit the airlock because Dr. Glamet^vorį was digitally and retinally approved for the bird lab, which shares the same security program. I have said before that we need tighter security."

"Security is arranged to keep the enemy out, not our scientists in." And doing anything else would be incredibly cumbersome. Some scientists and soldiers went between the domes half a dozen times each day. Half of Monterey Base's inhabitants weren't military, and that was before counting Colin's Settlers. In such close quarters, it was impossible to physically separate facilities for Army and civilians, as would have been done on a pre-Collapse post, and how much martial law would the civilians tolerate before they rebelled? Especially since the arrival of Settlers who recognized no military necessities?

Jason hadn't even been able to convince his own wife of military necessities.

He said to Duncan, "I'll take it under advisement."

"Yes, sir."

Hillson's voice sounded in his earplant. "Sir, permission to come up. I talked to more of the hunting party, and I think there's something else you should hear."

"Proceed to command post, Sergeant."

Now what?

The lab tech had done a good job of staining the brain-tissue slides. The microglials were tiny round purple-and-pink balls packed between neurons. Astrocytes shaped like stars, oligodendrocytes with their spidery, irregular tendrils. All were glia cells, which played important roles in brain development, functioning, and recovery from injury.

There were too many of them. Way, way too many.

Toni said, "No signs of previous injury to either of their brains, before the bear."

Brain injury caused a proliferation of some glials, which then carted away dead or injured neurons. Other types of glials released chemicals that "pruned" excess synapses to create more efficient communication among neurons. That happened primarily during embryonic development and again during adolescence, when the frontal cortex was rewiring itself for adult functioning. Too much pruning of synapses could lead to such brain diseases as Alzheimer's and Parkinson's.

But neither Glamet^vor¡ nor Kayla Rhinehart were embryos, adolescents, or victims of neurological disorders. Although—

Toni said, "Kayla's bipolar disorder may have been worsened by whatever is going on with all these glials, but Marianne said she was probably bipolar all along, even before the spore cloud hit World. And nobody ever said there was any anomaly in Glamet^vor¡'s thinking."

"But we've had *R. sporii* here for over thirty years and nobody ever reported anything like this!"

"No. But World wasn't exposed to only *R. sporii.*"

Then Zack saw it.

The virophage. Everyone on World had been exposed to the virophage, which killed *R. sporii.* But what else did it do in the bodies of its new hosts? Microbes that modified brain structure and functioning filled a long list: rabies, tertiary syphilis, toxoplasmosis, even Lyme disease. *R. sporii* itself had modified fetuses to produce enhanced auditory abilities in infants like Colin Jenner. But no one had ever seen a microbe that caused such unrestrained multiplication of glial cells, which could be as destructive to brain tissue as it could be useful.

He said, "Has anyone detected C1q or C4 or—"

"That's the next step," Marianne said. Her face looked gray. The lab techs stood awkwardly by their benches, listening but not saying anything.

Glial cells released complex cascades of a variety of proteins. Some signaled synapse pruning to begin; other molecules caused synapses to form. Zack wanted to know—and it seemed to him that he'd never wanted to know anything more in his life—what this promiscuous proliferation of glials was doing to brain neurons. Kayla and Glamet^vor¡ could not tell him. He would have to depend on the presence, absence, and amounts of the molecules that glials produced.

Then, all at once, he wanted to know something else even more.

"Marianne—was the virophage on World transmitted only by breathing it in? Is person-to-person transmission possible?" *Are we all going to get it?*

Marianne said, "I don't know. We left World soon after the virophage was released. And for all these weeks, I didn't know we . . . but everyone from the ship has been having headaches. I still do, but much fainter than before."

"Any other symptoms?" Zack could barely get the words out.

"Well, I seem to sleep longer."

Headaches.

Sleep.

The plasticity of developing brains, due in part to the presence of glial-produced molecules almost never found in healthy adult brains. But not just in fetuses, either.

Zack said slowly, "I think person-to-person transmission of the virophage may be possible. We need . . . we need to check out all the children in both domes. Ask their parents about headaches and over-sleeping and any changes in behavior.

"Now. Right away. Now."

Hoofbeats drummed across his brain. *Zebra.*

Hillson appeared in the command post with Private William Landry. A troublemaker, Landry was one of those who'd never gotten over the loss of what he referred to as "the real army," in which he'd been a lifer. In his forties, he'd seen action in Brazil; he acquitted himself well in ground war but chafed under the off-again, on-again, mostly remote war with New America. Jason had inherited him along with the base, and neither liked nor trusted him. But Landry was the best shot on base and always included in the hunting parties.

Hillson said, "Sir, Private Landry was the first one to spot the bodies of Kayla Rhinehart and the Worlder scientist. He reports something strange."

"I shot the bear," Landry said. Pause. "Sir."

Hillson said, in the tone that had wrangled out-of-line soldiers into line for thirty years, "Report, Private."

"I seen the bear charge and a second later I seen her cubs. She barreled on over to them two aliens and laid into 'em. But they didn't fight or nothing. In fact, they didn't even react. I couldn't see real clear, but it looked like they was both asleep. Maybe they was.

"But the funny thing was, I don't think they woke up when the bear started clawing away. Neither of 'em woke up. They just lied there. I fired, but the bear'd already slashed open the woman's throat. Bear turned to me and I fired again, and still the alien didn't move. That bear was hit, all right, but she was tough and mad. She bellowed and made one last slash at the Reddie before she come for me and I dropped her with a hit to the head."

Reddie. The same word Perry had used. What other slurs did his men call Worlders? Jason said, "So the victims didn't react to the bear because they were already dead?"

"Didn't look dead to me. Corpses got a whole different look to 'em."

"Perhaps they were freshly dead?"

"From what?" Landry said contemptuously. Hillson said sharply, "Private," and Landry added, "Sir."

"Dismissed," Jason said, and Landry sauntered out. But his question had been a good one. Jason said to Hillson, "Drugs?"

"Could be. Or could be Landry's lying. Although I don't see any reason why he would."

"Nobody else saw the bear mauling?"

"No, sir. Landry was point. Also, sir, outside patrol received a message from the signal station, a general bulletin to all bases. Colonel Hahn has died and General Strople is now commander in chief."

"Okay." Jason paused a moment. He hadn't known Colleen Hahn well, but he'd respected her. An able soldier and fair officer. Jason still wondered how she could have contracted RSA, but it was not his place to question that. He said, "Tell Dr. Holbrook I want an autopsy on the two bear victims."

"I think that one is already in progress, sir."

"Oh?" Holbrook had the authority to make that decision. Although . . . did World culture permit autopsies? The *Return* was a Worlder ship and, technically, Ka^graa led a diplomatic mission, even though there had been very little diplomacy going on so far.

"Hillson, have Jane sent to me."

"Yes, sir. Is she in Lab Dome?"

"Probably. Send her here."

Despite everything, his heart lifted at the thought of seeing Jane again.

Jane had spent another hour with Colin in the infirmary. She wanted to know about life in the Settlement, but he was curious about World. Jane insisted, and he had become both enthusiastic and theoretical, while she concentrated to keep up with his English.

He said, "Before the Collapse, in developed countries the total energy to produce food was more than the caloric value of the food produced, if you count in all the energy used in everything from tractors to fertilizer to plants. Agriculture was the most energy-intensive segment of the economy. But in preindustrial societies, energy produced as food was typically *ten times* larger than the input in terms of the labor of people and animals. It was a much better relationship with nature."

This wasn't what Jane wanted to know. "But how did you live, each day, to produce the food?"

He told her. As he spoke, she could feel the air between them shifting, tightening, becoming something more than air. When he said, "Now you tell me about World," she struggled to explain her former life to him; so much that seemed obvious to her, beyond needing explanation, was strange to a Terran. Finally, she said, "I don't know how to say . . . what simply . . . simply *is* . . ."

"Like a fish not noticing water," Colin said, and grinned, and just like that she tumbled all the way into love with him. And even that—"falling in love"—was a Terran expression that had taken her a while to fit to feelings and actions that certainly existed on both planets, but not in exactly the same way. At home, mating choice was a complex alloy of individual preference, the needs of the lahk, and bu^ka^tel. But simple desire, and the copulation it often led to, was a personal and unquestioned right.

Jane desired Colin Jenner.

She blurted out, "Who is Mary?"

"Mary who?"

"When you became injured, you asked if Mary was all right."

He smiled. "Did you think it was a woman?"

"Is it not a female name?"

"Yes. Mary is a beautiful and very bright child I have been teaching to raise kelp."

"Okay." She felt herself blush, and blushed more when he laughed at her, his eyes warm.

When Colin tired, she left his room and went to La^vor's. Had Jane been neglecting her friend? Yes, she had, but her translation duties kept her so occupied. And Glamet^vor¡'s tiny cubicle was jammed next to La^vor's. Since his tirade against Terrans, Jane had felt even more un-comfortable around him. How strange it was that two people should have such different reactions to Earth!

"I greet you, La^vor. I greet you, Belok^."

La^vor broke into a huge smile. "I greet you, Jeng. . . . Jane! Belok^?"

"I . . . greet you," Belok^ said.

He squatted beside his sister, twelve small circles of karthwood stained in various colors on the floor in front of him. Standard toys on World and nearly indestructible, they served babies to chew, toddlers to pile and knock down, older children to be taught their first math. Every small Worlder had a set. Virtually indestructible, kiki were often passed down through generations of a lahk. Belok^ looked huge beside the blocks intended for little children.

La^vor said, "We work on totals and reductions. See, Belok^, here are two kiki and there is one kiki. How many kiki have we here?"

"I tired," Belok^ said.

"You just woke!"

"I tired." He stretched out on the floor, jostling La^vor, and closed his eyes.

"Wake up, Belok^!"

He started to snore.

"I do not know what to do with him. He sleeps too much. But Claire-mak says he is not ill."

"Let him sleep," Jane said. "I want to talk to you."

La^vor smiled. "You glow, Jane. Has something good happened?"

"Yes. No. I don't know."

"Tell me! Come, sit on the bed!"

The two women stepped carefully over Belok^ and climbed onto La^vor's narrow bed, each sitting cross-legged with her back against the wall. The Army blanket, an unattractive bilious color, scratched rough against Jane's legs, bare in her brief wrap. La^vor wriggled to get comfortable. She was unusually short for a Worlder, her body stocky, her skin too pale and eyes too small to be pretty. She was the kindest person Jane knew, with the gift of being happy whatever her circumstances.

Too bad her older brother was not more like her.

"I think," Jane said, turning to look at her friend and choosing her words carefully, "that I would like to copulate with someone, and maybe even sign a mating contract, if he is willing."

La^vor smiled. "With Glamet^vor¡?"

"No. I told you that is finished."

"With who?"

"With Colin Jenner."

La^vor's lips parted in surprise—and then the top lip lifted more. "With a Terran?"

A small shock ran through Jane. So it was not only Terrans who could be disgusted with humans who were different. Her face must have shown . . . something, because La^vor said, "I regret that unkindness. Please forgive me."

Formal words. La^vor meant them . . . and yet she *was* being formal, and her gaze didn't meet Jane's. Jane took her hand. "Please, La^vor . . . this is my choice. You are my friend."

"Yes, until the end of time. If he is your choice, then I am . . . I am hopeful that the Mother approves. Jane, you must give to me some time to fit myself to something so unseen!"

"Of course. We are friends until the end of time. I don't even know if Colin will wish this."

"He is gravely injured?"

"He will recover. And he was not injured in his mating parts," Jane said, poking her friend. She suddenly felt full of lightness, mischievous as a child.

La^vor laughed. "You already know this?"

"No!"

"But you want to discover it?"

"Yes!"

"Will his lahk mother consent? Marianne-mak?"

"Terra does not . . . yes, I hope Marianne will consent." Jane had learned long ago that although La^vor's heart was loyal and generous, her mind was not elastic.

"When will you ask Colin-mak?"

"I don't know."

"How often do you think he will visit you?"

La^vor assumed that matings here would be like matings on World: each partner would stay with his or her lahk, and the children would be raised by the mother's lahk. Jane had observed that it was different on Terra. Zack and Susan lived together; Toni and her wife lived together; the parents of the six children in Enclave Dome all seemed to be caring together for their offspring. Jane had doubts about how well that could work—coming from different lahks, wouldn't the parents sometimes have different ideas about their children, with no lahk privileged over the other to make decisions? Marriage rooted only on the partners, not in their society—how could that endure? No plant, even the most brief-lived, could flower without roots.

But La^vor was right, too. Jane could not go with Colin to a new Settlement; she was not immune to RSA. She doubted that Colin would stay longer at the base than he had to. If they moved beyond just copulating and signed a contract for two years, it would be more like a World mating than a Terran marriage.

"I hope he would choose to visit often. But, beloved heart, he has not yet even agreed to simple copulation!"

"He will. Men always love you!" La^vor said, without the least tinge of jealousy.

Jane hugged her. "But if the—" Someone knocked hard on the door. La^vor said, "Enter, please!" And then, "I greet you, Ka^graa."

Jane, quicker, said, "What is it, Father? What has happened?"

Ka^graa, his face creased with grief, said, "I greet you, La^vor. Come from the room, Jeg^faan."

Jane scrambled off the bed. Her heart thudded against her chest. In the corridor, Ka^graa gently closed the door behind them, took his daughter's hand, and led her to her own cubicle.

Inside, he said, "Glamet^vorɪ is dead. Also Kayla Rhinehart. They left the dome and were killed by a wild animal."

Jane cried out. Unreality took her; for a moment the room spun wildly and nothing was itself. Then the universe righted itself. "Outside the dome? Why did they go outside the dome? Are you sure?"

"Yes. They both left notes. I saw his. They planned to steal the spaceship and return home."

It made no sense. They didn't know where the spaceship was, Glamet^vorɪ couldn't pilot it—or could he? He had watched Branch Carter, who hadn't known much about the ship, either. But Glamet^vorɪ was desperate and Kayla was unbalanced in her mind. Or maybe they'd both been unbalanced.

Ka^graa said, "Claire-mak performed autopsies without permission. I was only informed afterward. All this time, and not even Marianne-mak understood that you are the temporary lahk Mother while we are on Terra and they should have asked you. Or maybe she did know and thought that you would deny permission due to some primitive custom. We are not primitives. I am a scientist, Jeg^faan."

Jane saw how angry her father was; otherwise, he would not have spoken so. All the Worlders—except Glamet^vor¡—were so aware that they stood now on Terran soil, not their own. They had tried to adapt themselves to Terran custom. But it was hard to be so disrespected. Her father was among the most eminent scientists on World.

It was disturbing, too, that he had stopped calling her "Jane."

She said, "They don't know better. I will speak to Colonel Jenner."

"That will not help."

"It may."

"I think not. Tell him that we must have a farewell burning, outside, and the ashes of Glamet^vor¡ must go back with us to World."

"I will tell him. But, my father—if they know that Glamet^vor¡ and Kayla died from a wild animal, why did they do an autopsy?"

"I don't know. Maybe it is their custom to always do so when someone dies."

There had been no autopsies on the people killed at Colin's Settlement. She did not say this. Her father looked, for the first time that Jane could remember, very old.

CHAPTER 12

Jason waited in the command post for Hillson to send Jane to him. She didn't come. Instead, two of the scientists arrived with Elizabeth Duncan.

"Sir," she said, "Doctors McKay and Steffens request to speak with you. They say it's urgent."

Why were the virologists being escorted by Jason's second in command instead of a soldier on guard duty? Duncan's face was as impassive as ever, but McKay's twisted with emotion and Steffens's had been wiped of her usual sneer.

"Permission granted. Major, remain here, please. Dr. McKay, what is it?"

"Autopsies were performed on both victims of the bear attack," McKay began.

"Already? With or without permission from Dr. Ka^graa?"

"Without. The medical research team suspected an anomaly that it seemed vital to examine without delay."

The words had a stilted, rehearsed feel, as well as vagueness: "the medical research team." It wasn't like either McKay or the brash Steffens to evade responsibility. So it had been Jason's grandmother who had made the decision to autopsy, and McKay was trying—ineptly—to shield her. Jason let that go, for now.

McKay said, "Brain tissue from both people showed anomalies. Excess gliosis—that means too many glial cells of different kinds. This kind of gliosis in healthy adults usually means an injury to the brain: an infection or other neural distress."

"They *were* attacked by a bear."

"No, the gliosis was well advanced. *Really* well advanced. Kayla and Glamet^vorį had this going on before they left the dome. They may have had it going on since they left World. Glial cells release complex cascades of a variety of proteins. Some cause the destruction of neural synapses—the connections between brain cells—and some cause formation of new synapses. Essentially, they rewire the brain in fetuses, in early childhood, in adolescence, and after brain trauma."

"Are you saying that Ms. Rhinehart and Dr. Glamet^vorį's brains were being rewired? Why?"

"One possible explanation is the virophage they contracted on World. Everyone from the ship has experienced symptoms of infection, notably headaches and oversleeping."

Oversleeping. Jason's eyes met Major Duncan's. *I don't think they woke up when the bear started clawing away. Neither of 'em woke up. They just lied there.*

McKay's face twisted. "The other people experiencing headaches and oversleeping are children at Enclave Dome. I checked with the parents. Kids' brains are still developing. If the virophage is transmissible person to person, and if—"

"Don't you know if it's transmissible that way? Haven't you looked?"

"It's not that simple. We don't even have a culture of the virophage. The cultures aboard ship were destroyed by atmospheric contamination when the survivors were transported from the Settlement."

Jason tried to sort out all this medical information. "You're telling me, Doctor, that my base has been contaminated for weeks by a disease that might be transmitted person to person, so that everybody might have it. But everybody isn't having headaches and oversleeping."

"No. It may be progressive, with the star-farers exposed longer and the children more vulnerable because of the greater plasticity of their brains. It also may be that not everyone is infected with the virophage.

Another possibility is that some people have the virophage but experience no symptoms, some have symptoms for a while but no permanent changes—they throw off the infection and that's that. And some are susceptible and develop the kind of gliosis seen in Kayla and Glamet^vorį. Many contagions are like that, including flu and Zika. There may be genetic susceptibility. Right now, we—Toni and Marianne and Claire and I—think that's the most likely possibility with this."

"Why do you think so?" Coldness was creeping up Jason's spine, from tailbone to neck.

"We talked to everyone from the *Return* and the parents of all six children on base. Of the star-farers, all of them had headaches, which have mostly gone away, and three of those are oversleeping. Of the kids, all had symptoms but now only two do, and those two have both headaches and oversleeping. Devon Jones and . . . ," McKay's voice caught briefly, "my daughter Caitlin."

Two of six kids, four of ten from the *Return*. If McKay was right, over a third of the base might be susceptible to whatever this thing was. If it even was a thing. Jason said, "What's the next step, Doctor?"

"Continue research on the autopsied brains. There are proteins to check for, molecules known to be involved in rewiring brains after injury. Run gene scans on the sleepers. And we need to . . . to watch what happens with everybody else."

"Who are the adults whose headaches didn't go away and who are sleeping too much?"

"Branch Carter—"

The spaceship pilot. Christ.

"—Belok^, who is Glamet^vorį's brother—but not his sister, La^vor. Also—"

"The brother but not the sister? So it's not genetic who gets this thing and who does not?"

McKay looked astonished. Steffens jumped in. "You're thinking that siblings share the same genes, but in fact they only share fifty percent on average. Susceptibility might indeed be genetic, or partially genetic. We don't know."

Jason knew this, but the science had momentarily slipped his brain. Steffens, whom Jason had never liked ("Imperator" and "the Praetorian Guard" were hers), wore the carefully impassive expression of someone trying to not show superiority. Forget her; Jason had a larger picture to think about. He said, "Who are the other two from the ship whose headaches didn't go away?"

Silence. Then McKay said, "Marianne Jenner."

Jason hadn't expected that. But somehow, he knew what was coming next. "And the other person with headaches who isn't oversleeping, or at least not yet?"

"The translator," McKay said. "Jane."

Marianne insisted on attending the funeral pyre for Kayla and Glamet^vorɪ. There were reasons why she should not, all of which she ignored. For one, she hadn't actually liked either Kayla or Glamet^vorɪ. But that was trivial; they had been her shipmates.

More important was the overwhelming work in the lab. Old Dr. Holbrook was left as physician to nine hundred people, including the injured Settlers, since Claire and Lindy were co-opted for work on what the virophage might have done to human brains. Everyone with any notion of lab techniques, both civilian and military, had been reassigned to Zack McKay's day-and-night research push. Necessary, but it was all too familiar to Marianne: from the *Embassy* on Earth, from the clinic on World. How many times could humanity take on microbes and win? Marianne had no faith in this work. Or maybe she was just, after all these decades, too burned out.

Which was the third reason to not attend the funeral. All she really wanted to do was sleep. Her head throbbed just behind her forehead, and her eyelids felt like six tons of lead. Her neck ached from holding up her head. Her spine sagged, looking for something to lean against.

Nonetheless, she donned an esuit, passed through the airlock, and walked between Jane and Ka^graa, also esuited, to the pyre that had been built between Enclave Dome and the dark woods where Kayla and Glamet^vorj had been found. The sky, overcast, seemed to press down on the group of mourners led by La^vor and Belok^. Their military escort carried what looked to Marianne like entire arsenals.

How many such burnings had she been to? Too many, on World. But World had survived, and right now Marianne was not at all certain that Terra would. Microbes were such formidable enemies. Maybe Terra should just give up.

She was so tired.

But she straightened her spine as they reached the wooden pyre topped with the bodies wrapped in Army blankets. Beyond, trees blew in a rising wind. A flock of birds wheeled overhead, calling shrilly. Jane, lahk Mother to this temporary and displaced lahk, recited an ancient ritual in her own language. The musical cadences rose and fell as La^vor wept and Belok^, who may or may not have understood, looked frightened. Jane didn't translate, but Marianne had been told, light-years from here, what the chant meant. The bodies of the dead were being returned to the soil, the planet, the universe from which they were formed. Energy flowed through all, and all were one, and all existed forever.

The pyre was lit, and the mourners turned back to the dome. Ordinarily, Worlders did not bury the ashes of their dead, nor scatter them. They let nature do that. In this case, however, La^vor wanted the ashes to carry back to World. Soldiers would stay until the bodies were consumed, put out the fire, and gather the ashes.

Marianne could barely lift her feet. She was so tired.

Jane, dry eyed but taut as guitar strings, walked beside her toward Lab Dome. "Marianne, you need to sleep."

"Must . . . work."

"No. You'll be more of use to everybody in the lab after you sleep. The—"

"Go! Run—now!"

An officer—Marianne could not remember his name. He grabbed her hand. "Go, go!" Then she heard it: the rush of planes overhead. Jets? But Jason had said that neither the Army nor New America had jets anymore, they had all been destroyed or there was no one to fly them or no fuel or something . . .

The droning grew louder.

How could there be jets?

She stumbled, was picked up, was dragged on. The airlock opened and everyone jammed into it, packed in a solid ball like microglia. The outer door closed. Just before it did, Marianne glimpsed something rising swiftly above the horizon in the distance, slightly darker than the clouds.

Jane said to her, "Are you all right?"

"Yes." Emerging from the airlock into decon, she sagged against the wall. Only it was Jane she was somehow leaning on, Jane concerned for Marianne despite her own grief. Such a sweet girl, she would be wonderful for either Colin or Jason, Marianne didn't care which only . . . only . . .

Then she was asleep on the floor of decontamination.

Jason had been watching the funeral from the clear dome of the command post when the call came over his earplant. A soldier of J Squad on close patrol at the north airlock must have darted inside as soon as he received notice from the signal station. "Incoming, sir! Three planes, probably F-35s, three minutes away!"

F-35s? There were no more of those flying. But—

"Get everyone inside." He watched through the dome. Yes, there they were, coming in fast from the northwest . . . the direction of Sierra Depot. How the fuck had New America—

His grandmother. Jane. J Squad . . . but they all made the airlock. A moment later, the jets swept low over the dome and strafed it. Shells exploded harmlessly against the alien ceiling two feet above Jason's head. The vibrations didn't shake the dome, exactly, but he could feel it in his bones. To Colin and the other superhearers, it must have seemed like the end of the world. Trees in the woods burst into flame.

The jets flew off, banked, and returned.

If New America had gotten the launch codes from the quantum computer at the depot. . . . but those were codes for ICBMs, not plane-dropped bombs. Still . . . if the jets carried nuclear weapons, then there was nothing Jason could do but wait for the end of Monterey Base.

It didn't happen. The jets dropped bombs but they were not nuclear. They exploded against the dome, and the dome held. Whoever those super-aliens were who'd designed these domes, they'd known physics that Terrans hadn't suspected existed.

The jets flew away. Somehow the eerie silence of the entire operation made it seem even more sinister.

A whole section of forest to the east had caught fire.

Jason couldn't have it put out. He didn't have the resources. There were only two things he could do. The armory in Lab Dome held shoulder-mounted missile launchers that could take down planes; he would have to set up a constantly-manned station in the woods. He could also surprise-attack Sierra Depot with everything he had and hope to destroy the jets or the fuel tanks—and where had New America gotten jet fuel in the first place? Or the jets? Pre-Collapse, there had been no F-35s at the depot.

Jason said to captain Goldman on a closed channel, "Send someone outside to contact the signal station and make sure it wasn't hit."

He waited. Duncan appeared at the door of the command post.

Goldman said, "Signal station secure."

"Good. Stand by." To both Duncan and Goldman he said, "I'm going to report to HQ."

He saw the quick consternation on Duncan's face and knew she was thinking that he should not risk it; she should go. But this time Jason had to go himself. If New America forces were hidden in the woods to follow him and take out the signal station, they'd be thwarted. He was going to call HQ from the spaceship.

He said to Duncan, "Take command while I'm gone. Relay anything important through the signal station. Captain, ready a FiVee with troops from J Squad, but you stay here, keep a force outside both domes, and stand by."

"Yes, sir."

Duncan said, "Sir . . . do you know whether Lieutenant Allen has enough control of his ship's communications system to contact HQ specifically? When it first approached, contact was with us only because we were the closest viable receiver."

"I don't know. But I'm going to find out."

The spaceship might not be weaponized, but it was up to Jason to find ways to use it to maximum advantage. He tongued his mic back on. "Goldman, prepare to relay orders to the *Return* via the signal station."

"Yes, sir."

The command post dome had shed the dust from the explosion as if it had never occurred. The fire in the woods was being fanned by wind but away from the dome rather than toward it, and the heavy cloud cover looked as if it carried rain. If New America were smarter, they would have dropped their bombs on a dry windy day, and they would have dropped them to the east, so that flames spread over both domes. That might not have harmed the domes, but it would have trapped the inhabitants in hot air, which might overwhelm the domes' built-in climate controls and be filtered through the dome walls to inside. Or not. Nobody actually knew.

The funeral pyre for Kayla Rhinehart and Glamet^vorį, a small man-made echo of the forest fire, was dying down.

Rest in peace.

Jane followed the soldier carrying Marianne Jenner through the Decontamination airlock into Lab Dome. Marianne was old; had she had klefic? Jane didn't know the word in English, but Jane's grandmother had klefic when Jane was six. After she woke up, she could not speak, and her brain was never the same, and she had drooled and stared vacantly until she died. The doctors hadn't been able to do anything.

Oh, please the ancestors, not that for Marianne, so intelligent and so kind . . .

Claire Patel waited outside decon. "What happened . . . bring her here, please."

The soldier carried Marianne through the makeshift corridors to the infirmary and laid her on a bed in a tiny cubicle. Colin's room was only a few doors away. Claire said, "Jane, what happened?"

"I don't know. She just seemed very tired, and then she wouldn't wake up."

Claire straightened from Marianne's limp body. "Wouldn't wake up? Did you see her eyes roll back in her head? Did she gasp for breath?"

"No. She just fell."

"Like a faint?"

"I don't know that word."

"Never mind. Did she hit her head?"

"No, I don't think she hit her head."

Claire returned to examining Marianne, checking her pulse, counting breaths, shaking her shoulders, peering under her eyelids. Jane held her breath.

Marianne didn't wake up.

Claire frowned and turned back to Jane. "Did you know . . . did anybody tell you . . . that Caitlin McKay can't be woken up, either?"

"What?" The words didn't make sense.

"Do you know of anyone else so sleepy that they can't stay awake?"

"Belok^. Belok^ was very sleepy . . ." But Belok^ had been at the Burning and had come with Jane and La^vor through the airlock . . .

Claire said, "Where is Belok^ now? I didn't see him."

"I don't know. Wherever the soldiers took him. He and La^vor don't live in Lab Dome."

"I'm going to call a nurse for Marianne and then we're going to find Belok^."

When they did, the boy lay curled on his side in the middle of a corridor, a soldier standing helplessly over Belok^'s huge form, La^vor shaking her brother. "Come awake! Come awake!"

Claire bent over Belok^ and examined him the same way she had Marianne. "All his responses are normal, but . . ." She didn't finish the sentence. La^vor, too frightened to speak, clutched Jane. La^vor had just lost one brother, and now the other slept as if he were the breathing dead.

Jane thought of Claire's curious Terran phrase: *Never mind*. Would Marianne, Belok^, little Caitlin never be in their minds again? And would this happen to more people?

She wanted to talk to Colin, hold his hand, draw warmth for her suddenly cold body. But La^vor needed her. Jane put her arms around her friend and murmured to her, searching for words of comfort she could not find.

Her headache grew worse.

Four people were now comatose: Caitlin McKay, Devon Jones, Marianne Jenner, Belok^. Two from the ship who'd been infected with virophage; two children from the base. But not the other four children in Enclave Dome, not Claire Patel or Mason Kandiss from the *Return*. Not Ka^graa, La^vor, or Jane.

Zack and Susan sat by their daughter's bedside, Susan's face swollen with tears. All four coma victims had been moved to Lab Dome, carried in esuits by gurney bots through the tunnel system. A special area of the infirmary had been closed off and divided with curtains into cubicles. One of the three physicians was always on call nearby. No one knew what would happen next, but Zack's stomach had clenched when he saw that space had been left for more cubicles. Nurses were ready-ing more beds.

Caity, with her beloved Bollers beside her on the bed, didn't look ill. Her face, pale when she'd been awake and complaining of head-aches, now flushed lightly with the rosiness of a healthy child fast asleep. Her little chest rose and fell. Her eyelids fluttered—was she dreaming? They had no MRI equipment on the base, which had been designed for research, not trauma treatment. They couldn't tell if what had happened in Kayla's and Glamet^vor¡'s brains was happening in Caitlin's. They had no way to help her, and no answers.

It was Zack's job to find them. He had already stayed too long be-side Caity. Now he had to leave her with Susan and resume work. There had to be a way to fight this. If the cause was the virophage, which Zack suspected it was, then maniacal work must find a way to defeat the mi-crobe. Humanity had defeated microbes before: with antibiotics, with antivirals, with widespread eradication programs like those that had eliminated malaria from the United States and smallpox from the en-tire world. There was a way to cure Caitlin of whatever pernicious mi-crobe had seized her brain.

There was.

There must be.

CHAPTER 13

Jason strode into the armory with two members of J Squad; more met him there. All wore full armor. They were going to meet the *Return* when it landed. Li had sent precise instructions to the ship where and when to set down in order to minimize the time it was vulnerable. The chosen rendezvous was far enough away to avoid the snipers and missile launchers undoubtedly hidden in the woods around Monterey Base.

The armory motor pool always seemed to Jason a pathetic remnant for an Army that had once had transport capabilities to deploy a brigade anywhere in the world within ninety-six hours and a full division in a hundred and twenty. It consisted of six FiVees—five here now—three quadcopters, and two Bradleys. Ten years ago, as the world fell apart, Jason had taken considerable risks to get the Bradleys to Monterey. Army research bases did not ordinarily stock armored fighting vehicles, not even older ones. Jason had also secured modification kits for the Bradleys, which were now as good as Bradleys got, although he still regretted that he hadn't been able to secure any Strykers. Neither Bradley had as yet left base, and the enemy didn't know they were here.

One was now prepared to roll. Jason was doing everything possible to neutralize possible attack by New America.

It wasn't enough.

The Bradley roared out of the airlock and accelerated to its top speed, which was not very impressive, across the perimeter. Even before it reached the road, it was hit by a rocket-propelled grenade. The vehicle jerked violently, throwing Jason against Corporal Wharton. The reactive armor installed between the armor plates exploded as it was supposed to, neutralizing the incoming fire.

"Direct hit, sir," Private Kandiss shouted, unnecessarily. The Bradley bulldozed through the cloud of dust thrown up by the hit and kept going. The gunner was kept busy. Noise like falling mountains assaulted eardrums. Two more RPGs, and the Bradley turned off-road toward the river.

Immediately the ride became even rougher. The soldiers crammed into the small space bounced and clutched. Jason kept his eyes on the video display. New America had FiVees much faster than the Bradley, but no FiVee could go against the Bradley's chain gun. He saw no FiVees. The armored vehicle crunched over saplings and rocks, keeping to open country.

The river finally came in sight, a dull ribbon under the low sky. The rain, which had stopped, began again.

"Okay, river ahead," Jason said. "We turn north along it and—"

A Stryker tore toward them from a grove of trees.

No—New America did not have Strykers! Except, they did now.

The Stryker had slat armor; it could withstand any ordnance that the Bradley could fire without stopping. Nor could the Bradley outrun the Stryker; tracked vehicles were just not as fast as wheeled ones. But they were more stable, with better mobility over rough terrain. And—

"Make directly for the river, Sergeant. Gunner, if anything moves, shoot it."

"Yes, sir."

The Stryker gained on the Bradley, firing constantly. Jason lost track of the hits. The river, when they reached it, ran a few feet below a rocky bank. "Go! Go!"

The Bradley plunged over the bank, swaying wildly. Jason held his breath. Then they were in the river, powering across at maximum water speed of eight miles per hour. A Bradley was not an amphibious assault vehicle. *Please don't let the water level be too high. . . .*

It wasn't. The Bradley lumbered across the light rapids and emerged, climbing the bank as it shed water, on the other side.

Jason had hoped that the Stryker, wheeled, would flip when it dived over riverbank. It didn't, but it hit a rock, bounced, and came down mired in mud.

On the video display, the *Return* descended from orbit. If the Stryker had a lucky warhead shot . . .

"Go! Go!"

They raced toward the ship. It set down silently, rain sliding off its silvery hull. Jason and his troops were already out of the Bradley and running. They were barely inside the airlock when the *Return* lifted, soaring high above the rainy land beneath and the missile from the Stryker that just missed the hull.

Jason gazed down at the dwindling Bradley. New America would claim it, of course. But not for long.

Information Tech Specialist Ruby Martin waited just beyond the airlock. "Sir, welcome aboard. Lieutenant Allen instructed me to tell you that something has happened aboard."

"What?" On the wall screen, Earth fell away. Now the sky was black above a band of deep violet shading into grayish-white below them and blue on the horizon, which curved away in every direction. Already they were well into the stratosphere.

Martin said, "Major Farouk has passed out and can't be revived. We don't know what drugs he might have taken or if this is a suicide attempt or—"

"It's not." *Christ, another one.* "Did Major Farouk learn anything useful about the ship before he went comatose?"

"I don't know, sir."

"Did he leave notes?"

"No, sir."

"Have you learned anything more about the ship's communications capability?"

"A little more, yes, by experimenting."

"Do you think you can contact HQ at Fort Hood, if we fly there?"

"Yes, sir," she said, with noticeable pride. "I think I can."

"Good. Take me to the bridge. Sergeant, keep the squad here."

The ship seemed vaster inside than out, although Jason knew that was impossible. Jane had explained to him that the insides had been built for Worlders to found a colony, with animal pens and seed stores and food supplies, none of which remained. The inside of the *Return* had been scoured and stripped before she launched for Earth. All that remained were wooden partitions—no metal ones—that Worlders had erected to divide the space into rooms and corridors, with far fewer of each than in the two domes at Monterey Base. In that respect, the inside of the *Return* resembled Colin's Settlement.

But only in that respect. Jason walked past the FiVee that he had ordered, along with a lot of ordnance, loaded onto the ship during its previous landing. He said abruptly, "Specialist, did Major Farouk mention having headaches before he went unconscious?"

"Yes, sir."

"Have you had headaches or sleepiness? Has Lieutenant Allen, or Corporal Michaelson?"

She looked startled. "No. Sir?"

"Never mind."

The bridge was a surprisingly small and unpretentious space ringed with strange machinery and three wall screens, only one active. It showed Earth, now the blue-and-white globe familiar from a million pictures and holos. Seth Allen sat on a wooden bench that looked as if it had once been a low table, topped with a cushion woven of rough cloth. More cushions were heaped in the corner. He and Michaelson stood and saluted.

"As you were. Lieutenant, is that supposed to be a captain's chair?"

He grinned. "Sir, the Worlders like to sit on heaped-up cushions. I don't."

"Understandable." Jason realized that he had no idea how the Worlders lived at Monterey Base; he'd never been in any of their quarters. Did Jane sit on cushions instead of chairs, eating or studying English at a low table? "Where is Major Farouk?"

Martin said, "We dragged him to bed, sir."

"Good. Lieutenant, can you fly the ship at this altitude to HQ at Fort Hood?"

"At a lower height, yes. I need to navigate visually, unless I can home in on a long-range signal."

"No signal, not until we get there. Take the ship down to above a hundred thousand feet."

"Altitude is difficult to calculate, sir—I don't understand their measurements."

"What do you understand?"

He pointed to a small screen. "This shows symbols that seem to correspond to air temperature. The high troposphere is much colder than the stratosphere above it. Stratosphere starts at about forty thousand feet, at this latitude."

Jason didn't ask how he knew that; Allen possessed a curious mind interested in any branch of science with military application. It was why Jason, lacking a trained pilot, had assigned him to the *Return*.

"I want the ship low enough for rough visual navigation but still as high as you can—high enough to avoid attack by F-35s."

His eyes widened. "Yes, sir. I can try."

"What is the fuel situation?"

"I haven't been able to determine that, and neither had Captain Carter or Major Farouk. Our best guess was that it's some kind of cold fusion, at least during conventional flying. When it jumps . . . well, anybody's guess. Branch thought maybe it utilized dark energy or dark matter."

That was also what Farouk had speculated. Not useful. "When we arrive above HQ, initiate contact."

"Yes, sir. But we don't need to be right above them. There's a range— you'll remember that the *Return* contacted Monterey Base from space without knowing exactly where it was."

Jason did remember—it was one of the few pieces of luck he'd had. What if the *Return* had instead made contact with New America? It could have happened that way. He said, "Proceed, Lieutenant. Martin, has HQ restored visual communication?"

"No, sir." And then, in a sudden burst, "That should have been an easy patch. I don't understand why it hasn't been restored. A monkey could do it, sir."

Allen began touching various protuberances. Only the one active wall screen told Jason that the ship moved; there was no sensation of motion. The screen showed Earth becoming larger again, its features more distinct. The Pacific Ocean, clouded out to sea and quite a way inland. Then mountains—how fast they were flying!—followed by desert. Somewhere down there, dead below the returning wilderness, lay deserted towns, ruined cities, overgrown farmland. However, in various places RSA survivors had banded together to form small settlements, mostly ranches and farms with a few towns that cannibalized industrial machinery. Those that managed to avoid New America's troops were growing. The United States was building again.

In Colorado lay the radioactive ruin of Peterson Air Force Base and Cheyenne Mountain. The complex had been built to withstand a thirty-ton nuclear blast, an EMP, and airborne biological warfare. NORAD had held out for a long time, waging the deadly war that finished off what *R. sporii avivirus* had begun. But eventually personnel had had to emerge, and RSA had been waiting. Survival rate there had been less than 2 percent. Jason didn't know what had happened after that; information from Fort Hood about NORAD had ceased three years ago.

Jason had never served at Fort Hood, which had once been one of the largest military installations in the world, home to two full combat divisions as well as various other commands. 55,000 troops had been stationed there, many being readied for deployment around the globe. The grounds had included the world's biggest concentration of armored military vehicles: Abrams, Bradleys, Strykers. The air had been alive with Blackhawk copters on drill, with Apaches bristling with weapon mounts, with Chinooks like whales. There had been a live testing area for antitank guns and equipment. Just before the Collapse, three domes had been built at the southern end of the base, replacing the old administrative buildings.

The domes had survived. Nearly all of the rest was gone, although Jason knew that one entire dome still housed vehicles and rescued equipment. Much of the rest of Fort Hood's 150,000 acres was reverting to wilderness, growing amid bombed wreckage. Desert scrub was almost impossible to kill.

"Yes, that's Fort Hood," Jason said. "Maintain high position over the fort, and open contact. They already know we're here."

"Yes, sir," Allen said.

Jason prepared himself to face—metaphorically, anyway—General William Strople.

"Fort Hood, come in. This is the spaceship *Return*, US Army, Colonel Jason Jenner in command. Come in, Fort Hood."

A startled young voice said, "This is Fort Hood."

"Colonel Jenner wishes to talk to General Strople."

"Access protocol, please."

Jason gave the classified codes and waited. Five minutes later, Strople's voice sounded on the bridge. They were a long five minutes. Jason dismissed everyone from the bridge except Lieutenant Allen. Finally Strople said, "Colonel Jenner?" Still no visual.

Jason said, "Yes, sir. I'm talking to you from the bridge of the spaceship *Return*. I've had it flown here because I suspect New America of instituting the recent attack on Monterey Base in order to lure personnel to the signal station to report to HQ. They could then follow, discover its new location, and destroy it."

Silence. Jason could almost hear Strople thinking. Unease formed in Jason's stomach.

"Very clever. However, Colonel Jenner, you have neglected to inform HQ that the spaceship can be flown over the planet in this manner. The only intel I have is that it landed near Monterey Base and has since been flown only back and forth to orbit."

"Sir, I reported to General Hahn that the *Return* had been used to bomb New America after their attack on a farming settlement nearby. The ship has been contaminated with RSA."

"I did not receive that information."

What? Allen turned in his chair to throw Jason a wide-eyed look. If Hahn had not shared such vital intel with her next in command . . .

Strople seemed to realize his mistake. He covered it with an attack. "Colonel, you are reprimanded for not reporting vital war intelligence directly to me. A letter of reprimand will be included in your file. The weaponized spaceship is now classified as the property of HQ. Land it immediately."

Jason pressed his lips together; his spine stiffened. Colleen Hahn had not trusted Strople with crucial intel. She had, supposedly, died of RSA, which no competent CO would risk contracting—and she had been very competent. Strople had jumped several ranks in too short a time. Information tech specialist Ruby Martin said that restoring visual should have been simple for HQ techs. Jason didn't know what was going on at Fort Hood, but every instinct in him screamed that something here was very wrong. Right after the Collapse, there had been Army bases taken over by sheer force by ambitious survivors, as if the newly fragmented United States military were some South American dictatorship.

But he could not disobey an order.

However, if he landed the *Return* now, there was no guarantee that it would ever take him and his soldiers back to Monterey Base. Or if it did, Strople might send a higher-ranking officer with them to take command from Jason. Would that first-star general permit Colin's misguided Settlers to stay at the base? How would HQ treat the four Worlders whose ship this was? Jason was well aware of the prejudice in some

Army circles, including top brass, against Worlders. He had even heard, through Hillson, reports of ugly prejudice at Monterey Base.

But he could not disobey an order.

But . . . the *Return* technically didn't belong to the Army at all. It was a World diplomatic vessel. Strople could not command it. Jason seized on this, even as he knew that he had commandeered the ship. Ka^graa, however, had not protested.

"Colonel Jenner?" Preemptory, threatening.

"I'm sorry, General, we're having technical communications difficulties. Your last few sentences were badly garbled. Repeat, please."

"I said the weaponized spaceship is now classified as the property of HQ. Land immediately."

"We can't, sir, I'm sorry. We're speaking to you from orbit. The captain has explained to me that the ship—which, as you know, is of neither Terran nor World design—is preprogrammed to execute only two maneuvers: fly in orbit, as I am now, or else move laterally within only a hundred-mile radius of where it first landed. That seems to be a feature to conserve limited fuel."

"Let me talk to the alien captain."

"He does not speak English, sir. And the translator is not with us. She is ill."

"RSA?"

"No, sir. Some . . . alien disease. Which is something else I need to report."

"And you can't land the ship here?"

"No, sir. Frankly, sir, we have very little control over the spaceship."

Strople snarled, "Of all the ass-fucked operations . . . you are still reprimanded, Jenner."

"Yes, sir. But about the alien disease, which may be a reason you wouldn't want the *Return* to land here even if it could. We have a possible medical emergency at Monterey Base."

"What kind of 'possible medical emergency'? And don't you *know*?"

Jason described the bear attack, McKay's findings about anomalies in the victims' brains, and the unexplained comas of not only Belok^ but also two Terran children at Monterey Base, and possibly Major Farouk. When he finished, Strople said, "So you think this thing might spread? That more of your people might fall into comas?"

"Medical personnel don't know."

"It appears you don't know much, Colonel."

"No, sir. But I haven't yet reported"—*because you gave me no chance*—"the main reason I came here. New America has obtained and is flying F-35s. Three of them strafed Monterey Base."

"Do you know where they came from or where they went?" In contrast to his previous utterances, Strople sounded neither surprised nor alarmed. Jason thought: *He already knew.* Was this somehow connected to the surprise visit of the two HQ captains to Monterey Base? To access ordnance, or form covert alliances?

Jason said, "No, sir, not for sure. But I think their likely airfield is Sierra Depot."

"Casualties at Monterey?"

"None."

"Do you know how many planes they have in total?"

"No. We observed three."

"Keep me informed if you actually learn anything useful. About anything."

"Yes, sir."

"HQ out."

Jason drew a deep breath. Allen gazed at him, waiting, face professionally impassive. Queasiness took Jason at the lies he had just told, but he would not have done anything differently. Nor did he owe his officers any explanation. Nonetheless, he said, "The *Return* is a World diplomatic vessel, under the command of Ka^graa." Or possibly of Jane; Jason did not understand the whole lahk Mother system, which seemed insane to him. Jane was a young woman, not even military, and Ka^graa was her father.

"Yes, sir," Allen said.

"Lieutenant, you will not repeat anything you just heard. That's an order."

"Yes, sir."

"Now take the *Return* back to Monterey Base."

Whoever the hell the ship belonged to.

The *Return* set down at a different location from its previous landing and only long enough to drive off the FiVee, leaving aboard Allen, Martin, and Michaelson. The ship lifted to a safe orbit. The FiVee drove to the base without attack and through the armory airlock, where Farouk was loaded onto a gurney.

Lindy and an Army nurse waited just outside the armory. Immediately she bent over Farouk, examining him with the instruments always in her pockets. "How long ago did he lapse into the coma?"

"I don't know," Jason said. "Where's Holbrook?"

"In surgery. One of the Settlement kids broke an arm falling off a crate. Nurse, have this patient taken to the v-coma ward."

Jason said, "The what?"

"Virophage coma. We've got a dedicated ward now. Colonel Jenner, a word, please."

She addressed him as CO, and she hadn't rolled her eyes at meager medical intel about Farouk. Neither of those things boded well. Jason followed her to a temporarily vacant alcove formed of two properly installed walls and one large, empty, splintery crate smelling of beets.

"Jason, there is some bad news and I wanted to tell you myself. Your grandmother has fallen into the same sort of coma as the others. There are six now, with Dr. Farouk."

His grandmother. Instantly a hundred memories flooded Jason: Grandma cutting his and Colin's PB&J sandwiches into triangles and stars. Grandma taking him and Colin to hear a bridge make noises—although, of course, only Colin could hear that. Grandma teaching him and Colin about microbes, about mice, about ecology. The Marianne

Jenner of his memories was much more real to him than the woman who had returned to Earth twenty-eight years later. Lindy knew all of Jason's memories of his grandmother; he'd told her when they'd been married.

Which raised a whole other set of memories, especially when she took his hand.

"Jason, there isn't reason yet to despair. We don't know what we're dealing with here. Marianne and the others may spontaneously come out their comas. There doesn't seem to be any trauma."

"Do you have the equipment to know what's going on in her brain?"

"If you mean an MRI, no, we don't. CAT scans are inconclusive. The base infirmary was never designed as a trauma center; you know that. The best thing we can do is a spinal tap to see what's going on in the cerebral-spinal fluid. I need your permission for that, since you're the next of kin."

"Yes. Okay. Will you do the tap?"

"No, Holbrook will. He's much more qualified. He'll tap the others, too."

"Is it dangerous?"

"Not very."

"What can I do?" The moment he said it, Jason remembered Lindy's charge against him: *You always think you can control everything.*

But she didn't frown, or even drop his hand. "Nothing. Me, neither, not really. All we can do is wait while the virology team works. And hope there aren't too many more headaches-cum-sleepiness that turn into comas. Jason—"

Now she did frown, but it didn't look like disapproval—more like uncertainty.

"What?"

"Nothing." She dropped his hand. "Now it's all up to Zack McKay and his lab team."

It must be a genetic variation. Had to be.

Zack stood with Susan by Caitlin's bed in the curtained infirmary cubicle, one of a row of curtained cubicles holding v-comas. The curtains, made of some heavy material of an oppressive olive green, shut out light from the corridor. Under the dim overhead, Caity looked so small on the adult-sized bed with Bollers by her side, and so much like a healthy sleeping child instead a victim of a condition no one understood.

There must be a mutated allele, a genetic variation somewhere amid the fifteen million base-pair variations known to exist in the three-billion-pairs human genome. Maybe one of those fifteen million variations had occurred as a result of some human encounter with the virophage in the far distant past. The mutation had been passed along, a silent passenger until this child, Zack's child, contracted the virophage. Then what? What genetic sequence had been triggered by the phage? And what was it doing to the brain of someone who had been affected in the womb by the ubiquitous *R. sporii*, but had never contracted RSA?

Because so far, that was their only clue. None of the coma victims was an RSA survivor. It was almost nothing to go on. They needed to run full-genome comparisons, ASAP.

Amy Parker, head nurse, entered the cubicle and turned up the light. "Major Holbrook will be here in a minute."

Stupidly, Zack thought, *I'd feel better if she called him Dr. Holbrook.* But this was a military base, Holbrook was an Army doctor, Amy was Lieutenant Parker. And Zack was an ass.

When Holbrook arrived, Amy turned Caitlin over and held her, pulling up her gown to expose her delicate little back. He prodded the ridges of her spine and selected a spot between two lower vertebrae. After cleaning the spot, he inserted a long needle—Zack winced—and advanced it until clear fluid filled the syringe. The needle was withdrawn, Amy put a bandage on the spot, and the whole thing was over. Caity had not so much as changed her breathing pattern. Holbrook nodded and left for, presumably, the next v-coma.

Susan said, "I'll stay. You need to get to work on those fluid samples."

"I do, yes."

Until answers were found, Lab Dome was Zack's new home. He would live, sleep, work there, not leaving until this new horror was vanquished. "Will you—"

"I'll send someone with your clothes and things. Bye, love."

Zack set off for his lab at almost a run. But as he barreled into the room, Toni grabbed his arm. "Zack!"

"What is it?" Worse—from her face it was worse.

"Three new comas. Two are soldiers here in Lab Dome, and one of them is an RSA survivor."

There went the only clue he had.

"Who are they? Do they bunk together?"

"Yes. Privates Lawrence Larriva and Mark Buckley. Both bunked with Mason Kandiss, that Army Ranger from the *Return*, so that's the suspected transmission path."

"Yes, probably. Who's the third victim?"

Toni's expression changed.

"Who? A civilian? One of our research team?"

"No." Toni paused. "It's the translator from World. Jane."

CHAPTER 14

Over the next four days, five more people fell into comas, all soldiers. Jason visited McKay's lab, a scene of purposeful and focused activity, to see if isolating Mason Kandiss would help. "Probably not," Toni Steffens told him; McKay was "unavailable." "Preliminary transmission diagrams indicate that there are secondary and even tertiary carriers."

"Have you found anything? Anything at all?"

Dr. Steffens stared at him. "We've found a lot of things, Colonel, but so far none of them are going to pull your soldiers out of their comas or keep more from falling into it, if that's what you mean."

"It isn't." Jason held on to his temper; the scientists were all overworked, overstressed, and absolutely necessary. "I'm going to ask some basic questions. Are you any closer to understanding what happened here?"

"No. Not yet."

"Are you closer to predicting how widespread the problem might be?"

"No."

"Can you predict anything about who might or might not be susceptible to the condition—any shared physical qualities, for instance, in the victims?"

"Not yet."

"Look, Doctor, I'm going to be frank here. You don't like me, and I'm not crazy about you, either. But I need to be kept up to date about anything you find. You're a civilian, but this base is under martial law. Now is there anything else I should know?"

"Only that 'what happened here,' 'the problem,' and 'the condition' are no ways to refer to human beings who may die if we can't help them."

"Don't talk to me in—"

McKay appeared at Jason's elbow. "Toni, please get back to work. Please." And when Steffens had stalked off, "Colonel, I apologize for my colleague. We're all unraveling a bit."

"That is no excuse for disrespect." He'd almost said *insubordination*.

"Her wife, Nicole, collapsed into a coma a few hours ago."

"I hadn't yet been told that." Jason felt his adrenaline ebb. "How is your little girl doing?"

McKay looked surprised. Why? Did everyone on the science side think that Jason knew of the coma victims as only nameless statistics? Jason added pointedly, "Caitlin."

McKay said, "She's the same."

"I'm sorry. Please let me know if you make any advances at all."

"I will."

Jason left, glad to escape the lab. Although his next visit proved worse.

He pulled aside the curtain in front of Jane's cubicle. A second v-coma ward, as close as possible to the first, had been carved out of a hallway plus a few storerooms. The ward held, ominously, room for more patients.

Like the others, Jane looked deeply asleep. An IV with nutrients ran into her arm. Her dark curls spread across the pillow, and occasionally the lids over her big eyes fluttered. Dreaming? Of what?

This was Jason's second visit. He didn't even know why he came; he could have just requested reports on her condition, on all their conditions. On his previous visit, Ka^graa had been sitting by his daughter's bed. Today Colin, with a bandaged side and a large cast on his leg, sat in a powerchair that badly crowded the cubicle. He looked up.

"Colin. How are you feeling?"

"Better. Does anybody know anything about how to cure this thing?"

"You mean, with the technological advances you despise?"

Colin said, "Cheap shot, big brother."

"Accurate shot." They were bristling at each other like cats . . . no, not cats. Colin was holding Jane's hand. So—like horned elk in spring-time.

I didn't know, Jason thought. He didn't know that Colin and Jane . . . but was it mutual? And what was Jason doing even thinking about her when he had so much else to think about?

Colin must have seen something on Jason's face. His own expression softened. He said gently, "No, Jace. She and I belong together. And she wouldn't have been good for you anyway, or you for her. You need some-one who will push back, like Lindy."

Rivalry vanished from Jason's mind, replaced by rage—the pure product, directed against one of the two people who would push back at him. The rage came out cold, because that was how he had been trained and how he had trained himself.

"You aren't exactly the correct person to dictate my life, Colin, when yours wouldn't even exist if it weren't for my intervention. I thought you might have learned something from the violence that lost you a third of your precious Settlement."

Colin's gentle expression vanished. He had always been equal to Jason's attacks. "I didn't need to learn it, because I already knew. Vio-lence is never the answer, not yours and not New America's."

"How can you—"

Colin rolled on, raising his voice, holding his brother's gaze with one just as fierce. "You think violence is an instrument you can control, like your tech, using it only for 'good and sufficient' reasons. But violence is not an instrument; it's a cancer. You can't turn people into killing machines with the power to end life, and then expect them to behave humanely in the rest of their lives. Humane empathy is always the first victim of war, or soldiers couldn't kill at all. Once violence gets started, it always escalates. It can't be controlled."

"We didn't start it. New America did. And Congress declared war on them." Just before Congress itself became a victim.

Colin said hotly, "Your Army equipped New America with all their stolen weapons *and* their stolen destructive imperialism. Fighting over territory that doesn't belong to either of you, only to the Earth! Did you know that a hundred years ago in World War II, sixty-five percent of the casualties were civilians? And in Iraq and Brazil, it was ninety percent?"

"Of course I knew that. Don't patronize me—I know more military history than you ever dreamed of. But I'm defending people here, and I have no choice."

"There's always a choice, Jason."

"Only for those as smugly self-righteous as you are. You get to have a choice because people like me make that possible. Without my Army, your entire precious Settlement would no longer exist, and you wouldn't, either."

"I know," Colin said, with one of the truthful and humble swerves to facts that made him so endearing, and so exasperating. "But, Jace— you don't have to actively go after New America. You can just wait them out. They'll destroy themselves eventually, because violent societies always do."

Jason said carefully, "Why do you think I'm planning to 'actively go after New America'?"

"Aren't you? Before you lose so many soldiers to v-coma that it's too late?"

"I—"

"Annhhh," Jane said, and opened her eyes.

Instantly Colin bent toward her. "Jane?"

But her eyelids fluttered closed again, and Colin's gentle shaking didn't make her stir.

Jason slipped through the curtain. He didn't want to watch Colin gazing like that at Jane. And if she opened her eyes again, he didn't want to see how she gazed back.

Before going to the beds of his soldiers in v-coma, Jason went to find a nurse or doctor and report Jane's brief, futile, apparently painful awakening.

Analyses of Caitlin's cerebral-spinal fluid revealed several proteins nobody had seen before. The other v-comas' samples confirmed that. The proteins contained expected amino acids, but they were folded in unique ways. "What the fuck do you suppose they're doing in there?" Toni said. Since Nicole had become comatose, Toni's language had deteriorated below even its usual obscene level. She barely slept, and definitely didn't bathe. Zack breathed through his mouth around her, hoping that she didn't notice.

At 2:00 a.m., bleary with lack of sleep, Zack said, "I think the proteins are rewiring their brains. Along with all those glials and the chemicals that we know either create or prune synapses." There were many more synapse-forming chemicals than synapse-pruning ones, the direct opposite of the autopsy tissue from Kayla and Glamet^vorɪ.

"But rewiring to what end, fuck it all? To *what?*"

"Toni, get some sleep. Please."

"No. Not till the genome matching is done."

With the available computing power, it seemed to take forever to run the matching program. The base's main system sat dark and unrepairable. The most powerful consoles that were still running had been commandeered for this, over the completely unreasonable protests of the immune-boosting team, who claimed they needed it more. There was no "more" than researching the v-comas, and Zack had told Major Vargas so, forcefully. Jessica Yu had backed Zack.

Tissue samples had been sequenced to provide full genomes for Belok^, Jane, Caitlin, Devon, Marianne, Branch, Farouk, and the soldiers in v-comas. The matching program was comparing their genomes with control samples, cycling through all fifteen million possible genetic variations in each genome, looking for sequences that they all shared.

Zack said, "We'll find the allele that triggers the comas."

"You don't even know for motherfucking sure that it *is* an allele!"

Zack didn't answer. He turned away before he said something too sharp.

Toni put a hand on his arm. "Look, I'm sorry. I'm just—"

"I know. We all are. But go sleep, Toni. And *shower.*"

A tech rushed into the room. "Zack! The matching program finished!"

The matching program was printing its results—damn the shortage of paper and ink. Zack seized the densely covered sheets as they came from the printer. Toni studied the display screen with three lab techs crowded behind her.

The six v-coma genomes shared thirty-two alleles not found in the control samples, most in junk DNA. Six of those were insertions, genes incorporated into the genomes somewhere in, probably, the distant past. One of the six might have been activated by the virophage to set in motion the cascade of proteins and chemicals now rewiring brains. Or might not have been. Only 4 percent of polymorphism affected gene expression. That was the figure decided on just before the Collapse, when most basic science pretty much stopped.

Toni said, "The v-comas might be multifactorial inheritance disorders, rather than monogenic." She said it reluctantly; she wanted there to be a single-gene explanation as much as Zack did. The chances were better for coming up with some sort of gene therapy.

Although in no case were the chances high.

The lab tech said, "If it's a single variant, we can at least predict who else might fall into a coma. If you don't have any of those six alleles . . ."

If I *don't have them*, was what the tech really meant. This research was intensely personal. Zack said, "I have a sample to sequence next."

"Yours?"

"No." It was Susan's. If he lost her as well as Caitlin, he lost everything.

Toni said, "We have a lot of samples to sequence and match. Let's get started. Zack, the new v-comas from today have to be first, as confirmation—you know that. Anyway, it might help further narrow down the allele. If there is an allele."

Her skepticism was the correct attitude. Zack knew that. He went to find the tissue samples from the v-coma soldiers. Before he had even prepared the samples for the sequencer, someone came into the lab. Zack didn't turn; Toni talked to whoever it was. After the visitor left, Toni touched Zack's shoulder. Her eyes looked almost as big as a Worlder's, and compassion moved in their depths.

"Zack—there's one more. Susan."

Bright morning light assaulted the top of Enclave Dome, throwing everything in the command post into harsh relief. Jason could have closed the tentlike curtains installed on rods overhead, but he didn't. He needed the glare, he needed coffee, he needed everything he could get to combat the sleeplessness of a bad night. A nightmare reliving the Collapse, another filled with sweating anxiety, a wet dream about Jane.

He cradled the coffee mug in cold hands. After ten years, the base was officially out of coffee, but a small amount had been hoarded for both the signal station and the CO. Jason refused to feel guilty about this. Hillson, his pipeline to the barracks through careful cultivation of selected recruits, had told him that the troops drank some sort of tea steeped from a plant gathered by hunting parties. The United States Army was reverting to Paleolithic hunter-gatherers.

Well, no, it wasn't quite that bad. But the hunting parties were more frequent now, and vegetables and dried seaweed concoctions from Colin's settlement would have to be stretched farther than before, to feed more people than before. The base cooks were endlessly inventive, but it was still going to be a problem. One of so many.

The first thing for today was to issue an OPORD to—

"Sir," Hillson said in his earplant, "coming up."

It was the first time that the master sergeant had announced entry instead of asking permission. Jason braced himself.

Hillson's face had the rigid, impassive expression that meant he was furious. "Sir, we've had an incident. A hunting unit left at dawn, ten troops led by Lieutenant Sullivan. They just returned. Two of them are dead."

"New America?"

"No. They were shot by Private Kandiss."

Jason blinked. Mason Kandiss, the soldier off the *Return* that Jason had assigned to J Squad, had performed so well that Jason had had the luxury of forgetting about him. "Tell me as much as you know, and how you know it."

"Kandiss told me himself. I have him in custody in the stockade. I also talked to the seven other members of the hunting unit and to the prisoner-at-large."

Tommy Mills, of New America? What the fuck did he have to do with this? Jason waited. Hillson would produce the story in his own way, each word weighed and measured before being released.

"The hunting unit divided into two squads. They preserved, as far as I can tell, proper communication and support distance. Kandiss was assigned to lead one squad; Sullivan had the other. When the two had reached maximum permitted distance apart and were out of line of sight, the four other members of Kandiss's squad turned their weapons on him. They told him he was a traitor, bringing the virophage to the base, part of a conspiracy to kill everyone. They—"

"Was this 'conspiracy' supposed to be created by World or by New America?"

"They didn't say. Sir—you knew that in some quarters there's a lot of anger and fear about the aliens, and about the v-comas, and about bringing the Settlers here, and about . . . everything."

Of course Jason knew. Anger and fear were to be expected after ten years of claustrophobia, of boredom broken by rare bouts of combat, of crowding now made worse by the Settlers, of a war that seemed to go nowhere. There had been incidents before, but no one had died. He said, "Go on."

"Kandiss told me that the four others said he deserved to die, along with all traitors, and they were going to take him out. They didn't. He killed two of them. A third is in the OR now with a knife wound in the belly. The fourth threw down his weapon and raised his hands. The other squad heard the commotion and came running. Kandiss surrendered."

"He took down three of his attackers? Who were the four?" Not J Squad, surely.

"Privates Landry, Guerra, and Madden. Landry and Madden are dead. Madden was a new recruit who grew up on base. Landry was always a troublemaker and Guerra a broke dick, always whining. Private Drucker surrendered. Lieutenant Sullivan shouldn't have put them together in a squad."

"But they were all armed and in full gear—how did Kandiss take them down?"

"Sir, you may have forgotten—Corporal Kandiss was an Army Ranger. The only one we have."

Jason heard the respect in Hillson's voice. He said, "Is Kandiss injured?"

"Minor bruises."

"How extensive are these sort of conspiracy theories?"

"As far as I can tell, not very. But there *is* resentment about the aliens and the v-comas. Some about the Settlers, too, although as long as we have enough food, that seems pretty low level. Especially since some of the Settler women don't believe in monogamy and they've made it their business to try to convert soldiers to their Mother Nature ideas, which they're doing in a sort of free cathouse combined with ideological lectures."

Jason tried to picture this enterprise, and failed. "Why did you talk to the prisoner-at-large, Tommy Mills?"

"He's been assaulted a couple of times—war enemy and all that. Mills says that Kandiss started to protect him. Which made Kandiss even more suspect to a lot of our people with bad attitudes about the aliens."

It was the third time he'd used the word. Jason said, "Hillson, they aren't 'alien.' The aliens are the ones who took them from Earth a hundred and forty thousand years ago, the same ones who left them the spaceships and domes. Worlders are as human as you and me."

"If you say so, sir. I'm just saying that a lot of soldiers don't see it that way. We could have more assaults."

Jason tried to think. He needed more sleep. Hadn't he learned once that Rangers were trained to function on a few hours of sleep for a week or more? Probably Jason, who had been competent but not outstanding at physical training during basic, could not have qualified for Ranger School.

"Kandiss is housed with J Squad? Any trouble there?"

"No, sir, never in J Squad."

Good—Jason needed to trust his elite unit. "Quarter the prisoner-at-large with J Squad. Put Drucker—and Guerra, too, as soon as Major Holbrook gives permission—in the stockade to await court-martial. Keep me informed of any further conspiracy theories or other problems you hear of." Hillson must have a hell of an informant system, and Jason was grateful for it.

"I may not hear of anything in time to stop it."

"I know. Pick men you trust for twenty-four-hour guards on Dr. Ka^graa and the other three Worlders, including the two in v-comas. Don't use anyone from J Squad—I'm going to need them."

"Yes, sir." Hillson didn't ask what Jason planned for J Squad.

"And send Kandiss to me."

"Yes, sir."

Colin's words ran through his mind: *You think violence is an instrument you can control. You can't.*

Colin had no idea how much more violent things were going to get. But then, before Jason could put his plans in motion, New America attacked.

CHAPTER 15

Blatt . . . blatt . . . blatt blatt blatt. . . . Sirens in both domes sounded an attack. Zack hardly noticed. Deep in lab work, protected by the invulnerable domes, he didn't need to react. Alerted by the signal station, the patrols would get everyone inside in time. A few more missiles would shatter themselves against one or both domes. If the signal station was hit, Jenner would erect a new one, as he had before. And nothing mattered as much as this lab work.

Susan had fallen into a v-coma as she sat by Caitlin's bedside. Four more people had also gone down. Then had come a caesura, in which everybody had hoped the virophage had run its course, having infected everyone susceptible. All eighteen victims shared only one unique allele. Uninfected people had been tested, including the other four children who had played with Caitlin and Devon, as well as the research scientists. Zack did not possess the mutation, which by now they referred to simply as "the allele."

Neither did Colonel Jenner.

"I think the epidemic is over," a lab tech had said.

"Shut the fuck up," Toni had snapped. "It's not over until we bring them out of v-comas."

To what? Zack wondered. But he only glared at Toni, before taking precious time away from work to pacify the lab tech. Still, Toni was right, even though having no further victims was a blessing.

Then there were more victims.

In the three weeks since Susan had fallen into a coma, so had three of the Settlers. They had arrived last at the base, which meant that they'd been easily infected, without long exposure. The evidence was at least predictive: If you had "the allele," you fell into a coma. If you didn't have it, you were infected with the virophage—probably they all were, by now—but you didn't get your brain rewired by a microbe from antiquity.

All research on the vaccine, immune boosters, and gene drive had ceased. Zack hadn't visited the bird lab in three weeks; all his time was spent in Lab Dome's main facilities, researching the virophage. Presumably lab techs were still caring for the sparrows in the underground annex, but he no longer cared. All that mattered was finding a way to help Susan and Caity.

More and more of Lab Dome had become a hospital. Lieutenant Amy Parker, head nurse, had recruited Settlers to carry out the basic care of those in a coma, so that she and the trained nurses could keep the IVs delivering nutrients, monitor the v-comas, and nurse those still recovering from the destruction of the Settlement. All facilities and resources were strained almost as far as they could go. Meals had become mostly soup, and soup had become mostly fresh meat, dried vegetables, and seaweed. Last night Zack had dreamed of fresh raspberries with crème fraîche.

Blatt . . . blatt . . . blatt blatt blatt . . .

The experiments he was running told him nothing. For one thing, analyses of consecutive spinal taps from the same patient kept turning up new proteins. Zack could discover what the proteins were made of, he could discover how they reacted in solution with other substances, but he didn't know what they were doing in a human brain. He didn't know what inactive genes were being prompted to become active, other than the allele that had begun the metabolic cascades. He didn't know how to wake up the v-coma victims, or what would happen when he did. He didn't know anything.

"Dr. McKay," a lab tech said.

He didn't even look up to see which lab tech it was. "Ignore the sirens. The missiles can't affect the domes."

"It's different this time."

Then Zack did look up. "Who are you?"

"Ben Corrigan. Dr. Steffens assigned me to you. I've been assisting you for two days now."

The man was clearly a Settler, sunburned and muscled and dressed in homespun. Yet he had prepared slides deftly and . . . yes, the notes on Zack's tablet were clear and complete.

Corrigan said, "I was a high-school biology teacher. Before the Collapse."

"And you joined Colin Jenner's Settlement?"

"Yes." Corrigan's expression said he didn't want to talk about it.

Blatt . . . blatt . . . blatt blatt blatt . . .

Corrigan winced. Zack said, "You're a superhearer." Victim of a different microbe, *R. sporii*. Corrigan's brain had been rewired in the womb. Virus and virophage, enemies, had coevolved to make use of different parts of the same organ in their hosts, presumably in competition but with different effects.

"Yes, I'm a superhearer," Corrigan said. "And whatever is going on out there, this attack is different."

"Different how? What do you hear?"

"Ground and air—you know that already. There are large disturbances out there, and more coming."

"The domes are impregnable to anything short of nuclear energy."

Corrigan said nothing.

He had waited too long to act.

Jason watched helplessly from the command post as New America assaulted the base with weapons that he had not known still existed. The three F-35s emerged from the clouds and swept low overhead, dropping bombs. These exploded spectacularly against the dome's energy shield, producing noise and fury but so far no damage except to the already charred forest beyond the perimeter. Although—what would happen if one of the jets flew a kamikaze mission directly into a dome? As far as Jason knew, that had never been tried.

The F-35s flew off, but they were not the main offensive.

Eight Strykers lumbered over the horizon, armored moving buildings. Each could hold eleven soldiers. The Strykers' slat armor could withstand RPGs, and their ordnance, including the biggest guns ever fitted to this type of vehicle, could take out anything from a soft target to concrete bunkers. Jason had not known so many Strykers were left; there had been none at Sierra Depot. These had come overland from somewhere distant, plowing slowly through saplings and over rubble, skirting the ruins of cities. Where had the fuel come from? And did HQ know?

Jason couldn't contact HQ, or anything else. The Strykers took positions facing all six airlocks and began firing. Any soldier who stepped outside to communicate with the signal station would be instantly reduced to a bloody pulp. After they had done trying out the Strykers' ineffectual 105mms, the Strykers would simply wait in position, with New America's troops bivouacking behind. Eventually Monterey Base, already low on food, would either starve or surrender. It was a siege, as if this were the thirteenth century and Monterey Base some medieval castle. But unlike thirteenth-century fortifications, the base had neither arrow slits and parapets from which to fire, nor rats to eat when the siege got too bad.

So it all came down to the tunnels from the annexes. New America would know the tunnels existed; all domes had one underground or underwater airlock. It was built into the incomprehensible alien design. But did they know where the base's tunnels terminated? If so, a force would be waiting there. If not, they would have troops and snipers covering as much of the surrounding area as possible, waiting for someone to do what Jason had waited too long to do: get a message to the signal station to deploy the *Return*.

Assuming the signal station had not already been taken out.

Then, an added insult, a Bradley lumbered from the woods. A Monterey Base Bradley, the one that Jason and J Squad had abandoned to board the *Return* for the trip to Fort Hood.

Hillson came up behind him. "Sir."

Jason didn't answer. If he had carried out his plan before now, this might not have happened. If he hadn't waited to attack Sierra Depot because he didn't want to reveal to HQ that the *Return* was capable of more than he'd told Strople . . . if he hadn't waited to see how many of his troops would be stricken with v-coma . . . if he hadn't waited for definite orders . . .

"Sir . . ."

Jason turned from the ineffectual bombarding of his alien castle. "Do we have any intel about the signal station?"

"No, sir."

"About the tunnels?"

"Captain Goldman listened at the exit. He didn't hear anything, but that doesn't mean squat. They'd wait quietly."

"Send one of the superhearers with Goldman."

"We don't—"

"The Settlers have three of them, plus one kid." Sergeant Tasselman had registered all the Settlers, with as much information as he could pry out of them.

Hillson didn't convey his surprise, but a pleased look crept into his eyes. "Yes, sir. Permission to accompany the superhearer."

"Permission granted." Jason turned back to the clear dome. "Hillson, you ever fight in a Stryker?"

"Yes, sir."

"Me, too." Jason could almost feel the inside: hot metal, the stink of too many bodies in too tight a place, of urine and bad breath and ammo, the Congo jungle vivid on the view screen. But remembering the inside of a Stryker was better than remembering what the outside had done to an enemy village.

To Hillson he said, "The three adult superhearers are Sarah Waters, Colin Jenner, and Benjamin Corrigan. Take Corrigan."

"Yes, sir."

The bombing had stopped now. The Strykers sat motionless, waiting. Jason sent for and briefed Elizabeth Duncan. "Sir," she said, "there's no need to go yourself."

"I'm going. Take command."

"Sir—"

"That's all, Major."

Her expression didn't waver. If she disapproved—and of course she did—it didn't show. Once again, Jason marveled at her self-control. It was an admirable military trait, but it also made him uneasy. She would back him up on this counterattack, but how far would she back him up on a direct defiance of HQ? He wasn't sure, which is why he hadn't as yet told her his entire plan.

And, of course, she was right to disapprove of his going outside. He could have used any of J Squad to convey orders to Li, and Li would accept them. Impossible to explain to the hyper-correct Major Duncan why Jason had to go outside himself. He could barely explain it to himself. But this mess was his responsibility, and he was going to fix it.

Lindy's voice in his head: *You think you can control everything.*

Uncharacteristically, Duncan tried again. "Permission to speak, sir."

"Go ahead."

"You should not go yourself. Sir. Send me."

Was she offering a genuine strategic assessment, or was she starting to take control of J Squad? Jason suspected that what had happened at HQ had been a junta-style takeover. General Hahn had been killed or imprisoned by Strople, who had his own agenda for the war. Strople could not have done that without convincing control of HQ officers. Was it possible that Elizabeth Duncan also—

No. He was being paranoid.

He said to Duncan, "Dismissed, Major."

She left. Half an hour later, Hillson returned. "Sir, Corrigan was in Lab Dome. One of the scientists found out he had some sort of biology background and they're using him in research. Captain Goldman took him through the tunnels. He says he heard troops near the exits of both tunnels, but not directly above either exit."

Shit. "Did he hear any heavy vehicles?" Not that Corrigan's report would be conclusive. A Stryker could be in place already, quietly waiting. Or just heavy ordnance.

"No, sir. Sir, with all respect—you shouldn't go yourself."

Sometimes Hillson seemed to reach into Jason's head and extract his thoughts. It could be very annoying.

Jason said. "If this doesn't work, it won't matter who goes. Not in the long run."

No one would be left to care.

He waited until well after nightfall. In full armor, Jason was a walking metal can equipped with the best sighting, communications, and killing tech of ten years ago. The J Squad soldiers with him looked equally formidable. But if there was another Stryker waiting at the top of the tunnel, they would all be hamburger in five seconds.

The unit stood, helmets off, going through weapons check in the storeroom at the bottom of Enclave Dome staircase. Jason had chosen Enclave tunnel precisely because it was used more, bringing in supplies and game, and so more likely to be known to New America. They would expect him to use the Lab Dome tunnel exit, which they might or might not know the location of.

The storeroom smelled of onions, but there were too many empty crates around. It was October; ordinarily, Colin's Settlement would be supplying pumpkins, apples, pears, late tomatoes. Not this year, and not ever again if this plan didn't work.

Jason and Kandiss, the only members of J Squad who were not RSA survivors, activated esuits.

"Okay," Jason said, "listen up."

Zack dozed on a pallet in a corner of his lab. He was dreaming something formless but menacing when someone shook his shoulder, hard. Instantly he bolted upright and lashed out.

"Jesus, Zack, don't assault me!"

Lindy Ross, crouching over him. Zack looked wildly around. No one else was in the lab, and only a dim night light burned.

"What the hell are you doing, Lindy? What time is it? What's happened?" Fear spitted his guts.

"It's not Caitlin or Susan," she said quickly. "It's midnight. I need your help."

"My help?"

"Yes. I have to move Colin Jenner and I can't do it alone."

That made no sense. "What? Move him where? You want an orderly." And then, "Is he dead?"

"No, he's not dead. I can't move him alone with his injuries and tubes unless I use a carry-bot, which can't go down stairs."

"Down stairs? Why would Colin go down any stairs?" Was Lindy delusional?

"I'll explain later but I need help *now*, while I can do this in secret, and you're the only one I trust. Come on!"

She tugged on his arm, and Zack rose, befuddled by sleep or its lack but responding to the authority and urgency in her tone. They moved swiftly through the artificially night-dimmed corridors to the infirmary. When Zack tried to whisper a question, Lindy put her finger to her lips.

Colin Jenner waited in a powerchair. Lindy whispered to Zack, "If we run into anybody, say that you need tissue samples from Colin for your research. Come on."

They moved, a silent ghostly group, past the cubicles with v-comas, who were beyond hearing anything. God, so many of them! From a side room came night nurses' voices, weary and yet strident, arguing about something. Beyond the infirmary, the corridors were empty. They went through the first door to the tiny enclosure at the top of the staircase, Lindy squeezing in Colin's bulky chair. She closed the door behind them.

Zack said, "Are we going down to the bird lab? Why? And where's the guard?"

"Went comatose a few hours ago. Zack, you can get down there. Give the security system your scans."

"Not until you tell me what's going on!"

Colin said, "I'll tell you. The underground annex will have a small airlock and then a long tunnel to the outside, as an emergency escape hatch and—"

"I know that, Jenner!"

"What you don't realize is that there's a whole New America army camped all around us, with tanks or something like tanks, and—"

"How do you know?"

"I *looked*," Lindy said. "Observation deck is off-limits now, but I'm a *doctor*. With a good enough story, soldiers let me go places they won't let other people go."

"And anyway, I hear them," Colin said.

Of course. Zack hadn't put it together. If Ben Corrigan could hear "something different out there," so could Colin Jenner.

Lindy said, "We're going to take Colin through the tunnel to its exit somewhere in the woods. We need you because you have security clearances for the airlock scanner—you've gone outside to obtain sparrows. Colin's going to listen to find out whether there are New America troops right above, waiting for us to come out like rats from a burning sewer. If not, I'm going outside and try to call the signal station. I have an earplant and mic, you know—doctor's privilege. Mine aren't military but maybe the signal station will hear us. Otherwise, there's no way to tell them what's going on."

Zack was appalled. "New America will hear your message, too. They'll pick up your location instantly."

"I'll walk a long way from the tunnel exit before I signal."

"Lindy, they'll mow you down!"

Lindy said, "Help me with Colin's chair. We can't jiggle him too much." She took off her long white coat. Under it she wore a jacket, military pants, and boots. An assault rifle was strapped across her chest.

Zack said "And even if you reached the signal station, what good could they do?"

"Send missiles. Jason can't fire outside, and we're just sitting here like caged sparrows in the bird lab. And if the signal station can't fire missiles, they can at least send the *Return* to rescue us."

"No," Zack said. "It's an insane plan."

Lindy moved so close to him that their feet almost touched. Her eyes, inches away, bored into his. He smelled her musky female odor, overlaid with smells from the old jacket. "Let me tell you what's insane, Dr. McKay. It's insane that my ex-husband didn't foresee this. I would verbally flay him up one side and down the other except that I know beyond a grain of doubt that he's already doing that to himself. It's insane that New America found antique weapons that what is left of the entire United States Army didn't find, or at least didn't find here. It's insane that we live in structures we didn't build, don't understand, and can't alter by so much as a molecule. It's insane that the only way the formerly greatest military machine on Earth can only communicate with itself is through one lousy comsat or else with human signalers through one relay station, like a nineteenth-century telegraph office. It's insane that New America can hold us in a state of siege until we either starve, or all fall into v-comas, or start eating our comatose patients, whichever comes first. All those things are insane. Getting a signal to the *Return* so they can rescue us is the only thing not insane."

Rescue—how? All at once Zack realized that Lindy had lied. She was keeping secrets. Colin Jenner probably believed the *Return*, which had conveyed him unconscious from the Settlement to the base, was going to swoop down and carry everyone off to safety. Lindy knew that the order would be to bomb the hell out of New America and everything else in a mile's radius.

Or did Colin know that, too, and was still willing to help Lindy even to the point of her own death?

And how long could the overcrowded, underprovisioned domes hold out without food coming in from the forest or Colin's Settlement?

Zack closed his eyes, opened them, and began easing Colin's chair down the steep, narrow stairwell.

Kubetschek took point. J Squad moved through the airlock that the "super-aliens," whoever the hell they'd been, had designed, and into the bot-bored tunnel beyond. A generation ago, on the *Embassy*, the analog of this airlock had served as a submarine bay under New York Harbor. In Colin's Settlement, it had led to a wide tunnel that slanted sharply upward to bring in stored crops. In domes used as Army bases, the tunnels went downward first so they could be more deeply buried, and were fortified with steel and concrete.

Jason walked directly behind Mason Kandiss. The only light came from their helmets, and the Ranger was a huge dark silhouette. They all moved quietly, but if New America was above them, and if they had among them a superhearer, then the enemy knew what Jason was doing. No way to calculate the odds.

At the end of the tunnel, Kubetschek and Goldman mounted the stairs. The others covered them from shallow alcoves built into the tunnel walls. However, that wouldn't help much if strong enough explosives came down from above.

Goldman tapped in the code to open the hatch. The old, familiar tension tautened the base of Jason's skull.

The two men touched the mechanism that raised the heavy, camouflaged hatch at the top of the stairwell.

It made a shocking amount of noise as soil, bushes, small rocks slid off the rising hatch. Dirt and pebbles clattered down the stairs, mixed with fat droplets of rain. But no larger noise of enemy fire. Kubetschek sprang through the hatch, followed by the other three members of J Squad. They took up defensive positions while Jason, at the top of the stairs, spoke urgently into his mic to the comsat somewhere above.

"Signal station, come in—code red, repeat code red!"

"Signal station here," Li said, sounding startled. "Sir?"

"Execute Operation Flamingo in five minutes. Repeat, execute Operation Flamingo . . . verification code Delta Whiskey Alpha. Repeat, Delta Whiskey Alpha."

A bullet whizzed past his helmet.

Instantly Kandiss was firing. Goldman covered Jason's body with his own as he shoved him back down the stairwell. Jason yelled, "Go! Go!" and all of them scrambled through the hatch, followed by a torrent of rain splashing down the steps. Goldman stayed to lock the hatch as the rest of them ran back through the tunnel.

Something heavy rumbled overhead.

A sniper . . . the stray bullet had come from a sniper, but more of the New America force had not been that far away. And now they knew where the hatch was.

Ten minutes. They had maybe ten minutes . . .

Boots rang staccato on the metal plates of the tunnel floor. Behind Jason, Goldman pounded along until he caught up to the others. The tunnel was wide enough for only three raggedly abreast.

Go, go, go . . . ten minutes. He didn't know what would happen if they were still in the tunnel when the *Return* dropped down from orbit.

In the other dome, Zack and Lindy bumped Colin's powerchair down the steps, one at a time. Colin winced but didn't cry out. "Christ," Lindy said, "you'd think the Army would have sprung for powerchairs that can climb up and down steps!"

Zack puffed, "You don't want . . . my opinion . . . on what the Army chooses to spend on or . . . not." God, he was out of shape. Lindy was lifting and hauling easier than he was. "Jenner, you okay?"

"Yes."

"I'm trying to not . . . sorry! . . . Okay, we're down."

"That's the airlock and decon to the tunnel," Lindy said, unnecessarily. "Zack, scan it open and then you stay here."

"I'm an RSA survivor and—"

"We don't need you. Colin will listen at the tunnel hatch, and if it's safe, I'll go out and contact the signal station."

"This whole idea looks stupider now that I consider it."

"Good, I'm glad you think so, because you're not participating any farther than this. Just wait on this side of the airlock to help with Colin's chair after we get back."

"If there's a hatch, what makes you think you can lift it alone?"

"It will have hydraulics."

"Do you know that for sure? You don't. And, Lindy—what if there's a code to open the hatch?"

"There is. I know it."

Zack didn't ask how. She'd been married to Jenner; she could have been told, or have stolen, any number of supposedly restricted things. He said, "I don't think you should—"

"Zack, now!"

Zack put his eye and finger to the scanner. It said, "Retinal scan and digital chip match. Dr. Zachary McKay." The airlock/decon chamber slid open.

Colin powered himself inside behind Lindy and raised his hand to the CLOSE DOOR button. The door closed.

Zack sagged against the wall. Would he ever see either of them alive again? And if Lindy succeeded in this mad scheme to alert the signal station, would either the soldiers there or the *Return* act without orders from Colonel Jenner? In fact, could anybody even pilot the *Return* now that Branch Carter was in a v-coma?

Spaceship, Monterey Base, signal station—each locked separately, unable to reach the others except by desperate measures, no better than the caged sparrows in the bird lab. Was this any way to run a war?

Decon could not be rushed, but without decontaminating everyone, RSA would win. They all went through the decon process at once, a tight fit for so many bodies. Jason counted each agonizing minute, squashed against Goldman and Kandiss. Kandiss's AR-15 jammed into Jason's side.

When decon was done and the airlock finished cycling, they exploded into Enclave Dome's storage area.

Thirty seconds. They'd made it with thirty seconds to spare.

Zack couldn't see Lindy and Colin—why didn't the airlock have some sort of wall screen to the tunnel beyond? Or something like that? Or—

The world shook and screamed and threatened to break apart.

Zack threw himself into the airlock and slammed his fist onto the DOOR CLOSE button. Another explosion shook everything—an earthquake? *Now?* It seemed long minutes before the airlock opened on the other side. Colin, the superhearer, sat just beyond the airlock with his hands pressed tightly to his ears; tears made trails through the dirt on his face. But he cried out to Zack, "Get her out!"

Lindy lay a short distance along the tunnel, which rained dirt and stone from gaps between the sagging ceiling plates. Zack grabbed Lindy, who was conscious but looked dazed—had she hit her head? She screamed when he grabbed her under her armpits and dragged her, but Zack had no choice. If that had been an earthquake, there could be aftershocks and the entire tunnel could collapse. He shoved Lindy into the airlock, closed the door—thank the gods that it still closed—and pushed START DECON. *Come on, come on . . .*

Decon hadn't finished when everything shook again. But the airlock was part of the original alien structure and didn't crack. Lindy moaned. Zack said, his voice too loud and too shaky, "Earthquake!"

"No," Colin gasped.

No? Then what?

"Bombs."

Whose? Did New America have those kinds of weapons? The dome had held . . . but what if it didn't go on holding?

Lindy moaned again. Then silence.

Jason said into his mic, "Major Duncan?"

"Operation Flamingo successfully executed, sir."

"On our way up."

J Squad, too disciplined to cheer, nonetheless looked as if they were hallooing and slapping each other on the back and high-fiving. But there was only Goldman saying, "Well done, sir."

They climbed to dome level and dispersed to stations per the OPORD. Jason, ignoring the frightened civilians—J Squad would explain and reassure—climbed to the command post and looked out through night-vision goggles.

The *Return*, its mission finished, had already lifted back to orbit. The bombs it had dropped, the most powerful nonnuclear weapons ever developed, had incinerated everything around both domes in a quarter-mile radius. In the eerie night-vision green, the scene was something from a nightmare. Forest burned, although the thickening rain would take care of that. It was already bringing down the dust and smoke of the carnage. The twisted metal of Strykers gleamed wetly. Debris lay everywhere, along with what was left of bodies. It would take days to clean up everything and refortify the tunnels.

Jason had gambled that the domes themselves could withstand the ordnance. The bombs had been experimental ten years ago; no one knew how powerful they still were. Now Jason knew. The *Return* would be back at first light. This job was only half finished.

He wasn't going to report to HQ until it was. Strople wasn't going to stop him.

Colin said shakily, "Can you get Lindy up the stairs? You can leave me here and put her in the chair!"

"No," Zack said. "I don't dare move her any more without a doctor—I have no idea where she's hurt. I'm going for help."

Lindy quavered, "*I'm* a doctor, I—" but Zack was already sprinting up the stairs. At the top, he found himself unable to unlock the door at the top. *Christ!*

Colin called, "What is it?"

"The door isn't recognizing me—I don't know why not!" It must have something to do with the earthquake, or bombs, or whatever the fuck had happened. He pounded on the door with his fist; nothing happened.

Colin called, "Come back down. She has an implanted mic and earplant."

Of course she did. Cursing himself for an idiot—Colin, who es- chewed technology, had remembered the mic and implant and Zack had not—he sprinted back down the stairwell. He bent over Lindy. She was speaking in short gasps, her voice full of pain. "Jason . . . help me . . . Lab tunnel . . . please . . ."

"Lindy, no—Jenner will be over in Enclave Dome, he can't hear you! Call someone else . . ."

But someone heard. Maybe the mic, or the frequency, was tuned to more than just Jenner. A few long minutes later multiple footsteps pounded down the stairwell. Claire Patel said, "What happened?" at the same moment that an Army sergeant thundered, "What the fuck are you people doing down here?"

Zack wished he had a good answer. He no longer knew.

Anything.

CHAPTER 16

When Dr. Holbrook came out of the operating room, Jason was there. Three o'clock in the morning, and Dr. Holbrook's eyes drooped with exhaustion; he was not a young man. He pulled down his mask and said, "Sir, she'll be fine. A broken rib punctured a lung, but she'll be fine."

"Will there be any permanent damage?"

"No."

"Can I see her?"

"She's sedated. They'll take her to . . . wherever they can find an empty bed, I guess."

A nurse found, or made, an empty bed in a tiny room whose empty shelves on three sides said that until recently it had been a storeroom. Lying on a gurney, Lindy looked small and vulnerable. Jason smoothed her hair, matted with dirt, away from her forehead. She didn't stir. Her left hand lay on top of the blanket. Bare—what had she done with her wedding rings? Probably put them in a drawer somewhere, as he had with his.

She breathed regularly, her small breasts rising and falling under the hospital gown. Was the 3-D printer still making gowns? He thought he remembered hearing that the raw material had all been used up, but maybe not. There was so much going on in these two domes that he did not, could not, keep track of it all.

When had he and Lindy lost track of each other? At the Collapse? No, they had still been working together then, overwrought and terrified and furious in those first few days when Jason had been snatching scientists and equipment, trying to outrun the spread of RSA in order to create an outpost of military research. He and Lindy had worked together at the start of the war, too. He had held her as she cried when they'd gotten the news of the nuclear strikes that had wrecked what was left of civilization.

So when? He had done only what was necessary to defend the base. To defend her. And, somehow, that had made him lose her.

Just as he had lost Jane to Colin. Although Jane, unlike Lindy, had never been his to begin with.

"Lindy," he said softly, "what the fuck were you trying to do in that tunnel?"

Actually, he already knew. The patrol, outside in the nightmare wreckage, had received the message from Captain Cooper, acting CO at Lab Dome. Jason had gone over there, picking his way through twisted wreckage and body parts in the streaming rain, and had learned the whole stupid story from Zack McKay.

Lindy had been trying to save the base. Jason had actually done so, by taking a terrible risk, and armed with bombs and military knowledge and a fucking *spaceship*. She had had nothing but courage and heart and a willingness to die if necessary.

He took her limp hand. So much emotion shook him that the floor seemed to waver. *Lindy.*

A noise behind him, and Jason turned. Colin, in his powerchair, sat in the doorway.

"Jason—Colonel Jenner—I need to talk to you. Alone."

Zack crept onto the bed beside Susan, who didn't stir. Sometimes v-coma patients twitched when touched, but not now. The curtained cubicle held two beds; Caity lay on the other. Zack put his arms around his comatose wife. Susan had lost weight. Always slim, now her bones felt as fragile as a sparrow's, as fragile as Zack's heart.

Everything in him ached: muscle, bone, brain. Colonel Jenner himself had questioned Zack about Lindy's plan, about the tunnel, about the entire disastrous enterprise, and the more Jenner questioned, the stupider Zack felt. Why had he ever agreed to help Lindy?

Because somebody had to do something, and Zack had not trusted that Jenner and his military were capable of that. Well, Zack had been wrong. The attacking forces had apparently been pulverized. The base was safe, and Zack was lucky he wasn't in prison for violating a military area or something. If they had a prison. If he wasn't so desperately needed in the "research effort." Which, like Lindy's plan, was going nowhere.

In the last twelve hours, another soldier, a civilian, and a Settler had fallen into v-comas.

He was, paradoxically, too tired to sleep. But eventually the sound of Caitlin's and Susan's breathing calmed him, the only things that could.

The only things that mattered.

Colin said to his brother, "You need to take me with you to Sierra Depot. It will be today, won't it? You need me with you."

It took all of Jason's self-control to not betray surprise. "Sierra Depot?"

"Come on, Jason—the attack you're planning."

"Why do you think there will be an attack on Sierra Depot?"

"I made it my business to know. I'm not stupid, even though you think my ideas about the Settlement are stupid. And unlike you, I'm not isolated by military protocol from talking to anybody at all. Nurses, cooks—do you know how much information cooks and kitchen help overhear in the mess? Your off-duty soldiers talk to the Settler women, who report to me. Soldiers speculate about what you're going to do with them. Some might even know."

Christ—Colin's intel network was as good as Hillson's. Maybe better. "I don't discuss strategy with civilians. Especially not civilians that engage in violations as stupid as the one you just did."

"It was stupid," Colin said, with his disarming candor, "but that was Lindy's plan. This will be yours and so I'm sure it will be well thought out and effective. The reason you need me with you is my hearing. I can hear things way before any of your officers can."

"We have technology to 'hear things.'"

"Not on the *Return*, you don't. Or if it's there, you don't know how to use it. Because you're going to go on the *Return*, aren't you? To bomb the jets at the depot the same way you bombed New America here?"

"Again, as I said—"

"I know, I know, you don't discuss strategy with civilians. But I can be an added resource, Jason. You need all the resources you can get."

Jason studied his brother's face, that face he had known as toddler, child, awkward teen, grown man. And yet how much did he know Colin at all? It was possible to become so familiar with someone that you ceased to see him at all. And since Jason had chosen West Point, their lives had diverged so much.

"Colin, why would you even want to go on any kind of military operation at all? You disapprove of the Army, of our tech, of everything this base is trying to do. Why go on an attack, if there were to be one?"

Colin said simply, "The kids."

"What kids?"

For the first time, Colin showed a flash of anger. "Don't play dumb with me. Jason. The two kids of Sugiyama's that New America captured and are still alive. If they are alive still."

"How did you—"

"Tommy Mills. That boy is confused as hell. But he's been in Sierra Depot, he came from there, and he's another resource you're neglecting. Seeing what happened to the one Sugiyama child really shook him. He wants to help get the kids out of there. Lindy told me—"

"Lindy? Lindy talked to you about all this?"

"We got a little drunk one night. This is all a huge strain on her, too."

Lindy and Colin 'got a little drunk one night'? A flash of jealousy seared through Jason like a first-degree burn. Jane, and now Lindy?

Colin, for once oblivious to Jason's state of mind, rushed on. "Lindy's having nightmares about the kids. About Sugiyama, too. I know you're not planning an extraction raid, but you've got Mason Kandiss, who's done them before. And Tommy says the Sugiyamas are housed separately and a little away from the main barracks. Even some of the New America soldiers are appalled at what happened to Frankie, and so General Blackwood moved them out of sight. And—why, Jason? What do they want from Sugiyama?"

So Colin didn't know everything. Not about the quantum computer, not about the launch codes for the Q14s. Colin's ignorance steadied Jason. He said, "What could you hear if you were on the *Return*? Nothing."

"Not until you open the airlock. I don't suppose that a Worlder ship comes with bomb-dropping equipment. You'll have to do it manually, won't you? From fairly low?"

Jason said nothing.

"I can hear a lot," Colin said, almost humbly.

Jason knew, had known all his life, how much Colin could hear. Plants making more noises than anyone had suspected. Imminent earthquakes, thunderstorms, air attacks. Mice underground, buried machinery, humans. The entire environment, which was why he was so sensitive to its fate.

"Please," Colin said. "Let me do something useful, Jason."

Jason tongued on his mic. "Hillson, escort Private Mason Kandiss and the prisoner-at-large to Lab Dome conference room immediately."

Marianne dreamed. Deep in v-coma, images formed in her brain, shadows born of new connections and new proteins, both built with old cerebral materials. But in that building, that unconscious construction, lay everything.

Gaze at the shadow of a building at midday and it looks sharp, well defined. Look at the building again at midafternoon and the shadows have gone soft and long, melting at the edges into other structures, connecting them in new ways. At night the shadows disappear, along with the building itself if the night is dark enough. But look by moonlight, by starlight. Look through night-vision glasses at the green images both familiar and infinitely strange.

It all depends on the light. On how much you can see, on how much appears connected to everything else.

Marianne rose almost to consciousness, stirred on her pillow, sank back into the shadowy depths.

The FiVee rumbled from Lab Dome an hour before dawn. The low cloud cover continued, although the rain had stopped and on the western horizon lay a thin strip of clear pearl gray.

Jason sat in the back of the FiVee with Mason Kandiss, two other soldiers with airborne experience, half of J Squad, Colin Jenner, the prisoner-at-large, and an exhausted Major Holbrook, who was too old to operate at midnight and do battle at dawn but who was the only Army physician they had. Only Kandiss and Jason wore esuits; the rest had already survived RSA, the invisible killer all around them. But Jason was more concerned with visible enemies.

The FiVee rolled over the charred and body-strewn perimeter of the base, then reached the rain-sodden forest. Smashing through and over saplings, bushes, hidden rocks, the vehicle was both noisy and easily spotted, but that no longer mattered, not until New America sent reinforcements. Jason watched Kandiss's lips move—a silent prayer? The big Ranger, 240 pounds and all of it muscle, sat on the parachute packs, with Colin's powerchair wedged between Kandiss and the truck wall. Tommy Mills crouched at Kandiss's feet.

The *Return* floated down to a new location, fairly close to the base. The troops jumped from the back of the FiVee almost before it had come to a complete stop. In five minutes everyone and the new equipment was on the ship and it was lifting. The most important resources were already aboard.

As always, Jason was struck by the amount of wide, empty space on the *Return*. This was a spaceship designed to carry people, their possessions, their animals, and their crops to colonize a new planet. Once, the United States had planned on doing that, too. Those plans had disappeared in the destruction of the Collapse and then the war, but maybe his country could have another chance. After all, it was to the United States that the Worlder ship had come. To Jason's base. It was his job to use and preserve it.

If Sierra Depot had acquired F-35s and Strykers, they might have acquired ground-to-air missiles that could take out anything below seventy-five thousand feet. And way below that was where Jason intended to go.

Corporal Michaelson escorted him to the bridge. Lieutenant Allen turned from the control console. "Welcome aboard, sir."

"Thank you."

"Awaiting orders."

He gave them. Allen's eyes widened. "Yes, sir."

"And maintain constant communications with the airlock, Lieutenant."

"Yes, sir."

"Do you know any more about the fuel situation than you did before?"

"No, sir. Unknown fuel source, presumably sealed inside somewhere."

"Then we'll just have to hope the ship doesn't suddenly run out of fuel and fall out of the sky."

"If so, I'll try to have it fall on Sierra Depot, sir."

Despite himself, Jason almost smiled. "Are you still navigating solely on visual?"

"Yes, sir. We'll have to drop out of the clouds at some point."

"I'll tell you when." Jason had maps and Allen had a compass; given a constant and known speed, he'd figured the time to Sierra Depot. Maps, compass, basic geometry—it was as if navigation had returned to the nineteenth century.

Jason returned to the large area near the wide airlock. Why so wide? Had the Worlders, whose "technology" Jane had described to him, brought beast-drawn carts through here, along with the sophisticated telescopes and other tech that their bizarre society permitted or the super-alien tech bequeathed to them?

Everyone was in position. The inner door of the airlock was already open. Colin and Tommy were both harnessed to the wall, close to the outer door; neither would fall out if the ship abruptly tilted with the outer door open. Everyone wore oxygen masks except Kandiss and the two airmen, who wore parachute harnesses. Just beyond, the designated bombardiers stood with the same lethal explosives that Jason had just dropped on his own base.

Tension prickled through the area like heat.

"Allen, *now*," Jason said.

There was no sensation of motion. But on the wall screen, the gray mass of clouds below them became a gray wall filling the screen, and then they were below the clouds, dropping low. The airlock door opened. Tommy and Colin leaned forward, into the cold air.

Below them, Sierra Depot lay in dawn light. Mostly a support facility, it had no dome. Once the depot had been a 34,000-acre, high-desert supply, maintenance, and repair facility, ideal for outdoor storage of rows and rows of vehicles along with its many buildings. Even before the Collapse, changes in weather patterns combined with budget cuts had greatly reduced the depot's stocks of everything. RSA had left so few survivors that much of the rest had been closed. When the war started, the remaining troops had defended the depot bravely until re-inforcements arrived. Before that happened, however, the commander had destroyed everything he could not defend, so that it wouldn't fall into New America's bloody hands.

The depot had been chosen to house the top secret quantum-computer project precisely because a supply depot was not a place an enemy would look for it—but that was before the enemy included ren-egade pieces of the Army itself. Sierra's CO had been prepared to blow up the buried quantum project, too, but that hadn't been necessary. The depot had held until New America had captured it a few weeks ago.

Jason asked Tommy Mills, "Where are they being held?" The *Return* hovered over the remains of so many battles: rows of blasted vehi-cles, charred barracks, twisted metal storage units. An area to one side, circled by an electric fence, held lighted buildings. Tiny, antlike figures patrolled, undoubtedly raising alarms.

Tommy shook his head, his young face squinched into fantastic anx-iety. Then he pointed. "That building there . . . by them trees . . . I think that's it. . . ."

"Allen, sixteen degrees north from current position . . . *Colin?*"

Colin, eyes closed, bit his lip. "I can't . . . no, wait . . . yes. That build-ing there, the one off by itself." As the ship dipped low to fly over the building, Colin sagged in his chair with efforts Jason could only imag-ine: straining his hearing to take in everything below, filtering out what he didn't need, searching mind-deafening noise for one muddied signal. No time to ask if he was sure. F-35s could scramble in three minutes. Missiles could launch even faster.

"Allen, hold position. . . . Now!"

The *Return* hovered briefly and the three airmen jumped. Only three . . . But Jason had no time to think of that now. Kandiss would have to make what he could of surprise. The *Return* lifted and flew quickly back over the base to the airfield. Small figures ran toward the jets. Three men, five . . . Jason had no time to count them before bombs from the *Return* dropped and obliterated them all.

They crossed the base again, dropping bombs as they went. Jason peered out the airlock. Christ, they had rows of Strykers . . . from where? He watched them all go up in smoke and flames. The explosions sounded like the end of the world. Debris leaped into the sky, almost immediately obscured by smoke.

A surface-to-air missile whizzed by the ship, slowed, returned. Heat-seeking.

"Lift!" Jason shouted and the *Return*, faster than he would have thought possible, rose higher than the missile could go. The outer air-lock door closed. Jason felt O_2 flow into his mask.

"Allen, again," Jason said. There were more buildings. This time it would be more dangerous, but it had to be done. He had no idea what weapons, brought at who-knew-what time and distance, had been stored in which buildings.

Nor did he know under what structure the quantum computer was housed, or if it could withstand the pounding that the depot was receiving from the *Return*. It might be that Jason was destroying his own last, most powerful weapon, even as he destroyed the enemy.

They dodged two more heat-seeking missiles. But when Jason finished, there was nothing left of Sierra Depot, except for the one building beyond the trees.

"Allen, land on my command, ten degrees . . . now."

The *Return* set down north of the building. J Squad ran out. Half took up defensive positions; half ran toward the building. Over the tops of the trees, oily smoke and orange flames rose lurid to the dawn clouds.

Eight of Jason's best soldiers disappeared into the building. Jason said, "Colin?"

"I don't hear any gunfire. No, wait . . . I do now."

The minutes seemed like hours.

Ten figures left the building. Two of them carried children; two had adults slung over their shoulders. Gunfire erupted from the trees.

J Squad returned the fire, and in a hail of bullets Jason's unit returned to the ship, which immediately lifted. He closed the airlock. Colin cried,

"No . . ." a second before the ship took a hit and the impact rattled Jason's teeth. "Allen, go! Stay low but go!"

If they could . . .

The *Return* listed, as shocking as if the ocean had suddenly rose from a calm sea to a fifty-foot tsunami. But then the ship righted itself and flew off, barely reaching a thousand feet.

"Can you keep it flying at this height?"

"I don't know, sir!"

"Try to lift."

"Ship won't go any higher."

"Okay. Go back to base."

Colin said, "Open the airlock and let me listen. I can hear any machinery on the ground."

Jason did. It seemed to him only a slim safety, but if there were missile stations along the way and if Colin couldn't detect them, the *Return* would be shot out of the sky. And this was the only way home.

At a thousand feet up, the *Return* glided over desert and forest and hills, rising and falling with the terrain, just as if the ship did not have an open airlock and a huge hole in her side. Air whooshed through as in a hurricane.

"Allen, slow down before we're all sucked out!"

"Sorry, sir." The ship slowed and the wind became less than a gale. Jason watched Holbrook bend over the prone figures on the deck.

Corporal Wharton was dead, shot as the three airmen breached the building. Kandiss had carried Wharton's body; Rangers never left a comrade behind. Dr. Sugiyama, also carried out, was unconscious, and when Jason saw what had been done to the physicist's face, he felt sick. One of the children, the girl, lay gasping and batting everyone away. The little boy clung to the airman who had carried him out, even as the soldier tried to pass him to someone else. The child started to scream, which set the girl screaming too.

Holbrook, opening Sugiyama's shirt, said tightly, "Take them away. They shouldn't see this."

Christ alone knew what they'd already seen. But Jason said to Ku-betschek, "Take them to another room," even as the girl started to shriek, "Daddy! Daddy!" and the boy screamed even louder.

When the children had been forcibly removed, Jason knelt by Sug-iyama. "Doctor . . ."

"He isn't going to make it," Holbrook said. "What they did . . . he will die soon."

"Can you revive him enough for questioning?"

Holbrook grimaced. "No. And it will be a mercy if he stays oblivi-ous to the pain."

Jason stood. Kandiss sat beside the dead airman, the Ranger's lips moving in prayer. Wharton would be buried with military honors in the base's expanding graveyard beside Private Sendis, the soldier who had died defending Colin's Settlement.

Flying low and slow, it was noon before the crippled *Return* reached Monterey Base. There had been no further attacks. The dead and wounded were carried inside through the carnage and debris around both domes, and Jason and a guard took the FiVee to the signal station. Before it left, Colin grabbed Jason's sleeve.

"What happens now?"

"I report to HQ." He yanked free of his brother.

"And then . . ."

"We clean up the base. Patrols check out the woods. We hunt and forage. Maybe you get to be the founding father of another quixotic settlement. Jesus, Colin!"

"I meant what happens to you."

"Court-martial," Jason said briefly, and climbed into the truck.

CHAPTER 17

Jane dreamed.

A voice came to her speaking her own language, sounding as if from a great distance and yet filling the inside of her head, a voice calm and measured as oceans: "You do not choose your enemies; they choose you."

I want no enemies! Jane tried to cry out, but her own voice was muffled, wrapped in thick folds of flesh that clogged her throat.

A closer voice, startled, said, "She tried to say something!"

"No, she . . ."

She what? Was Jane "she"? Who was she?

Then voices and identity both disappeared, sinking into velvet blackness, into even deeper sleep.

Zack, bleary, looked up from his lab bench, where it seemed to him he'd spent days, weeks, possibly years. Claire Patel stood in the doorway. From her face, whatever news she was bringing him wasn't good.

"Zack, three more v-comas. Do you want to test them for the allele?"

"No. They'll have it." But three more comatose people affected the allele frequency rate. "How many does that make, total?"

"Thirty. Plus Kayla Rhinehart and Glamet^vorⱼ."

Thirty-two out of about seven hundred people: roughly 4.5 percent. "Who are the new v-comas?"

"A kitchen worker, a soldier, and a lab tech from Dr. Sullivan's team."

The lab tech was faintly surprising: Lab personnel had been exposed earlier to the star-farers than had the Settlers, yet this tech was just now lapsing into v-comas. But, then, there were always variations in innate resistance.

He focused more sharply on Claire. He didn't know her well; his insane hours working meant he'd barely interacted with anyone from World except Marianne. Claire was small, pretty, drooping with fatigue even though it was only around noon—wasn't it? He'd lost track of time. He said, "Aren't you supposed to have an Army bodyguard with you? Where is he?"

"He's the soldier who just went comatose." She took a step forward, hesitated, raised a hand and let it drop, and then it all burst out of her. "I can't do anything for them. Nothing. The nurses keep them clean and turned and hydrated. But we're running out of nutrient solution, and then what? And there is nothing I can do for the v-comas. I can't do anything for anybody else, either. The soldier brought in from the raid was dead, Sugiyama died twenty minutes ago, and the children won't let anyone near them."

"A raid? What children? Wait . . . Frank Sugiyama the *physicist*?"

"You didn't know that Colonel Jenner attacked Sierra Depot this morning?"

"No! I've been—"

"The Army destroyed those fighter jets that New America's been strafing us with, plus everything else at the depot, or at least that's what Colin Jenner said. He was there. They brought back Sugiyama and his children, but Sugiyama had been tortured and his kids are traumatized beyond belief."

Colin Jenner? A raid? Why didn't Zack ever know what was going on?

Tears, silent and the more terrible for being silent, slid down Claire's cheeks. She swiped them away. "Sorry. I just feel so . . . helpless."

"We all do."

Except, apparently, Jenner. Zack tried to catch up to events. "Then New America won't be attacking the base anymore?"

"Well, not from Sierra Depot, anyway. Zack—are you any closer to finding out anything useful about these comas?"

"No. We—"

A newly recruited nurse, very young, dashed into the lab. "Doctor! They need you now! The alien—the boy—"

"Belok^?" Claire said sharply.

"Yes! A few minutes ago, nobody was there except his sister, but then I—"

"What is it, Josie? Is Belok^ dead?"

"No. He woke up."

A flock of birds nested on bushes just outside the new signal station. The station had been hastily dug by a bore-bot into the side of a sloping ravine. Jason, accompanied by Captain Goldman, tried not to slip on the muddy hillside on the way to the camouflaged entrance. Rain sparkled on tall weeds; at the bottom of the ravine a brook murmured. He paused briefly to scowl at the birds.

They were sparrows. Until RSA, Jason could not have told a sparrow from a goldfinch, but everyone had learned about sparrows. Native to Eurasia, the small, plump, gray-brown house sparrows were now found on every continent except Antarctica. Some idiot had introduced them into the United States in 1852. They weighed about an ounce, liked to bathe in dust, hopped rather than walked on the ground, ate seeds and insects. House sparrows were mostly monogamous, although adultery occurred often. They laid two to seven clutches of eggs every year. They would build their domed nests almost anywhere—in bushes, under eaves, in cacti, on top of streetlights for the warmth. They liked to be near groups of humans.

This group was settling down to roost. They chirruped to each other: *orphilip orphilip orphilip*. A few tucked their heads under their wings, preparing to sleep. An adorable illustration from a children's book, deadly with unseen plague. Jason restrained himself from pulling out his sidearm and shooting them.

Inside, this version of the signal station was small and crude, the worst one Jason had seen yet. Two muddy pallets on the floor, rations in plastic bins, three buckets of water, and the sophisticated console connected to the even more sophisticated equipment hidden somewhere in the forest outside.

Li and DeFord saluted.

"As you were. Lieutenant, Specialist, you are both commended for carrying out your part of Operation Flamingo perfectly."

"Thank you, sir."

"I need a link to HQ."

"Yes, sir," DeFord said, grimacing. He knew—they both knew—what was coming. Jason had chosen DeFord carefully, knowing that he needed someone here that he could trust as much as Li. A member of J Squad, DeFord was one of those men who make unlikely but excellent soldiers: short, weakly muscled, able to think outside of Army boxes, bright as hell, and fiercely loyal to Jason, who had saved his life during the Collapse.

When he had the comm link to General Strople, he stepped back and Jason seated himself at the console. "Sir, Colonel Jason Jenner reporting a successful raid on Sierra Depot."

"Proceed."

There was no way to tell how much Strople already knew. The radar at Fort Hood would have tracked the movements of the *Return*. But unless there were additional comsats that Jason didn't know about, something he would once have thought impossible but now was not so sure of, Strople didn't know the rest of it.

"As per your orders, sir, I made the decision to attack Sierra Depot based on my knowledge of the situation. The enemy was using the depot as a base for their newly recovered, or imported, F-35s and armored vehicles. A concerted attack on Monterey Base from both air and land led to the start of a siege. We destroyed the force surrounding the base, but our supplies are depleted and New America could have mounted a second siege from the depot. More of my troops are lapsing into comatose states, from which medical personnel can't extract them. My intel, as per my prior report, was that Dr. Sugiyama was being held at the depot. That raised the possibility of his cooperation with the enemy in accessing the quantum computer without its self-destructing. For all these reasons, I determined on the attack, which was carried out at oh-six hours this morning. The depot has been destroyed. An airborne unit extracted Dr. Sugiyama, who has since died of injuries inflicted by torture. Also extracted were his two young children. Sugiyama was not conscious at the time of extraction and has provided no useful intel."

"What is the situation of the quantum computer? Is it intact?"

"Unknown, sir."

"So you don't know if it can still launch the nukes."

"No, sir."

"How did you destroy the force surrounding Monterey base?"

"With bombs dropped from the spaceship *Return*."

"And how did you destroy everything at Sierra Depot, possibly including the quantum machinery?"

Jason closed his eyes, opened them again. Here it came. "The same way, sir."

"You told me in a previous report that the spaceship was not capable of flying laterally more than a hundred miles if it was not in high orbit."

"I did, sir."

"Are you telling me, Colonel, that you deliberately lied to me?"

"Yes, sir."

The voice fifteen hundred miles away remained calm, but Jason heard in it not only the anger he expected, but something like triumph. "Repeat that, Colonel."

"I falsified information supplied to Headquarters."

"Why?"

Because I don't trust you, you bastard. Something is going on at Fort Hood that looks a lot like a military coup, with you as the leader of a South American–style junta.

"The *Return* is a diplomatic vessel, sir. It does not belong to us, and its use is predicated on the consent of the leader of the World expedition, Dr. Ka^graa. Turning it over to Fort Hood would have violated international law."

"You do not get to make that decision, Colonel. Was your second in command, Major Duncan, a part of these acts?"

"No, sir."

"Was she aware of the raid before it was carried out?"

"No, sir." Another lie.

"You are hereby relieved of your command, Colonel Jenner, and are under arrest for actions that may have aided and abetted the enemy."

A stretch to get treason out of falsifying information, but Strople could make it stick. After all, there was no one above him to dispute the charge.

Strople added, "I wish to speak with Major Duncan."

"She is at the base, sir, and I am at the signal station. I thought it advisable for her to remain at base in case my FiVee was taken out by New America on my way here or back."

"You're going to wish it had been, Colonel. That would be better than what's going to happen to you now. The signal station personnel must have been involved in directing the spaceship."

"Information Tech Specialist David DeFord aided me. Lieutenant Li was overpowered and restrained."

"Where is Li now?"

"Here, and still captive, sir."

"You will release him at once, and he will arrange for me to speak to Major Duncan. Specialist DeFord is also under arrest. Who else is with you at the station? Identify yourself."

Goldman stepped forward. "Captain James Goldman, sir."

"Did you have prior knowledge of Colonel Jenner's deceiving HQ about the capabilities of the spaceship?"

"No, sir."

"Did anyone else know?"

"I have no knowledge of anyone, sir."

Jason said, "General, no one else knew. The decision was mine. Everyone else acted on my orders, assuming that I had received them from you."

"No one else was involved in this conspiracy?"

So now it had become a conspiracy. "No, sir."

"Uh-huh. Captain Goldman, you will take custody of both Colonel Jenner and Specialist DeFord, relieve them of their weapons, and immediately transport them to base. There you will imprison both until further orders concerning their courts martial. Do you understand?"

"Yes, sir," Goldman said.

"Lieutenant Li, you will remain at the signal station. Contact your perimeter patrol at the base and arrange for me to speak to Major Duncan as soon as she can be transported to the signal station."

When the farce had finished, all the actors playing their parts, Jason turned from the console. Li, Goldman, DeFord. Plus Duncan, Hillson, and the perimeter soldier on duty, Laura DeSoto, a lifer who was also a member of J Squad. And, of course, Jason himself. Benjamin Franklin had famously written that two people can keep a secret as long as one of them was dead. This was seven people. He trusted every one of them.

In the Army that Jason had joined, this cabal would not have been possible. Personnel, information, legal documents, orders all had flowed across the country—across the *world*—in rapid, verifiable, closely surveilled streams. But this was not the Army that Jason had joined. This was the army of nineteenth-century isolated forts, of twentieth-century cabals and juntas, of a stray and damaged spaceship, of an enemy on American soil made up of Americans with no police to stop them from seizing whatever they wished.

I have violated my oath as an officer in the United States Army. Except—
he did not believe that. Now his duty to his country lay in preserving
the scientists at Monterey Base and the diplomatic mission from World,
so that together they could find a solution to what had destroyed the
old Army along with everything else.

The penalty for treason in wartime was death.

But maybe there wouldn't be any court-martial. Maybe the order
would come later today to summarily execute Jason and DeFord. If so,
nobody but the seven of them would hear it.

"Jim," Jason said to Goldman, "we're returning now to base."

Belok^ sat up on a pallet, in a row of pallets divided by inadequate curtains. La^vor crouched beside him, holding his huge hand. The boy
blinked his large dark eyes, looking dazed. Zack hung back as Claire
knelt on the floor beside the rumpled blankets.

"Belok^? Kar^ judilᵢ?"

La^vor spoke rapidly in World; Zack couldn't tell if Claire understood her. Claire listened to Belok^'s chest, shone a small light into his
eyes, tested his reflexes. Belok^ said nothing, but the skin between
his eyes wrinkled slightly.

La^vor stroked her brother's hand. It seemed to Zack that Belok^ was
gathering himself, trying to pit his challenged, mostly wordless mind
against circumstances. He looked slowly around the cubicle, then directly at Claire, at La^vor, at Zack. Some emotion moved in the depths
of his eyes.

Zack felt the hairs on his arms prickle.

La^vor went on murmuring to her brother.

Belok^ stood up. He staggered, stiff with not moving for so long, and
Zack saw how thin his arms had become in his coma. La^vor jumped
up and let him lean on her. From his great height he looked down at
her upturned face. "La^vor," he said slowly.

She answered in World, something reassuring. Zack braced himself.

Now Belok^ would say the name of his dead brother, Glamet^vorj, and she would have to tell him that the only other pillar holding up Belok^'s universe was dead.

Belok^ looked all around once again. Then, haltingly, he said something in World: something of several words, something that might have been an entire sentence, something he had never been able to say before. Then a second entire sentence.

And none of the other three, frozen by surprise, managed to say anything at all, until Zack said in a voice that didn't even sound like his own: "Caitlin."

Caitlin had not woken, nor Susan, nor any of the other v-comas. When Zack had finished checking, he returned to Belok^'s cubicle. The boy was sitting up, broad back against the wall, while a clutch of medical personnel peered at him from the corridor. Claire said, "La^vor, kar^ . . . I mean, hee^kan . . . no . . . we need Jane for this!"

Zack said, "I'll go get Ka^graa. He can't translate like Jane, but he's the best we've got. Besides, he's the head of the World expedition."

"No, he's not," Claire said crossly. "But go get him anyway."

Zack didn't want to leave. In the corridor, a young Army nurse, Josie Somebody, hovered at the edge of the silent crowd. He said, "Please go find Dr. Ka^graa and bring him here. Right away."

An expression of distaste flitted across the girl's face. But she said, "Okay," and walked off. A soldier rounded a corner of the corridor and said something to her, but she shook her head and moved on. Zack returned to Belok^.

He was still speaking, fluently and without hesitation.

Claire, who'd rocked back on her heels, looked as if she'd been hit with a two-by-four. La^vor was weeping. Zack got out, "What is he saying?"

Claire said, "He's hungry."

"Is that all?"

"I can only get a few words, but mostly, yes, it seems to be that he's hungry. Also that he wants to see Glamet^vorį. She hasn't told him yet. But, Zack, it's not what he's saying . . . it's that he's talking so much and so easily."

"I know." And then, "Colin Jenner and the others . . ."

Claire nodded, understanding without Zack's finishing his sentence. Colin Jenner and the other superhearers had had their auditory centers rewired in utero by the original *R. sporii*. The infants, hypersensitive to sound, had cried nonstop until drugs were developed to tamp down their ability. Some had stayed on the drugs for life. Some, like Jenner, had been bright enough to learn to compensate, as bright children learned to compensate for dyslexia. They had learned selective attention, still hearing the incessant background noise but paying attention only to those they chose at a given moment.

Microbes in the fetal brain had done that. Microbes, that for two billion years had been the dominant form of life on Earth. That had evolved complex and sophisticated signaling techniques, gene-swapping techniques, interdependencies, antibiotics to kill each other. Microbes that, through the union of two prokaryotes, had begun the long evolutionary march toward the multicelled organisms that eventually became humans. Microbes, that still made up one-third of the cells in the human body, outnumbered humans on Earth by a factor of 10^{22}, and could produce a new generation every twenty minutes and so had adapted to—and modified—every available ecological niche on Earth, clear through the stratosphere, solely to aid their own survival.

What had microbes created for themselves in Belok^'s brain?

"Zebras," he said aloud, and Claire looked at him as if he were crazy.

CHAPTER 18

By the time Jason reached base, Elizabeth Duncan had her orders from Strople, brought in from the perimeter by Private Laura DeSoto and delivered as if both of them didn't already know the orders would not be obeyed.

Jason jumped out of the FiVee in the armory airlock, went through decon, and left Lab Dome for Enclave. Between the domes, soldiers grunted and swore as they cleared away wreckage from New America's attack. Jason didn't ask what they did with the enemy bodies; he could see the mass grave at an edge of the charred forest. Carry-bots trundled body bags and sacks of lime. Amid the devastation, the twin energy domes shone almost obscenely bright in the afternoon sun.

At the command post, Elizabeth Duncan said, "You look like shit, sir."

Jason blinked; she had never spoken to him with anything approaching such informality. He said, "You don't look great yourself, Major."

"Do you think Strople will promote me, now that you're in stockade?"

"Probably."

But neither of them could sustain the banter. He had been up for thirty-six hours and sagged with fatigue, and banter was foreign to Elizabeth Duncan's nature—had she rehearsed it to try to reassure him of her loyalty without any embarrassing sentiment? Unwritten rules forbid them to name what they had actually done: falsified information and retained control of a United States Army base after being relieved of command. To name things was to give them greater power—although it was difficult to see how this situation could have more power over either of them than they had already committed to. But they had made their decision, they'd made it together, and for good and sufficient reasons.

Still, Jason had been unwilling for as good a soldier as Duncan to go down with him. If it came to that, he and Specialist DeFord would go alone to court-martial, and Strople would never know that Major Duncan plus four others had collaborated with Jason. But it was not going to come to that.

She said, "Sir, General Strople has ordered me to bring him the *Return*. I told him the ship is too damaged to fly that far."

Which might, for all they knew, be true. "Did he believe you?"

"I don't know. But he pretended to. He's sending a unit here for the court-martial and to take control of the base."

"Sending? How?" If they had somehow acquired more planes or functional choppers and the fuel to fly either . . .

"FiVees. A convoy of eleven vehicles."

Jason blinked. "You're kidding."

"No. I calculate about ten days."

Over the broken roads, through the desert and up the shattered coast . . . no way to refuel except with what they carried with them, the possibility—no, the certainty—of attack by New America. . . .

"They want the *Return* that bad," he said, and it wasn't a question.

"Yes. Or they don't believe that I wasn't complicit in your decision."

"Fuck," he said, knowing that she had never before seen him lose control, "fuck, fuck, *fuck*."

"Yes, sir."

"We can't catch a break."

"You took out Sierra Depot."

Her voice held uncharacteristic admiration, in which there was nothing personal. In another world, Jason thought, she could have commanded the entire US Army; she had the necessary toughness, control, and intelligence. If the Collapse hadn't happened when it did, she'd have risen through the ranks faster than he did. Instead she stood a chance of going down with him.

He said, "Elizabeth, when the convoy arrives, I'll be in the stockade along with DeFord and you will disavow any knowledge of—"

A scuffle outside the closed door. "No!" said the soldier on duty, and Duncan's hand moved to her sidearm. But when the door was flung open, Claire Patel stood there.

"Sorry, sir . . . she insisted and I didn't want to . . ."

"It's all right, Private. Dismissed."

"Colonel Jenner—I'm sorry to burst in like this but you have to be told now . . . Belok^ is awake."

For a disoriented second, Jason couldn't remember who Belok^ was. Then he got it. "Out of his coma?"

"Yes!"

"The others?"

"No, but they're all being closely watched. There's more. I examined him, and he's changed. He can talk now."

"The coma made him able to talk?"

"It did something inside his brain. No, don't ask for details because we don't know. But he's different now."

The other v-coma victims had already been able to talk. Jason's exhausted mind fumbled at Claire's unspoken ideas. She moved forward a step. "We don't know what it means, no. But Zack McKay's spinal-fluid analyses seem to indicate massive alteration of brain chemistry. The kind of chemicals that usually indicate more formation of synapses, more pruning of synapses, the sort of profound changes that are usually seen only in small children and adolescents."

"Doctor," Duncan said, "do you mean that the v-coma victims will wake up with increased verbal fluency?"

"We don't know, Major. That's the whole point."

Jason said, "Monitor the situation and keep me informed. Dismissed."

Claire grimaced; too late, he recalled how much the civilian doctors and scientists disliked it when he addressed them as if they were soldiers. Well, tough. He had more important things on his mind than civilian touchiness.

But then Claire's face softened. "Colonel," she said, gently and yet with the note of defiance that said she knew she was overstepping boundaries, "I'm sorry to say this, but you should get some sleep. You look like shit."

Zack thought that the next v-coma to wake up would be Caitlin, since she had gone comatose at the same time as Belok^. But it wasn't Caitlin. At evening, the little girl still lay comatose in the same cubicle as her mother, and the nurse said there had been no change in either of them. Zack gazed down at his wife and daughter, reached out, touched Susan's hand. It felt so warm, so alive . . .

"Dr. McKay," said the same nurse he'd sent to find Ka^graa. Only now she looked oddly defiant. "There's another v-coma awake."

"Where?"

"Bed on the end." The nurse turned away . . . sneering? Why?

The bed on the end held Toni Steffens.

Head Nurse Amy Parker bent over Toni, who batted her away. "I'm fine. Nicole?"

"Still comatose," Amy said. "Dr. McKay, Major Holbrook will be here in a minute."

"Zack," Toni said, wonderingly. And then, "I have the motherfucker of all headaches."

Well, whatever had been going on in Toni's brain had not changed her personality. But her broad, intelligent face looked puzzled. Holbrook strode in.

"Dr. Steffens? How do you feel?"

"Headache."

"I'm going to examine you. Everybody out, please."

Zack waited, fidgeting from one foot to the other, just outside the curtain, until Holbrook emerged. "Vitals are all fine," he said. "I don't think it's wise to give her anything for the headache until we—"

"I can hear you, you know," Toni said. "No, I don't want anything for the headache. And no, I'm not a superhearer now, you're just loud. Be quiet and let me think."

Think? Zack pushed his way into the cubicle. Toni struggled to sit up, her nutrient IV bobbing, her puzzled expression replaced by such intense concentration that she seemed frozen all over again. Holbrook said, "It would be good for you to walk now, Dr. Steffens."

Toni didn't answer. Eventually she said to Zack, "Tell me what's happened while I was comatose."

Where to begin? "New America attacked the base with fighter jets and—"

"Not that." Toni raised her newly thin arm and waved it, brushing aside New America, the base, and the fighter jets. "What happened in the lab. Not with the v-coma analysis—with the avian gene drive."

"Nothing. Toni, you know that." Had her memory been affected? "All work on the gene drive was dropped to investigate the v-coma and try to—"

"Shut up now."

Zack held on to his temper. He and Holbrook glanced at each other, neither knowing just what they were dealing with, uncertain how to proceed. A minute passed, two. Then five very long minutes.

Toni pushed back her blankets and tugged at her IV. "Get me out of this thing. Out of here."

"Be careful," Holbrook said, "your muscles will have partially atrophied and—"

"Get me out and to the lab. Zack, I need your help."

"With what?"

Toni looked at him. Her puzzlement was gone. She gazed at him with what looked like . . . was it pity?

Toni said, "I'll try to explain in terms you can understand. Stop me if I go too fast."

Jane stirred on her pallet, caught in the twilight between sleep and wakefulness, where the real and the imagined cannot be told apart because all things have become possible. She was with her lahk sisters in their house of curving karthwood; she was on Terra under a dome; she floated free in a dark space of cold, glowing stars. Creatures scampered through the walls, through her blankets, through her brain. Voices rose and fell, or were they waves on the beach at Kle^chov^olı̧? No, they were the stars themselves, rumbling before they exploded in novae of gas and speeding particles and the end of everything. . . .

"They're killing us," a star said.

"And he's letting them."

"Nah, Josie, the old man's all right. He stopped the attack by the Newsies and pulled off that raid on Sierra that—"

"And he let in them fucking aliens that're killing us!"

"Nobody dead yet—"

"Might as well be—"

"For two cents, I'd—"

"Watch your mouth, Carl."

"Quiet, you guys, my head nurse is coming . . ."

But no one was coming, Jane was alone except for the things scudding through her brain: leelees . . . no, Terran "mice" . . . no, something else . . .

Then nothing, and again she slept.

Another morning, after another long and mostly sleepless night. It might, Jason thought blearily, be an interesting experiment to see how long he could go sleepless without losing the rest of his mind. Parts of it seemed gone already. His thoughts moved slowly, through tarry mud, and in circles.

Eight days until the convoy arrived.

Court-martial.

Running out of supplies.

Toni Steffens. Belok^.

Eight days . . .

"Sir?" said the private on duty outside the command post. Jason hadn't even heard the door open. "Dr. Ross asks to see you."

"Dr. Ross?"

"Yes, sir." The private peered at him; did Jason look that bad? Probably.

"Let her enter."

"I'm already in," Lindy said, pushing past the guard.

Jason said, "Dismissed."

Lindy closed the door. There were still bruises on her face, but unless she wore some sort of brace or bandages under her clothes, she didn't seem to be suffering from her reinflated lung. She wore her determined look. Jason straightened for the blow. "What is it? Have v-comas died?"

"No. And nobody else has revived, either."

"Dr. Steffens?"

"I haven't been to the lab—Claire Patel is there, examining her yet again. Or trying to, since Toni won't stop working long enough for much examination. She's got everybody over there doing things and she's barking orders like General Patton."

"Working on what?"

"I don't know, I'm not a virologist. I'm also not there, I'm here."

Jason snapped, "Why are you here? I didn't send for you." The snappiness, he dimly realized, was cover for a barrage of emotions fired by just seeing her.

"No. I'm here to examine you. Jason—Colonel, sorry—you're showing disturbing signs of sleep deprivation. Two different people have told me so. And—"

"Who? Who told you that?"

"—as your physician—"

"You're not. Major Holbrook is. Where—"

"With the v-comas. They're not waking but they're stirring. I'm it, Colonel, and I'm going to examine you. Now." She pulled out a porta-lab and moved toward him.

Jason submitted. She could give him drugs to keep him going, maybe something that would last until the court-martial was over. Even at West Point, where designer pharmaceuticals had been ubiquitous to ward off sleep, to keep the body going through the physical punishment of training and the mental fog of studying while exhausted, Jason had avoided drugs. He hadn't wanted to surrender control of his faculties, not even to something that was supposed to enhance them. He'd kept to the same puritanical policy while in combat in Congo. But this was not West Point and the combat here couldn't be worked out in physical activity, and Jason could see the end of his strength rolling toward him as inexorable as the convoy coming up from Fort Hood.

"Dr. Ross—"

"Be quiet, I'm not done. I'm taking a quick blood sample."

Could she see how much her nearness disturbed him? She moved close to lift one of his eyelids and he could smell her, that spicy female odor . . . How long had it been for him? Masturbation was not the same. . . . He felt his cock rise and how could that be when everything else on him was barely functional? Christ, let her not notice. . . .

"Jason," she said quietly, "you have to sleep. Your reflexes are off, your skin is sallow and your eyes puffy. You have way too much corti-sol in your blood. Soon you're going to have tremors, impaired concentration, and forgetfulness, if you haven't already. I'm going to give you something that won't put you out so completely that you can't be roused in case of emergency, but will nonetheless let you sleep. And Major Duncan is perfectly capable of taking over for a few hours."

"Okay," he said, and watched her eyes widen with surprise.

"Okay? Well, good. You should take two of these at—"

"Sir!"

Hillson, flinging open the door with no announcement, no ceremony. The master sergeant's face wore the wooden expression that meant extreme rage. His shoulders looked carved from granite. Jason said, "What is it?"

"A homicide, sir. Corporal Winfield is dead. Private Dolin is under arrest."

Winfield? A member of J Squad, he'd been on the raid at Sierra Depot, he'd parachuted down to extract the Sugiyama kids. . . . Jason's mind fumbled at trying to place Private Dolin, and failed. He said, "What happened?"

"Corporal Kandiss—"

"Kandiss was involved? Did he kill Winfield?" A sour stickiness formed in Jason's throat.

Lindy said, "Is a doctor needed?"

Hillson ignored her; perhaps he didn't even hear her. "Sir, what happened was that Dolin drew his sidearm on Kandiss, who wasn't armed, but Dolin didn't know that Winfield was there, too. Winfield tried to disarm Dolin and Dolin shot him. Then Kandiss disarmed Dolin."

"Where did all this happen?"

"At the brothel, sir."

The brothel, where Settler women tried to spread indoctrination of Colin's nature philosophy. A weird arrangement, but you couldn't lock soldiers, most of them male, into two domes without a brothel developing, however informally. Colin had found out about it within days of arriving at the base. Jason hadn't asked its location.

"Where's Dolin?"

"In the stockade."

Where Strople thought Jason was. Or maybe not. Did Strople have suspicions that more was going on at Monterey Base than he'd been told? Of course, Jason thought, more was also going on at Fort Hood than Jason had been told. Unless . . . Christ, he was so tired.

"Sir . . ." Hillson said, looking suddenly uncertain.

"I'm fine, Sergeant. Begin a formal investigation immediately. Report to me no later than this evening. Dismissed."

"Yes, sir." Hillson left.

Lindy said, "An investigation? Are you going to . . . will there be a court-martial?"

She didn't understand. Jason passed his hand over his eyes, even as a detached part of his mind thought: *That, that thing I'll have to do—I have never done that before in my life.*

"Jason? Will there be a court-martial?"

"No. We are at *war*. Dolin shot a fellow soldier. The investigation will find out why, but it doesn't really matter why. He did it."

"And you . . ."

Jason opened his lips to order her out, to stop her questions, to remove the scent of her that brought back so many memories, but no words came out. He felt his knees give way. He staggered, caught himself, sagged against the desk.

"Jason—"

"Go . . . away."

She didn't. She took another step forward. He stumbled again—how could he stumble when the floor was supporting him?—and she caught him.

Her touch undid him. All of it undid him: the long months, years, of trying to hold together a base of military and scientists who were needed—both groups—to save the world but did not trust each other. The murder of Winfield, which Jason should have somehow prevented. The murder by torture of Sugiyama's little son and Jason's failure to rescue Sugiyama in time. His looming court-martial, into which he had dragged six good soldiers. The fruitless work of the scientists in stopping RSA, the mission to which Jason had sacrificed his military honor by defying orders. The wreck of the *Return*, the wreck of the United States he'd sworn to serve, what he was going to have to do to Dolin, all of it all of it all of it . . .

Then he was in Lindy's arms, the sobs shaking his whole body but

nonetheless silent because a colonel in the United States Army did
not cry.

"Shhh," Lindy said, "shhhh, it's all right. . . ."

The stupid statement sobered him. It was *not* all right. He pushed
her away, but she caught at him, her small hands surprisingly strong.
He remembered that.

"Listen to me, Jason," she said, but without a trace of either command
or plea. Maybe she still remembered that the best way to deal with him
had always been with calm facts. "You are under enormous, even su-
perhuman strain. You've done an incredible job, but no one can control
everything, especially not in such an insane situation as this. If you keep
blaming yourself for every single thing that does not go perfectly, you
will drive yourself mad. And you can't do that, because the base needs
you. And I need you."

That last was said in the same steady, reasonable voice as the rest,
without emphasis. For a moment Jason wasn't even sure he'd heard it.
But he had; Lindy was letting the need show in her eyes.

So she was braver than he was, after all.

"Right now, you must sleep. I'm going to give you something for
that. Hillson can conduct his investigation and then you can . . . do what
is necessary. You have to have Dolin executed, don't you? Yes. I'm sorry.
But I'll tell you this—he didn't kill Winfield over any fight in a brothel
over a girl or money or drink or whatever else anybody claims. Dolin
was after Kandiss because some of your soldiers blame the star-farers
for bringing the virophage to the base and causing the v-comas. They
can't reach Marianne or Jane or the other comatose because you have
guards on the infirmary, but they could reach Kandiss. And Dolin
wouldn't have even tried it if he didn't have more soldiers ready to lie
for him about it."

"I know."

She smiled, a complex smile he couldn't read. "Of course you do.
Jason, you're doing the best possible job under the worst possible circumstances. Now, take these."

She handed him two pills. He took them without water, a pointless piece of macho toughness, and sagged into a chair. Lindy stood over him. He closed his eyes, but she was still there.

"Lindy," he managed to choke out, "Lindy . . ."

She went still beside him.

He reached out, groped for her, and pulled her down on top of him, even as he rolled both of them off the chair and onto the floor.

"Lindy . . ."

"Shhh," she said.

"I can't . . . I want . . . You've always been . . ."

"Shhhhh." She reached for his belt, tugging with her small, strong hands at the buckle.

It took a while for the sleeping pills to work.

CHAPTER 19

Zack watched Toni. It was unsettling to not know what he was see-ing. He was unwilling to admit that he had become a little afraid of her.

He saw his old friend and colleague, looking physically unchanged. Toni wore the same tee and many-pocketed pants she had always fa-vored, although now they hung on her; during the v-coma she had lost weight. Her gray-streaked brown hair was pinned back in its usual care-less bun. She bent over the lab bench with the same round-shouldered stoop.

He saw her unchanged concern and love for Nicole, whom Toni vis-ited three or four times a day, each time striding from the lab to the v-coma ward to stand wordlessly at the end of Nicole's pallet. Toni never stayed more than a few minutes. Once, she whispered something in Nicole's ear. The comatose body on the bed didn't stir.

He saw Toni's intense concentration as she worked, as she had al-ways worked. The researchers in the next lab, Drs. Sullivan and Var-gas, worked on the samples taken from Toni's and Belok^'s bodies. Toni worked on the avian gene drive. To carry out her experiments, she'd commandeered as many lab techs as she could. The problem was that she couldn't work with them. Zack saw her frustration that not even he could follow what she was doing.

Toni would bark out a sentence—sometimes just the fragment of a sentence—about her work. The problem, Zack eventually figured out, was that she was giving a report that left out several things: the intermediate steps to get to her process, the results of those steps, the scientific hypotheses that had led her to those processes in the first place. It was as if she expected Zack and the assistants to grasp those from what she'd said. And none of them could.

"Go back, Toni," he said, so often that he grew even more impatient than he was afraid. "Start at the beginning of what you did, and why." And she would look at him as if he were a not-very-bright fifth-grader instead of her department head. *Explain?* her look said. *Why would I need to explain to you how to add sixteen and seventeen: add the six and seven to get thirteen, put down the three and carry the one . . .*

Then she would try to explain, and that was even worse. She was apparently holding several different strands of thought at once—that's what she called them, "strands"—as graphics in her mind, enormously complicated and detailed graphics. That let her see connections among them that she was pursuing both mathematically and experimentally, each step of which changed a graphic in ways that in turn changed all the others. She couldn't, or wouldn't, draw it for him: "Too complicated." And he could follow only a small part of it.

It made him humble.

It made him resentful.

Humbly and resentfully, he worked the intricate process of modifying DNA. The genes they modified would be injected into sparrows in the subterranean bird lab; the gene drive would incorporate itself into the sparrows' reproductive machinery. The birds, artificially brought into mating readiness, would copulate and lay eggs. If Toni succeeded, embryos inside the eggs would carry a gene drive that would render all male offspring sterile.

If.

"Denatured random coil one sixty-four, with molecule fifteen," Toni said, and Zack was supposed to know what she wanted him to do about the engineered folding of a protein he had never known existed.

Then all of it—proteins, genes, eggs—fled from his mind. An

Army nurse entered the lab, protected by his scrubs from Toni's scowl. "Dr. McKay," he said, "your daughter is waking up."

Caity had climbed off her bed and onto Susan's, trailing her IV. When Zack dashed into the cubicle, she looked up at him fearfully. "Daddy! Mommy won't wake up!"

He lifted Caity in his arms. "Yes, she will, honey. She needs to sleep now. Come on, let Mommy get her rest. Nurse, can this line come out of her arm? Can she . . . oh, Caity!"

The nurse detached Caity. Zack carried his daughter—where? There was no place to take her in this crowded makeshift coma ward, where now even the corridor held sleeping figures on gurneys. Zack clutched Caitlin as if she, not he, were a life raft. Her little body felt hot in his arms; she smelled of soap and a wet diaper, although she was far too old for diapers. He ducked with her into a supply closet, its shelves ominously bare.

The nurse followed, alarmed. "Dr. McKay, we need to . . . she must be examined! I've sent for Dr. Patel!"

"A minute . . . just give me a minute!"

"Daddy, I feel funny."

Alarm shot through him. "Funny how? Nurse! Come back!"

Caitlin vomited all over him.

Toni and Belok^ hadn't done that when they woke—had they? "Nurse!"

Then Claire was there, taking Caitlin from him, laying her on a clean bed somewhere—how had they gotten to this cubicle? Zack, paralyzed with fear, didn't remember. But Claire was saying, "It's all right, Caitlin, your tummy just hurt for a minute. . . . Zack, there was almost nothing in her anyway, I'm not finding anything abnormal . . ."

Caitlin lay quiet on the bed, gazing solemnly at the three adults clustered around her, at the small crowd visible in the corridor beyond.

This was an event: a third v-coma victim had revived, the first child to do so.

Claire said gently, "How do you feel now, Caitlin?"

"Good."

That same unblinking gaze, Caity's eyes traveling from Claire to Zack to the nurse, from the nurse to Zack to Claire. The stillness of her small body, as if everything in her was concentrated in her eyes, or what was going on behind her eyes. The adults all holding their breaths, waiting . . . for what?

The suspended moment spun itself out longer than Zack could stand. "Caity, sweetheart . . ."

"I'm good, Daddy," she said in her high child's voice. "I'm not sick.

"I'm just thinking."

Jason had never had to do this before. Had never expected to do it. There was no protocol. There were only eight soldiers and a doctor on a charred stretch of land beside an alien dome, in a gray dawn.

The day before, after sex with Lindy, whatever drug she'd given him had let him sleep nine hours straight. He'd woken to a message from the signal station, addressed to, and delivered to him by, Major Duncan. The convoy, five days from Monterey Base, had been attacked by New America. There had been a firefight, and New America had won.

Duncan, her lips drawn in such a tight line that words barely fit through them, said, "General Strople says he will send another convoy, more heavily fortified, but he can't do so until next month. He says to keep you and DeFord in stockade and to turn all available resources to the repair of the *Return*. He wants that ship, sir, and he wants it bad."

"Yes." Bad enough to cause the deaths of a convoy of his troops. New America did not take prisoners, not unless the prisoner was someone who, like Sugiyama, they thought could be of use to them. Had the convoy been underfortified? Or did New America have more scavenged weapons, more powerful weapons, that Jason didn't know about? He knew for sure only one thing: the annihilation of the convoy had bought Jason more time. Time paid for by the deaths of yet more men and women, because of him.

And now he was going to cause another death.

They stood on the east side of Lab Dome, just beyond the armory airlock. Gray clouds seemed to hang directly overhead and a light drizzle fell on the burned-out woods. Jason was the only one in an esuit. If he had permitted himself, he would have felt at a disadvantage, a commander more vulnerable than his troops. He did not permit himself to feel that, or anything.

"Lieutenant, conduct the prisoner to the . . . the pole."

Dolin staggered a little as he was walked to the shoulder-high stake driven firmly into the ground twenty feet away. The pole was the trunk of a dead sapling, dragged from beyond the woods and stripped of its branches and leaves. The exposed wood where branches had been torn away looked pale against the remaining bark.

Dolin lurched again, and his escort clasped him more firmly. Jason had instructed Holbrook to give Dolin some sort of drug to dull anxiety and pain. Maybe it was keeping Dolin quiet as well, although Jason had not asked for that.

He had the results of Hillson's investigation. He had conducted a hearing as well—not a formal court-martial but more than Dolin was entitled to under the rules of war. He had Dolin's confession, offered not only freely but sneeringly, with all the vitriol of a man who knew he had nothing more to lose: "I shot the fucker defending Kandiss, and I tried to shoot Kandiss too. Them cunts brought the sickness to the base and if you wasn't an alien-loving traitor who don't deserve to command a *latrine*, you'd of shot them all out of the sky before they even landed on Earth. Fucking lily-livered coward!"

The lieutenant tied a blindfold around Dolin's eyes, then walked away.

Jason said, "Raise weapons."

He didn't know any other way to do this. The United States Army was at war, by a valid vote of Congress even if Congress no longer existed. He was commander. He would not order a backroom lethal injection, or anything else that could give rise to rumors of torture. The five men with raised rifles were all volunteers, but all carefully vetted. None, as far as Hillson could tell, were likely to lie about what they were doing, or to turn and shoot the base commander. None of the five was Kandiss.

Dolin sagged slightly forward in his bonds, straightened, sagged again. Maybe he was drifting in and out of consciousness. Jason had not specified how high a dosage Holbrook should administer.

This man had willfully murdered a fellow soldier, while trying to murder another.

The United States was at war.

"Fire," Jason said.

Five weapons laid down fire. If any of the guns were aimed to miss, Jason didn't need to know about it. Dolin's body jerked, jerked again, blossomed into red. The guns fell silent.

"Lower weapons," Jason said.

Holbrook declared Dolin dead. The body was cut down. The burial detail moved into action, covered by the others.

Jason and Holbrook returned to the airlock. Just before he went inside, he heard a flock of sparrows somewhere begin their morning song.

Zack sat in the conference room of Lab Dome, beside Colonel Jenner—an unwelcome juxtaposition he had not planned. The room, as always, held more people than it should. Someone had moved out the table (putting it where?) and brought in more chairs. These were packed in so close that Zack could smell the mustiness in Jenner's uniform. He tried to edge away, but it was impossible.

Did all these people really need to be here? Maybe not, but everyone wanted to hear the first results of the team analyzing the awakened v-comas, and apparently Jenner had okayed this as an open meeting instead of a military briefing. So in addition to every scientist on the base and some of the techs, the room contained all three physicians, as much of the nursing staff as could be spared, Ka^graa—although no one to translate for him—more officers and, standing against a side wall, two privates who had recently awakened from comas. Zack, like everyone else, took furtive little peeks at the man and woman, whose faces showed no hint of whatever they were thinking.

The only significant people missing were the other three who'd awakened from comas. Caitlin was a child; Belok^ was a functional child; Toni had refused to leave her work on the gene drive. "His Highness can do without me."

Major Denise Sullivan made the presentation. Her broad, kind face looked pinched with exhaustion, but she stood straight and spoke without either notes or polite preliminaries. Everyone here was well beyond preliminaries.

"Analysis of cerebral-spinal tissue from those who awakened from v-comas"—she nodded at the two privates—"hasn't, so far, turned up much more than we knew from samples taken when they were asleep. There are proteins we haven't seen before, as well as different and new folds in proteins commonly found in the brain. Proportions of various proteins are different. Specifically—"

She went into details. The presentation was pitched badly: too simple for Zack and the other scientists, who already knew all of this, too technical for the military. Without turning his head—he didn't want to be rude—Zack watched the two soldiers standing against the side wall. They were the most interesting people in the room. What was going on in those altered brains? Their faces gave nothing away.

"So in summary," Denise finished, "at the cellular level, we cannot yet explain much. What we do know is that only people with what we're calling 'the coma allele' go comatose. In the coma, profound

changes occur in the brain that may indicate both increased neural connections and altered neural connections, and that the result, according
to IQ tests administered to all awakened subjects, seem to show a leap
forward in intelligence.

"If the increased brain activity resulted only from increased
density, length, or thickness of neurons, there would probably be a
problem with overheating of brain tissue, since the brain would then
use more energy and so generate more heat. Human cortical gray-
matter neurons already had axons that were pretty close to the
physical limits. Therefore, the most likely situation is that the greater
proportion of the changes in brain functioning are due to revised
connections and functioning among the neurons that were already
there."

Suddenly she threw her hands into the air and let them fall. "But we
have no idea how. It may be that different receptors that affect how the
brain works are being inhibited or activated, just as the dCA1 receptor
is activated in memory formation. Or it may be that the v-coma patients
are undergoing acquired savant syndrome. This all needs much more
work, and that work requires, in part, equipment we don't have."

Major Duncan said sharply, "What is acquired savant syndrome?"

"Sometimes trauma to the left side of the brain—always the left
side—results in people acquiring savantlike abilities they didn't have
before: to do mathematical calculations in their head, remember long
strings of numbers, that sort of thing. The theory is that the ability was
always there, latent, and the trauma destroys whatever mechanisms
were inhibiting it. But savants often have trouble with social relations,
too, and as far as we can tell, the v-coma subjects do not."

Caitlin, cuddling in Zack's arms, asking for a story, giving him a
flurry of kisses. No, she had no trouble with social relations.

Duncan was not done with her questions. "Why did privates
Ramstetter and Veatch, who fell into comas later than some other victims, revive earlier?"

"We don't know."

"Does that mean their brains underwent less rewiring than did others because they were comatose a shorter time?"

"We don't know." Denise hesitated; Zack knew what she was not saying. The gain in IQ *was* less for the two soldiers than for Caitlin, Belok^, and Toni. But IQ tests had always been suspect, and here the other three subjects were a child, a boy who had been mentally challenged before, and an already brilliant scientist. Not good data, and Zack saw the moment that Denise decided not to mention it.

Duncan asked another question, and now her hostility to the entire presentation became obvious. "And you—all of you scientists—are telling me that the human brain was remade by some tiny microbe? By a *germ?*"

All of Denise Sullivan's apologetic uncertainty vanished. She stared steadily at Major Duncan. "Rabies, which destroys the human brain, is caused by a 'germ.' Toxoplasmosis, which causes humans to choose riskier behavior than they would otherwise, is caused by a single-celled parasite. Superhearing, a profound rewiring of the auditory areas, was caused by *R. sporii*. The ATCV-1 virus—"

"Thank you, Doctor," Colonel Jenner said. "Is anyone else going to speak?"

Marissa Freirich rose hastily. She was one of the two schoolteachers in Enclave Dome, although lately no school had been held in the general disruption. At the Collapse, she'd been a twenty-one-year-old, brand-new fourth-grade teacher at the elementary school on Monterey Base. Now she worked with Caity and Belok^. It was clear that lecturing to this group of scientists and top brass intimidated her, but she plunged ahead.

"Before his coma, Belok^ spoke only a few basic phrases. Now his speech level is about that of a four-year-old, in both English and World, and he is learning to read. Caitlin McKay, who *is* four, could already read simple picture books. Yesterday she read aloud the first few paragraphs of *Alice in Wonderland*. In the original, which includes words like 'conversations' and 'marmalade.'" Marissa bit her lip. "She doesn't even know what marmalade is. Sounding out words isn't the same as experience. But she has definitely gotten smarter. She—"

Colonel Jenner interrupted, but not with the sharpness that Major Duncan had shown. "Is it your sense that the intelligence of these children will just keep on growing? That they'll get more and more intelligent over time?"

"I don't . . . of course I'm not a scientist and it isn't for me to say if . . . all I do is . . ."

"You work with those children," Jenner said, relentless. "What do *you* think?"

Marissa said, "I think they had a big leap in intelligence and now they're learning to use that. I don't think that each day they're getting smarter than they were the day before."

Without twisting his body on his chair, Jenner turned his head to look at his two soldiers. All he did was blink once. The female private said, "Yes, sir. She's correct."

The male said, "Yes, sir. Agreed."

Then Marissa, displaced schoolteacher, said outright what Dr. Denise Sullivan had only tiptoed around. Marissa said, "Either way, some of my students are getting a lot smarter and the rest are not."

There. She had named it, the elephant in the room. Humanity bifurcating. If the changes in neural structure or efficiency were permanent and also inheritable, the human race was on its way to becoming two species.

Not an elephant in the room. A swamp's worth of dinosaurs. Or—

An entire herd of zebras.

CHAPTER 20

Two weeks after the meeting with the scientists, neither Jason nor Elizabeth Duncan had been told anything about a new convoy heading north from Fort Hood. This was surprising: Why was Strople delaying the start of a second convoy? Jason's best guess was some sort of internal upheaval at Fort Hood. Duncan had no opinion, or at least none that she offered aloud.

The two of them stood in the command post, watching the horizon. Beyond the stumpy woods charred in the destruction of New America's siege, trees blazed red and gold and orange, bright spots among the more somber pines. Somewhere farther north, on a flat field defended by nearly everything in Monterey Base's arsenal, a crew of specialists and civilians repaired the hole in the *Return*.

They worked under an Army engineer and a sergeant who had, in his youth, been a welder. They used supplies of metal found on the huge ship, guessing at how to use those to seal and heat-proof and whatever else you had to do to the hull of a spaceship to let it rise higher than a thousand feet. Both men admitted they had no real idea what they were doing.

"Sir, if the bastards had hit any of that there alien machinery," Sergeant Lewis Dunfrey had said during one of Jason's visits to the site, "it woulda been all up with that flying boat. But the RPG didn't hit nothing vital." After a minute he'd added, "I hope."

Duncan said, "If Major Farouk were awake . . ."

"Yes," Jason said. More people had come out of v-comas, but not the physicist.

Jason had chosen not to be present at the repair site when Lieutenant Allen tried to lift the ship. If the entire vessel exploded, he would be needed to come up with a different strategy.

He half expected the *Return* to destruct. Not because he had the wispiest idea of the physics or engineering involved, but because the total destruction of the *Return* would somehow match the total destruction he had visited on Sierra Depot. Not that any of that made sense.

"Here she comes . . ." Duncan said. Jason felt her tense beside him.

A gleam on the horizon. Sunlight reflected so directly off the hull that Jason's vision blurred. He looked away and when his gaze swung back, the *Return* was rising, rising, a streak in the blue sky like molten silver on the sea. Silent, swift, so beautiful his heart stopped. Then the ship was gone.

He barely dared to breathe. Long minutes later, she fell back out of the sky, slowed, hovered, and rose again. Whole, functional, returned from orbit.

Jason turned to his second in command. To his surprise, tears stood in her eyes—Elizabeth Duncan! He pretended not to notice, and the next moment the tears were gone.

"It worked," she said in her usual dry voice.

"Yes."

One thing gone right.

The duty guard knocked on the door. "Sir, a message from Lab Dome. Dr. Farouk has woken up. You said you wanted to know when it happened."

Jason glanced at Duncan. She said, "Better late than never."

"Like so much else," he said.

Days later, Jason arrived at the command post early in the morning, after a night with Lindy. The night had not gone well.

It had been his fault. They hadn't been together since the day before Jason had executed Dolin. She was kept so busy with the awakenings—eleven of them now—and he with running a base short of supplies, routine, and answers. But last night's tension had not come from those inescapable cares. "You're avoiding me," she'd said to him yesterday. "Why?"

Sometimes he wished she were less direct. "I'm not."

"Yes, you are. I waited for you to . . . never mind that. You've got something on your mind, Jason, something you're not telling me. What is it?"

And less perceptive.

She repeated, "What is it?" but now her tone was softer, more concerned, Lindy at her most gentle. Damn her! Accusative Lindy he could have resisted; merely sexy Lindy he could have enjoyed. But this was Lindy evoking the kind of bond they had once had, in which they told each other their deepest desires and fears, as Jason had never told anyone else. This was the Lindy of long sweet conversations in bed after orgasm, wrapped in each other's arms or propped up on pillows with glasses of wine or making the kind of silly jokes that grew from a long marriage. But he could not tell her that in the eyes of the United States Army, he was no longer in command of Monterey Base, was under arrest, was facing court-martial. That deception was known only to six other people, all bound to silence, and he could not be the one to break the secrecy that was eventually going to endanger so many. He had, after all, been its architect.

So he said, "It's nothing," and watched disappointment and then hurt darken Lindy's eyes. And still she didn't give up.

"All right. I don't believe you, but I'm not going to press it."

Lindy! When hadn't she pressed, pried, burned through his reticence with a laser cutter? That was why he'd been able to be himself with her in the first place, why he had fallen in love with her. She had pushed him into love, and he had landed into more happiness than he'd thought possible. Until the war began.

He still loved her. He knew that now. Jane had been a momentary attraction; it was Lindy he wanted, needed. But it wasn't fair to her to reconnect, not when chances were that Strople's troops would execute him for treason. It would be too much like soldiers who quickly married before deployment, only to create widows and widowers. Jason had always considered that selfish behavior. Better to wait until you could offer, if not security, at least a living body. Until you were a little more in control of events.

Lindy said, "Spend tonight with me anyway, Jason. I just want to feel you next to me, inside me." And she'd touched him, quickly and furtively, in that special caress only she knew that he responded to, and then tossed him a mischievous smile over her shoulder as she walked away.

Maybe his reasoning was wrong.

So he'd gone to her, and they'd tried to make love, and it had been a failure.

"It doesn't matter," she'd said, "it happens to all men occasionally. Look at the strain you've been under . . . it's all right."

"No."

"Jason, love, you can't control everything."

The old accusation, and even though this time it hadn't been an accusation, just a sweet reassurance, Jason had shut down. It was not all right with him. He'd said, "I think you should go now, Lindy." His tone had been wrong and, stony-faced, he hadn't corrected it. Lindy had left his quarters hurt and angry. He hadn't gone after her.

Not fair to her, none of it. The rest of the night had been sleepless.

Dawn broke, pink and gold and angelic, over the burned forest. Then a knock on the door—Christ, this early? Hillson must never sleep. But it wasn't Hillson.

"Sir," said the guard, "Major Sullivan to see you."

The scientists almost never requested to see Jason, especially at the command post. The daily reports to Jason from Lab Dome all said the same thing: no more information about brain changes. More v-comas were awakening, and all showed the same increased intelligence as the first ones. Dr. Steffens was working day and night on the gene drive for birds, with no results. No vaccine, no boosted human immunity. Nothing changed. And yet, here was the head of the vaccine team. Hope surged in Jason.

"Show her up."

Major Denise Sullivan appeared at the command post with a sheaf of printouts and a puzzled face. "Sir? Something major to report on the virophage."

"Proceed, Major. Do you have—"

"The vaccine? No. I'm sorry, I shouldn't have started like that, it's not the vaccine, it just has to do with virophage transmission, but I thought you should know . . ."

It wasn't like her to be this flustered. Jason waited.

"We've been looking at how the virus affects those who don't fall into comas. The controls, you know. The epidemiological graphs, which I've printed out for you in incremental time units, plotting blood samples versus—"

"Major," Jason said, summoning patience, "cut to the chase. I don't need the graphs. Just tell me what the graphs say about transmission."

"Yes, sir." She tilted her head slightly, obviously thinking how to phrase this simply enough for Jason, and he thought that she looked in that moment like a large bird.

She said, "Everybody is infected with virophage. Everyone here. But if you don't have the allele, the virophage seems to leave your body after a period of time ranging from two days to seven. Your immune system fights it off. Like a rhinovirus."

"A . . ."

"A cold. But if you are, or were, a v-coma, the virophage stays in you. And then you can go on infecting other people."

"For how long?"

"Unknown. But from the contact diagrams we constructed, the transmission goes on after you come out of the coma. That seems to be how subjects twenty-nine and thirty-one contracted it. If you look at graph sixteen-A—"

"I will. But let me see if I understand this. I had the virophage, but it's gone from my body now, and I can't infect anyone else. Dr. Steffens, who was in a coma and is now out of it, can go on infecting people and if they have the right genes, they go into a v-coma and come out smarter."

"Well, there are nuances that you haven't . . . but yes, sir. Basically, yes. Metabolic cascades . . ."

"Major, I don't want this discussed with anyone who doesn't already know about it."

"But, sir—"

"That's an order, Major."

Jason was thinking about Dolin, Winfield, Kandiss. If this intel entered the base's rumor factory in some twisted form, it wouldn't change who could or could not fall into v-coma, but it might fuel the anti-starfarer sentiment out there. Without the *Return*, after all, there would not be any virophage on Earth, nor any division among those who could spread it further and those who could not.

Jason said, "Leave those graphs with me. I want to study them. Anything else?"

"No, sir." She left. But before Jason had time to study the virus-transmission graphs, Hillson appeared. The master sergeant's entire body was so rigid it looked as if he were encased in invisible cement. This was Hillson in his most extreme rage.

"Sir," Hillson said.

Jason said, "The second convoy has started from Fort Hood. Finally."

"Yes, sir. I just received the encrypted call from Lieutenant Li."

So whatever turmoil had been going on at Fort Hood, delaying a second convoy, had been solved, or subdued, or killed, and Strople was still in command. Or again in command. Either way, he was confident enough of his troops to now send a detachment rumbling north to claim the *Return*.

"How long?"

"I estimate ten to fourteen days, sir, but of course it depends on weather, on if New America attacks them, on the state of coastal highways."

Those had not been maintained for ten years. Rock slides, forest encroachments, bridge collapses. The Strykers could pretty much go through or over anything, but not fast. And thanks to the climate shifts of global warming, which had been halted but not reversed, parts of the terrain between here and Texas were rainier and muddier this time of year than they had been in centuries.

"Did Li say anything else?"

"No, sir. The signal station will monitor the convoy's progress via the *Return*. But there is something else."

Of course there was. Hillson was not in this stiff, contained fury because the convoy had left Fort Hood. Jason waited.

"Six soldiers have deserted. Gone." Hillson listed them, spitting out the names as if they were rotten fruit pits. "They took weapons, supplies, bivouac tents, and gear. Sometime in the night."

Jason said nothing, a little surprised to learn that he was not surprised.

"Sir, I can organize a search party in half an hour. With quadcopters, or you can bring the spaceship down to—"

"No."

Hillson blinked. "No?"

"No. Let them go. They can either be picked off by the enemy or found a settlement that—I assume all six are RSA survivors? They didn't take any esuits?"

"All survivors. But, sir—they are *deserters*. In time of war."

Jason understood what Hillson was not saying: Jason had executed Dolin but was taking no action against these six. Inconsistent, bad for discipline, bad for morale, Army regs . . .

"Hillson, let them go. In ten days I won't want them here anyway."

Hillson's face crinkled into a fantastic terrain of bewilderment. Was there contempt there, as well? No, not yet. But Jason couldn't tell, didn't know, what Hillson would think about the much larger decision that Jason had to make soon. Hillson, loyal and tireless and meticulous, nonetheless lacked imagination.

In less than ten days.

But not yet.

"Yes, sir," Hillson said unhappily.

The duty guard opened the door. "Sir? Dr. Patel is here."

Christ, it was practically Grand Central Station in here. "Send her in. That's all, Sergeant Hillson."

"Yes, sir."

Claire Patel walked in, her small upright figure stiff with determination. "Colonel Jenner, a word, please."

"Certainly."

"I'm concerned that the Awakened in the lab are working too hard. Doctors Steffens and Farouk, and the two lab techs who were in a coma before. Their bodies now require more energy and maybe more sleep—we don't know why—but they're hardly sleeping and they're eating only when forced. All four of them are losing weight and starting to show signs of sleep-deprivation psychosis. The medical staff has tried reason, argument, and orders, and none of them will listen. As commander here, you could order them to preserve their own health."

"How would I do that, Doctor? Except for Dr. Farouk, aren't they all civilians?"

"We're under martial law, aren't we? Lock them in their rooms, or somewhere else, for six or seven hours and they'll sleep. Put food in there. You could order that."

"I could. I will not." Didn't she see the kind of resistance that imprisoning civilians—civilians!—"for their own good" would cause on a base already fragmented into military and scientists, those who welcomed the star-farers and those who resented them, those emerging as superintelligent and the rest of us poor slobs? She did not. All of them, Patel and Hillson and even Lindy, saw the situation here through their own lenses, and no other way.

"You won't intervene to save their lives?"

"Are they in danger of imminent death?"

She hesitated. "No."

Claire Patel was always honest; that was why he'd asked her that question. Jason said, "Is their work yielding any useful results?"

"Not yet."

"Will it?"

"I don't know."

More honesty. Jason almost said, "Dismissed," but not only should he not do that, it wasn't necessary. Dr. Patel turned to go. But she had one more parting shot.

"Colonel Jenner, your grandmother has woken up. She's not young. I hope she doesn't overwork herself in the lab, as well."

Marianne was not in the lab. She sat with Colin in the conference room. A group of Settlers had been in there with him, discussing plantings for the garden that had to be created all over again outside the dome since, while Marianne had been comatose, there had apparently been a terrible battle. Colin asked the Settlers to leave the room and they had, trailing children and bits of environmental conversation. Colin sat in a powerchair, his injured leg in some sort of cast, regarding his grandmother with intense curiosity.

"No," she said, "you first. Tell me everything that happened while I was comatose. How were you hurt?"

He did. Part of her mind listened intently, although it was an effort to slow comprehension to the speed of his words. The rest of her mind kept evolving the thoughts that had seized her since she'd woken up four hours ago.

Night in the dome—dim lights, soft breathing beyond closed curtains, solitary footfalls in the corridor. She lay in the v-coma ward, yes.

A narrow bed, a green Army blanket that was too warm. She didn't move it yet. She lay absolutely still, mental fingers that were still Marianne tentatively touching her new mind, as if it were a lab specimen.

It was not. It was her. She was not fragmented, not fundamentally different. But her thoughts ran on parallel lines simultaneously, and the tracks crossed and recrossed, making connections she could not have made before. The image came to her of a yarn sculpture she had seen once, long ago, so intricately and fantastically knotted that each strand seemed to connect to every other in ways that her linear mind could not conceptualize.

Linear no longer.

She lay there for three hours, making neither movement nor sound, knotting strands. Her old watch, still on her wrist after journeying to the stars and back again, glowed with the time. Eventually, a nurse moved silently through the curtains.

"I'm awake," Marianne said.

The nurse brought Lindy Ross. Marianne submitted to Lindy's examination but said little. Lindy finished by saying, with unnecessary force, "Marianne, you must eat. Your brain is now using more glucose, and you are already in ketosis. I'm going to send food in here now."

"All right," Marianne said, and for the first time, Lindy smiled.

She ate. She walked up and down with an orderly, until he was satisfied that she would not fall. She dressed in her own clothes, which she found in a plastic bag under the bed. She wanted to talk to someone, but not Lindy, who had seemed agitated and distracted. Someone who might understand the thoughts in her head. Zack McKay was, Lindy said, asleep—"Finally!"—and shouldn't be disturbed. Jane was still comatose, Ka^graa too hard to talk to without Jane's translations. Claire, the nurse said, had gone to Enclave Dome. Dr. Steffens was here, but apparently she would not leave her lab work to talk to anyone, even Jason. Jason himself was out of the question. He would listen, but he would not care about the topics knotting themselves fantastically through her brain.

Ryan? No. Marianne loved her son, but he was now more frail than she had ever been.

She slipped out of the ward and asked a startled soldier on his way to the mess, "Where can I find Colin Jenner?"

"Ma'am?"

"Colin Jenner," she said patiently. "Please find him and then take me to him."

He hesitated, evidently weighing his choices. She was, after all, the CO's grandmother. He said, "Yes, ma'am," and delayed his breakfast long enough to hunt up Colin in his Settler meeting and take Marianne to him.

When Colin had finished his recitation of attacks and counterattacks; of his and Lindy's supremely stupid, brave attempt to get a message to the signal station; of ship repairs and comas and awakenings, he said, "Grandma, tell me how it feels."

That was Colin—feeling before all. She said, "It doesn't 'feel' like anything. I just think differently. Faster, more deeply. Colin, do you remember when you were small and were fascinated with elephants?"

"Of course. I drew them all the time."

"You did more than draw them. You made up stories about them, you talked to pretend elephants, you dreamed about rescuing an elephant in a basement, like in your favorite picture book."

He smiled. "I remember."

"I want to tell you about genetic evolution. After all, that's what I am, an evolutionary geneticist, the only one here at the base. Evolution is a process, but not an evenly paced one."

"I know that much," Colin said.

"I'm rehearsing here, Colin—trying to find the one strand to explain it simply." And each idea—almost each word—led to other strands, other ideas. Her task now was to separate out the ones that would make sense to nonscientists. This was urgent.

He said, "You're trying to find the words to explain it to Jason, when he's being Colonel Jenner."

Even as a child, Colin had been quick to perceive the cues in human relations. Marianne took his hand where it rested on his knee, above the cast on his shattered leg. Her deeply veined hand squeezed his muscular fingers, on which his Settlement sunburn had mostly faded. She unknotted strands of thought in her mind, knotted them again, pruned and simplified.

"There are three parts to what I want to tell you. First, that punctuated evolution led to long periods where nothing much seemed to change in human beings, followed by rapid change. Five or six million years ago, proto-humans diverged from apes. Two hundred thousand years ago, by some estimates, toolmaking began. A hundred thousand years ago, modern humans emerged in Africa. Seventy thousand years ago, the first cloud of R. *sporii* hit Terra, wiping out most of humanity except those with natural immunity—which is why Worlders aren't immune. They'd already been taken from Terra to World by the so-called super-aliens. About forty thousand years ago, the Great Leap happened—Colin, are you following this?"

"Every word. I already knew it, you know. And so does Jason."

"Just bear with me. Humans had had a long period of cultural stagnation. Really long. Then, during the Great Leap Forward, modern humans started burying their dead with funeral rituals, making clothing with bone needles, carving buttons and fishhooks, creating jewelry and art. By thirty-six thousand years ago, they had fertility figurines and cave paintings and musical pipes.

"Some equivalent of the Great Leap must have occurred on World, too, or humans there would have stayed at an earlier stagnant level. I'll come back to that."

Colin nodded. He turned his head slightly—hearing something that she could not? Marianne didn't interrupt herself to find out. She wouldn't lose her line of thought, but he might.

"That's the history, or a brief version of it. Second comes the genetic part. This is all known science. Our divergence from apes correlates with multiple mutations in a region of the genome called

HAR1—human accelerated region one. The human brain developed a much wrinklier cortex, to mention just one change. Other mutations in other genes correlate with other advances. One of them—this is important—is a gene called ASPM, on chromosome one, which has mutated fifteen times in the last six million years, and the mutations seem to correlate with milestones in human evolution. The last mutation occurred along with the development of agriculture and sophisticated writing. Of course, mutations can be destructive, as well—an ASPM allele causes microcephaly in fetuses, who are born with small brains—in fact, brains exactly the size of *Australopithecus africanus* a few million years ago. And changes in one gene can affect others. ASPM is *seminal*. It affects the division of cells in developing brains. It affects other cells. It affects coding in IQ domains of the human genome."

Colin's face crinkled in concentration. "So you think that everybody who went into a v-coma had this mutation? In that one gene?"

"Yes, yes. Or maybe in two copies of the gene. I can talk to Zack McKay about that."

"But what does this have to do with—"

She said, "I think the virophage tweaked the ASPM gene. The v-comas are the next stage in human evolution."

Colin opened his mouth, then closed it again. When he spoke, the sentiment was pure Colin, the democratic populist. "But not for everybody? That's not fair."

"No, dear heart. Evolution never is. This may or may not be evolution, depending on whether it gets into the germ line and can be passed on to the next generation. But there's one more thing."

He said unhappily, "Go ahead."

"Microbes."

"*R. sporii?*"

"No, its virophage. The fact that some humans, those with—maybe—a given mutated allele—fall into a coma and others don't—that means something important. It means we've encountered this virophage before, or we wouldn't have the genes to react to it. And since some of those in comas are Worlders, humanity encountered the virophage before a hundred and forty thousand years ago."

Colin frowned. "Are you saying that the virophage caused humans to . . . oh, I don't know . . . diverge from apes? *Millions* of years ago?"

"I don't know. I'm not sure we can know. But that's the wrong question."

"Grandma, you look tired. Maybe you should—"

"No, let me finish! We've been asking ourselves the wrong question for decades now—ever since Worlders first landed in New York Harbor. We've been asking 'What do we want?' How can we develop a vaccine against the spore cloud, counteract the virophage, eliminate RSA— they're *all* the wrong questions."

Coin shifted his weight in his powerchair. "What's the right question?"

Marianne leaned forward, swayed, caught herself. "The right question is 'What do the microbes want?'"

"Microbes don't 'want' anything! They're not sentient!"

"No. But natural selection leads to the proliferation of traits that aid their survival. So why select for a strategy that essentially results in rewiring their human hosts' brains? What does the virophage gain when it does that? There are a lot of potential answers.

"Maybe they need some protein found in neurons or synapses or brain-chemical cascades, and the rewiring causes more of that protein to be made.

"Maybe they've evolved to hijack our cellular machinery to aid their reproductive success, as a lot of viruses and parasites have evolved to do with all kinds of animals.

"Maybe they use us to carry them elsewhere so their territory is increased and so their numbers grow. Like cherries, who use mammals to eat their fruit and excrete the seeds in new places, or burdocks that cling to fur to get seeds somewhere else. That's how both smallpox and measles pathogens got to the United States—humans brought them."

Colin said, "So which is it? What does the virophage 'want'?"

Marianne shrugged. "I don't know. But I always thought that we humans would someday transform ourselves with genetic engineering. What if the opposite is true—if microbes are the dominant force? If genetic engineering, at which microbes are expert, transforms us? It always has created new life-forms, from the moment the first fermenting bacterium merged with a swimming bacterium. But—there's still a strand missing!"

"A strand of what?"

"Something I haven't figured out. Damn it, I don't have the math!"

"Math? What has math got to do with it?"

All at once Marianne's vision blurred and she sagged in her chair. "I am tired. I think I better rest now."

Colin powered his chair to the door, opened it, and shouted down the corridor. "Hey! Anybody! Will somebody help my grandmother back to her room?"

A civilian on janitorial duty stuck her head from a doorway, a plump older woman with hair like electrified wire and a cheerful smile. "Just a sec!"

"Thank you," Marianne said.

"Grandma, just one quick question. Why are you telling all this to me, instead of to the brain-change scientists? Especially the ones with enhanced intelligence?"

"I will tell them. But they all want to know how the virophage changed the v-coma victims' brains. I want to know why."

Now Colin looked totally bewildered. "Is there a why? Doesn't evolution just happen?"

"Yes. But there's a missing piece, and I don't have the math—Jason!"

"Are you all right?" Her other grandson, tall and stern in his uniform, the cheerful janitor hovering behind him. He scowled at Marianne and Colin. "I was coming to see you—what are you doing out of bed?"

"Take me back, please," she managed to get out. Again her vision had blurred; exhaustion felt like a physical weight on her shoulders, her chest, her brain. But she heard Colin repeat his question, and even as

Jason lifted her in strong arms and half carried her from the room, she smiled at Colin.

"Grandma, why *me?*"

She said over Jason's shoulder, "Because scientists think in performable and replicable experiments, and you drew elephants."

CHAPTER 21

"Sir? Permission to have a word with you?"

Private McNally, one of the awakened, saluted. Jason was on his way to the mess in Lab Dome. He had resolved to have a larger presence at the other dome. Although he would never have Hillson's intel network—and didn't need to, as long as he had Hillson—he could at least walk around and see more for himself. And be seen. Also, perhaps the scientists would be less formal with him, less guarded, if he went to them instead of either summoning them to the command post or staging formal presentations.

And maybe he would happen to run into Lindy.

McNally stopped him in a crowded corridor. Beyond lay an open area, or what passed for an open area in the crowded dome, where three shouting Settler children played a game with a ball. The ball bounced off crates, most empty, off chairs where two Settlers sat talking, off a nurse hurrying to the infirmary. McNally's salute had been a half-hearted swipe at his forehead. Or maybe not halfhearted as much as preoccupied.

McNally said, "I want to show you something, sir. I don't have nothing on me but if you come with me to the armory . . ."

A trap? How unpopular was Jason with his own troops? And McNally was not an ordinary soldier; his brain had been tampered with by the virophage. Dr. Sullivan had said that the tampering could have different effects on different people. And why did McNally seem so hesitant?

Jason said curtly, "No. Tell me what you have to show."

"It's a weapon, sir. An A15. I modified it."

"Who gave you permission to do that?"

"Nobody, sir. That's how come I want to show it to you."

Which made no sense. But looking at McNally's thin, serious face, Jason saw that it made sense to McNally, that some kind of reasoning Jason didn't understand was going on in that semi-alien brain. How alien?

Two off-duty members of J Squad, privates Tarrant and Kandiss, walked through the shrieking children toward the mess. Jason called to them. They stopped, surprised, and immediately came to him.

"Sir?"

"Private McNally has a modified weapon he would like to show me. You will accompany him to the armory and then to Lab Dome's conference room, with the weapon. Lieutenant Jones is on duty at the armory. I will arrange clearance."

They understood instantly; that's why they were J Squad. Unlike McNally, both carried sidearms. If this was a trap, conspirators would have to be very good to take out Tarrant and Kandiss. McNally smiled faintly.

The conference room was empty, although copious crumbs and three dirty cups of what passed for coffee littered the table. Scientists. If it had been soldiers, their squad leader would have roasted them. The stuff was undrinkable, anyway.

Jason waited, studying formulae and diagrams scrawled on the whiteboard. None of them was intelligible to him, but he could tell that none looked biological. Jason needed to find time to interview Major Farouk, the physicist, about his theories on the *Return*. Not that Jason had understood Farouk's specialty even before the physicist had gone into v-coma.

A lab tech ambled in, spotted Jason, and retreated hastily.

Eventually Tarrant and Kandiss arrived with McNally, who carried a canvas weapon sling. Tarrant gave Jason a faint nod: *All okay, sir.* McNally laid the sling on the table, unzipped it, and stood back. Kandiss removed an A15 with odd mountings on the underside of the barrel.

McNally gave the impression of hunting carefully for the right words—or maybe it was for words simple enough. "I modified it so it can be fired remotely, sir. If a soldier falls and drops the rifle, this device here, it automatically orients the weapon in the direction of the last shots. Then the controller—this doohickey here—can keep the weapon laying down fire in bursts, if you want to. The rounds probably might not hit nothing, but if the down soldier isn't visible, maybe it'll convince the enemy that the position is still being held."

Kandiss stared at the A15 beside the coffee mugs as if it were a snake. Lena Tarrant said, "Sir, we tested the weapon. It performs as described."

Jason said to McNally, "Private, have you had ordnance training?"

"No, sir."

"Were you an engineer of any type before the Collapse?"

"No, sir. Didn't finish high school."

"Have you ever studied mechanical engineering or weapons manufacture, or received any kind of advanced training in those areas?"

"I been reading on the computer in the enlisted library, sir. Since I waked up."

"And that reading taught you to invent this?"

"No, sir. This isn't in any reading."

"How did you invent it?"

For the first time, an emotion flitted across the private's face, gone in a nanosecond: disgust. He said, "I looked at the A15, sir. And I thought about it. And I experimented."

"Did you have permission for these experiments?"

"No, sir."

"Did you have permission to be in the armory, removing weapons?"

"I belonged there, sir. I was on armory guard."

"Which did not include any form of removing, and certainly not of modifying, an A15 without an OPORD to do so."

Now McNally looked Jason straight in the eyes. "No, sir. But I thought you might find it pretty useful, sir. That's how come I brought it to you."

The unsaid words were: *And risked disciplinary action to do so.*

Beside Jason, Tarrant shifted uneasily. Kandiss stiffened. Jason knew without looking at them, what each was thinking. Tarrant was impressed with the weapon. Kandiss, the spit-and-polish ex-Ranger, was focused on the breach of regulations. But McNally had brought this to Jason voluntarily, at personal risk, because he thought it would be valuable to the Army.

Jason made his decision. "Private, you are reprimanded for taking unauthorized action. However, this could be a useful modification if a hunting party is surprised by an enemy patrol and takes casualties. In the future, you are to bring any ideas for weapons modification to me or Major Duncan before you implement them. Failure to do so will result in disciplinary action. Am I making myself clear on this?"

"Yes, sir."

"You will take the A-15 outside, along with Sergeants Kandiss and Tarrant, and demonstrate it more fully than you were able to do in the armory. If they find it satisfactory, you may be asked to modify more A-15s."

"Yes, sir."

"Dismissed."

Jason didn't go to the mess, after all. He was no longer hungry. Walking around Lab Dome had been a good, if uncomfortable, idea. There were more Awakened here, and every one of them could, like McNally, outthink Jason, even in areas in which they were not trained. This was, as his father used to say when Jason was a child, a whole new ball game. Could Jason put it to advantage? He should interview more of the Awakened. He should find out what they were thinking—if he could follow it—before the convoy arrived from Fort Hood and everything changed.

The Settler children, oblivious of rank, knocked into him as they chased their ball along the corridor. "Sorry, man!"

Jason turned his path toward the infirmary. While he was doing this observational walk-around, he should discover who else had awakened from v-coma.

Jane had.

She woke, lapsed back into sleep, woke again with a start, slept fitfully. There were dreams, and when she woke completely she was not sure what had been dreams and what had happened during the brief period of wakefulness. There had been monstrous trees overgrowing World, there had been Glamet^vor¡ pursuing her with a knife, there had been a leelee she'd had as a childhood pet and her lahk Mother and Colin . . .

Colin sat by her pallet in a chair with wheels, his leg wrapped with some contraption of cloth and plastic.

"Jane?"

"Ne¡ . . . jinn grat^ . . ." And then, clearer in her head, "I am here."

He smiled. "Where were you before?"

She stared at him dumbly. His smile disappeared. "Are you all right?"

"I am . . . not me."

His warm brown eyes took on that look of understanding, the look that always reminded her of home, where there was so much less struggle to understand. "Yes, you are you. But while you were in the coma, the virophage did things to your brain. You're . . . well, if you're like the others who have woken up, you're smarter."

Smarter? Jane didn't feel she knew more than before. But . . .

She said slowly, "Things look more clear."

Colin leaned forward in his chair. "You mean your vision was affected? Your eyes?"

"No." What did she mean? Her mind was racing and yet standing still, like a skalethi quiet in its pasture, patient wisdom in its dreaming eyes. "I see . . . you more clear."

He laughed, stopping abruptly. "That sounds alarming. See me clearer how?"

"I don't have words. You are a shape, a color . . . no, a feeling made of shapes and colors. The feeling of you." She felt the inadequacy of the sentences, and then their sexual connotations. Warmth mounted from her neck to hairline. "I didn't mean . . ." Oh, words were so inadequate!

But Colin had always been good at knowing what she meant. "Your increased smartness is . . . psychological? You have a sort of intuitive grasp of what people—or at least me—are like?"

"No. Yes. It's . . . hard to explain."

It was impossible to explain, and not only because she didn't know the World translation of some of the words he had used. Her thoughts had always been tinged with color, but now ideas, sights, had deeper and complex shadings and more profound shapes, and—this was, she realized, completely new—the shapes were connected to each other in ways they had not been before.

She said, "Tell me of the others who are awake."

Colin pointed a finger at her. "See, right there—you are the only one of the Awakened who has asked what the other Awakened are like now. This might be half-baked because I just thought of it this minute, but maybe what happens in the comas is that you guys are smarter mostly about whatever you spent a lot of time thinking about before? Like paths through the woods—the brain paths used the most get the most changes in the coma."

The possibility shimmered and shifted in her mind.

Colin plunged on, "So Toni Steffens is spending all her time in the lab since she woke up, and the kids are learning to read faster, and my grandmother is spinning theories about evolutionary biology. And you're being Jane, focused on people."

He was alight with clear, bright colors, entranced with his idea, and in love with her. Jane saw him, all the way through. She felt dizzy, even though she was lying on a pallet with tubes stuck in her. And then, behind Colin, standing in the doorway, she saw his brother.

"Jane," he said, coming into the curtained cubicle. "Colin. How are you feeling, Jane? Did you just wake up?"

"Yes," Jane said. She saw Jason Jenner, too. Every line of him, every shape he made in her mind, was tense and jagged. His face looked older than Colin's by at least a decade, even though she knew they were only a Terran year apart in age. This was a man carrying huge burdens—in her mind they were gray harsh shapes of enormous density—and buckling under them. No, not buckling—not yet. But add a little more, and he might. Or not. In Jane he called forth pity, along with a desire to not add to his cares.

"I feel fine," she lied.

"Good. Has a doctor checked you over?"

"Not yet."

"I'll send one." He vanished. A few minutes later Claire appeared. In those few minutes, Jane looked again at Colin, and the shapes/colors of the brothers shifted and shimmered in her mind, along with what Colin had said about those who woke up becoming more intelligent pursuers of whatever had preoccupied them before. Her thoughts widened out to include everything she knew about the base, about Jason Jenner, about the terrible Terran war, about Colin's destroyed Settlement and the displaced Settlers she had talked to, about World.

"Jane—what is it?" Claire said. "Am I hurting you? What are those tears about?"

But Jane could not tell her. Sorrow swamped her, but she couldn't give it words. Jane might be wrong. Other shapes were possible, other colors from other people.

But she didn't think so. One pattern was so much clearer than all the rest—a pattern based on what Jason Jenner was, what Colin Jenner was, what she herself had become, and the others like her. People acted from what they were, and from how their essential natures shifted and colored the situations around them. Also, the pattern in her mind was not only the clearest and most likely, it was the best.

If that pattern did indeed come to pass, she would never see Colin Jenner again.

Marianne left the infirmary, with Dr. Holbrook's reluctant permission. She had wanted to leave yesterday but he had forbidden it. "You aren't a young woman anymore," said this Army doctor who was older than she was. What did he see when he looked at her, knowing and yet not knowing what changes had come to her neural structures?

So people had come to her: Ryan, her grandsons, Ka^graa. Zack McKay, whom she'd sent for. Zack and she had talked for a long time, Marianne slowing her thoughts and words so this very intelligent man could follow them. Zack had left looking dazed.

Now Marianne walked carefully, right hand on the wooden wall that had been hastily erected to create this makeshift corridor. The wood no longer smelled raw, but the unsanded surface felt uneven, with bumps and ridges rough under her palm. To her left, rows of curtains hid equally makeshift cubicles, each holding a bed or gurney or pallet with a v-coma sleeper. Some cubicles were empty, their patients already awakened.

A carry-bot trundled past, laden with towels and basins and cleaning supplies. The nurse walking beside it, a very young woman in faded scrubs printed with daisies, smiled at her tremulously. Too young to be an Army nurse and still faintly suntanned—she was one of Colin's Settlers, overcoming her aversion to tech enough to help out the overworked medical staff.

The sight cheered Marianne. People adapted. Hand still on the wall although she was feeling stronger, she moved toward the end of the corridor, where a soldier stood guard at the door dividing the infirmary from Lab Dome's commons. "Commons"—a term from another life, academic teas in an oak-paneled, pseudo-British room at the university. Funny she should think of that now, when—

A man in a hospital gown erupted from the curtain to her left, screaming. Before Marianne could react, he grabbed her arm hard enough to topple her from her feet. "Run! Run! They will— Run!" He threw back his head and howled like a wolf.

Then it all happened at once. The soldier pulled a gun from the holster on his thigh. The young Settler nurse turned from the carry-bot and gaped. Lindy Ross flung aside the curtain of the next cubicle, where Susan McKay lay comatose. The screaming man thrust Marianne between himself and the soldier's gun, whatever paranoid fantasies his mind was prone to now strengthened, justified, stronger and wilder in his stronger and wilder brain. He howled again, and his arm tightened across Marianne's throat.

The soldier, uncertain, didn't fire, but he kept his gun trained on them. Marianne could see his lips move in subvocalization to his mic. The deranged man's arm tightened further, and she struggled to breathe.

Details were suddenly scalpel-sharp: the soldier's lips moving, the antiseptic smell of her captor's arm, the worn geometric design in the cubicle curtains, the realization, sharpest of all, that these might be the last things she experienced before she died.

Then something hit them from behind, hard. The man fell, dropping Marianne. She gasped for breath. The nurse shoved the carry-bot to slam into her captor's back. The soldier sprinted forward and grabbed the man, who started to cry. Lindy bent over Marianne.

"Are you all right? Oh my God—"

Marianne couldn't talk. She was still gasping for breath, trying to get air down her bruised throat, wheezing in desperate wrenching pants. But the thought she couldn't utter was clear in her mind:

Some people cannot adapt, not to changes in their own brains.

Then everything went dark.

She woke back in bed. Lindy sat beside her.

"Marianne?"

"What . . . how long . . ."

"Only a few minutes. Your oxygenation is fine, and except for a bruised neck, you shouldn't suffer any consequences from that attack. If you hadn't already been so weak, you probably wouldn't have blacked out at all. Does your throat hurt?"

"Yes."

"That'll go away."

Already Marianne could talk more easily. A little more easily, anyway. "The attacker?"

"He's a soldier. Jason will deal with him." Lindy's face was grim.

"He isn't . . . entirely responsible. V-coma strengthens . . . whatever pathways . . ."

"I know. Major Holbrook will advise Jason. Marianne—where were you trying to go?"

"Dr. Farouk."

Lindy's eyebrows lifted. "The physicist? Why?"

"I . . . need to see him."

"Well, you're not going to. Not unless he comes to you, because you're not going anywhere for a while. You're not a young woman, you know."

Like Marianne didn't already know that? And yet people kept telling her. But it wasn't like Lindy to be condescending. Lindy looked distracted, and purplish circles blossomed under her eyes. Something was hurting her. Jason?

Marianne didn't ask. She said, "Send Dr. Farouk to me."

Lindy stood. "I can try. But I doubt he'll come. He's working on something important and will hardly stop to eat. Just like Toni Steffens. Are you, too, going to start behaving like your health is irrelevant?"

"No."

"Well, good. We need at least one sane Awakened around here. And a few more sane un-Awakened wouldn't hurt, either."

"Tell Dr. Farouk . . ." What? Nothing that Marianne could put into a neat, short message for Lindy to carry.

Lindy waited.

"Tell Dr. Farouk I have something new about time."

Lindy's forehead wrinkled. "Time? What do you mean?"

"Just tell him. And that it's urgent."

"I don't see how the—oh, Ryan."

Marianne's son thumped into the cubicle as fast as his cane would let him. "Mom?"

"I'm fine, Ryan."

"They told me that you—"

"I'm fine. Really." But before she turned her attention to Ryan, Marianne directed a long look at Lindy.

"Please. Dr. Farouk. Now."

CHAPTER 22

Zack was frustrated. He'd carefully repeated to Toni all of Marianne's speculations about the ASPM gene, the mutation carried by all the v-coma victims, and human accelerated region 1. Toni had barely listened—or maybe she had. How would Zack know what this mentally enhanced Toni was doing? Maybe she was capable of following multiple pathways of thought at once. Or even all possible pathways, like electrons in an uncollapsed state. Or maybe she really wasn't listening to him.

He finished with, "So maybe we should look more closely at the ASPM gene."

"Okay."

"'Okay'? That's it?"

"You look at it," Toni said, and went back to her own work. If her attention had ever really left it in the first place.

He started to work, but after only an hour, Claire Patel came into the lab. "Zack—"

He knew. From the tone of her voice, the wideness of her eyes, his own half-dread, half-eager anticipation. He said, "Susan is awake."

"Yes. She's asking for you."

"Is she all right?" *Is she still Susan?* Caitlin, to his immense relief, had emerged from her coma a brighter, more thoughtful child, but still Caitlin. She had pouts, she had tantrums, she liked snuggles, she still carried around Bollers, who now had stuffing oozing out of his fuzzy neck. But

Caitlin was four. Her brain was expected to be highly plastic, her personality in flux. Susan was . . . Susan was his heart. What if she had changed in some important way other than intellectually, what if she no longer needed him, what if . . .

Claire said, "She's as healthy as someone can be who's been in a coma this long."

Not what he'd meant. Zack rose on suddenly unsteady legs. "Tricia, can you finish this?"

The lab tech nodded. "Sure."

When Zack reached the infirmary, someone had already brought Caitlin to her mother. Susan sat up in bed, Caity nestled beside her, and Zack thought his heart would split along its seam. Susan was thinner, her cheekbones sharp beneath shadowed eyes. She smiled at him.

"Zack."

"Is it you?"

What a dumb thing to say! But she seemed to understand.

"Yes, it's me."

"How do you feel?" Also pretty dumb, but complexity seemed to have deserted him. There was something in her eyes . . . Claire tactfully withdrew.

Caitlin said, "Mommy is awake now, too. But she can already read good."

"So I can," Susan said. "Zack . . ." She stopped but not, it seemed to Zack, because she didn't know what to say, or how to say it. She was waiting for him.

He walked carefully, as if something in him might break, to the side of the bed. There was no chair so he stood, putting his hand on her shoulder, looking down at her. *Please, Sue—help me.*

She did, just as she always had. "I feel fine, Zack. Shaky physically and mentally, but I'm hoping both will pass. I just need to get used to thinking . . . like this."

He wasn't yet ready to ask what "like this" meant for her, or to compare it to what had been said by those who'd awakened before her. That wasn't what he wanted to know, anyway.

Susan continued, "What are you afraid of?"

He blurted out, "That now I won't be smart enough for you."

Her eyes widened; he'd surprised her. That he could do that was oddly reassuring. She wasn't omniscient.

She said, "Of course you are. But I didn't marry you for your admittedly formidable intellect, you know. That was never why I loved you. It still isn't, and I still love you."

Caity hugged Bollers, listening hard.

Susan added, "Nothing will change that. Not even if I were Einstein—which I'm not—and you were a block of wood."

Caity said seriously, "If Daddy was a block of wood then he couldn't talk."

Zack said, "And from what I remember, Einstein didn't treat his wives particularly well." Relief filled his body, sweet as fresh strawberries in the sun, light as helium.

"Mommy, I want to write a story about a block of wood that talks. Where's my tablet?"

Susan said, "She can write now?"

"A little," Zack said, "and read a lot. Oh, Sue—"

"Yes," she said. "Now tell me everything that's happened since I fell asleep. Then I'll try to describe what this is like for me."

"Mommy, Daddy, I want you to help me with my tablet!"

"You will have to wait your turn," Susan said in her no-nonsense, don't-mess-with-me voice. That, even more than what she'd said, reassured Zack. Susan had always been the one to discipline Caity, Zack the one to spoil her.

They were still all themselves. They were still all here. They could ride out Marianne's leap of punctuated evolution, or anything else. Together.

"Zack," Tricia said, barging through the curtain. "Oh, hello, Ms.

McKay. Zack, sorry to intrude, but Toni says you should come to the lab right away."

"Not now."

"Now," Tricia said.

Lab techs did not command department heads. Zack looked up, irritated until he saw Tricia's face. He hadn't known the usually quiet woman could look like that. "What is it? What's happened?" Another Awakened gone crazy, like the man who'd attacked Marianne? An escape of live sparrows with RSA? A breach of the dome by New America?

Tricia said, "Toni says she's made the gene drive. To wipe out the birds. She's got it, and it works."

"We were tinkering with the wrong thing," Toni said. "We were trying to modify the DNA in the gametes. I modified the histones instead."

Zack scanned the rest of her notes. She'd done an amazing job. Histones, spool-shaped proteins around which the DNA in a eukaryote was strung, were more tractable than genes. Histone modification could radically alter the activity of a gene without altering its DNA sequence. When the cells divided, the alterations were passed on to the daughter cells. Virology already possessed a gamut of proteins capable of altering histones, but Toni had found a new one. More: she had found a way to exploit epistasis, the effects of genetic mutations that depend on other mutations. Her notes—much clearer than before she'd Awakened!—showed how her modified histones affected other histones, changing the behavior of cell signaling, pasting the genemod into two copies of all cells.

He said, "The birds . . ."

"Yes. I've been inserting trial gene-drive mods into frozen sparrow embryos. They paste themselves beautifully into both chromosomes. I mated the offspring with another nest brought into artificial readiness.

From the males—nada. Nothing. Zilch. The males are sterile. The females reproduced, and of their offspring, all the males were healthy but sterile. We'll get a selective sweep, Zack. Within a few decades, there will be no more sparrows left in North America—and no RSA. Eventually, the disease will be gone from the entire world."

He had to sit down. It wasn't her conclusion that staggered him—they had known that was what a successful gene drive would do—it was her science. How had she done that so *fast*? She'd had to breed two generations of sparrows . . . of course, sparrows mated very young, and hormones could bring them into fertility out of season. Still, she must have had viable gene candidates ready to go shortly after she awakened.

He looked at her with awe.

She frowned. "But the other gene drive, the one to eliminate RSA directly instead of going through reproduction—I haven't cracked that one yet."

He nodded. She would crack it. All they needed now was time.

"I'm tired," Toni said abruptly. "I'm going to sleep. Will you come get me if Nicole wakes up?"

Zack nodded again. Toni left. Zack sat still a long time, ignored by everyone working in the lab around him.

He saw what Toni, for all her new brilliance, did not. Toni's incredible intelligence was focused on science—as it always had been. But there was more than science involved. Inserting this gene drive into more birds and then releasing them into the wild was a political decision, with enormous ecological implications. Look what had happened thirty-eight years ago, when the original *R. sporii* had nearly wiped out eight species of mice. Entire economies had been shaken.

Probably, given the way things were now, releasing the birds would be a military decision, made at Fort Hood. He didn't trust military decisions. Not anybody's, no matter how much "military intelligence" they were based on—

"Oh my God," he said aloud, suddenly *realizing*, and everybody in the lab stopped and stared at him.

Hillson said to Jason, "The deranged corporal who attacked Dr. Jenner is under restraint."

"Good." They had no psychiatrist at the base, although that was the least of the problems represented by Corporal Douglas Porter. Hillson, however, didn't yet realize that.

The master sergeant stood by the doorway of the command post, making his twice-daily report. As always, Hillson's uniform looked rumpled and slightly askew, as if assembled in the dark. Which it might have been; Hillson seemed to need almost no sleep. His homely, intelligent features gave away nothing, but Jason heard volumes in his voice, most of it either bewildered or disapproving.

"The convoy from Fort Hood is still eight days out," Hillson said. "It was attacked by New America just west of the Los Angeles nuclear zone. Lieutenant Li relayed what the *Return* picked up of the convoy's radio signals to Fort Hood."

Jason, startled, said, "The *Return* can do that now?"

"Yes," Hillson said, disapproval lapsing very briefly into Army pride. "Specialist Martin is getting pretty good with that alien hardware. She figured out more of the communications capabilities than that lab tech did. That Branch Carter."

"Good. What did Li say about the attack?"

"The convoy leader, a Major Highland . . . do you know him, sir?"

"We were at West Point together." And Highland had been a prick even then.

"Oh," Hillson said, with the enlisted man's disdain for the academy. "Anyway, sir, the convoy wiped out the enemy. But it slowed them, for repairs and medical and burials and such. So eight more days, maybe more."

Another reprieve.

And then, "What else, Hillson? You don't look that grim because New America lost a battle."

"No, sir. Ten more deserters."

Ten. Well, that might actually be a good thing, although he couldn't say that to Hillson. Not yet. Unless . . .

"Give me the names."

Hillson did. Jason hid his relief; none of them were Awakened. He said, "They've gone off to start their own little army? I assume they took supplies and weapons?"

"Yes, sir. They stole what they wanted."

And you wonder why I let them. But Jason's reasons would have to wait a short while yet. Hillson was going to be troubled enough when that conversation happened.

"Sir—"

"Anything else, Sergeant?"

"No, sir."

Hillson, deeply unhappy, left. Unhappy but completely loyal. He passed Major Duncan entering the command post. She said, "Sir— Doctor Farouk wants to see you."

"Farouk?"

"Yes, sir. I was at Lab Dome and he stopped me, practically sputtering. It took me five minutes to get him to speak in normal English instead of formulas or equations or whatever the hell they were. I brought him here to see you, but what I got from him, I thought I'd tell you first. I could be wrong, but . . ."

"Major? What is it?" He had never seen her look like that.

"Sorry, sir. Dr. Farouk says—at least I think he says it, he indicated that it needs more work—but he thinks he understands the physics of the starship. Of the engine, I mean. He thinks that in another few years or so, we might know enough to build ones that can be bigger or smaller or different. He's very excited, sir."

Another few years. Jason—and Duncan as well—knew they did not have another few years. Their eyes met.

"Good news," Jason finally said.

"Yes, sir," she answered.

Neither of them meant it.

And then, before Jason had even seen Dr. Farouk, Zack McKay appeared, asking to tell Jason something about Dr. Steffens.

And about sparrows.

Jane sat on a child's chair beside Belok^, who sat on the floor. Monterey Base had nothing like the thick, richly embroidered cushions of home, nor World's low tables of polished karthwood. The items Jane had brought with her lay on the floor at her feet.

La^vor crouched beside Belok^. Jane knew that La^vor was afraid of what might happen to Belok^. La^vor had lost one brother; she needed some of her lahk to hold on to, here in this strange place that had never, not once, felt like home. The patterns and colors that La^vor made in Jane's mind were unfocused and gray.

And Belok^? Jane needed to find his patterns. She held up the first of her items, a flattish, more or less rectangular stone. In World, which he'd understood even when he couldn't speak much of it, she said, "Belok^-kal, what could you do with this?"

The giant child looked puzzled.

"What things could you do with this stone?"

He took it in his big hands and turned it slowly over and over. Jane waited. La^vor put the tips of her thumbs together, a World gesture of anxiety.

Finally Belok^ said, "Build. Build a thing."

"What kind of thing?"

More waiting. The pattern in her mind was a cloud, colorless and formless but filled with light. She watched it take form as Belok^ answered, his words slow and thick, like tree sap emerging after a long winter.

"Build . . . house. Build . . . cookstove . . . build path build table build steps."

La^vor gasped. The formless pattern in Jane's mind took on tints and lumps. She said, "Can you do anything else with the stone besides build?"

Again the puzzled face, creaking into understanding. Belok^ looked at the stone. Next his gaze roamed around the other items Jane had brought: a cup, a blanket, a hammer, a length of wire, a small 3-D printer. Belok^ stared at the tablet on which La^vor had been teaching him to write his name. He picked up the tablet pen, put it down again. His childish brow crinkled into sand waves. A full minute passed.

Belok^ reached into his pocket. He pulled out a soft white stone; Jane had seen Settler children play with these in some complicated game. Belok^ scratched the white stone over Jane's rock. Three symbols, crude but recognizable: his name in World.

La^vor burst into tears.

Immediately Belok^ dropped the white stone and put his arms around his tiny sister, folding her to him, murmuring comfort. And in her mind, Jane saw Belok^'s shapes: whole and brightly colored, kind and loving and frighteningly innocent.

She almost cried, too. Belok^'s pattern in her mind was a simpler, cruder version of Colin's.

She went to him, straight from Belok^ and La^vor, almost running along the corridors to his room. He wasn't there. She found him conferring with gray-haired Sarah Waters, from the Settlement. "Colin!"

"What is it?"

"I need to talk to you!"

Sarah, startled, faded tactfully away. Jane didn't talk. She seized his chair and tried to push it. Colin made it roll by itself, following her along the narrow, clogged corridors as swiftly as possible. Jane kept her head down so no one could see her face. She ignoring Colin's repeated, "Jane? What is it? Jane?" At his room, she closed the door, climbed onto the bed, and lay down. She pulled up her wrap.

His face changed; his pattern shifted. He whispered, "Are you sure?"

"Yes!"

"I haven't said anything, Jane, because I didn't want you to feel that in a place strange to you, you were in any way pressured to . . . I wanted to give you . . ."

"I know. Don't talk now. Later, but not now."

Colin ducked his head, and she couldn't see his face. Then, carefully, he heaved himself from chair to bed. Jane, in an agony of desire that was sweet as Terran honey, sweet as World mef fruit, sweet as home, reached for him.

For a while, then, the patterns were all shining, and she didn't have to picture what must inevitably come.

CHAPTER 23

Two more v-comas, one a soldier and one a civilian, had awakened. Jason had reports brought to him hourly, from many people. He walked the corridors. He visited the infirmary wards, the labs, the armory, the mess. He put on an esuit and talked directly to the outside patrol. Elizabeth Duncan took over the command post. Jason talked, but mostly he listened. Command had always involved invisible tentacles resting lightly all over the base, sensing every movement in every corner, trying to anticipate the next shift. Too often he had failed. But now the tentacles vibrated constantly, hot with detail, so that sometimes it seemed to Jason that he stood in every bit of Monterey Base at once. That he could see the freckles on the Settler children kicking a ball in the Commons, smell the deer roasting in the kitchen, hear the squawk of sparrows in the bird lab underground.

The one thing he could not do was sleep. He wouldn't take any more of Lindy's sleep-inducing drug; he needed to be sharp. Night after night he lay awake, alone in the dark, going over the plan again and again, trying to find an alternative. Failing.

Failing, too, to still the ache for Lindy. But it wouldn't be fair to her, wouldn't be fair, wouldn't be fair . . .

Nothing was fair.

Then back to walking both domes of the base, tentacles vibrating, people watching him from eyes that were fearful or hostile or speculative or sympathetic. Listening. Learning.

His grandmother had been shut up for days with Dr. Farouk. They were "working out equations" that they would not, or could not, explain in terms that Jason could understand.

Private McNally, he of the spotty education and no specialist training, had invented two more improvements to ordnance. Another Awakened soldier, Specialist Kelly Swinford, had joined him. She was not, Dr. Holbrook told Jason, quite his intellectual equal—but then the old man had thrown both hands into the air in a completely unmilitary gesture and said, "I can't really tell. They are *different*. No, not different, they all still have the same personalities but they are . . . different." Jason had not pressed him. He understood.

Five people were still in v-coma, including Branch Carter and one child, Devon James.

The convoy from Fort Hood was a week out from Monterey Base.

Jason's father and brother were planning a new Settlement, because *We can't live like this for much longer.* Ryan, Jason suspected, would be glad to go on doing so, but Ryan would go where Colin led.

Major Sullivan and her team were closer to a vaccine against RSA, but not close enough. Nor had Major Vargas's team made any progress on a way to tweak the human immune system to fight off RSA.

And Dr. Steffens . . .

Ah, not yet. Give him a few more minutes before he had to go to Toni Steffens.

Jason walked into the kitchen of Lab Dome mess. Big pots bubbled on a stove. Two Settlers, teenagers, rose hastily from the floor, straightening their clothes. The boy's ears blushed bright red. Jason said, "As you were," even though neither was a soldier, and withdrew. The little incident cheered him. Those kids, who had been small children at the time of the Collapse, had found pleasure, maybe even joy, in the midst of crisis. More power to them.

Hillson was increasingly wooden to Jason, and Jason knew he couldn't hold off Hillson much longer. Hillson's loyalty was beyond question, but the decision Jason had come to might shatter that loyalty beyond repair. Or not. Either way, Jason would talk to him next.

Right after Toni Steffens.

He made his way to the labs, only to be told that Dr. Steffens was in the underground annex. At the corridor leading to the stairwell, the guard saluted and opened the door. Jason put on an esuit and descended the staircase, his boots ringing on the alien metal. He entered the negative-pressure bird lab.

It was pandemonium down here. Cages and cages of noisy sparrows, none of them happy. Wings flapped, beaks opened, bird shit fell through bars, females squawked as he approached caged and artificial nests. Full-grown birds, fledglings, eggs. How had Dr. Steffens got them to breed so fully in captivity?

Not that Jason would understand it if he were told.

A harried lab tech nodded as he scattered seeds into cages. Jason called over the noise, "Where's Dr. Steffens?" The man pointed.

Behind a stack of cages, she bent over a lab bench, a short dumpy woman with lethal bird shit on her pants, the brain of a genius in her head. Jason had a sudden incongruous picture of Toni Steffens accepting a Nobel Prize, standing in her bird-stained outfit at the Stockholm Concert Hall before the king, in a room full of chirping sparrows.

"Dr. Steffens."

She looked up, startled. "Now?"

"Yes." He hadn't told anyone, not even her, when it would happen. Benjamin Franklin, again, with his wise counsel on secrets.

"I need a few minutes."

"Yes." Jason headed for decon, glad to escape the bird lab. He waited in the small space outside the airlock. To his left was the stockade, in which sat the deranged Corporal Porter, who had attacked Jason's grandmother. Porter was another problem. Holbrook was trying different meds, although so far all they had done was reduce Porter to zombielike quiescence.

Eventually Toni emerged from the bird lab beside a lab assistant and a loaded carry-bot. The assistant wore a look that Jason recognized all too well: terrified but determined. He'd seen that look on the faces of new recruits in Congo, some of whom had never made it home. Five trusted soldiers from J Squad, fully armed and armored, clattered down the steps.

The eight of them went through the airlock to the tunnel beyond. Parts of the tunnel walls and ceiling had shaken loose during Jason's relentless bombing of Monterey Base, but the carry-bot was able to navigate three-quarters of the way to the hatch. When rubble blocked the bots' progress, everyone carried the cages of birds over the debris. J Squad opened the hatch and took up defensive positions, with more soldiers covering them in the woods. However, as Jason had expected, the trees were empty of enemy. New America, reeling from the destruction of Sierra Depot, was most likely regrouping, or concentrating on attacking the undomed convoy.

The cages were lugged up the stairs, one by one. There should have been, Jason thought, some kind of ceremony. What Jason, Toni, and the lab assistant were doing would change the world just as fundamentally as anyone who had ever won a Nobel: Alfred Nobel with his dynamite, Salk with his vaccine, Crick and Watson with their double helix. Just as much as anything since the spore cloud.

One by one, Toni and her assistant opened the cages.

Jason watched the last of the sparrows flap off into the trees. Probably some would die, eaten by predators. But in the spring, most would mate. The males, all sterile, would fail to impregnate their wild brides. The females would also mate, producing sterile male offspring and females who would carry the drive into the next generation. As the sterility spread, helped by Toni Steffens's other, diabolically clever gene tweaks, there would be fewer and fewer sparrows. A "selective sweep," Toni called it. Sterile males would have to go farther afield to find mates. They could—because they had, once before—cover two continents and, eventually perhaps reach Asia from Alaska. It had happened before.

Fewer and fewer sparrows. Eventually, there would be none. And RSA would die with them.

How long? Toni Steffens had not known for sure: too many variables. What she had known for sure was that Jason's decision to release the birds would change Earth's ecology even more profoundly than had the temporary elimination of eight species of mice by the original spore cloud. Sparrows filled more ecological functions than mice. Jason even knew what they were, but in case his knowledge was incomplete, there were going to be outraged scientists eager to shout it at him.

This evening. Time was running out.

For now, he stood quietly, watching a genetically altered sparrow, unwitting time bomb to its own species, perch on the branch of a blue oak. Finally he said to Toni Steffens, "All right. Let's tell them." And into his implant, "J Squad—all troops back to the dome. Perimeter patrol—all troops inside. Repeat, all troops inside."

"Sir?" said a startled voice. Perimeter patrol was always maintained, in case of messages from the signal station.

"All troops inside."

He tongued off the implant. To Toni he said, just as if she had been one of his soldiers, "Game on."

Above the trees, a quadcopter hummed. Lieutenant Li, Specialist De-Ford, and Corporal Michaelson, all undoubtedly mystified. The signal station had never been left empty before. But Jason wanted everyone here, no exceptions.

He opened the hatch to the tunnel. The sparrow on the blue oak spread its small wings and flew off.

The armory was the only space large enough to hold everyone, and then only when the FiVees and Bradley were jammed into one corner with the quadcopters on top of them. No room for many chairs; except for the old, people stood or sat on the floor. Jason and Toni climbed onto the hood of a FiVee, where everyone could see them. Half of J Squad stood in a solid line against the ordnance lockers; the other half made a cordon in front of Jason's FiVee dais.

While people were being escorted from Enclave Dome to Lab Dome, while everyone was being brought through the open internal airlock to the armory, Jason had talked to Hillson. It had not gone well. Hillson stood now by the front left wheel of the FiVee, scowling. Whenever Jason glanced at his master sergeant, his stomach tightened.

The only people not here were the five v-comas who had not yet awakened, a nurse to watch over them, the tranquilized Porter in his stockade cell, the three soldiers on the *Return*, and Elizabeth Duncan in the command post to maintain surveillance. Duncan already knew what Jason would say. The others would be told right after the meeting.

"You don't have to introduce it this way," Duncan had said. "You're the commander."

"Yes, I do," Jason had said. "Otherwise, if I tell it piecemeal, rumors and exaggerations will get completely out of control."

"True. But, sir . . . you'll be inviting ugly debate."

"They're entitled to debate."

"And then you'll carry out the plan anyway."

Jason hadn't replied; they both knew he had no real choice about the overall strategy.

He scanned the crowd. Faces curious or apprehensive or hostile. Some of the hostile ones were his own troops. Some still resented his allowing the star-farers to infect everybody, resented his bringing the Settlers to the base, resented the war going on so long without much real action, resented their lives cooped up in two domes. Others of his soldiers waited blank-faced, reserving judgment.

The scientists stood together by the airlock, Dr. McKay next to his Awakened wife, holding their little girl. Dr. Ka^graa was with them, along with Jane, her cousin La^vor, and the giant teenager Belok^. Jane caught his eye and then looked away. In that moment, Jason understood that she *knew* what he was going to say. How? A little shiver ran down his spine.

Colin, in his powerchair, sat beside Jane, with Jason's father seated on a folding chair, one hand on his cane and the other on Colin's shoulder. Ryan looked very old. The Settlers clustered behind Colin. Jason looked for his grandmother, but couldn't find her or Lindy in the press of bodies. He spotted Claire Patel, Dr. Holbrook, and one of the young teachers from Enclave Dome with Dr. Sugiyama's two children clinging to her. Holbrook had told Jason that the teacher was the only one who could deal with their trauma, and they would not leave her. The little boy, trembling, had his face buried in the teacher's neck.

Lieutenant Li, standing by the ordnance lockers, stared steadily at Jason. Did he guess? Maybe.

The rest of Jason's officers, both line and staff. None of them among the Awakened.

The enlisted troops who were Awakened: McNally, Swinford, Ramstetter, Veatch, Larriva, Buckley.

Mason Kandiss, standing impassive with J Squad.

Beside Jason, Toni Steffens sat down on the roof of the FiVee's cab. She must be exhausted. Her work on the gene drive had been unceasing. But, then, so had Jason's work.

He braced himself. Everyone was here, 660 people. Time to begin.

"People of Monterey Base," he said, knowing the term sounded both pompous and faintly comic but unable to think of anything better, "we are all here together because I have two announcements that you all need to hear. They affect everyone, military and civilian alike."

Someone coughed. It was the only sound. Well, that wouldn't be true for long.

"Neither announcement will, or can, be reversed, although I know you will have a lot to say about both. Here is the first: Dr. Steffens developed a gene drive to spread sterility among the sparrows that carry RSA. She and her team bred birds carrying that drive, and we have released them into the wild. In thirty to fifty years, by best estimate, the United States will be free of RSA. It will no longer exist here."

Babble of voices: Done what? Released what? What does he mean? But at least half of the crowd knew enough. Colin shouted, "You can't!"

Zack McKay started to say something, stopped, stared at Jason as if at a mirage. Voices rose. Jason raised his hand, but no one stopped talking. Over the din—*as bad as the birds*—Colin's voice prevailed; he was, in his own way, as used to command as Jason. People quieted to listen.

"Are you insane? You've wrecked the entire ecology! Do you know what happened a hundred years ago when the Chinese tried to eradicate sparrows? Insects swarmed out of control because no birds were eating them, the insects ate the crops, twenty million people died of starvation! And now with the ecosystem already so fragile—"

"We haven't got twenty million people," Jason said. "There aren't twenty million people left in the entire country. Look, I know this is a huge meddle with the—"

"It's irresponsible! It's criminal!"

All at once, Jason had an image of Colin as a small child during one of their brotherly fights: "Dad! He hitted me! It's cwimial!" God, the betrayals of memory!

He looked at Colin's non-childish face and said, "It's done, Colin. It was a choice between the ecology and the population dying of RSA."

"But out in the—"

"You have no right to—"

"No idea of—"

"No authority for—"

Half the crowd glared at him; the other half asked bewildered questions of their neighbors. Here and there were a few understanding faces, chief among them Jane's. She was translating for her father and cousin, but her eyes were on him.

He'd expected this. But he didn't expect Colin's next shout, or the sudden pain it gave him. Colin said, "So how are you any different from the Gaiists, taking the fate of the Earth into *their* own hands?"

Relative silence. Now—he would have to finish this now. He called loudly, "There is more."

The murmuring and questioning quieted but didn't stop, and Jason kept his voice raised to just below a shout. Everyone needed to hear this.

"There's another reason I released the birds. *Listen*, everyone, this is the larger of my two announcements, and it affects all of you. Our scientists will no longer be able to work on the gene drive, or to create a version that stops RSA without eliminating sparrows. They won't be able to do that because we will no longer be here. And neither will the domes."

The crowd stilled as if shot.

This was it. He needed to make it simple enough for the teenage Settlers to understand, convincing enough for the scientists, strong enough to command his army.

"The people coming out of v-comas have increased intelligence. Most of you already know that. They fell into v-comas in the first place because they possess a certain gene. I'm sure most of you have already heard that, too. This gene doesn't only exist among people at Monterey Base. It's a human gene, found in both Terrans and those from World. About four and a half percent of all humans possess it— possibly more, because Monterey Base is a small sample size to generalize from. Four and a half percent of *all* humans, including the New America enemy."

On some faces, growing comprehension.

"All of us were infected with the virophage from World. Everybody. However, most of us didn't even notice, or had just a slight headache, and then we got over it, like you do a cold. But those with a special gene who are exposed to the virophage go into comas and come out changed. The virophage activates the gene. After the v-coma, those people are still carriers and can infect others who have the special gene. And after the v-coma, when you awaken, your brain is different. Rewired. More intelligent. And so what you will infect others with is increased intelligence.

"I want to say that again—every single one of the Awakened can infect anyone else who carries the right gene, and the result will be that that person, too, becomes much smarter.

"People, intelligence is a weapon. It is the most formidable weapon there is. Intelligence lets us create ever more effective weapons, ever more effective strategies to perceive and exploit our enemies' weaknesses. Intelligence—in both uses of the words, information and smartness—is what wins wars.

"We can't let New America win the United States. We can't let those among the enemy who possess that special gene become more intelligent. That means we can't let them be exposed to those among us who are v-coma carriers."

Dead silence.

Jason continued, "This means we can't ever, ever allow any of the Awakened to be exposed to anyone in New America. Nor can we allow anyone from New America access to the domes of Monterey Base. Because although we know that those of you who never went into v-comas are free of virophage by now, there are still dormant spores of the virophage in the domes. They're apparently just as tough as *R. sporii*.

"I repeat, *enhanced intelligence is a weapon*. We can't leave that weapon to New America. What we can leave, what we are leaving, is a planet that somewhere down the road will be free of RSA. But neither the Awakened nor the domes must remain where New America can get at them."

Someone in the crowd yelled, "Kill all the Awakened!"

Jason did not see who yelled, but the shout was taken up by a few others. J Squad drew their weapons. Jason shouted, "There will be no killing!"

He saw Colin jerk his chair to shield Jane. Marianne continued to gaze directly at Jason. Hillson, with the agility of a much younger man, had climbed to the roof the FiVee cab, directly behind his commander, assault rifle on his shoulder.

Jason said, "Here is what we will do. Listen carefully, because most of you will have a choice to make. Three days from now, the *Return*, the World spaceship, will go back to World, who owns it. Every single Awakened will be on it. No exceptions. The rest of you may also choose to travel to World, or you may choose to stay here. However, the domes will be destroyed."

Gasps. There was only one known way to destroy an alien dome.

"If you choose to stay on Earth, you must leave Monterey Base tomorrow. Civilians will be provided with FiVees, supplies, tech, some weapons. You can return to the Settlement dome if you choose, although I don't recommend it because New America will attack there again and you will be vulnerable to siege.

"Army troops have four choices. You may come on the spaceship to World, under my continuing command. You may separate from the army and accompany civilians. You may stay with this battalion, which will now be commanded by Major Mainwaring, and will move into the mountains. Or you may join a convoy now on its way here from Fort Hood, although I should tell you that I believe Fort Hood to be under an unstable military dictatorship. All of those choices are more physically dangerous than accompanying us to World, but the decision is yours, except for the Awakened."

It was Ryan, his usually meek and depression-prone father, who called out loudly, "'Us'? Are you going on the ship to World?"

"Yes," Jason said. "I am. So is Major Duncan, Captain Goldman, Lieutenant Li, and others." All his coconspirators. "I urge you all to come with me to World, but I will not issue orders even to the soldiers among you. The decision is yours."

Someone called, "You're going to *nuke* the domes?"

Chaos erupted. Before anyone in the crowd was hurt—Jason hoped—a single shot was fired, echoing in the enclosed area. *I'm hit,* Jason thought a nanosecond before the pain started. A second shot, close on the first. Jason toppled forward off the hood of the FiVee. *What son a bitch got a gun in here to—*

Then he landed on the heads and shoulders and arms of people below, and knew no more.

CHAPTER 24

Zack thrust Caitlin into Susan's arms and pushed himself forward to shield them both. But there were no more gunshots. Caitlin screamed; everyone screamed, it sounded like. The McKays stood near the open internal airlock, and Zack shoved Susan into the stream of panicked people. "Go! Go!"

"Zack—"

"I'll be all right! Go! Take her to . . ." The lab might be attacked. Anywhere might be attacked if there was some sort of insane riot against the Awakened. But all at once one of Jenner's J Squad was there, strong arms opening a passage for Susan.

"I've got her, Doctor."

For one terrible moment, Zack thought: *And what if you're with the gunman?* But, no, this was J Squad, Jenner's personal Praetorian Guard, as Toni called them. Toni—

"Go!" Susan shouted, and he didn't have to tell her where he needed to go. She knew. Susan always knew him. He let the soldier usher his wife and child to safety as he turned to fight against the crowd, toward the FiVee.

It was like trying to pole upstream in rapids, but he got there. Jenner, surrounded by grim soldiers, lay on the ground. Holbrook bent over him—or at least Zack thought he did. Jenner was not Zack's goal.

Toni stood in a narrow passage between the FiVee and the armory wall. A soldier on the vehicle roof pointed his rifle at Zack, whose heart stopped. But then the soldier recognized him and nodded. Zack slipped behind the truck.

"Toni! You all right?"

"Nicole? Will they attack the infirmary? Will they—"

"Jenner's men seem to have it under control. They took Susan and Caity to safety, they'll protect everybody at risk . . . are you okay?"

"Yes. Jenner?"

"I don't know."

She said, "I was on the cab to answer questions, and then he fell and I jumped back here. I saw J Squad take down the gunman but I didn't see any more. I think he might have acted alone."

Relief flooded Zack, even though Toni could be mistaken; what did she know about the mood of Monterey Base? This was her first time out of the lab since she'd awakened. The lab . . .

"Toni—*why*? The birds—"

"Jenner told you why he released them. He's right."

Words that, coming from Toni, were almost as shocking as Jenner's own. Her deep brown eyes caught and held his.

"Zack, he *was* right to release the birds. We were right."

"The whole ecology will be wrecked!"

"Changed, not wrecked."

"Wrecked. At least, in the short run."

"We were thinking long run," Toni said, and from her tone, Zack knew that the subject was closed. He knew, too, that Jenner's plan would be rammed through, even if Jenner himself was dead. Major Duncan and J Squad and whoever else Jenner had brought into his strategy would make sure of that. The gene-drive birds had been released; the domes with remaining virophage spores would be nuked; the Awakened, if no one else, would go aboard the *Return* to the stars.

Wherever Susan and Caitlin went, Zack would go, too.

His breath caught at the thought. A spaceship, a new planet, they would have to have all their microbes changed, what did he remember about World, a K-something orange dwarf star . . .

Toni said, "I'm going to find out if the colonel is dead."

And an alliance, however temporary, between Toni Steffens and Colonel Jason Jenner, US Army. That might be the strangest thing of all.

When there was no more gunfire after the first shot, panic subsided a little. Soldiers funneled everyone out of the armory. As the crowd thinned, Jane looked for Colin. Two soldiers had pushed Jane, her father, La^vor, and Belok^ into a corner and stood in front of them, guns raised, to protect them. But no one tried to hurt them, and when the armory was almost empty, Jane said to the back of one of her protectors, "Can I go now?"

The soldier turned. Through the faceplate of her helmet, the woman looked middle-aged, which still felt so strange to Jane. On World, she would be a Mother. The soldier nodded.

"Stay here, please," Jane said to the others, and slid past her protectors. At the far end of the armory another line of armed soldiers stood in front of the huddle around Jason. Ryan was among them, and Colin's powerchair. Jane caught a glimpse of Colin's face and knew, from the Colin-patterns in her mind, that Jason was not dead.

Colin looked up at her. "I saw the military guarding you . . . but Jason . . ."

"How bad is it?" Jane knelt by his chair, felt his outrage in her mind and bones and heart.

"He'll live. The fucker hit his chest but Holbrook said he missed everything vital. Oh, Jane—"

She knelt by his chair. "Do you need to stay with him? Or with your father?"

Colin glanced at the huddle. The press of bodies had shifted, and now Jane could see Lindy bending over Jason. She, not Holbrook, was injecting something into the colonel. A nurse came through the airlock wheeling a gurney. Jason's eyes were open; he said something to

Lindy that Jane couldn't hear. Blood stained the entire front of his uniform.

Colin said, "I can go. But the soldiers—"

He hadn't even finished his sentence when the middle-aged female soldier appeared beside them and said, "This way, ma'am." The other guard was leading Ka^graa, Belok^, and La^vor.

Jane said, "Colin, too."

"All right."

She took them out of the armory and to the secure quarters where all the Awakened slept. Jane crowded into Colin's room beside his chair and closed the door. He said, "Did you know?"

"About the birds? No."

"I don't know what Jason tells you."

"Jason and I don't talk," Jane said. She felt grief pressing in on him, jagged pieces, sharp as scalpels, and knew that not all the grief was for the ecology.

She said, "We have two days."

His eyes filled with tears. Like the men on World, Colin was not afraid to cry. He said, "You know, then."

"That you must stay here? Yes. And I must go."

"I want to be with you. But Earth is going to need people who are not New America. Who are not military, not killers, not destructive, not . . ."

She took his hand. "Colin, I want to say something. I have been thinking about this. It is possible to want a thing too much. Even a good thing. Wanting it too much makes you rush after it, chase it hard. And then, like anything being chased, it runs away."

"I don't understand what you're trying to tell me."

Jane struggled to find words. The pattern, so clear in her mind, was wordless, and this was not her language. But nothing had ever been so important to communicate.

"You want Mother Terra, as we have Mother World. But let Her come to you. And if She comes with some technology necessary to keep you alive, let Her. You don't have to grab technology, like Monterey Base does, but you don't have to push it away, either. Just receive it, as a gift."

"I want to live without tech, free with nature."

Jane said slowly, "Nature is not free. Or pure."

"Jane—"

"Don't be disappointed in me, Colin. Just listen. I have been practicing reading English. In the library. Do you know what 'kintsugi' is?"

"No." His face wore a stubborn look, and Jane saw the resemblance to his brother, and to his grandmother.

She said, "It is from an art in a place called 'Japan.' They made earthenware pots, like ours on World. Sometimes the pots break in the firing of them. Then kintsugi comes. It means to stick the fragments of broken pots together with a golden lacquer, to make something even more beautiful because it was broken and mended."

There was a long silence. Then Colin said, "I love you."

"I know," Jane said, and felt that knowledge, too, as patterns in her mind, full of sorrow and joy and the weight of two planets.

She crawled onto his lap, careful of his injured leg, and held him.

Marianne and Ryan walked beside Jason's gurney, with Lindy on the other side. Orderlies wheeled it from the armory to the OR. Soldiers, and no one else, filled the corridors along the way. Dr. Holbrook had gone ahead to scrub. The bullet was still in Jason and had to come out.

Just before Jason disappeared into the OR, Lindy stooped and kissed his lips. Jason's eyes were closed, but Marianne watched his mouth form a brief curve.

She had always thought of Colin as the fragile one. Colin was the one who'd had a ruptured spleen from a schoolyard bully. Who had had to learn to compensate for the superhearing that for the first three years of his little life had tormented him and made him cry constantly. Who had sobbed over the deaths of countless pet gerbils. Who'd carefully watered every plant that he heard "clicking" from dryness. Who had tried to found a quixotic, impossible way of living in harmony with nature.

But Jason turned out to be the one who was most vulnerable.

She said, "How badly is he hurt? I want the truth, Lindy."

"Not very. Of course, surgery is always a risk, but he should be okay. He should have been wearing body armor, but he probably thought it would send the wrong message—Marianne, they shot him! One of his own men! Don't they know how hard he's struggled to hold this base together, to do the right thing, even now that . . . Did you know about this? The birds and the forced exodus?"

Exodus. Biblical. No, not biblical—older than that. What Jason was forcing on Earth was Promethean science, an ambitious experimental enterprise to counteract a major threat, a science which pits potential pay-offs against huge risks. Marianne, who had herself engaged in Promethean science on World, understood.

She said truthfully, "If I had thought about it, I would have known what Jason would do. But I've been thinking about something else. Thomas Farouk and I . . . Lindy, I need to talk to Jason. Can I do that before he goes under anesthesia?"

"No, of course not. What is it? Tell me."

"I can't. On second thought, it will wait. It's already waited a hundred and forty thousand years."

Lindy stared at her. "Are you okay?"

Was she? Were any of them? "Yes. Just get Jason well. We only have two days."

Someone tapped her on the shoulder. Marianne turned to the sergeant who seemed to always accompany Jason, an older man with bristly gray hair above a face that gave nothing away. Except right now.

"Dr. Jenner, ma'am, I'm Master Sergeant Hillson, Colonel Jenner's aide. Will he be all right?"

"I'm told that he will be."

Hillson nodded. "Good. I need to talk to you, ma'am. About the Awakened."

"What about them?"

"They're all leaving on the *Return*," he said, with no uncertainty. "All of them, no exceptions. Colonel Jenner was going to talk to them to make sure they understand that. He can't, now. So you have to."

She considered him. Hillson was going to carry out Jason's orders even if he, she, and everybody else died doing it. Marianne had barely had time to consider those orders, including what it would mean to return to the alien planet she had left, in her personal time stream, less than three months ago. Three months and twenty-eight years.

"Ma'am?" He was immovable as mountains.

"All right," she said. "Get all the Awakened together in the conference room."

"Yes, ma'am," he said. It was fortunate that he didn't salute; she might have tried to slug him. From nerves, from fear, from frustration. When was the last time her life had been under her own control?

Maybe it never had. She no longer knew, not since she and Farouk had worked out their theory.

Twenty-eight.

Jane didn't need to count how many people had jammed into the conference room. She felt the shape and color of the crowd, and she knew. She felt, too, the colors and shapes of their bafflement, fear, and rage, as well as her own sorrow over leaving Colin.

Twenty-eight people: twenty-five of the thirty who had already awakened. Three parents of v-coma children: Zack McKay, and Fiona and Karl James, whose little boy lay comatose in the infirmary, under guard. The twenty-eight sat on chairs or leaned against the walls, scientists and soldiers and Settlers and a kitchen worker. Facing them, looking determined and exhausted, stood Marianne Jenner. Her determination was jagged-edged and dark blue, and in it Jane felt clearly her resemblance to Jason.

"I am here on behalf of Colonel Jenner, who is in surgery," Marianne said. "I'm here to listen to all your ideas about leaving Earth. but I need to tell you up front: This is not an undecided debate. We are all going to World. We—no, wait, please, give me a moment to finish—represent too great a threat to Earth. As Colonel Jenner said, if we transmit the virophage to New America, whoever contracts it will gain the same enhanced intelligence that all of you have. They will devise new weapons and new ways to cause destruction, because their intelligence—like yours—will grow along whatever pathways are already prominent in their brains. Those are pathways of aggression and hatred. If you think that Terra is hell now, it is nothing compared to what three or four generations of vicious and narcissistic conquerors can make it. Sadists equipped with the physics of Dr. Farouk, the biology of Dr. Yu's team. They will—"

"I don't care!" Karl James shouted. "We're not leaving Earth! We'll take our chances here!"

"I'm not going, either," Toni Steffens said, more quetly but with even more determination. Jane wanted to shrink from the deadly shapes that Dr. Steffens made.

"Marianne, consider," Toni Steffens continued. "If Earth is going to recover, it needs the intelligence that the Awakened can bring. We can use it to counter New America's wars, to aid in Earth's ecological recovery, to return humanity to a viable civilization much more quickly. If intelligence is a weapon, it can also be a force for good. Surely even Colonel Jenner can see that!"

"Yes," Marianne said, "he can. But it's a question of risk versus benefit. The risks here outweigh the benefits. And, Karl James, your child was born in Monterey Base and isn't immune to RSA. How could you stay here with him anyway?"

"Use your so-called super IQ to figure that out instead of kidnapping us!" Karl yelled, and Jane saw that he was past rational argument, beside himself with fear and anger.

For the first time, she saw the use of that strange Terran phrase. Karl James was two shapes in her mind, superimposed on each other: one spiky and the color of blood, the other muddy and puddled as dirty water.

A woman near the back of the room cried, "I'm not going, either!"

Then everyone was talking, voices rising higher and higher with objections, with reasoning, with emotion, with such overwhelming noise that Jane slipped from the room, slightly surprised that the soldiers guarding the door let her go. And then not surprised at all. . . .

It didn't really matter what was said here. Jane knew what would happen. She'd known it the moment she'd seen the shapes of Marian Jenner. Of Zack McKay, of the two members of J squad who were Awakened. All of them felt like Jason.

The decision had been made.

CHAPTER 25

"No pain pills," Jason said.

Lindy frowned. "You were *shot*. You are not going to feel good for a while. If pain interferes with your thinking and—"

"It won't. Is the bullet out?"

"Of course the bullet is out! You just had fucking surgery! Oh . . . no, Jason, you can't . . . stay still!"

Jason stayed still. Lindy stood beside his bed in the infirmary. She was the first, but Jason knew that beyond the door would be a whole horde of people who would want to see him: his father and grandmother, Hillson, Colin, Duncan, Li, Ka^graa. But Lindy first, Lindy always first, and he took a minute he didn't have to meet her eyes steadily and ask.

"Lindy . . . are you going with me? On the *Return*?"

Her eyes opened wide. "You're going? I mean, you're really going to do this insane thing?"

"It's not insane and yes, I'm going."

She said slowly, "There is a rumor that the convoy from Fort Hood is coming to arrest you and take over Monterey Base. That there isn't any other reason they would send so many troops. Is that true?"

"Yes."

"Is that the—"

"*No*, it's not the reason I'm going on the ship. I'm going because I started this and I need to finish it. I'm going because I have to be sure that everyone who could spread the virophage isn't in a position to do so. World is already infected, the entire damn planet. I'm going because Major Farouk thinks he's cracked the spaceship physics and we can, in time, build more ships and colonize the stars. I'm going because—"

"All right, I get it. For somebody just out of anesthetic, you're very articulate. You're going to direct the whole operation from this bed, aren't you?"

"I'm going to get up."

"No, you're not. Not yet. Speaking of Farouk, she and Marianne are desperate to see you. Something about equations."

"Equations can wait. Send the guard for Major Duncan, please. And send in Sergeant Hillson, if he's out there."

"Of course he's out there—when is Hillson not ready to do whatever you need him for?"

But I wasn't sure this time. He didn't say it aloud. Instead he said, knowing that he was begging, "Lindy?"

She shuddered, a long visible jerk the entire length of her body. She still scowled: his prickly, independent, maddening wife. If she refused, if the past lay too heavily between them for her to overcome it, he didn't know if he had the heart to colonize World. The will, yes, but maybe not the heart.

"Lindy, I need you. Desperately. And I love you. I always have, despite . . . everything. Your choice is your own, but . . ." He couldn't finish. All he could do was hope.

"Yes," she said, her voice thick. "I'll go with you. You seem to keep needing a doctor."

He fumbled for her hand, but she snatched it away. "Not now—neither of us has time. I love you, you idiot. Now I'll get Hillson. Do not try to get up!"

He stayed flat in bed, although he hated it. Pain mounted steadily in his side; he tried to ignore it. Hillson, who seemed to have aged ten years since yesterday, said, "Sir, Major Duncan asked me to make a report to you, she's directing the evacuation. Lieutenant Li went back to the signal station, and the *Return* reports that the convoy from Fort Hood is maybe six days out."

"Moving too fast."

"Yes, sir."

"Go ahead, Sergeant." It hurt even to lie still, to focus on what Hillson was saying. How much blood had Jason lost? Tubes ran into him in various places, but none of them were red. So maybe he had all the blood he needed. It would be nice to have all of something he needed.

"The Awakened, military and civilian, were all talked to by Dr. Jenner and Ms. Ka^graa, and given the chance to ask questions about World. We have nine Awakened troops, including Corporal Porter, who attacked Dr. Jenner."

"Porter is still drugged?"

"Yes, sir. As per your orders."

"Who shot me?"

"Private Perry."

A perpetual troublemaker, Hillson had said weeks ago. Jason didn't have to ask what had happened to Perry; he knew. You did not get to shoot your commanding officer in front of J Squad and live.

Hillson continued, "All eight soldiers have agreed to be transported to World. You wanted agreement, sir."

"I did." Hillson had wanted only orders: *This unit is being deployed.* But this was hardly a normal deployment.

"Three of them have family members here, who will also go. Of the remaining troops, those whom you are allowing to choose deployment or separation from the service, the division is about fifty-fifty."

That surprised Jason. He'd expected far fewer to choose World. A sudden pain seared his side; briefly he closed his eyes.

"Sir?"

"Continue, Sergeant. The officers?"

"Major Duncan, of course. Captain Goldman. Lieutenant Li."

None with a choice; they were all coconspirators.

Hillson continued, "Lieutenant Allen. Lieutenant Parker and some of her nurses. The rest—captains Frazier, Gardner, Vargas, and Sullivan and Major Holbrook—all are staying here. Majors Sullivan and Vargas are furious that you released the birds and that you're going to destroy the dome. I have a detail loading up scientific equipment onto a FiVee under their direction."

"Go on," Jason said.

Hillson spieled off more names, finishing with, "The civilian Awakened are . . . in a lot of disagreement."

Of course they were. "Who else will leave?"

"All the aliens, of course."

Jason would never get Hillson to think of them as anything but aliens. But Jason was relieved that Jane agreed; she might have tried to stay with Colin. But on second thought, perhaps Jane, with her increased insight, understood better than any of them.

"Dr. Jenner and Dr. Farouk agree to go, of course. Also Dr. McKay—his wife and child are both Awakened. He's not happy, but he'll go. Also some of the civilian scientists who are not Awakened, and a lot of the civilian base staff. They don't want to try to live here without the base. A child, Devon James, is still in a coma, and his parents have finally agreed to go with him, but they're not happy. In total, a hundred and three people have agreed to leave Earth. But some of the Awakened are saying they won't go."

"Who are . . . the holdouts." Damn, he hadn't expected to be this tired so soon. It wasn't as if he hadn't been shot before, in Congo. But he'd been younger, and hopped up on combat drugs, and not striving to move an entire Army base off-planet.

Hillson said, "Holdouts among the Awakened are two Settlers, one parent of a Settler girl still in coma, and Dr. Steffens."

That shocked him. "Toni Steffens?"

"Yes, sir. She wants to stay here and continue her bird experiments. And to keep her wife here. The wife is in a coma."

Jason thought rapidly. He hated the only alternative he saw. Toni Steffens was so intelligent, so stubborn, so commanding that Jason would have hated to face her in battle. But she could not stay. "Have her straitjacketed by force, and then drugged. Get Holbrook to do it, on my orders, with whatever troops it takes. She gets put on the ship, along with Nicole."

"Yes, sir. Dr. Patel wants to stay here. She wants to go with the new Settlement your brother is planning."

A loss. But Jason had allowed the choice, Claire had not been in a v-coma, and Colin's people would need a doctor.

Hillson said, "Your father is going with the new Settlement, too."

Expected.

Hillson coughed. "I haven't talked to Dr. Ross."

"Dr. Ross has agreed to go with us."

Hillson nodded. "Yes, sir. About the Settler child in v-coma and her parents . . ."

"They have to go. Put the kid aboard the ship under armed guard and the parents will board. The other two Settlers get the same treatment as Dr. Steffens." Colin was going to have a fit. Jason didn't like it, either; he was kidnapping two families. But he had no choice. "Do it as quietly as you can, Hillson. And as soon as you can."

"Yes, sir."

"Good job, Hillson. Has the . . . *Return* . . . landed?"

"Should I get the doctor? You're—"

"I'm . . . fine. The ship?"

"She's landed, sir. Supplies are being loaded. The deserters . . . sorry, sir, the *evacuees* are being given transport and supplies and weapons. They leave tomorrow."

"Good. Hillson . . . you didn't name yourself."

Hillson straightened, which would have seemed impossible given that he was already straighter than a rifle barrel. His homely face looked even more wooden than usual. "I go with the United States Army, sir."

Cold slid down Jason's spine. "Which army? Staying or going?"

"You are my CO, sir. You are deploying this unit. I go where you send me."

"Thank you," Jason said, and Hillson scowled at the breach of protocol, the gross violation of chain of command, as he had not outright scowled at any of the other fantastic and unprecedented things Jason had said so far.

Lindy bustled in, took one look at Jason, and said to Hillson, "Out. Now."

Jason said, "I have people to—"

"No, you don't. Not yet. I shouldn't have even allowed Hillson in. Bye, Sergeant."

Jason managed, "Dismissed." Hillson would carry out all his orders. So would Elizabeth Duncan and the rest of his officers. But—

"You can't control everything," Lindy said. "Isn't it enough that you're bringing off this insane plan?"

"I need . . . a drug to stay awake."

"No," Lindy said. "You need to sleep."

Against his will, he did.

When he woke again, it was the next day. Had Lindy given him something in his IV that made him sleep? He would have been furious with her if it would have done any good, but it wouldn't. And Jason did feel stronger. Hillson reported that the convoys leaving the base were nearly ready to roll. "Convoys?" Jason said. "Plural?"

"Yes, sir. Major Duncan authorized it. One is heading south, to join the convoy from Fort Hood. Mostly military and their families, with some base civilians. They have transport and weapons. The other convoy has Settlers, some military, and a lot of base civilians. Colin Jenner will found a new village of some kind. They're heading up into the mountains, to someplace able to be defended, and Major Duncan equipped them with most of the supplies not put aboard the *Return* and most of the transport."

Colin had accepted military? And considering defense? "Are they equipped with weapons?"

"Yes, sir."

Well, well. The mountain finally recognizes the reality of avalanches.

"Is the *Return* on schedule for departure?"

"Ahead of schedule, sir. Major Duncan wants to see you. Also Mr. Jenner."

"The major first."

Elizabeth Duncan entered. Jason said, "Major?"

"Operation is proceeding smoothly, sir. Both convoys to depart in a few hours. Prisoners are aboard the *Return* drugged and under guard: Private Porter, Dr. Steffens—"

Jason said sharply, "Only Porter is a prisoner."

"Yes, sir. Sorry, sir. All the Awakened except Dr. Jenner are aboard, and so are the v-coma patients, including the parents of the Settler child. They're under guard, too, but not drugged. The Settlers fought the two families' removal, sir, but no one was injured. Lieutenant Li has loaded the signal station equipment. Loading everything else proceeds. So does ship modification for time during the flight."

Jason didn't ask what modifications she meant; it didn't matter. If the trip to World was like the voyage of the *Return* here, they wouldn't be in space very long.

In space. He tasted the words; they felt metallic on his tongue. He'd barely had time to think about the voyage, or the planet that would now be home. Getting there had taken all his thoughts.

"Anything else, Major?"

"No, sir. We can proceed whenever you so order."

"Thank you, Major."

She left, and Colin stormed in. Out of his powerchair, he leaned on a cane. "Jason! You kidnapped four of my people! Including a child!"

"Colin—"

"I want them back!"

"Col . . . I *can't*."

"You mean you won't!"

"I mean I can't. No one capable of transmitting the virophage can stay on Earth."

Colin took a step toward the bed. All at once Jason realized that if Colin bludgeoned him with his cane, Jason was helpless. Unarmed, alone, all he could do was scream. And who was still out there? Lindy, his grandmother . . .

Colin said, more quietly, "I don't do that, Jason. Stop thinking like a soldier."

"I am a soldier, Colin. That's why I have to do this."

"Protecting your country by destroying it? Wasn't that military tactic thoroughly disproved several wars ago?"

"I'm not destroying it. I'm ensuring that New America doesn't do so. They'll consume themselves in fighting each other. Haters always do."

They stared at each other. Between them lay gulfs of perception, crossed only by the fragile bridges of kinship and history. Colin knew he could not stop Jason, who had all the power on his side. Jason knew that Colin might never forgive him.

Jason said, "I'm told the ship can return to Terra. We'll only be a short time in space. People can come back."

"And twenty-eight years will have passed here."

"Yes." Colin would be the age their grandmother was now. Their father would be dead. Jason would be only a few years older. And probably the spaceship would not return to Earth anyway, unless there was a good reason.

Colin said, "Good-bye, Jason."

"Good-bye, Col. I'm sorry."

After Colin stormed out and Lindy came in, Jason said, "Tell my father and grandmother to wait. I'll see them in fifteen minutes."

He turned his face to the wall.

CHAPTER 26

Marianne never had gotten in to talk to Jason. He had been too occupied and too weak. "Later, please," he'd said, and then she'd been taken up with her own good-byes to Claire, to Ryan, to Colin. After the last two, the son and grandson she might never see again, Marianne had gone straight to her berth on the *Return* and stayed there until liftoff. She had always hated for anyone to see her cry.

Her shared quarters, thrown up hastily of plywood and metal and used mattresses, looked eerily familiar. As a small child, Marianne had been taken on an overnight train trip to visit relatives in Chicago. That compartment, like this, had had four berths with curtains in front of them and a single chair at the end. Here, however, there were no windows, not even a wall screen. If she wanted to see Earth left behind, she would have to go to the Commons.

She didn't want to see it. From the moment the *Return* had landed in California months ago, Terra had not felt like home. Cities destroyed, populations wiped out, wilderness returning . . . no. She had never been outside without an esuit. World would be as much home to her as Terra was now, except for the loss of Ryan and Colin.

But she would have Jason. And on World, Noah and her granddaughter Lily. Although World would be God-knows-what after twenty-eight years of infection by the virophage.

Marianne put her hand on the windowless alien wall. She pushed her grief away—and how many times in her life had she had to do just that?—and concentrated on what she'd gained. She and Farouk had combined their knowledge, his physics and her biology, into a theoretical structure with details so complex, and so beautiful, that she felt dizzy just bringing it to mind.

She knew who had created this ship. Who had brought humans from Terra to World 140,000 years ago. Who the "super-aliens" were.

She had always wondered about that initial transport of humans to World. An experiment, yes. But not a random lifting of a few thousand people who happened to roam the same geographical area. Any band of hunter-gatherers must have included a leader bellicose enough to stand off challengers, some aggressive hunters, other hunters willing to take subordinate positions, and some very yielding people at the bottom of the pecking order. Hierarchy was built into primate genes, and all carnivorous mammals had alpha and omega members of both genders.

And yet—all, or at least most, of the humans brought to World shared a genomic profile strong on tendencies toward cooperation, mildness, aversion to risk.

Somebody had *chosen* humans for those traits. Somebody had understood human genetics very, very well.

She had told Colin that life on Earth had always been transformed by microbes, from the first prokaryotes on. Serial endosymbiosis had, along with survival of the fittest, been evolution's earliest tool. The virophage was an unconscious entity in itself, no more sentient than an amoeba. But over the vast oceans of geologic time, different microbes had evolved to control their hosts in ways that aided their own survival. They used more complex animals as reproduction sites, as food, as a means of being carried from a site of exhausted resources to one with fresher resources.

Earth had, before the Collapse, become a place with rapidly exhausting resources. Years ago, Jonah Stubbins had been building his spaceship for that very reason: to escape an Earth that in a few more generations would be unsustainable for human life. It was a matter of species survival.

But which species—humans, or the microbes they carried? Or survival of an advanced species able to see ahead, to forecast what Terrans would do to their world and so seed another, as survival insurance for *Homo sapiens*? And if World had been seeded with humans, how many others as well?

And by whom?

Beings with enough intelligence to plan megamillennia ahead. Beings who perhaps began as raw material for a virophage that could—in its own interests—cause a second "Great Leap Forward" that made the first one, seventy thousand years ago, look like a not-very-bright child triumphant at piling just one block on another. Beings who understood human genetics very, very well. Beings who also understood that if microbes could evolve in ways that served their own survival, they could also be turned into tools to aid the survival of other races.

Marianne had gone to Thomas Farouk because she didn't have the math. Math was, always, the underlying key to everything that went on in the universe. For two hundred years, math had been blossoming, yielding a rich crop of theories usable and unusable: relativity, quantum mechanics, entanglement, multiverses, Gollancz equations. All of them, every one, had involved time. Time was basic to every process in the universe.

Farouk, with his virophaged intelligence, had done more than find a way into the equations for dark matter and dark energy that would eventually enable humans to build more ships like the *Return*. He had found a way into the equations of time. A new way that showed yes, under certain circumstances, time could be manipulated to allow travel backward.

Maybe.

Unprovable experimentally, at least with the materials and technology known so far.

But the equations were there.

And someone had known what would happen to Earth—even though they had not foreseen the human-created RSA—because maybe planetary destruction was what happened to all over-populated and over-civilized planets. But not to World, which had been carefully seeded with carefully chosen humans who valued cooperation over competition.

Who was that someone, symbiotic with the spore cloud and the virophage it produced?

Unknowable.

Unprovable.

But possible, because Promethean science was possible.

Marianne whispered, just to be able to say it aloud, "It was us."

Or not. The "super-aliens" might have been some other form of advanced sentience that had become one with the virophage, as living bodies always did merge. If not *Homo sapiens*, then another sentience that, like us, had started out simpler and had been changed to become more. Much more, because of microbes. As humans were on the way to becoming. The other species just got there first. If there was another species.

She didn't really believe there was. Not since Farouk, his face shining with disbelief and awe, had figured out the equations for time.

"It was us," Marianne said. "We are the super-aliens. Or will be."

Us. Them. Microbes.

All one.

CHAPTER 27

Jason lay on the bridge of the *Return*, in a newly installed "captain's bed"—Lindy's term—that he hated and was prepared to leave as soon as possible. Lieutenant Allen was at the controls. Major Duncan was there, and Sergeant Hillson, and Branch Carter, newly awakened and hovering somewhere between fascination and outrage at everything he had missed while in v-coma. Everything that could be tested, had been.

Just before dawn, Jason had traveled on a carry-bot from Monterey Base to the ship. Lindy and Hillson walked beside him, along with three members of J Squad, including Mason Kandiss. Before that, Kandiss had carried him up the stairs to the command post, with Lindy cursing colorfully that the dome had no elevator. Jason had set the necessary controls on a delayed timer. He looked out the clear dome one last time, at the gleam of Lab Dome in the brightening sky, the streaks of gold and pink on the eastern horizon, the forest burned by attacks, the graveyard beside the domes where lay Kayla Rhinehart and Glamet^vor¡'s ashes, the bodies of Dr. Sugiyama and all the troops killed by New America, and the soldiers who had been executed under the rules of war. Then Kandiss, moving more quickly now, had carried him down the steps and through Enclave Dome.

Little was left inside. Sticks of lumber, scrap metal. Everything that could be pried out of both domes, had been. Entire scientific labs, computers, kitchen equipment, furniture, supplies. Wiring had been torn out, partitions taken down, weapons crated, all of it plus the Bradley and quadcopters stowed on the *Return*. All but one of the FiVees and Bradleys had been given to the evacuees. Jason was carried through a littered but empty dome, a shell, only the alien walls still in place.

They had an hour.

A FiVee waited just outside Enclave for the short trip to the *Return*. Guarded by what was left of Jason's battalion, the ship stood in an open space by the river. Jason was carried aboard. The entire vast ship, of course, had been contaminated with RSA. A section, however, had been fitted with a transplanted airlock and decon chamber, sealed off, and decontaminated under Dr. McKay's direction. This section, which included the bridge, was where everyone who was not an RSA survivor would spend the entire voyage. Cramped, but necessary. Gratefully Jason shed his esuit.

Twenty minutes.

When they arrived at World, the RSA-contaminated ship might have to be left in orbit, although that would be a waste of good living areas. However, Jason was confident that with their virophaged-enhanced intelligence, Worlders would have devised ways to deal with such situations. After all, look what Toni Steffens and Major Farouk had come up with in much less time. Worlders would all have the same enhanced intelligence, and so they would have incredible tech.

"No," Jane said, "they won't." However, Jason wasn't sure he believed her. Twenty-eight years was a long time, even without v-coma enhancements. Twenty-eight years ago, he had been a child of ten, and the United States had existed as a real country, with real cities and an orderly chain of command and . . . no, he would not dwell on what had been lost. After all, he could not control the past.

He'd said, "Jane, the human mind is endlessly inventive."

Jane had merely shrugged, a gesture she must have learned from Colin.

All right—there were unknowns ahead. When hadn't that been true? As long as the next piece of tech worked . . .

"Lift the ship," he ordered, and the *Return* rose noiselessly straight up into the sky.

On the wall screen, the twin domes of Monterey Base glinted silver-blue in the sun. Then he could see the coastline, the river, the mountains. Colin and his people were down there somewhere, days away from the base, far enough out to be safe. And was that, glimpsed for only a second, a road, with moving vehicles on it? The convoy from Fort Hood?

Impossible to tell.

Fifteen minutes.

The ship, by what magic of physics Jason had no idea, hovered in the upper stratosphere. His hands gripped the arms of his bed, and he forced his fingers to loosen. The day was cloudless over what had been California, a mosaic of blue and brown and green. Jason did something he hadn't done since he'd been a small boy: He prayed. *Let the quantum computer not have been destroyed when I attacked Sierra Base. Let it still be operable, shielded under the rubble. Let the signal get through to the silos.*

Was that even a prayer? To pray for such destruction?

He knew enough military history to know he was not the first.

The first explosion, of the consoles in the command post, was too contained by the dome to be visible on the Return's wall screen. Nor was it visible on the transmitted image from the surveillance camera set a few miles from the domes. Those explosions, however, were mostly backup in case the main effort failed. Jason didn't know whether conventional explosions would destroy every last virophage spore at Monterey Base. He was taking no chances. Before it was destroyed, the command post had sent the signal to the quantum computer.

Five minutes later, Specialist Martin, seated at the radar console brought from the signal station, said crisply, "Incoming ICBMs from Alaskan silos, sir." Her voice sounded rich with satisfaction.

But, then, she was young.

Three minutes.

Two.

Please please please . . .

The transmitted image from the ground camera exploded into smoke and fire, eerily silent, before it disappeared. Images on the wall screen were smaller, no more than gray puffs. Still, Jason thought he glimpsed a mushroom cloud rising to the sky. But even if he hadn't, the domes—the two unshatterable domes built by unknowable super-aliens—were bursting into cleansing flames. Monterey Base was no more. And the virophage no longer existed on Earth.

On the bridge, no one spoke. The silence spun itself out, so long it became painful. Jason realized it was up to him to speak, not only to give the order but to set the tone for everything human to come. Even though he had no real idea what it would be, even though he could not control what happened, even though the order itself might sound like the cheesiest of clichés.

"Lieutenant Allen, set course for World. We are going to the stars."

ACKNOWLEDGMENTS

No book is written in isolation. I would like to thank my beta readers, Jack Skillingstead and Maura Glynn-Thami, for their valuable suggestions during the writing of this novel, and my editor, Beth Meacham, for her equally valuable revision suggestions after it was submitted to Tor.